Dzanc Books

# Best of the Web 2010

DZANC
BOOKS

1334 Woodbourne Street
Westland, MI 48186
www.dzancbooks.org
info@dzancbooks.org

Published 2010 by Dzanc Books
Book design by Steven Seighman


06 07 08 09 10 11 5 4 3 2 1
First Edition June 2010


ISBN – 13: 978-0-9825204-6-8


Printed in the United States of America

Dzanc Books

# Best of the Web 2010

**Guest Editor**
*Kathy Fish*

**Series Editor**
*Matt Bell*

**DZANC
BOOKS**

# Contents

Series Introduction · Matt Bell · **xiii**

Introduction: The Best of the Web 2010 · Kathy Fish · **xviii**

**Modern Love** · Stephen Graham Jones · **21**
*Everyday Genius*

**What We Tell Girl to Do with Us Brothers If We Ever Stop Making Mud** · Peter Markus · **24**
*Everyday Genius*

**Women in Wells** · Jac Jemc · **25**
*Juked*

**Martha Stewart Claims She Has Been Struck By Lightning Three Times** · Rachel Bunting · **28**
*Apparatus Magazine*

**Conservatory** · Chris Bachelder · **29**
*storySouth*

**Contemplations of the Saints** · Robert Bradley · **32**
*FRiGG*

**The Genius Meetings** · Elizabeth Crane · **34**
*Guernica*

**Touching the Spine** · Charles Lennox · **44**
*FRiGG*

**What Happened to Sheila** · Dan Chaon · **46**
*The Rumpus*

**Aesthete** · Mary Miller · **59**
*Wigleaf*

**My Sister, the Kite** · Amber Norwood · **61**
*Journal of Truth and Consequence*

**Arrgh Luxury Cruises: An Authentic Pirate Adventure** · Ravi Mangla · **62**
STORY*GLOSSIA*

**Foolish Creatures** · Frank Dahai · **70**
*Toasted Cheese*

**Muse** · William Walsh · **72**
*Night Train*

**Population: 41,685** · Mary Biddinger · **74**
*Memorious*

**When I Worked for Madonna** · Joanna Ruocco · **76**
*No Tell Motel*

**Skin** · Kevin Wilson · **77**
*Joyland*

**The Woman Down the Hall** · Lily Hoang · **94**
*Lamination Colony*

**He Has Juice** · Kim Chinquee · **108**
*Conjunctions*

**Pact** · Lydia Copeland · **109**
*The Northville Review*

**Suspended** · Kyle Minor · **111**
*Brevity*

**Laughter Incidence** · Ander Monson · **113**
*Spork*

**Swanbit** · Terese Svoboda · **117**
*failbetter*

**A Short History of Falling** · Pamela Uschuk · **120**
*Terrain.org*

**Jimmy and His Father and the Ways About Them** · J.A. Tyler · **123**
*>kill author*

**One Way to Cook an Eel** · Emily Bromfield · **126**
*Carve Magazine*

**Trouble** · James Scannell McCormick · **135**
*The Barefoot Muse*

**When I Say Love** · Meredith Martinez · **136**
*Contrary Magazine*

**How I Forget the Shape of Your Mouth When You Are Deep in Thought** · Alison Doernberg · **137**
*Eleven Eleven*

**Intercourse** · Robert Olen Butler · **140**
*Redivider*

**To A Place Where We Take Flight** · Anne Valente · **142**
STORY*GLOSSIA*

**Instructional Ghazal** · David Welch · **156**
*Agni Magazine*

**A Baker's Dozen of My Feelings about David Foster Wallace's** *Infinite Jest* · Elissa Bassist · **158**
*The Rumpus*

**How To** · Aaron Burch · **165**
*Everyday Genius*

**Tentacle Mind Report** · Stefani Nellen · **166**
*Conjunctions*

**Me and Theodore are trapped in the trunk of the car with rags in our mouths and tape around our wrists and ankles, please let us out.** · Mary Hamilton · **189**
*SmokeLong Quarterly*

**Great White** · Julie Platt · **191**
*Gold Wake Press*

**Karner Blue Butterfly Hunt** · Julie Platt · **192**
*Gold Wake Press*

**Samuel L. Jackson Is Not a Good Name for a Rabbit** · Elizabeth Ellen · **193**
*Wigleaf*

**After I Blew Through My Hysterectomy** · Kendra Kopelke · **195**
*The Potomac*

**Father** · Brian Evenson · **197**
*Wag's Revue*

**Caves** · Matthew Simmons · **198**
*Lamination Colony*

**Premises for an Action Plan** · Scott Garson · **208**
*American Short Fiction*

**If You See Buddha On The Road, Kill Him** · Barbara Yien · **214**
*Emprise Review*

**Proxy** · Emma J. Lannie · **215**
*>kill author*

**Pop Star Dead at 22** · Dave Housley · **219**
*Wigleaf*

**Translations of "My Refrigerator Light Makes Its Way Toward You" Into the 34 Languages Spoken in the Many Woods of Grief** · Lucas Farrell · **222**
*alice blue*

**One Day All Your Teeth Will Be Mine** · Sasha Fletcher · **227**
*Gigantic*

**The Sky as John Saw It the Night Kate Sparkled** · Molly Gaudry · **228**
*ABJECTIVE*

**From: Chorus from the Land of Grownups** · Donora Hillard · **230**
*Night Train*

**This Is Not To Say** · Amy Lee Scott · **231**
*Brevity*

**Ghosts and Monsters** · Angi Becker Stevens · **233**
STORY*GLOSSIA*

**The Reckoning** · Leigh Stein · **249**
*The Scrambler*

**Attending the Tasting** · Sarah J. Sloat · **251**
*The Literary Bohemian*

**Journey (Aigues-Mortes)** · Sue Standing · **253**
*The Literary Bohemian*

**Nostrum** · Michelle Reale · **254**
*BluePrintReview*

**Letter Written on a Paper Crane** · Dave Rowley · **257**
*The Literary Bohemian*

**Now, Right Now** · Jennifer Pieroni · **258**
*Wigleaf*

**The Taste of Mangoes** · Jie Li · **260**
*Cerise Press*

**Geomancy** · F. Daniel Rzicznek · **263**
*Guernica*

**Sounds of Silence** · Nanette Rayman Rivera · **265**
*carte blanche*

**The Girl Needs to Be Kissed** · Christine Schutt · **276**
*Blackbird*

**Ground Truth** · Claudia Emerson · **280**
*Valparaiso Poetry Review*

**Arizona's Lonely** · Rachel Yoder · **282**
*Necessary Fiction*

**Segue** · Lisa Zaran · **287**
*Juked*

**Glory** · Cami Park · **288**
*Staccato*

**Baby Love** · Sara Levine · **289**
*Necessary Fiction*

**A Companion Text to *Modernity and Self-Identity* by Anthony Giddens** · Angela Woodward · **294**
STORY*GLOSSIA*

**Selections from *Sucker Jane*** · Sean Kilpatrick · **298**
*Spork*

**Fifteen Unrelated Stories Titled "The Man Inside Her Pillowcase"** · Brandi Wells · **303**
*Keyhole*

**Crystal Castles** · Matthew Kirkpatrick · **306**
*Action Yes*

**Cube** · Amelia Gray · **316**
*Spork*

**Wife to Magrite** · Krystal Languell · **319**
*DIAGRAM*

**You wouldn't believe Me if I told You, but Me and Theodore built a time machine** · Mary Hamilton · **320**
*NOÖ Journal*

**Games Are Not About Monsters** · Christine Hartzler · **323**
*Fiction Writers Review*

**How I Became a Ghost** · Leslie Harrison · **334**
*Memorious*

**John Henry's Tracks** · Matthew Glenwood · **335**
*DIAGRAM*

**I Feel Better, And So Can You** · Matt Hart · **356**
*H_NGM_N*

**Family** · Jensen Beach · **358**
*Necessary Fiction*

**Photo Opportunities for a Dislocated Elbow** · Stokely Klasovsky · **360**
*Jellyfish*

**Field Notes** · August Tarrier · **362**
*DIAGRAM*

**Where the Glazed Girls Go** · Kasandra Snow Duthie · **371**
*The Summerset Review*

**Tricks** · Thomas Cooper · **378**
*Keyhole*

**Ideally Learnt French for Eavesdroppers** · Brian Baldi · **380**
*Matchbook*

**When a Furnace Is All that Remains** · Steven J. McDermott · **382**
*Necessary Fiction*

**Headlong for that Fair Target** · Eleanor Wilner · **386**
*Cerise Press*

**Penumbra** · David McLendon · **388**
*Everyday Genius*

**Flashlight Tag** · Kyle Booten · **389**
*storySouth*

**A Sigh is Just a Sigh** · Sean Lovelce · **392**
*Wigleaf*

**Pregnant with Peanut Butter** · Michael Czyzniejewski · **397**
*SmokeLong Quarterly*

**Requiem for the Orchard** · Oliver de la Paz · **401**
*Guernica*

**ex libris** · Kristiana Colón · **406**
*Our Stories*

**Maybe Visionary Sermon** · Ander Monson · **408**
*CEllA's Round Trip*

**Ashes to Undermine the Smell** · Josh Maday · **410**
*Lamination Colony*

**Wash, Dry, Fold** · Myfanwy Collins · **416**
*Mississippi Review*

**Notable Works** · **426**

**Contributors' Notes** · **432**

**Index** · **446**

# Series Introduction
## Matt Bell

Thanks to my father, I grew up around computers: I started hitting the keys on a VIC-20 as a toddler, played computer games on early Commodore and IBM machines, and typed my middle school papers on my mother's Apple IIc, the kind with that horrible, flickery green screen. Long before the internet, I learned to use a modem in the sixth grade, connecting to local bulletin board systems hosted out of other people's houses, even though there wasn't much reason to do so yet: a handful of files to download, a message board that moved glacially slowly, with only one user able to connect at any one time, and online gaming that was turn-based, as much about patience as it was strategy.

My first attempts at writing fiction included an awful fantasy novel I drafted in the summer between seventh and eighth grade, which I typed into that terrible blue screen text editor that used to come with MS-DOS because the hand-me-down computer I had in my bedroom wasn't quite powerful enough to run Windows. Among other things, this means I never had an attachment to notebooks or certain brands of pens, never stained my fingers with typewriter ribbons or correction fluid. I have never typed a single page on a typewriter. I do not, in fact, know exactly how they work or what one's component parts are called, although I'm sure I could look it up on Wikipedia.

I was in college for the second or third time before I began to read and write more seriously, and by then the internet had become a common part of everyday life. I was twenty and twenty-one and twenty-two, and looking for more books like the ones I was in love with—at the time, Denis Johnson, David Foster Wallace, Chuck Palahniuk, Kurt Vonnegut, Amy Hempel—and what I wanted to read I could not find in the few book stores available to me in the small town I lived in. Instead, I ordered books from Amazon and Powell's and other book stores that were online, and as I did so I somehow found out about literary magazines, something I'd never been exposed to by a teacher or friend.

The print journals that had websites looked great, but back then I didn't have extra money to buy literary magazines— around this time, I was living in my parents' basement, then failing to successfully move out West in my van, then living with a couple in a house that was too small for two people, let alone three—and even if I had found the money, I wouldn't have known what to buy. Instead, I turned to the internet, where I could read for free, where I could browse until I discovered something that resonated with me. It was early then, but there were already a number of great literary magazines in existence, publishing writers I'd heard of as well as ones I hadn't. Because I had never been part of any old guard of print magazine editors or readers, I held no loyalties to that form, and dived into reading online literature as if the computer were as natural a place to read fiction and poetry as any other. For someone who'd grown up around computers, it probably was.

I can still remember some of the first magazines I ever read, many of which are thankfully still around and thriving, like *failbetter, juked,* and *elimae,* and I can still remember the first magazine I ever submitted my own fiction to: a website named *Conversely* that has been "on hiatus" since 2005. The reason I submitted there? I had read Tod Goldberg's debut novel, *Fake Liar Cheat,* and recognized his prose as the work of someone who liked at least some of the same books I then liked. And so when I started searching for more of his work on the internet, I found *Conversely* and his story "Faith, Love, Hope," which they published in 2001. I can remember thinking, "If this magazine publishes Tod Goldberg, and I write kind of like Tod Goldberg, maybe they'd like my stories too?"

*Conversely* didn't publish that story, but when I finally did land my first publication, it was in another online journal. So were my second and third stories, as I recall, and certainly most of my first twenty or thirty publications. The first magazine that took a chance letting me work as an editor was online, as were all the other magazines I worked at, with the exception of *Mid-American Review* in grad school. My first book reviews were published online, and almost all of my writers' groups have been organized by internet, conducted via email as much as in person. There are dozens of other stories I might tell like the one above, and each of them is just one example of how the internet literary scene helped me become the writer and reader and editor I have become—that I am, of course, still becoming—by introducing me to the dozens and dozens of writers who have become my inspirations, my peers and my editors, and my friends.

***

Perhaps it goes without saying, but my story is not unique. There are now over a thousand online journals, and exponentially more readers and writers who have made the internet an integral part of their literary life, who have come into their own careers with online literature as a constant component of their day-to-day interactions with the written word.

In past years, much has been made of the "split" between the internet and the print world (as if nearly every print journal did not also have a website, as if every book is not also available for sale online, as if those spheres will ever be mutually exclusive ever again), but that is no longer a conversation I'm interested in having at great length. I do not believe an argument can still be made that the print journals are "better" than the web ones, or vice versa, or the argument that the internet literary scene is somehow diminished by the fact that "anyone" can start a literary journal, since that's no more or less true now than it was in the days before the internet. There is room—and perhaps even a need—for our literary community to have both print and online incarnations, and for both to thrive. We're lucky to have as many options as we do, arguably more than any generation of readers and writers has ever had.

Consider, for instance, the explosion of flash fiction as a form, which is, in my opinion, one of the hallmarks of current online literature: While the rise of flash has commonly been cited as a response to or panacea for the supposedly shortened attention span of contemporary Americans, I believe instead that the internet merely provided the room for new markets to arise, particularly those that might focus on the kinds of fiction or essays or poetry somehow less popular with already existing magazines, and that these new magazines used the accessibility of the internet to quickly gather and cultivate a community of like-minded writers. This sort of development can only be a good thing for the future of literature: I think of a writer like this year's guest editor, the incredibly talented Kathy Fish, and I wonder whether her work might have found so many readers if not for the online explosion of interest in the short-short, the flash fiction, the prose poem. (It's perhaps no coincidence that this is a growth she helped make happen as an editor at *SmokeLong Quarterly*, one of the form's most stalwart champions and a magazine that has appeared in every edition of *Best of the Web* so far: In every era, artists have founded new venues to both create and promote the kind of art that they loved making but for which they could not find an already existing home.)

\*\*\*

The big story this year has been what will happen to publishing now that people are reading on cell phones and e-readers and laptops everywhere they go, as if this represents some sort of shift away from "reading" toward some new, more nebulous and not yet understood activity. Maybe the marketing departments are right and it is some new paradigm about to explode, but every time I read another article about the rise of the e-book I wonder if this phenomenon isn't simpler than it's been made out to be. Isn't it at least possible that this is less a schism between the print world and some technology-driven future than it is simply a sign that there is some class of people who desire to read everywhere they go? The kind of readers who have always kept books in their purses and briefcases, but now also desire to turn the tools of work and drudgery—the company computer, for instance, or else the always-on Blackberry—into objects of intellectual and emotional liberation, points of entry into the online literary world, so capable of delivering stories and poems and essays at any moment?

I think it is possible. I think it's probably true, and that this sentiment will continue to spread in the years to come.

Thanks to the internet and the various ways we now interact with it, much of the world has become a book, and also a place in which to read one. The internet is an endless text that contains many other texts, all rearrangeable, mixable, sortable, so that readers can make their own literatures, their own personal libraries of essential writings. What we have collected here in *Best of the Web 2010* is just such a literature: a tiny shelf of a far-greater library, selected and organized to represent what we found most exciting about online literature in the past year. These are the works we would not have wanted to go through the year without, that we believe will continue to impress and inspire us in years still to come. *Best of the Web 2010* is a collection of our essential reading, and we hope that as you read these stories and poems and essays they might become part of yours.

# Introduction: Best of the Web 2010
## Kathy Fish

You are going to love this volume of Dzanc's *Best of the Web*. I don't say that because I guest-edited the anthology (though of course that contributes). I say it because I loved it, long before we had the final selections in place, long before the editors' nominations had rolled in. I loved this collection before it existed in the form you are about to read, because I'd read so much excellent literature on the web over the past several months that I knew that Matt Bell, Dan Wickett, Steven Gillis, and I could not possibly miss. Our challenge was not in finding enough great writing on the web. It was in keeping the volume to a reasonable size.

I knew I loved this future book when one morning, sitting out on my deck, laptop balanced on my knees, I fell upon this sentence:

*A man with such loneliness repels even the moon's face in water.*

That simply broke my heart. The sentence came late in a story I was already liking quite a bit and it completely stopped me. It's from Terese Svoboda's short story "Swanbit," published in *Failbetter*. I finished reading and, without further analysis, added the story to my list of nominations. I am so happy the story made it through the selection process and is included in the collection you're about to read.

There's an astonishing amount of great writing on the

web right now. How to even begin choosing the best? In the end, it's the subjective judgment of a handful of people and it depends on what they value most in literature. For me, I can say that the deciding factor was always the following: Did this writing open my eyes? Will I remember it months from now? Was it beautiful or strange or completely fresh and new? Did this writing unravel me?

A huge benefit of this gig, for me, was that the reading, the searching, led me to writers I'd never read before, or had clearly not read enough of. I was thrilled in the process to read then seek out more work by writers such as Jac Jemc, Charles Lennox, and Lily Hoang. And it seemed that everywhere I turned online there was literary greatness from the likes of Mary Hamilton and Angi Becker Stevens, among many others.

And I admit to being a huge, forever fan of beautiful sentences. I found myself compulsively cutting and pasting every gem I came across until I had pages upon pages.

This, from Molly Gaudry's "The Sky as John Saw It the Night Kate Sparkled" from *Abjective*:

*Kate's remains in the rolled up sky in his hands had been hot, and the rain had sizzled, and the rolled up sky in his hands had sogged heavy like corn starch mixed with water.*

Go and read every single sentence, each building and expanding upon the other, in the four beautiful sentences of Peter Markus's "What We Tell Girl To Do with Us Brothers If We Ever Stop Making Mud" from *Everyday Genius*.

This, from "Women in Wells" by Jac Jemc, in *Juked*:

*The soul music on the turntable hustles a circus into her muscles and he sits watching her dance, watching the glimmer of her watch-face can-can around the room.*

Just the phrase "watch-face can-can" makes me want to follow Jac Jemc around wherever she publishes and I hope and know she will publish a great deal.

I read Robert Bradley's "Contemplations of the Saints" in *FRiGG* so many times for the sheer wonder and strangeness of the dialog.

I also thrilled whenever I encountered a smashing title, such as Michael Czyzniejewski's "Pregnant with Peanut Butter" from *SmokeLong Quarterly* or Elizabeth Ellen's "Samuel L. Jackson Is Not a Good Name for a Rabbit" in *Wigleaf* or Alison Doernberg's "How I Forget the Shape of Your Mouth When You Are Deep in Thought" from *Eleven Eleven*. Sometimes a great title is just a single word, as in Cami Park's perfectly resonant "Glory" from *Staccato*.

Of course, all these fantastic titles crowned brilliant stories.

Every choice we made for this anthology moved me deeply, but none more than Don Chaon's honest and heartbreaking essay, "What Happened to Sheila" from *The Rumpus*. My own votes were always for those stories, poems, and essays that very clearly *mattered* to the writer.

For me, the highest praise I can give to any writing is that I wish I'd written it myself and that is true of so much that is included in this anthology. One such story is Sara Levine's "Baby Love" from *Necessary Fiction*. It is a gorgeous, odd, heartbreaking story. This is its last breathtaking sentence:

*For my feelings substitute the emptiness of a rain barrel, its wood drying out, its metal staves creaking; an unbidden, arid silence after two years of learning to hold the rain.*

Many thanks to Matt Bell and Dzanc for the honor of including me in choosing the material for this anthology. The works reprinted here are thoughtful, funny, wise, illuminating and all beautifully written. I am very proud of the book we've made for you. Enjoy.

# Modern Love

## Stephen Graham Jones

*from Everyday Genius*

1. My son's first-grade teacher doesn't shoot heroin anymore. If her pupils are dilated now, she says, it's with wonder. The children are supposed to have infected her with it. Maybe, I don't know. At dinner, anyway, my son wears long sleeves, to cover the ball-point pen track marks they all do to be like her. His breath through the baby monitor just five years ago is still so clear to me.

2. Once when it was Paint-Your-Baby day at the stadium I hid him in blankets and smuggled him to the park. I'd meant for us to sit on the grass and make talking sounds, but instead just stood, clutching him, watching four women with a tarp stretched between them, taut as a trampoline. Every few seconds a straw man would rise up limp from the tarp, hang midair for a few impossible seconds, then fall, smiling the whole time. There was a rhythm to it I couldn't deny. It was my son's first sunburn.

3. My father was the kind of physicist who, in his later years, wore his oxygen tank on his back when he came to visit. As if he was scuba-diving, just visiting from some higher place. Like this place would kill him if he were to accidentally breathe it in. In the science he taught my son, people didn't die, couldn't. His world was gluons and leptons and anafranil in controlled doses, when necessary.

4. In the garage last week I found a letter my wife wrote to my son when she was fifteen. She's thirty-four now. The letter starts out 'Dear Robert: Today the man who would have been your father died in a stock tank. He was the first one to dive in. It was beautiful. What can I tell you other than that he couldn't imagine breaking the surface of the water with anything other than his body?' The thing is, my son is named Robert. And my father was named Robert. It all seemed so natural a few days ago.

5. Picture this: a man sits in a bar after his father's funeral, and though he's hunched protectively over his beer, still, the fight raging around him slings a dollop of blood into his mug. The afterimage of the red arc lingers in the mirror longer than nature should allow. The man follows it down to his beer, now with blood blooming in it upside down. He looks from side to side, for who might be watching, and, when no one is, swirls his mug gently, keeps drinking.

6. The most terrifying moment of the twentieth century has to have been when I walked into the living room one night and sat beside my wife in front of the TV. We watched it together for a while and I didn't tell her that my love was like a wooly mammoth frozen beneath the tundra, a half-chewed daisy in its teeth, and she didn't tell me what I wanted to hear, that topiary gardeners dream of a naturally occurring shrub in the form of a horse. Instead I asked her if this was a commercial we were watching, and she shrugged, and we waited it out.

7. A strange attractor in a system of repetitive motion is a point which seems to be organizing the system when, in fact, it's the product of the organization itself. Which is an excuse, I know. But picture this: a woman's finger resting on the plunger of her cherished syringe. One day she pushes it down out of habit

and forces me up, through the green surface of the water, into another world. The grocery store, aisle after aisle, until there's the policewoman who patrols my son's school. Who keeps him safe. She's in the perfume aisle, trying on scents, as if any of them go with polyester. I fall so in love with her.

# What We Tell Girl to Do with Us Brothers If We Ever Stop Making Mud

## Peter Markus

from *Everyday Genius*

Bury us brothers here. Cover us up with the mud of this river. Let this muddy river run up and over us brothers, let it run its muddy waters up into the insides of our mouths. Let the fish of the river, let the mud too, nibble and gnaw us brothers down to bone. And the weeds of this river, those flowers growing up from the river's rivery bed, let them wrestle and wrap us brothers up into their leafy arms: so that we might be held here, down at the river's muddy edge, down here where there are stones for us to turn over, with our fingers and toes, stones for us to up from the mud pick up for us to throw: so they can float back up to that rivery hand, so they can rise up into that rivery sky—that nest of stars they fell out from back when they, the fishes of this river, back before they turned into birds, first learned how to fly.

# Women in Wells

## Jac Jemc

*from Juked*

The certainty clings to his smile from the minute she opens the door. They stare at each other, recognizing bits that have faded and others that have taken shape over the years. She makes some indecipherable gesture with her eyes, breaking the connection, and laughs, "You're too good to be true. They'll be home soon, I think. I'll wait with you."

He comes in, thankfully unable to think up an excuse not to. She puts on a record and never invites him to sit down. She asks if he wants something to drink. He nods and when she leaves the room he sits down. Everything around him is older now and the same. He remembers playing here as a child, with these brothers who are due back any minute. These brothers and this sister of theirs haven't changed the house at all since their grandparents died. He breathes in the smell of mothballs. The scent comes from all sides.

When she returns, the glass looks dusty, and he sets it on a coaster, already in place. The soul music on the turntable hustles a circus into her muscles and he sits watching her dance, watching the glimmer of her watch-face can-can around the room.

It's taken him a moment to figure it out, but this girl reminds him of someone. She reminds him of that woman in the well when he was a child, just up the road. That woman he told no one about, who'd spoken to him calmly, who'd seemed, not happy, but certain of her place all the way down there; that woman who'd just stopped speaking to him one day, and no flashlight could shine far enough down to see if she had gotten free or if she was just being quiet, and he couldn't tell anyone she'd stopped talking to him because they'd wonder why he never tried to help her out. This girl who answered the door? Who said just a few words as she let him in? This girl whom he's known forever, but not for a while? The voice this girl grew into is the voice of that woman in the well.

All the while this girl is dancing, trying not to color so exactly between the lines, slapping the walls every once in a while. She is wondering, beneath the beat, if this man won't get up and join her, what could he possibly be thinking about her while she willows and swipes around the room?

The music slows and she calms herself and sits in the rocking chair. This man, here. Her brothers, nowhere. This girl can't be still and because she can't be still? She begins to whip her tongue around her mouth, counting her teeth: 28. Wasn't she supposed to have 32? The number 32 sticks out in her mind.

He watches her, a lump moving around under her jaw-skin, and thinks about how he still sees her as a girl, but she is surely beyond that. Surely puberty has wrenched its way through her system and, by now, established well-worn patterns. She is still lithe, pale-looking, girl-like. They both have evidence in their minds of the other being younger.

He wants to hear that voice again, but now he's stuck in his mouth wondering what else can be said. For years his pride has named itself plainly around pretty girls, but with this one, each thing he thinks to say seems it would come out a high-handed sermon delivered from beneath a cartoon mask. He distracts himself with the newspaper from last Sunday lying on the coffee table. He leafs through to the crossword and fills in a few squares. He looks up at her and finds her eyes, a pleiad of sirens, curious and caroling. He never saw the woman in the well, but he knows this is how her eyes looked up at the silhouette of him against the daylight. Disconcerted, he reads her the next crossword clue: "River in which the heroine of *The Scamps of London* drowns?" This girl? She hums her elegiac response, lowly, "The Thames."

He escapes the wide openness of the room by disappearing behind the crossword again, eager to hide his excitement at hearing her voice. Yes, that was it. He was sure, now. It was full and vacant in the same ways the voice of the woman in the well was. How funnily life was able to fold on itself.

She tucks her feet up into the chair with her, happy to have company, but wasting the opportunity to make legendary decisions. She peels her nails and thinks of where her brothers might be. Until this guest had arrived, she'd repeated a mantra from nowhere, again and again, out loud at first, until it wouldn't stop itself even in the silence: "To become abandoned, you've only to extinct the others." These aphorisms had been showing up for months now. She watches the window, sure her brothers will pucker into focus at any moment.

The man will shift on the couch, squeaking against the plastic cover, and pretend to look at the newspaper while he threads her voice through his head. The girl will rip off her nails one by one and the same sentence will travel quietly into and out of her mouth. She will salivate and swallow it whole.

These two will be in this room together for hours, and what originally felt like a solitary stubbornness, slowly, will show itself to be spineless. The brothers will arrive back, with apologies, the girl will retreat, and the visitor will never admit what he's heard.

# Martha Stewart Claims She Has Been Struck by Lightning Three Times

## Rachel Bunting

from *Apparatus Magazine*

> *"Some people just attract electrical things."*
> —*Martha Stewart*

The first time I was in the kitchen washing
dishes when it sizzled into my stomach
with a single silver stroke. The lightning
flower still blooms faintly from my navel.

The next time it hit, I was watching the storm
gaining strength as it rolled in, centering
itself over my home. I was on the telephone;
my teeth played like the keys of a xylophone.

Finally, adjusting chairs in the garden, the spring
day giving way to an evening shower, I was racing
against the thunder. This time the electric fire
blazed through my feet to the ground.

Now my body burns hotter than the sun, a question
of impossible physics: how can this skin remain
intact, containing molten tissue without a rapid
evaporation of its organs, its muscles? Everything

has changed now, my hands no longer my most
trusted tools: muffin batter bakes within my glowing
palms on the way to the oven; leaf wreathes explode
into flames, scorching the lace runner on my dining table.

My body burns through my clothes, smoke escaping
from every loose-stitched seam.

# Conservatory
## Chris Bachelder
*from storySouth*

All day long Abbott and his wife have been arguing. By evening there is a fragile truce. The daughter has been put to bed, though her singing and babbling are audible on the staticky monitor. "I forgot to even ask you about the butterflies," Abbott's wife says, conciliatory in word if not tone. They are together in the family room, a designation they actually use. They are sitting as far apart as possible on the devastated couch, purchased at a furniture warehouse years ago, when Abbott was in graduate school, and now draped like a corpse by a mail-order cover. Besides Abbott's cocktail, the couch is the only adult item in the family room, which this and every evening looks as though robbers have ransacked it in an urgent search for a small and valuable item. Books, toys, coins, buttons, beads, and costume jewelry lie strewn across the stained carpeting. It's almost impossible not to fight with your life partner in this room. Abbott's wife has asked, sort of, about Abbott's trip to the butterfly conservatory, an outing he took this morning with their daughter but did not discuss afterward with his wife because she was too busy reminding him of things about which he did not need to be reminded. Today was Abbott's first trip to the butterfly conservatory. His wife has been twice before with their daughter, and she has reported that the conservatory is "neat" and "kind of peaceful," that it's "an interesting place . . . in the middle of nowhere." One response to his wife's inquiry is that the butterfly conservatory is a hideous travesty, a transparent example of everything that is wrong with everything. The twelve-dollar admission, accepted joylessly by a woman talking on the telephone to someone she clearly does not want in her life anymore; the cruel trap of the overstocked gift shop, selling stuffed butterflies, real butterflies, butterfly magnets and puzzles, butterfly nightlights and kites, along with entire aisles of bright toys thematically irrelevant but wildly attractive to children; the children; the lucrative imprisonment of thousands of butterflies, not to mention finches, turtles, lizards, fish, and a parrot, ostensibly in the name of appreciation and education; the *heat*, as one might find in a small bathroom after a long hot shower; the horrific music—hyperactive, flute-driven renditions of "Edelweiss" and "On Broadway," engineered to overpower visitors and create in them a stupor that might be mistaken for relaxation; the weird smell; the cafeteria with its dumb food names; the fellow adult patrons, all behaving as though they have never before encountered a flying insect; the pervasive sense of animal dirtiness; the chipper, ecologically ignorant staff members, who are in all seriousness referred to as *flight attendants*, and who spend their days trying to get children to pet a sleepy lizard—Abbott ponders this truce-obliterating response. It would no doubt feel good to take a big swing. But the truth is, he had a pretty good time at the conservatory. There were so many butterflies. Some landed on people's hands or shoulders. The large proboscises were easy to see. Butterflies are astonishing when you look at them, and when else would you ever look at them? The flight attendants had helpfully led Abbott and his daughter to a mounted board of cocoons, where they saw butterflies emerging, drying their wings, then flying off into the world, or at least into the hot dome. Abbott had never seen his daughter so engaged, so stimulated. He knows that the conservatory is, in addition to a hideous travesty, something like a spiritual center, operated by a dedicated team of citizen-workers. Who else cares about butterflies? Who else would attempt to mend their broken wings with a special wing glue? The pop of the ice in Abbott's glass reminds him—and probably his wife—that he has not, as a courtesy, desisted or at least curtailed his drinking during her pregnancy. This is a courtesy extended by quite a few Pioneer Valley men to their pregnant soul mates. Abbott has still not said a word in response to his wife's question, which, come to think of it, was not so much a question as a statement about forgetting to ask a question. His eyes are on a section of subtoy carpet in the shape of a rhombus. Either a rhombus or a parallelogram. He knows that any criticism of the butterfly conservatory would be a deliberate attempt to rankle his wife and renew the fight. This is what a married person can do, slander a sanctuary to provoke his beloved. But Abbott does not disparage the conservatory or its workers. His decision not to strikes him as exceedingly mature, though he knows that congratulating oneself on one's maturity is probably immature. Also, it comes as a tremendous disappointment to Abbott that his wife cannot know his restraint. If she could know, she would be touched. But he can't very well tell her how mature and restrained he's acting, for the maturity and restraint would evaporate upon utterance. Abbott and his wife can hear their daughter, through the monitor, singing an Australian folk song about a swagman who drowns himself in the billabong. She's waiting for an answer, his wife is. She's been waiting this whole time. Abbott clenches his jaw, stares at the dirty rhombus. When it comes down to it, he cannot bring himself to say that the butterfly conservatory was amazing, or even that it was neat, even though it would be at least partially true and would help salvage the evening. This is another small failure of spirit, and he knows it. The knowing of it might make things better, but probably makes things much, much worse. "It was fine," he says of his outing with their daughter. And then he repeats it: "It was fine." This is either an act of aggression or diplomacy, he's not sure which at this point. His wife is a separate person, large on the inside, capable of a very broad range of responses. She folds her thin fingers across her belly and gets ready to say something.

# Contemplations of the Saints

## Robert Bradley

from *FRiGG*

Nola is splayed on the wooden floor, her skirt hiked up high above her knees, playing jacks. She grips the ball in one hand, the jacks in the other. She won't let go of either. She says, "I'm experiencing boredom on an inhuman level."

Billie examines her breasts under her shirt, says, "I have a cyst. Thanks, God."

Lori says, "How can *anybody sleep*?" She's at the window, blowing smoke at the stars. "I'd pull them out by their roots if I could." Then there's a cloud of smoke and she's thinking of something else.

Devi slices into her thigh with a razor blade. She says, "Pain is incomprehensible to me. Mine as well as that of others, but still … it hurts."

Dora says, "I'll starve myself till starving becomes my only pleasure in life."

Margaret sitting in front of a mirror brushing brushing her hair, says, "We evolved from maggots and flies, forget monkeys."

Mattie says, "I saw a sign, I think, from God … it was exhilarating … and then tiring." She runs her hands down her face.

Jessie, waving a rolled up twenty, says, "The thing to keep in mind is that everything's alive; even the dead bones of your parents and grandparents, great aunts and uncles. Nothing ever dies. Brain cancer is life. Heart disease is life. Every second of every day whether you're completely unconscious, dreaming or blinking … life continues uninterrupted and without pause eternally."

"Fire or flood," says Jennifer. "It's not a question."

"I like fire," says Whitney. "It cleans and is clean."

Betty is practicing ritual hand movements. She says, "The act of speaking shows contempt for language; prayer contempt for God."

Kitty, looking up from her book, says, "Helen Keller said, Death is no more than passing from one room into another. Then she says that in that other room she can see."

"I can't make a fist," Amy says.

# The Genius Meetings

## Elizabeth Crane

from *Guernica*

We meet on Wednesdays. On the first Wednesday of the month we meet at one of our homes to discuss our achievements and share our profound and original thoughts. We have done everything from creating mathematical formulas to inventing technologies that will save your lives. We are architects, artists, physicists, and scientists. We are authors, composers, philosophers, and chemists. We are religious men and atheists. We are married, divorced, single, and straight. We know of a gay genius, but he does not attend the meetings. There are no women in our group. We are not saying there are no lady geniuses, but we sure don't know any.

We do not expect you to understand. We always knew we were different. For a minute Frederick thought he was the same, but he wasn't. When he was two, little Frederick sat down at the piano and composed his first sonata, the first to include a solo for the Jew's harp. He thought, Oh, how nice it will be to play this for my little friends! Then his mom came in and seemed surprised, which in turn surprised Frederick. When Marcus was four he discovered a hitherto unknown genus of insect while his brother was shooting spitballs. When Clifford was six he created a theory of abstraction just the title of which is ten pages long so we won't bother. Our dear friend William had both cross-bred a fig and discovered a dinosaur before the age of seven. These are just a few of the sorts of stories we share when we meet.

We meet to congratulate ourselves but we also meet to

purge ourselves. We meet to share things we cannot share with you. Smart things but also customs. Like the metaphorical value of sleeping in a nightcap to keep the genius in. Or the fact that many of us hold onto what we collectively refer to as our "lucky things" (ranging from typical things like shirts or socks we had on when we won awards, to typewriters that don't work, to small locks of hair purportedly from the heads of geniuses who went before us), though not one of us believes luck has anything to do with it. Or the value of saving entire volumes of academic journals, every article ever read that pertains remotely to our work, nay, every scrap of paper we ever touched, just in case, even if it means we must delicately move around the towers of paper in our homes and offices. Or the need for exactitude and precision, the importance of a regimen, and the malignment and misunderstanding of anal-retentiveness in contemporary society. We are aware that there are those of the mind that our disciplined ways of life are harsh, that our strict routines have consequences both mental and physical; to this we say, maybe so, but you sure seem to like that electricity we got you. We meet to have a safe place to use words like *ateleology* and *apotheosis* without confusing or embarrassing anyone, and away from your judgments of pretension. We meet to smoke pipes filled with tobacco we brought back from foreign lands and drink one brandy or liqueur that lasts us the evening. We meet to talk about that time the philosopher Eldred smoked marijuana, and to thank him for sparing us that horror. We meet to talk about one painting by Schiele or one article on Hindemith for two hours. We meet to discuss papers that do not get published and tenures that get passed over. (These things don't happen often, but when they do, the despair is often paralyzing.) We meet to talk about theories that don't pan out (or are disproven! the worst!) and novels that remain imperfect and therefore remain unseen and possibly published after our deaths (edited so thoroughly wrongheadedly as to diminish our genius when redemption is no longer possible) and discoveries made by those not among us, and the years lost on these projects. We meet to talk about how hard it is to be a genius. We discuss the difficulties of never being wrong, and the loneliness of being the smartest person in the room. We talk about the ones who died too soon, of the great works of art or science not to be. We grieve for Hubert, who took his life at the mere age of thirty-four while composing an opera that was sure to become a masterwork (a devastating loss to Frederick in particular, as Hubert had become a mentor of sorts). We weep for the great doctor Thirlby, who leapt to his death in the throes of a manic episode before finishing that remedy for autism. We talk about our personal lives, the lone area in which we do not always excel. We often suffer from depression and even mental illness. We make poor choices. We marry only the most beautiful women, models, and movie stars. One of us has married both a Miss America and a Miss Universe. Some of them are quite bright, some less so. There is nary a genius among them. That is not what we want. We geniuses love a gorgeous woman with a problem.

Take Winston the rocket scientist. Recently Winston came to the group with a broken heart. His wife Amaravati, a Bollywood star, left him for one of her co-stars. *I should have known,* Winston told us. *I know everything else.* We all nodded, knowingly. We asked if there were any signs. *Well,* he said, *perhaps when she told me that she could not promise to be faithful, I should have listened. Otherwise I can't think of anything.* We nodded again. *How could you know?* we told him.

Or take the time Eldred, who has suffered from often crippling depression since graduating college at age ten, came to ask the group whether or not it might be time for him to go off his medication. He posed to us the idea that since he had been doing quite well for several years on his lithium there seemed to be no reason to stay on it. The group had some differing opinions on this. Some of us fully agreed that this was a reasonable argument. Others were less sure, suggesting that a medical doctor would know best. Eldred ultimately made the decision to go off his meds with results that may have involved imaginary kittens with police badges providing dangerous directives, but we are happy to say he is now back on his meds and doing much better, although his choices in women still fit our general profile. His most recent fiancée was a woman he met in the psych ward. Theirs was a passionate but stormy affair, although they actually lasted longer than most of his relationships.

And the renowned architect Phillip has been living with his partner, the violet-eyed supermodel Elsabetta, for three years, trying unsuccessfully to cure her of her sexual abuse issues. It has been his belief that his sexual prowess and willingness to try anything to please would relieve her of these issues, but he has so far not met with success and cannot figure out why. We stared at him blankly. *We have nothing*, we told him.

Or take Geoffrey, the child of two academics, whose story resembles many a genius we have known. The pressure for young Geoffrey to achieve was immense, beginning as soon as he could hold up his head on his own. Although he was only two months old, it was at this time that Geoffrey's parents taught him sign language and began labeling the entire household inventory with large flash cards so that Geoffrey would learn to read before his first birthday. Passing that milestone at ten months, his parents began to read aloud to him from Tolstoy, Dickens, and Hemingway. Geoffrey was subsequently enrolled in everything from fencing to ballet class to tennis lessons. Tutors were brought in to teach him biophysics, dead languages, and medieval history. He learned to play the harp like a seraph. For fun, they would do the crossword or play chess. Geoffrey never saw a checker until he was thirty-one years old. He grew up to teach macroeconomics at Yale, but his secret shame never left him, and it was one nearly all of us shared. Geoffrey, in grade school, had once gotten a B. In penmanship.

Geoffrey hung his head when he told us this, but we had all been there. In fact, on this night, we took turns sharing our poor grades and the humiliation and fear they brought upon us. We recalled the harsh talk of permanent records and less than perfect GPAs* from our parents and principals and deans, and our long, carefully considered pleas to our professors to reconsider for the sake of our futures. We were aware that there were many who considered a B-plus to be a respectable grade, but this merely widened the gap between ourselves and everyone else. How could we live with a partner who believed such a thing? How would we raise our children? Would we go the other way and try to love them simply for who they were, as we had longed for at tender ages, as we often long for now? Or would we do as our parents did, pushing them toward the heights, at risk that our condition will again be handed down? Sandor the botanist pointed out that in the real world, no one mentions these things, that when the prizes are handed out, our A-minuses and B-pluses have long been forgotten by anyone but ourselves. And yet these are the things that shape us and haunt us.

The story of William is perhaps less typical, but ultimately most illustrative of our common plight. William was the only child born to a family of Nebraska fig farmers. His father was a stoic man, not given to open displays of affection, but dedicated to creating the perfect, juicy fig. His mother, who had hoped for a large family, five or six siblings for William at least, would suffer three miscarriages before sickly William was born. Worse, though, was the loss of their firstborn, Alma, who died of unknown causes in the night, just before her second birthday. William would never know this sister, only that he wasn't her.

William discovered his particular genius as a small boy.

---

* 5.0 GPAs became popular after our time, for which some of us give thanks to god.

Like many boys, he was interested in dinosaurs and could name all of the classes, subclasses, and infraclasses by the time he was four. By age five, having exhausted the meager selection of literature on the subject at the local library, he begged his parents to buy him a book he'd seen in the card catalog that wasn't on the shelves. His father dismissed this pursuit of dead things as irrelevant, but told him if he worked on the fig farm he could save up his money and buy whatever books he cared to. William eagerly accepted this challenge and unintentionally smote his father by cross-breeding what turned out to be the perfect fig (more sweet, plump, and moist than any before it, and readily identifiable by a tiny fragrant bloom on the bottom end), for which he was silently scorned. Nevertheless he bought himself a shelf of dinosaur books and by age six, theorized that there was a dinosaur that had not yet been discovered. By age seven he'd appeared on *Merv Griffin*, *David Susskind*, and *60 Minutes*, and by age nine, these dinosaur bones were unearthed in Peru, at which time William was honored by The Field Museum. His father made him work on the farm until he was fifteen.

He didn't have time to be awkward in high school, since he emancipated himself and graduated the year he turned fifteen, but he more than made up for that at college. One time, William drank three light beers and became wildly intoxicated (we relish these tales of debauchery as we cannot afford to be heavy drinkers; as much as we might like to cease our brain activity for an occasional evening, we cannot risk the long-term damage), informing us that he almost threw up and slept in until nine the following morning, earning him the nickname William the Lightweight for the duration of his time at University. Subsequent to this, William dated a number of emotionally withholding women, which he found to be an exhilarating challenge. After discovering yet another unknown dinosaur the summer after his sophomore year, he met his first wife at a sorority mixer. William was of course not in a fraternity, nevertheless his roommate, who had taken pity on him, invited him to this party, where he met Coreen, who, quite drunk on wine spritzers, thought William was funny and agreed to marry him. William, later noticing that she preferred wine spritzers to his company, divorced her shortly thereafter. This experience, however, did not deter him from marrying two more alcoholics, a professional cheerleader, and an especially stunning barista. He simply cannot stop getting married. William has been with his current wife, Marla (dean of a small arts college), for nearly five years (his longest by four and a half, and considerably longer than most of the rest of us, with the exception of Frederick, whose thirty-year marriage to Louisa, a renowned sommelier, is an extremely rare example of endurance, one we all admire and fear with equal fervor), and the problem seems to be, as far as we can tell, that she's basically normal, and smart, and wants to talk and work on their problems. William and Marla have one child, a four-year-old girl, and William would like to have another, but the couple's constant disagreements about parenting are a major concern. Marla wants to send their daughter to a Montessori school.

*Whoa,* said Clifford. *That is so not cool.* We all nodded at the great truth of this. *Also, she's very into this idea of "play" for children,* said William. Confused looks rippled around the room like the wave at a football stadium. *Marla doesn't think Zooey should have extracurricular activities until she's at least six and/or only if she expresses the original interest herself.*

*Well what does she do all day?* asked Marcus.

*Exactly,* said William. *I don't know. She just plays.*

*Oh man,* said Geoffrey.

*Plus Marla thinks it's fine for her to pick out her own clothes now.*

*Oh, that is no good,* said Winston.

*Really?* said William. *See, I just don't know sometimes. Do you know what I wore every single day until I was fifteen?*

We did know, but William told us again anyway.

*Overalls. Overalls and a red-checked shirt. Like a character from Hee-Haw. I wore that outfit on* 60 Minutes, *even.*

Hearing this again didn't lessen the impact. We did feel his pain.

*I mean, so my kid wears polka dots and stripes once in a while, at least she's expressing herself.*

*Mmm, I don't know about that,* said Clifford.

*Yeah, that's iffy,* said Philip.

*OK, but why?* William asked.

*It just is,* Philip said. Everyone nodded, but no one had a better answer.

*I don't think you can let this continue,* Geoffrey said. *Manipulate her* was his idea.

*Yes!* Marcus said. *Also, tell her one thing but do another.*

*Mess with her mind,* Philip said. *Tell her she's brilliant on Monday, and on Tuesday tell her she's obtuse.*

*Ooh, good one,* Clifford said. *I'd also advise backhanded compliments.*

*Control her,* Winston said. *Do not let her dress or feed the child. Or go to work. Or see her friends.* We couldn't argue with that. Well, Clifford tried to suggest it might be all right for her to have friends, but the rest of us shot him down. *Where do you think they get these crazy polka-dot ideas?* Winston added.

William reminded the group that we were geniuses, not misogynists.

*No,* some said. *We're both.*

This got us sidetracked for a while.

*Dump her ass,* Eldred said. *She sounds like dullsville.* We all vocally agreed. William told us that Marla suggested marriage counseling, and that he was really considering it. *Hmm,* we all said. *Not what we'd have done.*

*Let's take a vote!* Phillip said. *Raise your hand if you think William should break it off.* The vote was, of course, unanimous. William left the group disheartened but determined to break it off until he arrived home to Marla, who had baked him a pear tart and presented it to him wearing only an apron. Seeing his lovely bride holding the tart, William's heart softened, and he immediately agreed to go to counseling.

At the next meeting, William reported on his success in marriage counseling. He tried to explain about the tart and the apron. We understood the temptation. We have seen Marla. He told us of insights and revelations he experienced in their counseling sessions. That Marla actually had things to teach *him*. That compensation for his childhood feelings of inadequacy with a series of beautiful women had left him unfulfilled. He explained that when people do not have conflict in a relationship, it is considered a success. He used terms we were familiar with, but which baffled us in this context. He spoke of open-mindedness, communication, trust, and honesty. He spoke of serenity and spiritual awakenings. We mostly stared at him blankly as he made these reports. Sensing his imminent departure from the group, we snapped out of it and tried some last-ditch efforts to persuade him to end things with Marla. We suspected rightly that he was sharing our secrets. *She's going to get old,* we told him. *And ugly,* we said. *Hideously ugly. Also fat. Very fat. They all get fat, eventually. Bald, probably even. Oh, definitely bald.* We knew we were grasping at straws, that William was already gone. We were wildly jealous, but we kept that to ourselves.

We still take in new members every so many years, when we hear of a new genius. Now and again at the meetings William's name will come up. *Wonder how that William is doing.* We know, of course, that he's still married to Marla and that they have another toddler who is apparently only in preschool. *Imagine how fat Marla must be now*, we say. *So fat. And bald.* We have seen photos of Marla, who has to be near thirty-four by now, and she is neither fat nor bald. We speculate that his genius has diminished, but we know it is untrue. What no one wants to say is that we envy him. We secretly imagine our lives with one perfect woman who will take us away from ourselves, spirit us away on clouds and whales and the shoulders of giants, who will show us things we have never seen, and who we will stay with forever.

We meet to discuss whether or not to donate sperm. On this we are divided, even in our individual minds. Some of us believe the world could use a few more geniuses; others do not want to see more suffer as we do. We talk about how thinking physically hurts sometimes. How we wish we were dumb. How we look at the blissfully dumb people and we imagine what that's like, you who never think of killing yourselves just to have one quiet moment. We pity you, but we envy you. We think we are better than you and worse than you. We wish you could understand. Be grateful that you can't.

# Touching the Spine

## Charles Lennox

from *FRiGG*

This is the boy I know. You think you know this boy but you do not. He drinks strawberry lemonade from a coffee mug and does something like four hundred sit-ups in bed. He walks around the house in jeans and no shirt and stands a certain way whenever he sees himself in the mirror, hands on his bony hips, everything about him tight like rope. Then he caresses his stomach and says to the smooth glass, Feel the steel.

Tuesday is meatloaf night. Tuesday is when mother decides to no longer call this boy I share a room with by his first name. I have already forgotten it. He is just this boy to me. The one that grows taller as he sleeps. Who does something like seven hundred sit-ups after lunch and watches baseball through our neighbor's window.

It is summer when it happens and we are alone in the house and outside the day could be something beautiful but we do not bother to look. This boy I sound nothing like comes to me and points to his stomach and says, Go for it. Make a fist and unleash.

I say, My hands are fists and have never been anything else.

I punch him once and my elbow goes numb. I punch him twelve times and a trumpet is blown down the street. I punch him thirty-three times and there is a pyramid of sawdust on the floor and my knuckles are worn away.

This boy I want to hurt laughs at the ceiling fan. He brushes the dust off his stomach with the tips of his fingers and says, Who opened the door?

I punch him four times and hear the foundation of the world crack open. I punch him forty-two times and my left hand breaks.

I leave the room and open dad's drawer and pull out the brass knuckles and wear them on my good hand and when I come back in the room I start punching this boy who should not be my brother and concentrate on his navel. I punch him five times and break skin. I punch him nine times and unearth human tissue never exposed before to sunlight. I am the shovel and he is the dirt.

Get off me, is what he says, this boy I could erase.

I punch him twenty-seven times and see a tunnel of light. I punch him again and again and lose count and now my whole hand fits inside where his stomach should be. I punch him something like a thousand times and swear I can almost feel his spine.

# What Happened to Sheila

## Dan Chaon

*from The Rumpus*

"Don't worry, I'm not dying," said my wife Sheila.

But she was.

This was about three days before it happened, and she sat up in her hospice bed and gave me one of those complicated looks she had: comforting and teasing and scared and stubborn. She was a master of maneuvering through paragraphs of thoughts with a single expression.

"I'm not," she said, "dying."

"Okay," I said.

I believed her.

Lately, now that she's gone, I've been re-reading Sheila's work, the writer Sheila Schwartz. Her short stories, her essays, her novel.

There is this one particular story of hers which you ought to check out, it's called "Afterbirth," and it's in *The O. Henry Prize Stories, 1999*, edited by Larry Dark, and I've been thinking about it a lot.

It's a story about a woman on a plane that is probably going to crash, and it starts out like this:

> At first, when the captain's voice came on over the intercom and made the announcement, she felt almost glad. Not gleeful exactly, but a sudden ching! of recognition coursed through her; events fell into place. She was glad she'd had

her weekend at the hotel, glad for her swim in the hotel pool, for sleeping late, for the free hot coffee available in all the lobbies, tables laid out formally with linen napkins and china trimmed with gold leaf. She was glad, most of all, that she was flying alone; her husband and children hadn't come with her as they'd threatened to at the last minute. She was glad to be so selfless knowing that they were safe on the ground.

The story then goes on to follow the passengers and crew as they prepare for an emergency landing—the seasoned business travelers, an elderly couple, an angry teenager, the flight attendants and the captain himself, heard only as a voice with a "cheery lilt to it." Over the course of twenty pages, we observe the preparations and minor heroics and fears and squabbling, we observe as the main character considers the joys and mistakes of her life. As she braces herself.

But we stop before the plane actually makes its landing. Do they make it, or not? We never find out, though in her end notes Sheila says that the story was, to her mind, "...a kind of 'Occurrence at Owl Creek Bridge,' only higher up in the air." A story told by ghosts, I guess, though it actually ends in a state of hopeful suspension.

"Everyone still believed it couldn't happen to them," Sheila writes. "Not today, not with so much unfinished business, so much misunderstood, not with a husband and three babies waiting down below, their lives not yet unfolded, crushed up in cocoons of adoration, still wet with joy and love."

Not today.

That's what I'd been thinking for a very long time.

And why not? She'd been outrunning her illness for almost eight years by that point—stage four ovarian cancer, advanced ovarian cancer, a death sentence for most people, but not for Sheila. She recovered, after her initial surgery and chemotherapy, and then when it came back two years later she recovered again, so when it came back a third time, I told myself that it was going to be fine, basically, it was just another hurdle to get over.

Early on, a doctor told us that with this type of cancer "we don't really talk about being cured."

"Rather," he said, "We start to talk about the situation as a chronic illness. We look at you and we see that you're young, you've got a good weight on you, you've got a good coloring. There's reason to feel optimistic that, if the treatment is successful, you can continue on for quite a number of years."

"What does that mean?" Sheila said. "A number of years?"

"That's hard to say," the doctor said. "Two? Five? More, perhaps." He tossed off this last bit brightly, as if it was a festive indulgence—more, perhaps? Why not?– and I remember watching Sheila's pale blue eyes harden. She was a creative writing professor, and she had developed a particular politely dismissive expression when she thought you were wrong, a look with which she gently prodded her fiction-writing students. Do you really think that's the best ending for this story?

This was the gaze that she leveled at the oncologist, as if he were an apprentice writer who was insistently clinging to a bad plot device.

Two years? Five years? We both heard him say it, but we never spoke of it again.

"I've always believed in ghosts," says the narrator of "Conception," a story in Sheila's collection *Imagine a Great White Light*. "I've heard of all kinds of ghosts—frightened, desperate, lonely, evil, crazy, of ghosts who came back for no reason at all, for whom the earth is a piece of distant music behind a locked door they can't find...

'Just like the living,' somebody once told me. 'They don't know when to stop.'"

Maybe that was what we were like, I think now. Were we already ghosts, even months ago?

And yet we continued to make plans. We went on stepping gingerly into the future, expectantly. It seems crazy now that I look at the credit card bill, but we made plane reservations for a trip to Europe a year in advance. We worried over the flower garden, getting it ready for the winter so that it would be pretty when spring came. Sheila spent hours alone in her study, finishing the novel that she wouldn't live to see published, and she began to schedule readings and so forth. On her computer were the outlines of two new books of short stories, elaborate notes and drafts and tables of contents.

After she died, I found lists all over the house. She liked to write on blank envelopes, as if she were putting an address on a letter. Here: groceries and incidentals we needed. Here: texts she was considering for a new class she wanted to teach. Here: new chemotherapy drugs she hadn't tried, that she had read about somewhere...vinorelbine tartrate...etoposide... nedaplatin...irinotecan...

I guess I should have known. She had started doing chemo again in June, and by November she looked pretty terrible. Her coloring, her weight, all the signs that doctor had mentioned years before, these were obviously not good. Her skin was mottled and liver-spotted like an elderly lady's, and the hearty, swimmer muscles she'd been so proud of had wasted away so that her wrists were no wider than batons. The merrily spreading cancer cells bloated her legs and stomach, while her face grew gaunt: that sweetly prominent Jewish nose was now sharp and chiseled, like an Egyptian queen's.

She went in to the emergency room on November 1st, with terrible stomach pains, and after a few hours her oncologist, Dr. Wang, showed up. "I think it's time to consider hospice," the doctor told us, gently, and Sheila agreed.

"Just for a little while," she said. "I just need some rest

and then I'll get back on my feet."

Dr. Wang didn't argue, though later a social worker stared at us in disbelief when Sheila repeated this plan. The social worker was full of professional earnestness and compassion, with one of those gentle voices that oozed Midwestern niceness. The kind of woman who wore sweaters with cute animals on them. The sort of woman who, over the years, always took an instant dislike to women like Sheila, silently disapproving of her acerbic jokes, her lack of make-up, her ironic clothes and goofy jewelry, her unmanageable long hair and cavalier sexiness. Even in her hospital bed, even at ninety pounds and bald, Sheila still retained the authoritative aura that rubbed this social worker the wrong way. Her expression tightened.

"Ms Schwartz," the woman said, as if she understood that Sheila was probably delusional. "Ms Schwartz, you're in hospice. Do you know what a hospice is?"

Did we? I guess it was beginning to dawn on us, why we were here, but Sheila shook her head.

"Look, I'm not ready to die yet," Sheila said—and yes, she was, in fact, kind of blurry with pain medication at this point, but she spoke distinctly. "You have your agenda, but I'm not going along with it."

I nodded in agreement. "We want to go home," I said. "As soon as she's feeling a little better, we'd like to go home."

The social worker's mouth pinched, and I observed as she wrote something privately onto her chart. Agitated, she probably wrote. Illogical.

During the last year of her life, Sheila was working on a collection of stories called *In the Infusion Room*. A series of interconnected stories, all about people with cancer.

She knew, of course, that "cancer" was the easiest sort of cliché in stories, the quick fix for pathos, a beginning writer's mistake, a sorry genre in itself. Editors of literary journals begged: "Please: no science fiction, no horror, no cancer stories!"

It was her goal to reclaim the "cancer story" from the realm of Lifetime Channel TV—that bland, easy sentiment. She wrote a story about an oncologist who inherits his patient's houseful of cats, which won an award. She wrote a story about a woman who was recovering from cancer who wanted to climb Mt. Everest—mountain-climbing was an obsession of hers, and she loved doing the research; she wrote a story about cancer wigs and Beauty School students; she wrote a story from the perspective of an oncology nurse, and another about a teenaged girl with cancer who becomes, to her humiliation, the class mascot—a pet project for the school goody-goodies to dote on.

These stories are peculiar, quirky. A lot of times they are laugh-out-loud funny at unexpected moments, and full of bottled-up grief that seeps out through the edges. And rage. Quick bursts of anger that jump out and stab you right in the heart.

One of the great things about Sheila's writing—and about Sheila herself—was her ability to draw on a whole series of emotions at once without dissonance, her uncanny way of demonstrating just how complicated the concept of "humor," or "tragedy" actually is.

Of course, it's easier when things are neatly categorized, which may have been one reason that Sheila had such a struggle with Cancer Professionals.

People who say things like, for example, "The dying process can be an inspiring and beautiful journey."

We used to joke about the "uplifting" articles in her cancer magazines. CAN CANCER TRANSFORM YOUR LIFE?

That was one that she found particularly galling, full of quotes from perky cancer groupies: "Breast cancer enabled me to let things go," said one. "The everyday flow of things leaves you," said another. "I used to be a glass-half-empty person. Now I'm not. Now I'm a glass overflowing more than anything!"

I remember how Sheila would glance up from her

reading, her eyes bright with sarcasm.

"I feel so ungrateful," she said. "I'm missing out on all these great opportunities for personal growth."

I laughed. But as it turned out, most people didn't.

Most people don't like a sarcastic cancer patient, actually. It's scary and we discovered, as the years of her illness progressed, that even our dearest friends were reduced to platitudes. The idea that Sheila was dying was too painful for all of us, too unimaginable. Unacceptable. Nobody wanted to talk about it much. Acquaintances would ask: "How's Sheila doing?" and I would say, "Oh, great, fine," and it seemed more comfortable to leave it at that.

All of us learned, early on, that denial was the easiest route to take. It was such an effort, trying to conceptualize what was really happening, when all people really wanted was to be reassured, when there was such fervent hope for her to be well again. Thinking back, I can see that it had become such a habit we actually began to believe it ourselves.

We'd been married for twenty years.

We met when I was an undergraduate student, and she was a first-time teacher, straight out of Stanford, a former Stegner Fellow with a big teaching gig. She had a story coming out in *The Atlantic,* and I remember being impressed by that. I remember her teaching style, a kind of encouraging bluntness, the perfect combination of high expectations and high hopes. She would tell you honestly when something you wrote was awful, but you were always aware that she was looking for the best in you, that she believed that there was something precious in the simple desire to make art, that together you might be able to find it, that sweet spot where your own secret emotional life locked into a fictional world and made it come alive.

I know I'm only one of many of her students who fell madly in love with her, but I happened to be lucky. After my class with her was over, I used to write stories just so I could drop by her office to hear what she had to say about them, just to talk to her, to try to make her laugh that great bright, jolly, open laugh of hers, and—okay, I admit it—she was pretty voluptuous in her unassuming way, and I did find myself staring at her a little, her generous smile and her beautiful blue eyes, that look of child-like wonder and pleasure she would get when she talked about books or movies or works of art she loved.

There was a difference in our ages—she was eleven years older than me—and at first that was intimidating. I felt brave when I first asked her out to dinner, when we started meeting regularly at an Italian place near her house, purportedly to talk about my stories, but eventually just to spend time together. Looking back, I can see this as the major turning point of my life, I see how knowing Sheila created a pathway that I wouldn't have been brave enough, or wise enough, to have chosen without her. The year after I graduated from college, I asked her to marry me.

Sheila published her first book in 1991, a collection of stories called *Imagine a Great White Light*. A good introduction to her work, full of award-winning, distinctive stories, a collection that *USA Today* named one of the best books of the year, but it didn't bring her to the prominence that I imagined it would. We had two babies by that point, and she had a job as a creative writing professor at Cleveland State. She threw herself fiercely into motherhood and teaching, and began to work on a novel that she finished in the middle nineties. It was a brilliant book, I thought, but she couldn't find a publisher for it, so she went back and radically revised it again, and then revised it again, and then revised it again.

One of the things that I never could figure out was why Sheila didn't become a well-known writer. She was, herself, very modest and circumspect and philosophical about it, the world of writing was random, she said, but I was disappointed. Discouraged. She was so good, I thought, so brilliant sentence by sentence, paragraph by paragraph. She was doing things with tone and intensity that I thought were entirely original and brilliant. Her fiction walks this incredible thin line between hilarity and despair, between the absurd and the tragic, between detachment and compassion. She maneuvers with a dizzying, frightening grace—the way that Phillipe Petit walked the high wire between the twin towers of the World Trade Center.

When her novel was finally accepted for publication in early 2007, well over fifteen years after she'd first started that original draft, Sheila's life was so complicated that it was hard for her to take pleasure in it. Her elderly mother was living with us, and Sheila was busy ferrying her mother from one doctor's appointment to the other; and meanwhile Sheila was beginning to experience glimmers of her own health problems. The cancer was returning, aggressively.

Sheila's mom died in May, 2008, and in June Sheila started another regimen of chemotherapy in the hope that she could get a little more time.

Another year, we thought. Or maybe a little more? More perhaps?

She was so much looking forward to seeing this book published, this book that she'd revised and rewritten, over and over, this book that she'd stubbornly pursued for so long.
But she didn't quite make it.
Her novel, *Lies Will Take You Somewhere*, is a family drama, both tragic and darkly funny, with odd gothic undertones that emerge and recede as the story progresses. It's the story of the Rosen family: Saul, a rabbi; his wife Jane; and their three daughters. This was not the life that Sheila led, though maybe it was one that she once imagined for herself, back when she was a middle-class Jewish girl growing up in Philadelphia, back before she decided to marry a much younger gentile boy from the redneck end of Nebraska. The Rosens have the kind of life that maybe her mother would have nudged her towards, if Sheila had been less of a rebellious spirit.

Though the Rosens' life is not exactly idealized. Saul is self-absorbed and rigid; Jane is a wifty, aging flower-child who has settled but has never truly known what she wants from life. The daughters are a handful. And everyone, it seems, is adrift in a secret interior world, disconnected from each other, sneaking through their private existences even as they perform a public version of themselves.

The first scene sets up this theme in a gentle, comic way, though eventually it will become darker and more frightening. Jane catches Saul smoking in his study.

At first, because it's summer, she thinks it's coming from outside—the tail end of a barbecue, a gang of teenagers strutting by showing off with a bag of weed— but as she opens the door a cloud comes billowing out, yellow, misshapen. Saul leaps to his feet, startled, his face contorted, as if she's caught him with a lover.

"It's not what you think," he says, as the last puffs emerge from his lips.

"You're smoking!" Jane exclaims, but Saul shakes his head, I'm not. I'm not.

"Then what are you doing—eating incense?"

Saul shrugs. Laughs a little. "I don't know. I guess you caught me."

"I guess I did."

It would be funny, this blatant denial, except that Jane was just bragging to Dena, Saul's secretary at the synagogue, about how easily Saul quit three years ago, without even a whimper, and never smoked again. There was never any backsliding.

"Is this the first time?" Her voice tightens. "Have you been doing this all along?"

This is the first in a series of little revelations, small lies and concealments which grow larger and more complex as the book progresses. The novel's title, *Lies Will Take You Somewhere*, is taken from a Jewish proverb: "Lies will take you somewhere, but never back," and the book is a lovingly detailed depiction of the tangle of untruths and self-deceptions that we perpetrate in order to make our lives run more smoothly.

When the novel begins, Jane is getting ready to travel to Florida to deal with her late mother's estate—the house, which has been sitting unoccupied since her mother died six months before.

As Jane begins to explore the house, she discovers more and more evidence that she didn't know her mother as well as she thought she did, and her search to solve this mystery leads her into more and more surprising and ultimately dangerous territory. Meanwhile, back at home, Saul is struggling to deal with the children, particularly with their withdrawn, unhappy sixteen year old, Malkah—and he discovers secrets that Jane had been keeping from him.

The book has a kind of spiraling quality, both in its plot and in its emotional pull. With each turn, the novel grows increasingly menacing, and spooky, and these seemingly solid, ordinary middle-class lives unravel with unnerving swiftness.

And yet there's a gentleness in the book as well, a compassionate and tolerant eye for foolish mistakes, a tenderness for that desperate struggle we are engaged in to find meaning, somewhere—anywhere.

There's a passage early on in the book about Jane's mother that I'm particularly fond of, because it nails a certain kind of melancholy, tenderly comic tone that Sheila does so well:

> Jane can't help thinking about her mother's last moments. The neighbor who'd found her mother's body, before the EMTs came, didn't want to give her details. "Try not to dwell on it," she said. "Your mother's at peace. That's all that matters."

The chance to ask her face-to-face is gone now. The woman died too, from a fall, discovered on the concrete floor of her garage by another neighbor who herself died a few weeks after from a massive stroke—like a chain letter. Each time Jane made arrangements with a new neighbor to keep an eye on the house until she could come down, that neighbor succumbed, as if Jane were a curse, though Saul said this was nonsense, these were people well up in their eighties, their early nineties, this was the natural course of life, there was no curse, that was silly. But Jane still felt responsible. She kept the condolence notes they'd sent—"Our thoughts are with you"; "So sad for your terrible loss"—because she owed it to them, this last evidence of their existence, of their thoughtfulness even when they were so close to dying. She was moved by them, by their names at the bottom, their signatures as shaky as a ransom note—"Yours very truly, Sadie"; "Wishing you all the best, from Bernice"; or simply, "Your mother's friend, Ethel"—old-fashioned names no one would use again in Jane's lifetime, remnants of a different era.

I love this passage, with its "chain-letter" of vanishing neighbors, and Jane's pursuit of the "details" of her mother's death, as if the details might add up to some solution, like clues in a murder mystery. I love the way that these characters keep trying to put things together, to figure things out, like detectives, or archeologists sifting through debris.

When someone you love dies, it's hard not to look for them. To wait for them to come back to you. Where are you? Where are you? "Loss" is a good word, I think, because you spend so much time thinking that you can find them somewhere.

The fact that they are gone—vanished—is the most unreal thing you can imagine, and so part of you keeps searching. But there are gaps in the world, now. Places that she occupied that are just blank spots.

There is no writer who could blend the complicated, dissonant tones of comedy and sadness, irony and earnestness, satire and compassion, quite the way that Sheila Schwartz could do it.

Her students won't get another teacher who will give them the same kind of courage, that particular mix of demand and support, the intensity of motivating attention she could level upon her protégés, a transformative energy.

There is no replacement for her laugh, a low, sly, conspiratorial chuckle, comforting. A laugh that came naturally, even in the face of darkness, a laugh that enclosed you. Yes, things are fucked, but at least we're here together, aren't we?

I still have her voice on my cell phone, a message from months ago that I keep saving over and over. I have her letters and notes and lists, I have her clothes, still on their hangers, I have the white carbon bits of her ashes in a box, which she asked that I scatter over some pretty body of water, someplace where she would have wanted to swim.

And of course I still have her books, her novel, her stories, the words that she put together to create imaginary worlds. I know that she believed that a work of art was the one way for us to stay on in the world after we are gone, that was the urgency that she put into her students : this is the piece of you that will last, this is you, so you've got to do it right.

Re-reading her work, I think I can find her, just for a moment. A hint of perfume in the backyard, a tiny light outside in the distance, winking on and off like a firefly. Yes, she is there, briefly, I can feel her–though in the end, I'm sorry, I would rather have the flesh.

# Aesthete

## Mary Miller

from *Wigleaf*

I went to a wedding reception at the house of a man who painted with his ass. The largest of these paintings was in his foyer. People stood around it and said, that's his ass, because you couldn't tell it was his ass until someone pointed it out. I stood with them. I wore a black and purple check skirt, a belt cinched tight around my waist. People were surprised by the size of it.

After, a few of us went out.

I rode in the backseat with a boy I knew from school. He hadn't thought of me before but now he had his hand on my thigh, pinching at my pantyhose. I suspected he was gay. He only paid attention to the most beautiful girls, as if he could only comment on them aesthetically. His hand went up and down. It started a fire. I raised my ass and took my pantyhose off and stuffed them in the clutch my mother let me borrow. It was empty except for a twenty dollar bill, a tube of lipstick, and a bottle of clear nail polish for runs. She was teaching me how to be a lady. I was supposed to have already learned. The boy in the driver's seat was watching me in the rearview mirror, alarmed. He thought I was his precious flower. My brother was in the passenger seat smoking his silver cigarette, not offering it around like he normally did. The boy I suspected was a homosexual said I needed to shave.

We parked and got out. I went straight for the bathroom and hovered over the bowl and read the words I knew by heart. The sink was water-stained, the mirror missing a corner. I recognized myself in it right away. When I came out, the boy from the driver's seat was waiting with a can of beer. He was so tall his body had begun to curve back around. People were always asking how tall he was. I was short, but no one ever asked exactly how.

"Thank you," I said, and I stood there for a minute while he tried to open me up and then I went and sat down with the homosexual. I let him run his hand up my skirt. Touch my panties. The ceiling began to leak, the water accumulating on the table and I watched the drops swell and swell until they could no longer contain themselves.

# My Sister, the Kite

### Amber Norwood

from *Journal of Truth and Consequence*


Again I am running through the field at the college with
the geese who won't migrate and my sister, the kite,
her flying line wrapped through my fingers, which are turning
a shade of port, or eggplant. The sky, as usual, is heavy blue,

the sun a white circle punctuated by "m"s, and here
we do our battle. Her frame confronts the first day of spring,
spars outstretched and fingers wiggling. She turns back to smile
and ebb like she used to, waiting on both sides of the corner
at once, for me to catch up. And she is still

waiting, aloft in red sail. Her loud color marks
a contrast to morning; my sister, the kite,
in her blue jeans on air, and I attempt, from thirty yards,
to guide her. She twists against the keel and over the geese,
I can hear her laughing at how little I know I can do.

She grins through her hair, which today is her tail. This is resistance to air,
to me. She whips and she tugs, and I think of salvation. My fingers
swollen, and my sister, the kite, is teaching me physics
in connection. I can only hold the strings.

# Arrgh Luxury Cruises: An Authentic Pirate Adventure

## Ravi Mangla

from STORY*GLOSSIA*

DAY 1 — From the quay, their children flaunt miniature flags, all smiles and sunscreen. They arrange themselves along the narrow dock ramp, single-file, and wait for the captain to check their names off an admittance list that verifies their cash deposit—or as it was designated on the registration, "booty" deposit. The crew, in black uniforms with red waist sashes, fake earrings, eyepatches, hand out goodie bags filled with chocolate gold coins and tiny bottles of rum. One at a time, I guide them through the medical waiver and show them where to sign, right next to the X. They are dressed the part: in old t-shirts torn at the neck, skull and crossbones drawn on with marker. They wear bandanas and felt tricorns, brandish plastic swords (the kind you buy for your niece and nephew at toy stores and gift shops) or keep them ensconced in plastic scabbards. They have on fishing boots and snow boots under their ripped and tattered pajama pants. These are the kids who never grew up; or in some cases, the grown-ups who never had the chance to be kids. On the main deck, the planks creak and moan underfoot. The planks do not really creak and moan; the wooden planks are only a laminate. The ship is steel. Small speakers are concealed beneath the floorboards to simulate the sound of creaking and moaning. (This is what you get for the price.) Once everyone is aboard, the sails are raised. Black chests thrust out proudly. Birds scatter from their perch. However, again, the ship is not actually powered by the wind, but rather four 4860 kW diesel-electric engines (all together, maxes out at roughly twenty-seven knots). They are muffled with plumes of soundproofing material, which is so effective that even down in the engine room they sound at the very worst like a small hive of bees. The jackstaff is mounted at the bow, and the Jolly Roger, your standard issue black and white, is unfurled and hoisted. The sky is cloudless, the sun is shining—a perfect day to set sail.

DAY 2 — The first full day at sea is a festive occasion. I spend little time in the infirmary and most of it on the main deck with the others. Rum swells from bottles and tin cups. We pass them around the deck and sing drunkenly at the top of our lungs—"99 Bottles of Beer" and the soundtrack to Peter Pan. At night, under the star-pearled sky, we swap sea stories from our short time aboard.

DAY 3 — Two pirates in swimming trunks stop in for directions to the pool. I remind them where they are, and tell them that if they want something to do I saw some of the other pirates sword-fighting and wrestling on the quarter deck.

DAY 4 — A small pirate with a gimp visits the infirmary to ask for Tylenol for his pounding headache. I tell him that we don't have any Tylenol—this is a pirate ship. If he wants, I can prescribe him malt whisky. We get to talking and I find out his name is Leon Snackley—"Snack-Attack" among friends (owing to, I reason, his bite-sized proportions). He manages a direct mailing operation, and the gimp—which I assumed was feigned—is in fact the result of a snowboarding accident in Tahoe. I ask him how Tahoe is. He says it is nice. We exchange pictures of our families. I don't tell him that the smiling, blue-eyed blond in the photograph is my soon-to-be ex-wife, that the "mild pressure" he feels "just around his temples" is a blessing compared to the irremediable pain I feel in my head and heart. That sort of exposition is not for introductions. We agree to play a round of golf after we disembark.

DAY 5 — Aside from a few scratches and bruises, the infirmary is quiet, and I am left thinking about home. In my life on land, things have been stormy of late. Gwen, my wife of twelve years, found my trumpet rolled up inside of an old sweatshirt in our closet. She didn't understand why I had been keeping my trumpeting a secret. She asked how long I had been taking the lessons. I said four months—which was true. Previously I had been learning salsa dancing, and before that, ice skating. I would tell her I was working late, a dependable alibi. I don't know why a couple feels they have to share everything with one another. I like the idea of having a part of me buried away. I have never been unfaithful. I don't drink excessively or gamble. But I can't communicate everything; I need a little something set aside for myself. She made it so I would never have to share anything again: When I returned home from work the next day, Gwen and my two kids were missing. There was a post-it on the refrigerator saying that they had gone to stay at her sister's house. She called a week later to tell me they were flying down to Disney World, and we would file the divorce papers when she got back. I made my appeal, which, if I had the chance to repeat, I would have handled differently. I asked her what she would do for money—sell drugs? turn tricks?—and threatened to cancel her credit cards. She hung up. So while they are at Disney World, I am taking my own vacation. I needed to get away—from my medical practice, from the life we built together—and if I was lounging on some remote beach, I would wind up spending all my time thinking about her and the mistakes I have made. At least this way I am distracted.

DAY 6 — The first altercation takes place between a pirate and one of the waiting staff. He is tired of mutton and hardtack and wants a big porterhouse, medium-rare, and a glass of merlot instead of rum. The waiter informs him that neither of those items is available. They get into an argument, which escalates to some light shoving, and finally the pirate takes a swing. He is dragged to the brig, where he is chained and gagged.

DAY 7 — A pirate complains about having to defecate in public. He says he has a phobia about it. There is nothing the captain or crew can do about that.

DAY 8 — The first case of scurvy appears in a pirate: Caucasian, mid-forties. His gums are receding like a low tide. I prescribe him lemon juice and malt wort to be ingested three times daily. As for me, the early symptoms of homesickness are beginning to set in: I feel depressed and anxious, can't sleep (perhaps due to the rocking), and most of all, I am lonely. I wonder about the dog—who will get the dog?

DAY 9 — The pirates are unhappy about the lack of pool, the size of their cabins, the dearth of television and digital recorders, and above all, the terrible tasting food. The captain assures the pirates that their concerns have been taken into account; however, his words fall short of appeasing them.

DAY 10 — The seas of insurrection are brewing. Some of the crew suspect that the pirates are organizing. They observe them shuffling in and out of cabins, collecting in dark corridors, between the dim electric lights in sconces, scattering like rodents when approached.

DAY 11 — To date, according to my records, there have been six reported cases of scurvy (though one turned out to be a common cold), three cases of typhus, and one case of gangrene. The pirates with scurvy and typhus have been prescribed moderate to heavy doses of lemon juice, egg yolks, and malt wort. The gangrene patient was given a swig of whiskey and a sweaty bandana to clamp his teeth down on while I hacked off his left leg with a rusted saw. Even though it is not the pirate spirit, I can't help but think that were we anywhere outside of international waters I would have had my medical license revoked.

DAY 12 — The day is breezy and cool, and as I watch the wake roil behind the ship, I think of my wife. Beautiful, beautiful Gwen. I even wrote her a poem. I am no William Carlos Williams. Anyone who knows anything about poetry would call my rhyming couplets a crime to art, probably a crime to Hallmark as well, but it made me feel better to write them. I keep coming back to this charity dinner, a couple years ago, when I confused the ages of our kids and Gwen corrected me in front of two work colleagues and a city councilman. We made it through the night, but the next morning I told her never to undermine me like that again. She cried and said that I should know the ages of my own kids. I told her that I did know their ages, and that I had been tired. She undercooked my omelette, more than usual, and brewed the non-decaffeinated coffee, which she knew would irritate my stomach. I tried to make it up to her: I showered the bed with rose petals and hired a twelve-piece mariachi band to play outside of our window. How was I supposed to know she couldn't stand mariachi music? Make it up to your children, she said. They're the ones who need you.

DAY 13 — A scythe of moonlight slips out from beneath a bevy of clouds, only to be covered back up again. It is a dark and quiet night and the crew, including myself, has gathered in the captain's quarters to discuss defense strategies in the case of a mutiny. The captain warns us to stick together, travel in twos, and remain vigilant. Always vigilant.

DAY 14 — It is the shot heard around the ship. A pirate socks the captain in the mouth. The mutiny begins. Pirates climb the mast, swing from the gaff and bowsprit, brachiate from rope to rope, throwing eggs and rotten meat from the crow's nest onto the bewildered crew. All day long the infirmary is full of pirates and crew with concussions, black eyes, bloody noses, and broken arms. There is not a bed in the place without an injured body writhing in pain.

DAY 15 — The crew is overthrown and sent down to the hold. With his hands tied and plastic swords pressed to his back—a gloriole of dorsal fins circling below—the captain is forced to walk the plank.

DAY 16 — The pirates find a loaded pistol in the captain's quarters and a map leading to the safe with their booty deposits. They spend the day, map in hand, searching the ship for the safe. They have not yet discovered the cockpit or engine room (though it is only a matter of time), and continue adjusting the sails, even if it does little to vary their course. They determine the ship's latitude by measuring the distance between stars with their fingers.

DAY 17 — Reported cases of scurvy and typhus have risen twofold. Our supply of rum and malt whiskey is running dangerously low, and weevils have holed up inside the bread supply. The pirates are meeting to consider raiding a fishing yacht or cargo vessel and stealing the supplies they need.

DAY 18 — I meet with the new captain, an overweight man, late-thirties maybe, with a scruffy orange beard and stuffed bird, the mascot for a popular children's cereal, tied with fishing line to his right shoulder. He goes by the name of Calico Doug. He wants to know if he can trust me. I tell him that I am only a doctor. But he seems uncertain of this, and suspects I am harboring some hidden allegiance. I appeal to Leon, who stands to the left of Calico Doug. He looks down and fidgets with the drawstring around his waistband.

DAY 19 — I am confined to the hold with the rest of the crew. We trap the rats and mice that tickle around in the corners and divide them up twenty ways. (I would even take my wife's cooking over this.) All the cargo has been removed and taken to the main deck. Every few hours the pirates select two prisoners, usually waiters, to fight to the death for their entertainment.

DAY 20 — I talk with a young cabinkeeper named Becky. She is a pretty little thing with sandy brown hair like my daughter's. Before this trip, she says, she hadn't traveled farther than fifty miles from her hometown. After graduating from high school, afraid to fly, she took a job with the cruise company as a way to see the world. She tells me this as she picks the infinitesimal tendons and bones from her teeth with the sharpened tips of her nails.

DAY 21 — A violent squall lashes out. The ship bucks up and down on mounting waves. Most of us in the hold are disoriented and throwing up in fits. Thunder sounds and the rain comes swashing down. We look out the porthole and see the jagged flashes of lightning, close at hand, locking horns with a dark and livid ocean. Had the voyage gone as planned, we would have made port today.

DAY 22 — Sometime in the early morning, while we were still asleep, a speedboat pulled up alongside the ship and boarded. Its smooth egg-white hull is bobbing idly in front of the porthole. A fierce struggle rages above us, and we can hear the clangor of metal on plastic, the loutish grunts, the leaden thuds, the sporadic gunshots. The ship seems to be creaking for real now. We take turns lifting each other and peeking through a hole in the main deck left by a shotgun shell. The shrouds are torn, and the mizzen, main mast, and foremast have all fallen and lay cluttered together like a tangled handful of jacks. A thin sheet of water laps at our feet. We don't know who to cheer for; in any case, it seems unlikely we will survive this battle. Alas! Soon enough, we will be at the bottom of the ocean, with the other wrecked and barnacled ships, eels and rays threading up through a coppice of bones. I imagine, on a Disney-themed beach, artificial sand enough to fill a million hour glasses, my son is playing cowboys and Indians with a boy from New Jersey and a boy from Wales. From behind a sinewy palm, the Welsh boy shoots my son with his pointed finger. My son clutches his heart, dry heaves, and collapses to the sand, resisting the urge to smile just longer than the others.

# Foolish Creatures

## Frank Dahai

from *Toasted Cheese*

When the war was over and all the shelling stopped, Dan Barley set up a balloon animal zoo in a broken chemical factory. He displayed them on carefully labeled shelves: a fine translucent African elephant in blue, a red and green giraffe, infinite sausage dogs. He kept them tethered with string and fed them regular doses of helium from a baby bottle. Pins, knives and all other sharp objects were banned.

Children arrived, hesitant at first. They trailed in from disused cellars, rubbish dumps and sewers. They came from the burning remains of other people's houses. They were dusty, heartbroken and frightened. Dan took requests: sheeps! moo moos! His elbows carved the air while he worked on the new ones. The children squealed and squeaked in imitation. "And he will never deflate" he whispered as he put the final knot into a shimmering gorilla named George.

One morning the children knocked against the corrugated sheeting and were answered with silence. They pushed into the zoo to find it ransacked, destroyed and empty. Dan's pocket watch lay crushed under a boot print. Tiny cogs glittered in the dust. The children had been expecting this. They weren't surprised. They just set about hunting for any remaining animals.

Everywhere was checked: the pipes and rusting vats, the machines, ovens and bathrooms. It was some time before anyone thought to look up. And there they all were, still alive. A mass of colors, floating against the grimy glass ceiling, trying to escape to the sky and freedom. Foolish creatures.

The children used scaffolding and intuition to coax the animals back down. They slipped them under tiny arms, held them tight in grubby fingers and squeezed them into plastic bags. They brought them home and looked after them forever.

Even when they got smaller and smaller.

Even when they wrinkled up and collapsed.

Even when nothing remained of the whole project but dreams and patches of rubber.

# Muse

## William Walsh

from *Night Train*

Met her in a bar. *She* approached *me*. Those italics are important.

"Aren't you the poet?" she asked.

I waited a beat to answer, "I could be."

She gave me an envelope.

"What's inside?"

"Your next poem."

The bar was filled with shaved-head mommy boys, their crowns like newborns. I stood out with my hair curly on top and short on the sides.

"Open it," she said. "It's a title indicating a central image and a broad theme."

"Seamus Heaney said titles are meant to be thrown away."

"You can throw this one away."

"I just might."

"You won't."

"Fucking sure of yourself."

"Fucking sure of myself."

If she looked like anybody, she looked like Natalie Wood. Chestnut brown hair, shoulder-length, shiny. Her eyes appeared completely brown. That is, a dark brown very close in color to their pupils, and the whites of her eyes showed only when she opened her eyes extra wide. She was wearing a black leather vest with nothing underneath. Her breasts weren't big, but that's all right by me. Low-ride jeans, tight, little black boots. She was not dressed for church.

"Title to my next poem?"

"You just have to write it."

"Mine? No fees, dues, what-have-yous?"

She nodded her head yes, but said, "Or you could opt to sleep with me tonight."

The envelope was in my hands but still unopened. The television at the bar had on a reality show set in a tattoo parlor, which inspired those at the bar to begin showing their tattoos to one another, to share their subtexts.

"And if I do?" I asked.

"No envelopes. Plus you forfeit future envelopes."

"How many future envelopes?"

"Possibly an endless number."

\*\*\*

The envelope remained unopened until breakfast the next morning in my apartment, when I suggested marriage.

She could not hide her surprise. She smiled wide, a full-face of delight that I am sure mirrored mine.

"And babies," I said.

Her eyes watered. Clearly she had never thought about being a wife, a mother, raising a family. There was a shift in power. (I could write about that.)

My guess is she was one thousand years old the night we met. She had served hundreds of men like me—writers, painters, composers, and, more recently, a jazz trumpeter who is probably one of the three or four most famous jazz trumpeters. And some women, too, a ballerina, a stage actress, a field botanist.

She accepted my proposal, told me I could open the envelope.

So I got only one poem. One poem. But I've written that poem fifty, sixty times so far. And I will keep writing it.

# Population: 41,685

## Mary Biddinger

from *Memorious*


They tried to create something called a Republic.
In the back seat of a white van with no windows,

they passed a styrofoam cup and wore wool socks
on their hands, as if they'd been raised in row houses

not the cool myrtle subdivisions of white eye shadow
and glossy overcoats, mothers who pelted mailboxes

with gravel, peeling out after martinis with Joyce, Ruth,
the other one with the frosted hair and the habit

reserved for bathroom stalls and wedding receptions.
They had to write their manifesto on a night they both

remained clothed. They stole paper from her uncle's
butcher shop, running fingers along the Genoa ham

like it was a thigh, caressing the filigreed mortadella,
tagging *murder* on the sweaty refrigerator cases

then charging into the night with salty hands and dry
salami on their breath. She covered her sneakers

with quotations and burned the ends of her hair
accidentally, then called it intentional and ransacked

her sweaters in search of something torn, pilling
like her sister's skin at seventeen, pasty behind

dictionaries and other apocryphal texts that sucked
girls away from the highway overpasses and tracks.

Everything that happened underground was doctrine,
or at least subject to several lines of pink highlighter

and a flashlight beneath the chin, ghost stories over half-
eaten sandwiches. He stood still while she sketched

him in the nude, holding a can of gold spray paint,
a crimson vest hanging from the back of his chair.

# When I Worked for Madonna

**Joanna Ruocco**

from *No Tell Motel*

The bodyguards wear white
The bullets fly towards them
The bodyguards are clouds
The bullets do not penetrate
Kaddafi. The bullets are precipitation
After we drink coffee, we check
the bird feeders. Kaddafi has purple
martins on his shoulders. The bodyguards
are snowy egrets. Forget
in both directions from this moment
I am right in front of you
I have a rifle
I am sexually wonderful
like a horse

# Skin

## Kevin Wilson

*from Joyland*

Tonight, before they cross the street to their neighbors' house, Tommy and Margo wrap their seven-year-old boy, Caleb, in his winter coat and mittens and hat until he is not their son but a bundle of clothes in the shape of a boy. The wind carries the snow across the yard, thin, powdery curls snapping in the air, an angry cold. "It's just a short walk," Margo tells her son, who squirms inside the clothes, embarrassed that this much fuss is being made over him. "And it'll be worth it," his father says, patting the boy's coat to reassure himself that his son is inside. "We're gonna have fun."

The families have started getting together once a week to play cards and watch Hee-Haw, to drink beer and unwind. They are the youngest couples in the subdivision on Fawn Drive, each with a child, in houses nearly identical. Though Tommy and Margo have moved here less than six months ago, they can imagine themselves always living in this town, and they are happy to have other people to spend that time with, playing cards, watching Hee-Haw. It is a good enough life.

They walk through the snow with a six-pack of Pabst Blue Ribbon and a dip made with guacamole and beans and cheese and black olives covered in aluminum foil. Tommy carries the six-pack under one arm and holds Caleb in the other, holstered on his hip. They move through the snow and wind and cold fifty yards to the Kimball house, where they know they will be happy for a few hours at least.

Caleb wraps his arms tightly around his father's neck and watches through the slit of open space between his hat and scarf as they approach the house. He can see activity through the big window in the Kimballs' living room, the parents setting chairs around the card table, a fire already going. Kammi, the Kimballs' daughter, who is one year younger than him, is waving to them, inviting them closer and closer. "There's your girlfriend," Tommy says to his son, though the wind obscures his words. "I think she wants a kiss."

Though they mention it only in jest, to tease their children, both couples would be happy if Caleb and Kammi became sweethearts, got married, lived in a house close to them and carried on much the same way they have. It would suit everyone just fine and when they watch their children playing, bobbing up and down on the hobbyhorse and whooping like Indians, they look at each other and smile. They collectively think how nice it would be, how simple and perfect, which most simple things seem to be.

It is Margo especially who would like to see this happen, sooner rather than later. She is weighed down with vague flashes of her son and why he sometimes seems like a foreign object in her house. She has caught Caleb over the past year, crouched in the corner of his room, pants down at his ankles. She will open the door and find him positioned like that in the far corner of the room, touching himself in those places that she would rather not have to think about. Sometimes she closes the door softly and walks back into the living room and reads biographies of American presidents. She is up to Franklin Pierce, who was neither mediocre nor capable, merely a caretaker, which many of these men seemed to be.

Other times however, when the moment seems to fill up her lungs and flush her face, she grabs Caleb and spanks him, his pants already down and therefore convenient. She never tells him why she is doing this, only ever slaps at his legs and rear with a fierce silence. Her son never asks either, what it is that he has done wrong, because he has some vague idea, a notion, or else he wouldn't be in the far corner of his room.

It is what he reads that frightens Margo, his comic books always opened and spread on the floor around him while he sits there in the corner. After she has sent him out to the back yard to pull weeds or swing or just go away for a while, she gathers up the comics, looking at the pictures that make Caleb do the things he does. He always has the comic book of the Sub-Mariner opened, a muscular, pointy-eared man who lives underwater. He wears nothing but green, scaly swimming trunks and on his ankles are a pair of tiny wings, small like the wings of the tooth fairy. It is disconcerting to Margo in ways she cannot explain, obscene. There is something she does not understand about her son and these pictures of men in capes, bursting with muscles. Those tiny wings. Her son is mysterious to her, something she had not expected to happen for many years.

When they get inside, Sammy Kimball takes the beer and his wife, Tammi, takes the dip, while Margo and Tommy get Caleb out of his snow gear. The process is more time-intensive than any of them believe is necessary for a fifty-yard walk across the street.

After he has struggled out of his jacket and snow pants, Caleb sits at the counter with Kammi while the adults talk about the week, their jobs, and sit down for cards. The house is warm and smells of wood smoke and fried bologna. There is a George Jones song on the record player, singing something about not taking your love to town. Margo lays out the dip with some corn chips and Tammi sets out a plate of cold fried chicken and fried bologna sandwiches. Everyone opens a beer and the night seems easily understandable, something that can be held in the palm of their hands.

Once they've eaten their sandwiches, Kammi takes Caleb

into her room, the scent of eucalyptus and rosemary, and dumps a bucket of crayons onto the carpet. She shuts the door behind them and Caleb reaches underneath the bed for the flashlights. They crawl into the closet, a walk-in that is filled with Kammi's clothes and stacks of old magazines and newspapers that won't fit anywhere else. They take a handful of crayons and begin to draw on the walls, hidden behind the row of clothes hanging like a curtain.

This is something they have been doing for weeks, a secret they know will be discovered, which somehow makes it even more necessary.

After a few awkward weeks of playing, Kammi quickly losing interest and then yanking him into another game whether he wanted to or not, Caleb had shown Kammi a book his mother had given him, with Indians and these strange, simplistic figures drawn on the walls of caves. Actually the book was about some young brave who loses his favorite bow, but that didn't interest Caleb as much as the drawings. He and Kammi stared at the images, charcoal scribbles of stick figures riding lines that somehow suggested the form of a horse. It seemed like something manageable, a simple form of art. It was made all the more desirable by the fact that these pictures were drawn on walls, forbidden by parents. Kammi then walked into her closet and took a black crayon and drew a person walking over water, the waves of the ocean like a dozen shark fins. Caleb took a color that was called Ochre, which seemed Indian enough, and drew flaming arrows being shot over mountains, the peaks again looking much like the ocean waves Kammi had drawn, a school of sharks.

Now they have filled nearly the entire wall, simple strokes, lines of dark colors, bends and curves suggesting so much movement the wall seems to vibrate. Caleb draws a cloud, heavy with rain, spitting tiny dots of rain onto a group of grazing cows, heads bowed to the earth. Next to him, Kammi quickly scratches a quiver's worth of arrows into the body of a man, cowboy hat atop his head. She then reaches for the red crayon, worn down to a nub, to bring the blood flowing out of his body, pooling at his feet. Kammi's drawings sometimes scare Caleb, Indians falling off cliffs, dogs tearing a sheep apart, things spilling their insides. She holds the red crayon tight between her fingers and digs into the wall, laughing softly with delight.

The children hidden away, the couples switch partners. Margo stares across the table at Sammy, who is smiling at her, shuffling the cards. Tommy returns to the table with a beer for Margo and kisses her on her forehead, which makes Sammy smile even harder. The cards circle around the table, scooped up in hands and quickly arranged. Tommy bids four and Margo bids two; she could perhaps get four but she prefers to play it safe, to slowly accumulate points while the other team jumps up and down. Tammi bids three and now Sammy, looking at his cards and then at Margo, back and forth, until finally he says, "Margo, I'm going nil." Margo frowns. "I can only get two, Sammy. You can't go nil." Sammy places his cards down on the table and points to Margo. "You gotta be more adventurous, sweetie. Tell her Tommy." Tommy is concentrating on the cards in his left hand and biting into the chicken leg held in his right. "Be more adventurous, sweetie," Tommy says. Margo looks up at Sammy and he winks at her. Margo shivers and, unsure of what else to do, she starts rearranging the cards in her hand.

A month ago, at nearly two in the morning, Margo sat on the couch in the living room and read another presidential biography. They had gone out for pizza and then taken Caleb to the comic book store for the newly released books he'd been saving his allowance for. He and Tommy walked around the store, flipping through the comics, while Margo waited in the car. Caleb came back with another Sub-Mariner, a Marvel Team-Up with Spider-Man and Captain America, and something called Ka-Zar, a blonde, nearly naked, muscle-bound caveman of some sorts, riding a saber-tooth tiger on the cover. Tommy pulled the car onto the main drag and said, "The boy loves his comic books, no doubt about that."

Now, still awake in the middle of the night, both of the men in her house fast asleep, Margo went into the kitchen for a glass of milk. She drank it in big gulps, standing over the sink, staring out the window into the darkness outside. Out of the corner of her eye, she saw someone, standing in front of their bedroom window, a man standing on his toes, face pressed against the screen of the window. Before she could think better of it, to yell for her husband, lights going on all over the house, she opened the window and whispered into the night, "Hello?" The figure spun around, something in his hands, and stumbled away from the house. "Yeah?" he said, and Margo realized it was her neighbor. "Sammy?" she asked and there was a brief pause before she heard him reply, "Oh, Margo? That you?" Sammy took off his cap to further prove his identity, to calm her, but Margo still wasn't sure what was happening. "Are you okay, Sammy?" she asked, and she could barely make out the smile breaking across his face. "Couldn't sleep," he said.

Sammy was now standing in front of the kitchen window, Margo feeling the cold on her bare legs, one of Tommy's t-shirts hanging down to her knees. She saw that Sammy was holding a plastic ring of beer cans, only three left. "Are you drunk, Sammy?" she asked. He shook his head. "Not even close," he said. "I just couldn't sleep, nothing on TV, and I thought Tommy might want to have a few. He's asleep though, isn't he?" Margo nodded. "Sleeping like a baby," Sammy said, shuffling his feet. He pulled a beer from the plastic and held it up to the window. "You wouldn't want one, would you?" he asked. "It's late, Sammy," she said. "I'm going back to bed." Sammy popped the top on the beer and took a heavy sip. "You won't tell Tommy about this, will you?" he asked. Margo laughed, and then frowned at having done so. "I don't know what I'd tell him," she said. "I don't know what's going on." Sammy smiled and finished the rest of the beer. "Let's just pretend it was a dream," he said. He crumpled the can in his hand and slipped it into his jacket pocket. "Go back to sleep," he said and walked across the street to his house. Margo slid the window shut, but she couldn't walk away from the sink, gazing at the spot where Sammy had just been. She stayed awake for another hour, waiting for Sammy's face to reappear at the window, and she could not understand, or even acknowledge, the disappointment that she felt when he did not return.

Two go-rounds into the hand, Sammy throws down a king of clubs that Margo can't cover, losing the nil. Margo slaps the table. "Damn it, Sammy," she says, which makes everyone else laugh. Sammy holds his hands up in surrender. "We'll do it your way now," he says. "I'll behave."

Birds are falling out of the sky onto spikes jutting out of the ground, but Caleb tries to stay focused on the project as Kammi scribbles furiously beside him. Underneath the waves of the ocean, he draws a small figure swimming, arms outstretched, bubbles rising from his mouth. Caleb takes the Gunmetal crayon and draws two pairs of wings on the figure's ankles. Kammi notices the picture and draws an octopus near the Sub-Mariner, one tentacle moving closer and closer to Caleb's drawing. "Let's leave him alone," Caleb asks and Kammi stops drawing. She nods her agreement and it makes Caleb smile to have saved his drawing.

They crawl out of the closet, into the light of the room, and lay on their stomachs, sorting through the pile of crayons. The air is heavy with steam from the vaporizer, which the Kimballs keep on every evening during the winter because Kammi is always congested and slow with colds. They watch the machine's steady exhalations of steam, like a dragon crouched in the corner of the room. Caleb and Kammi line up the crayons according to shade, from dark to light, and then they select what they want to take back into the closet.

Before they go back, Kammi puts her crayons down and touches Caleb's face, strokes his cheek. Last week, Kammi pressed her lips against Caleb's and hummed, the thrumming of her voice tickling his teeth. Kammi likes to touch him, running her finger down the back of his neck, pulling off his shoes and socks and counting his toes. Caleb doesn't know how to respond when this happens, stands very still and counts to ten. "I don't want to draw anymore," Kammi says, and Caleb asks her what she wants to do instead. "Let's play house," she offers and he agrees, unsure of what to do next. "You lie down," she says, "and I'll get on top of you." They lie together in silence like this, their breathing not quite in rhythm. "Close your eyes," Kammi says, and Caleb does. He feels her pulling on his shirt, baring his stomach, and then she lies down on him again, the skin of their stomachs touching. After a few seconds of silence, the weight of Kammi pressing into him, he opens his eyes and finds her face less than an inch from his, her eyes wide open. "We're still playing," she says. "Keep your eyes closed."

Tommy and Tammi have won the last two hands and so they switch partners again, the men against the women. As they trade chairs, refilling their plates and opening fresh beers, Tammi asks if anyone wants to smoke some pot. "It's pretty good, Tommy," Sammy says, "This guy, some roofer who hangs out at the bowling alley on Wednesdays, gets it from Florida. And they get it from some island further south." Tommy looks at Margo who doesn't want to say no in front of Sammy and Tammi, but won't allow herself to say yes. Tommy nods in her direction, his eyes asking for her approval. "Maybe a small one," she finally says and Tommy pulls her close to him. "I only know how to roll big ones," Sammy says, "so I guess we'll only smoke half."

The door to the garage open, the four adults pass the

joint around, inhaling deeply and then directing the smoke out the door and into the garage, a cloud sitting heavy beside the Kimballs' car. "Let's hurry in case the kids come by," Margo says, and everyone laughs again. Margo wonders why she's so damn funny, but the pot is starting to calm her, relaxing the muscles in her face. She takes a solid hit from the joint and then hands it to Sammy, who licks his fingers and tends to the burning tip. "It's worth the money," Tammi says and everyone nods in agreement. They smoke it down to the end and then wander back to the card table, fresh beers in hand. Tommy deals the cards and everyone starts to sort their hands, focusing hard on the diamonds and clubs and spades and hearts, counting and recounting the numbers. "I don't know if I can get anything," Tammi says, "I can hardly read the cards." Margo notices Sammy catch Tommy's attention, motioning towards the two women. "Are you two cheating?" Margo asks, and Sammy and Tommy laugh yet again, but this time Margo admits that something about what she said, what exactly she can't say, is kind of funny.

"I was thinking, Tommy," Sammy says, "that maybe we could try that game I told you about." Tommy smiles and shakes his head, shuffling the cards in his hands. "I don't think that'd be such a good idea," Tommy says, avoiding Margo's gaze. "Is this that kissing game, Sammy?" Tammi asks. "Every time we get high, you have to think of some new game." The last time they smoked pot, burning a pan of Jiffy Pop on purpose in order to cover up the smell so the children wouldn't notice, it wasn't too long before they were all arm wrestling, Tommy and Sammy shirtless, flexing their biceps. Tommy had beaten everyone, round after round after round of hands clasped together, straining against each other, and the next morning none of them could raise their right arms without grimacing, their heads aching, nothing quite making sense.

Margo didn't like being the only one who didn't know about this game. "Kissing?" she said. "Who kisses who?" Sammy and Tommy looked at each other, giggling, and Sammy said, "You kiss everybody, if the cards say so."

Kammi kisses Caleb, flicking her tongue against his teeth when he opens his mouth wide enough, when he needs to catch his breath. His stomach is cramping and he shifts from side to side to try and slide out from under Kammi, but she is holding him down. "I wanna get up," Caleb says, opening his eyes, pulling away from her kisses. Kammi looks annoyed but she rolls off of him and lets him sit up. He stares at Kammi, her face bright red in patches, her nose starting to run. "I don't want to play anymore," he says, and she shrugs her shoulders. "It's fun," she says. "It gets fun." She kicks her leg out at the crayons, scattering them in several directions and Caleb is immediately grateful for something to do, gathering them up and sorting them again, making sure each one is lined up perfectly.

Sammy explains the rules quickly, already dealing the cards as he speaks. At the same time, everyone turns over a single card and if any of the numbers match, those people have to kiss. "What if all four of us put down matching cards?" Tammi asks. "Then it'll be our lucky night," Sammy says and Margo feels her face burn red. "I'm not sure if I want to play," she says, but Tommy leans over and rubs her arm. "We'll only play until our show starts," he says, "Just a few hands."

Everyone flips over a card, a seven of hearts, a jack of clubs, a three of hearts, and a nine of diamonds. Margo sighs, relieved. "Huh," Tammi says. "This isn't as fun as you said it would be." They flip over four more cards, no matches. "Give it time," Sammy says. "We'll work out the kinks as we go along."

On the fourth hand, there is a match. Tommy has a five of clubs and Margo has a five of diamonds. They stand and lean over the corner of the table, their lips meeting. Tommy holds the kiss a little longer than Margo would like, Tammi and Sammy chuckling beside them. "Well," Tommy says, "this isn't so bad."

The very next hand, Tammi and Tommy match up, both aces. "Here we go," says Sammy. Tommy scratches the back of his neck and looks over at Margo, who nods. "It's the rules, I guess," she says. Tommy and Tammi turn in their chairs to face each other, knees touching. Tammi kisses him, placing both of her hands on his shoulders, turning her head just slightly to the left, and then they pull away. Tommy touches the top of his index finger against his bottom lip, holds it there, and then places his hand back on his stack of cards. Sammy slowly claps his hands together in congratulations, pop, pop, pop, pop. "Now we're having fun," Sammy says and Tommy turns quickly to him. "It's just a game," he says and then looks over at Margo, who nods, her chin almost hitting her chest.

Caleb wants to go back into the closet, a fistful of crayons in his hand like a bouquet of flowers. Kammi shakes her head, her arms crossed against her chest. "It's my room," she says, "so I decide." Caleb ignores her, afraid of the games she will want to play instead, and so he crawls beneath the hung clothes and starts to draw a flock of birds, the letter M over and over in the sky. Behind him, the door clicks shut, the closet suddenly pitch black. He leans his shoulder against the door but Kammi will not let him out, has slid a chair under the doorknob. "Kammi?" he says. "Okay, I'm ready to come out." There is silence on the other side of the door, a faint wisp of light seeping under the doorframe like smoke. "Not yet," she says. "I'm thinking."

"It's dark," Caleb says, starting to whimper. He can hear the hiss of the vaporizer and then the click of Kammi's fingernails against the door, tapping a message he cannot understand. "You can come out," she says, "but you have to do whatever I say." He nods and then realizes that she can't see him so he whispers, "Okay." He hears the chair slide away from the door and then light spills into the closet and there is Kammi's smiling face, her arms outstretched, ready to hug him.

Two kisses later, a tentative, open-mouthed kiss between

Margo and Tammi, both of them surprised by the softness of the other's lips, and another, quicker, kiss between Tammi and Tommy, Sammy is the only person who hasn't kissed anyone. "I thought up the damn game," he said. "I should get to kiss whoever I want." Margo touches the tips of her fingers on her final playing card, the dread seeping into her stomach at the prospect of a match with Sammy, the taste of his mouth. They turn over their last cards, and there is a match, a pair of tens, Sammy and Tommy. Everyone laughs at the pairing, the game over, nothing broken or disrupted.

"Pucker up," Tommy says and Sammy kills the rest of his beer, smashes the can against his head, crumpling the aluminum as if it was paper. Tammi starts to sweep all the cards into one pile, but Sammy claps his hand on the table. "Well," he says, "let's do it." Tommy raises both hands in surrender. "I forfeit," he says. "Game over." Sammy is no longer smiling, a bright red ring forming on his forehead from the beer can. "Rules is rules, Tommy." Tommy looks at Margo, who looks at Tammi, who looks at the cards on the table. "It's just a game," Tommy says. "Right," Sammy says, "It's just a game. So let's go." Tommy laughs, his voice breaking. "Sammy?" he says.

Margo watches Sammy's face, the tiny beads of perspiration on his upper lip. He doesn't blink, doesn't flinch. She looks over at the clock, five minutes past Hee-Haw and she points to the time. "Hee-Haw's on," she says. "That's nice," Sammy answers, still looking at Tommy. "We'll watch it in just a second." Tommy, unsure of how to proceed or what to say to put an end to all of this, leans toward Sammy, his left eye twitching.

"Let's just go watch Hee-Haw, Sammy," Tammi says, her voice exasperated. A beat, silence, and then Sammy smiles, punches Tommy in the shoulder, hard, which makes Tommy wince. "You heard the ladies," Sammy says, "Hee-Haw's on," and then he pushes away from the table and opens the fridge for another beer.

Caleb hands his pants to Kammi, who carefully folds them and places them on the bed, next to his sweater. He is standing beside her, clothed only in his underwear and socks and he thinks, for the first time, how strange it would be for the Sub-Mariner on land, walking into a store or on a crowded sidewalk, wearing nothing but a tiny pair of swimming trunks. Things are better underwater, he imagines.

Kammi dumps the loose pieces of a puzzle onto the floor. She takes off her own clothes and sits with Caleb while they start sorting pieces by color, looking for the border of the picture. Caleb keeps thinking that he hears his mother coming to the door, the sound of footsteps in the hallway, but no one comes and he cannot decide if he is relieved or distressed by this. While Kammi hums to herself, running her hands through the pieces of the puzzle, Caleb finds it hard to stop glancing over at her, the lines of her body so similar to his, the sameness almost reassuring him. He connects two pieces, locking one into the other, and Kammi claps her hands, excited, and kisses him on the cheek, rubbing the tip of her nose against his face. He pulls away from her, but she curls her finger, commanding him to come closer. He leans forward and she kisses him again, on the lips. She tugs on his ear and then runs a finger along his right eyebrow, as if she is fascinated by each part of him. She throws her arms around his neck, squeezing him, and he pretends that he is drowning, sinking to the bottom of the ocean, and that the Sub-Mariner has swept him up in his arms, pulling him closer and closer to the surface, holding him so tightly that he cannot move. Kammi drags her fingers through his hair and he closes his eyes.

Kammi takes his hand and places it against her cheek, softly stroking the skin. Caleb tries to bend his mouth into a smile, afraid, and Kammi lets go of his hand. "Take off your underwear," she says and tugs at the elastic at his waist.

Caleb starts to shake, tears welling up and falling down

his face. He squeezes the muscles of his face, trying to stop himself, but the tears keep coming. "I can't," he says and Kammi purses her lips as if she's tasted something sour, the sight of Caleb's tears, a little baby. He starts to take in gulps of air, sputtering, and she backs away from him, crawls under the bed so that all he can see are her fingers and her eyes, shining, unblinking, waiting for what's next.

"Buck Owens is a handsome man," Sammy says, gesturing towards the man on the screen, who is strumming a guitar and smiling. Once the song is over, the cameras switch to a couple of men in overalls, crouched behind a patch of corn. "You're drunk, Sammy," Tammi says. "You shouldn't talk when you get drunk."

Margo waits impatiently for the end of the show so that they can gather up their son and go home, the evening making her more and more tired. She doesn't know what to say anymore, has exhausted the words necessary to say what she is thinking, and so she sits quietly while the show goes through the motions, knee-slapping, banjo-playing, joke-telling fun.

Before they sat down to watch Hee-Haw, she nudged Tommy and told him they should leave soon but Tommy didn't seem to hear her, his eyes glassy, his face pink and splotchy. Sammy had been sitting sullenly beside her on the sofa, unnaturally quiet, until this comment about Buck Owens, and Margo again doesn't know what to say. She does not find Buck Owens particularly handsome, the garishness of his clothes, the unflattering haircut, but Sammy, now leaning forward, points again at the TV. "If I was gonna go queer, I'd go queer for Buck Owens," he says, and there is silence in the room, no response that anyone can think of. Sammy leans back on the sofa and tries to take a sip from his empty can of beer. "Out of beer," he says, but makes no motion to get more, simply holds the can in his hand. "Buck Owens," he says, softly, almost a whisper.

When Caleb, shivering from the cold, starts to put on his clothes, Kammi, still under the bed, says nothing. He buckles his pants and feels safe again, protected. He hides in the corner of the room, away from the bed so Kammi cannot see him, and crouches beside the vaporizer, the machine softly rattling and hissing, changing water into air like a magic trick.

"Come under the bed," Kammi says, but Caleb doesn't move. "One," she says, waiting a beat before she keeps going, "two...three..." but Caleb leans against the vaporizer as if to hide, the warmth radiating from the machine, the hissing in his ear like someone whispering, someone with a secret to tell. He will not go to her, and his mind flips through the possibilities of escape, of gaining the upper hand. "You better come right now," she says, and Caleb presses his hand against the open mouth of the vaporizer, the steam moving so quickly from the machine that it seems to pass through the skin and out the other side of his hand.

Pain travels up his arm, all the way to his teeth, which chatter violently. He thinks he hears someone calling his name but his head is buzzing. "What?" he says, "What?" and his hand is numb, and there is the smell of burning, and when he pulls his hand away, the skin slides off the palm of his hand like a wet sheet of paper. There are ragged pieces of flesh hanging off his hand and he frantically tears at them, trying to make the skin smooth again, uniform. Kammi comes out from under the bed and sees his hand, what is left of it, and screams, the sound so high it chokes itself out while her mouth is still open. Caleb stares at her mouth, the perfect O her lips make, and he holds his hand out to her, the mess he has made, and she screams again, even louder.

When Margo reaches the door of Kammi's room, she finds the two children, Kammi nearly naked, her chest bare, and her son, standing quietly in the corner of the room, holding his hand out as if waiting for his palm to be read. Before she can ask what is going on, she smells burning flesh, the sharp scent making her flinch, and she finally notices Caleb's hand, the top layer of skin evaporated, burned away. "He touched the steam," Kammi says. "I didn't tell him to do it."

Tommy, who is now standing behind Margo and has sobered up just from contact with the situation, pushes past his wife, who cannot move, and scoops up Caleb, running back into the hallway with his son in his arms. "Do we call the ambulance?" Tammi asks. "What do we do?" Tommy grabs the keys off the counter and yells for Margo, who is still standing in the room, staring at Kammi, shirtless, her nose running. "Dammit, Margo," Tommy shouts. "C'mon." Sammy is still sitting on the sofa, drunk, oblivious to the activity. "You want us to come with?" he asks, but Tommy is already running across the street, towards the car in the driveway.

Tammi stands beside Margo and places her hand on her shoulder. "You should go, honey," she says. "Tommy's leaving." Margo, her hands clenching and unclenching like spasms, a rush of anger burning her ears, steps towards Kammi. "What happened, Kammi? What happened to Caleb?" Kammi backs away from her and whimpers, "It wasn't my fault." Tammi kneels beside her daughter and pulls a shirt over her head. "You should probably go now, Margo," Tammi says. Margo turns without a word and walks into the living room. Sammy raises his hand as she opens the front door. "See you next week?" he asks.

Standing in the doorway, her anger undiffused and expanding, Margo listens to the sound of the car horn, frantic and irregular. She wants to punch Sammy in the face, to set the entire house on fire, but then she remembers her son, the hand open and trembling. She steps outside, the shock of cold on her skin, and feels her anger harden, turning from a gas into a solid, heavy in her chest. She can feel it as she breathes, but she keeps running towards the car, the engine idling and then revving, the hi-beams blinding her, illuminating the snow as it falls.

The car moves slowly, the roads slick with snow, just starting to freeze. In the backseat, Caleb lays his head on his mother's lap. She holds his burned hand away from him to keep him from touching it, something he wants to do very badly. He can't feel anything. He stares at his hand, the skin glistening and wet, and he knows it is a part of him, but he cannot locate it. It is his hand and no one else's, right in front of his face, and yet hidden from him. The car bumps along the road, his mother holding him, the snow whipping against the windows, and Caleb falls asleep before he can feel the part of him that is damaged.

# The Woman Down the Hall

## Lily Hoang

from *Lamination Colony*

**An Introduction**

There's a woman sleeping down the hall.

Her hair isn't golden or flaxen or any of those perfectly descriptive words. Her nose isn't slight or bold. Her body isn't proportional or buxom. Her lips aren't full, but they are also not lacking. Her cheekbones are not defined or flat, but her eyes. Her eyes are full of gray, but really, that only means that they are neither light nor dark.

She isn't particularly striking in any way. Which is why she doesn't threaten me. She doesn't frighten me. I am not scared.

This woman sleeping down the hall from me, from us, she has slept for days and days and still will not emerge. She has snored and ground her teeth, and this disrupts my nights. But then, they also manage to disrupt my days, and it is for this reason that I wish to kill her. Now. While she is sleeping. Because lord only knows how long this woman can sleep.

I am certain that she can have little more than blistered gums by now. It's that sound of bone scraping against bone. It's not just a sound. It's really happening. This woman sleeping, she must have a burden that nestles like a bird, and hungry, it scrapes and scrapes and she must have nothing left in her mouth but the bloody remnants of that secret, whatever that secret may be.

I have never killed a woman, but I have often wondered how I would do it. Now, I wonder if her neck, which is not slender or thick, would be easy to grasp or if my large hands would simply slip from smooth skin. But of course I imagine that her skin would not be particularly smooth or rough. It is simply her way.

But I am not sympathetic. She disturbs me, and this is something I do not allow.

## The Cold Outside

Once, when I was old, I knocked on a door because it was snowing. Because it was cold, I was wearing nothing but tatters and fragments, and when the door opened, I asked to enter. I was very old back then and could barely walk and yet, somehow, I managed to travel quite a far distance simply to knock on this door. When the door opened and a maliciously smiling girl appeared I found myself suddenly energized. Her eyes were fire, and looking at me, I was warm.

To the small girl, I said, "It's cold out here, outside, but you have shared your warmth with me, and now I am no longer so chilled."

The child looked just beyond me. She barely bothered to notice that my lips were once again beginning to chatter, and although I wanted nothing more than to push her down and run towards the flickering fire behind her, I smiled the kindest emotion I could.

She said nothing.

To the small girl, I repeated, "It's cold out here, outside." I said, "Dear child, won't you let me into your house? It's quite warm in there I can tell. From your eyes, I can tell that there is warmth tucked directly behind you, if only you'd let me come in."

The child continued to look beyond me. I was certain that she did not flinch when I began to speak. This, I am quite sure, is no small feat because it has been a great while since I have had the pleasure to engage in oral hygiene. It is nothing personal. There is, in fact, little more that I would like than to be able to wrap some floss around my fingers.

I looked at this small girl with her vacant face, her eyes passionate about something entirely not me. I wanted to kill her. I wanted her to let me into her home so that I could do so without the neighbors noticing.

Once again, I tried, "I am an old lady, dear child. Can you not see that I am shaking, even now as I speak I cannot stop my teeth from banging violently together?" I extended my hand towards her.

I reached and I reached, and I was certain that eventually, either my limbs would extend no further or I would be able to touch her, but my hand kept moving forward and we never did intersect. Nor did she move. It was the strangest thing, how this child avoided my touch, a touch that we both knew would be lethal.

And my arm, by this point of acknowledgement, must have been nearly four feet long. It was a piece of salt-water taffy, only not so sweet or edible.

Finally, when my arm had reached its limit, the girl looked to me and said, "Old lady, you may enter my home, but only if you take out all of your teeth and both of your eyes. Then, you must peel away the nails from your fingers. When all of this is done, knock once again on my door, and I will come outside and strip you of your impure rags and bring you into a warm stew of bath, and there, I will clean you with my own small hands. After you are clean, I will set you by the warmest fire, and there, we will feast."

I looked at this girl. There was nothing left in her eyes, but she did not avoid my gaze. So I began, one tooth at a time.

## The Little Bird that Could

It is true that the little bird had lost nearly half of its left wing after the dog had had her pleasure with it. The man did all that he could to salvage the small bits of cartilage, pressing chunks of loose flesh back into the bone, hoping it would stick like putty if only he applied enough pressure for a long enough period of time.

He drove. He drove knowing that it wasn't safe for him to be driving while holding a dying bird in his lap, pellets of muscle staining his pants, but he was careful, and he knew that if he waited, the bird would not survive. For this, he is a kind man. It would be impossible to not think he was a kind man when he did, after all, leave his car running when he reached the animal hospital to ensure that the bird received prompt attention. Some would call this stupid, a man abandoning his vehicle like that, but those more foolish would call it kindness, but it matters little how he is judged because he did, after all, leave his car running and in doing so, it was stolen, but by then, the bird had been stabilized, and he cared more for the bird's health than a money-eating car.

He in fact had stolen it because it wasn't but earlier that day that some louse left his car unlocked with the key still in the ignition. This man, this kind man who saved the poor bird, out of dumb luck stumbled across this car, this car that clearly belonged to someone else, but not caring much, perhaps because of intoxication, he got in and drove away.

We're not going to call it karma or fate or any of these words, but it is impossible to deny that there is some kind of cycle involved because the moment he walked into his house, still intoxicated, although that may be too kind a description, he saw blood drizzled in chaotic trails. Out of curiosity, he followed these movements, which he alone could see. We have seen the house and the blood and sure as shit there's no way he could've seen any kind of pattern, and yet, somehow he did, and after he followed the trail to its end, he saw the dog and the bird. He's certain that at some point there was a struggle, perhaps even a war, but by the time he saw it, there were bits of dull bone protruding from this mass of flab and dirty feathers. The dog tossed it up and caught it. She tossed it up again and caught it midair. The man puked in his hand. Then, he called the dog, "Here Killer. Here boy." The dog's name wasn't Killer. The dog wasn't his. This wasn't his house. But the dog came anyways. The dog came and dropped the bird on his feet.

This is when the miracle happened, when the inebriated man picked up the pulsating carcass and crammed his own fingers over the missing pockets of organs and skin, exchanging his spare body parts for the ones it lacked for just a moment or two. The bird, recognizing a strange kindness, continued to breathe. This was perhaps all the little bird could do.

So the man jumped into the car that was not his and drove with the little bird dissolving in his lap to the animal hospital where the second miracle happened and the bird survived.

It was certain that the bird had only one functional wing and that the dog that damaged many of the little bird's nerve endings, although which ones in particular weren't quite clear. The man, now quite sober, agreed to care for the bird, which he'd become certain was some type of savior.

After eight hours of surgery and after he waited for another two hours for news that the bird had survived the anesthetic and all else, the man finally went outside, and he didn't even bother looking for the car, as he was sure that it had been stolen and if it wasn't, he certainly didn't have any respect left for a car that sat outside for ten hours with the keys still in the ignition that couldn't be stolen. He walked the many many miles necessary to reach his own home, his real home.

He was tired, but he didn't rest. He went inside and immediately began building a birdhouse. It had once been a bonding father-son activity, although he could hardly remember if it was between him and his father or him and his son, but his hands knew where to hammer, where to hold without instruction. And so he built and he built with great vigor until the house was complete. A two-story mansion designed specially for a bird missing a wing. Everything was slightly off, on this diagonal skewer, and the man, satisfied, slept. He slept for what must have been days and days and he never emerged, not even to go to the restroom, and it was not until the animal hospital called for him three days later that he finally woke, completely refreshed.

The man got into his own car and drove. He drove until he arrived and picked up his little bird, his own little bird. He was happy to see it standing, although the dog had almost lopped off a sizable portion of the bird's left leg. The man reminded himself to account for this in the birdhouse.

Joyous, the man drove home, eager to show the little bird his new palace.

## The Soundless Bloody Whistle

So I began one tooth at a time, and without anesthetic, it was difficult and bloody. My fingers became pliers, and they twisted and pulled with strength even I did not know I possessed. Perhaps it was out of desperation or out of coldness, but my fingers were icicles and pick-axes, and I performed the most skilled operations until all of my teeth were gone.

I took out all of my teeth, even the ones that had not yet formed, and I put them in a small pail for the little girl to inspect. They jingled a pretty melody, which I wanted to whistle but could scarcely manage a piddle of a sound without my teeth.

I took a swig of something that burned my throat, and it stung the corridors of my gums, but I didn't mind because there was some sort of numbing agent contained in it so I took a few more swigs until swigs became gulps and I was firmly intoxicated.

Intoxicated, I hastily plunged my icicle fingers into the sockets of my eyes and scooped them into the pail.

Without eyes, my hearing suddenly became muted, but I could feel vibrations in the ground with great accuracy. I could feel the little girl's little feet stomping down the stairs, skipping through the hallway, and pausing only briefly to unlatch and unlock and open the front door.

She did not invite me into her house, but this time, I did not wait for an invitation.

## The Unanimous Decision

For a woman to sleep days and days, she must be very tired. Or sick. Or perhaps both. For a woman to grind her teeth with such earnestness, she must be very guilty. Or sick. Or perhaps both.

I know that I should have sympathy for her. I know that women like her should be cared for and loved, but it is impossible for me to do so when she annoys me, and it is not just me. We are all annoyed. Her presence bothers us.

Only last night, we met in the tearoom, and although we had neither called a meeting nor extended invitations, everyone promptly arrived as though we knew the time had come for us to make a decision. Only last night, we all sat in the tearoom in solemn silence for minutes and minutes. We all closed our eyes, breathing in her grinding teeth and mucous-filled snores. I admit that I wanted to speak. I wanted to be the first to propose murder, but I restrained myself. It isn't proper for a lady to speak first, even if she is the designated killer. So I waited. I waited and waited, until the woman beside me inhaled a sigh and the entire room bounced with all the anger and frustration that had been muted for so long.

It is very difficult to order an overzealous crowd, but I sang a sweet song and they became enamored with the melody. One at a time, they stopped their screams to soak in the message of death, the calling for murder, and even though I created the song as I sang, we sang in unison, in perfect harmony, and that's how I knew the decision was unanimous.

## Weeping Beauty

The princess was very beautiful. This much cannot be disputed. She was so beautiful that her lips were veiled and her eyes shaded and every inch of her skin shrouded with death. It is said that this princess was so beautiful that any being that saw her would weep until they were sick with dehydration and even then, they could not stop crying.

Now this was a time before medical sophistications like diagnosis and needles so these people and goats and rabbits and lice were doomed to die. For a while, the king's cavalry tried to transport the more important people, like dukes and dames, to nearby sources of water, but submersion did little other than iron out wrinkled skin, but the discovery of the Fountain of Youth is an entirely different tale. Of course, even this mystical, magical fountain could not save these dukes and dames, but they were certainly the most attractive and youthful dead dukes and dames ever recorded.

Only no one suspected the princess for quite a while, at least not publicly. Even after the King and Queen and all the princes and princesses and dukes and dames and ladies and sires where dead, no one wanted to implicate the baby princess. That, they figured, would practically be sacrimonarchal, which was practically sacrilegious, and no one wanted God's scorning.

So the young princess continued to kill all the people who came to care for her, for simply looking at her was a death sentence, and it was only after she had unknowingly caused the death of her entire kingdom and adjacent kingdoms that a young knight suggested that perhaps she was to blame.

So this young knight, being the bravest of young men, volunteered to care for the princess, and after he traveled for weeks to reach her, he knocked on the palace door and used a thick blanket to cover his eyes.

He begged the princess to drape a curtain or several curtains over her head until not a single bit of skin was exposed. The princess complained of the excessive heat under all the cloth, but the young knight would hear nothing of it. He said, "Lovely princess, I am immune to your sweet words, but I am not strong enough to survive your beauty, and so I beg you. If you wish to eat today and tomorrow and for the remainder of your life, please, cover your entire body. Do not let even the slightest amount of skin reach my eyes."

She responded with a sweet song promising him that she would remain under layers and layers of curtains if only he would care for her

He reached to open the palace door. He knew that she was lethal and yet he desired nothing more than to see the face that had killed more than a thousand men. He dropped the thick blanket covering his eyes and saw the most majestic woman. It was then that he began to weep until there was nothing left to him but bone.

**The Little Bird that Couldn't**

He loved for the little bird. He cared for her. He chewed her food for her and drizzled slowly it into her little beak. Most of the time, the bird spit it back in his eye, but he was not offended. He loved the little bird.

Life was wonderful for this small family unit for days. He would often crawl into her birdhouse and spoon her when the nights were coldest.

Then, on the fifth day of their harmonious union, she fell out of a second story window and broke her neck.
Or maybe she didn't fall. Maybe she jumped.

## Promise

To the old haggard of a woman, I said, "Old haggard of a woman, you have almost done as I have asked. You have taken your eyes out and pulled out all of your teeth, but I still see a shard of shining white in your mouth, your mouth which is foul with blood and stink. I find you disgusting, but I can ascertain that you have indeed attempted to do as I have told you. I am a kind girl, old woman, and I will fulfill my end of the bargain, even though you did not. I will pity you with my kindness."

The old woman smiled and her mouth brimmed with slime.

## The Returned Gift

She was not an uncaring or cold princess and she, being lonely for so long, took the young knight in her arms and connected her lips to his. She transferred as much of her spit into his mouth as she could. She did this until her throat was coarse. The knight stopped weeping, but it was still quite clear that he was dying.

The princess ran to the fountain and scooped water out by the handful and ran to the knight and fed it to him. Slowly, he gained color. Slowly, he gained strength. And the princess continued her running from knight to fountain, which was no small journey, but she was determined to save him, her last hope for a friend.

It took many years for the young knight to fully recover, but it mattered not because he had consumed nothing but fountain water so he looked as youthful as the day he knocked on the palace door, and the princess, she had legs and hands of pure muscle from her many trips from fountain to knight. She was certainly kind and caring, but she was not smart, and for this reason alone, once the knight was strong enough to walk, he slapped her once across the face for not dragging his lithe body to the fountain, thereby saving nearly a decade of running, then he kissed her and returned all the sour spit she had so altruistically given him nearly forty years ago.

**Ever After**

He took a vow that day. He swore that never again would he save another being. In fact, he swore destruction on the world. It was his sole mission to kill all things sweet and kind.

That is how he came to reside with us.

They did not live happily after, but they did live together— he constantly reminding her how stupid she was for lack of education and she ever reminding him that though she may be dumb, she saved his life. In many ways, theirs was a peaceful union, and if nothing else, they were by far the most handsome and youthful rulers in the entire world, although none could actually see her.

But after centuries of rule, the young princess became quite bored with the young knight. She looked at him and said, "Darling, I've become bored with you."

He said, "And I with you. I can't believe there was once a time when your beauty killed men. Now, you're so average."

He said this without thinking, and she knew this instantaneously. So did he.

There was not a pause. She did it without hesitation. She dropped her veil and her shades, and all of her clothes fell off of her body, and he began to wail.

And that is how she came to reside with us. That is how she came to snore and grind her pretty teeth all day and all night.

The old woman smiled and her mouth was slimy, which I hate. I hate slime. I hate things that shine. But as quickly as she smiled, her mouth opened widely, as if she wanted to swallow me in one fell swoop, but then her eyes caught the empty holes where eyes once were directly behind me. Thousands of them. I hate to brag, but many beggars have come to knock on my door and I offer them a warm bath and company and they in turn remove their teeth and eyes and once they enter my home and I remove their slime, they no longer live. I do not kill them. They simply stop living.

This old woman though, she was different. I had a kinship to her. I felt a warmth that I have not felt since my dear brother stopped living. So I said, "Old woman, here are your teeth and your eyes. Screw them back into place, but only if you promise to live with me forever after here and play with me every day. Old woman, I make you this offer, but you must not try to eat me. You must play with me and all my dead old beggar men."

The old woman smiled and hungrily grabbed for her teeth. She sharpened the roots into screws and put them all back into her mouth. She said, "Now, dear girl, do you have any floss?"

**An Ending**

This woman sleeping down the hall, it is my duty to kill her. It is true that I live in a house filled with murderers and evildoers, and it is true that we take turns torturing our guests, and when there are no guests, we play games such as Monopoly and Trivial Pursuit to pass time. We are a family, and I have never killed a woman. Before I was an adolescent, I had seen scores of beggar men die, and I mounted their dead heads on my wall for decoration, but I did this only because my parents left me with no paintings when they deserted me.

But now I must do what I must do, and I wish to do it without an audience, so if you please.

# He Has Juice

## Kim Chinquee

from *Conjunctions*

It is a routine now: first the man will pour his coffee. She will drink her water before anything, and they will hear the other couples, however politely. Mostly everyone is not English.

They'll put on snowshoes.

And now their usual stuff is waiting: the bread and cheese, the boiled egg, sliced portions of a turkey. Ham, and creamer. Jam by his plate and she has butter. They'll take whatever bread and put it in their pockets: not for hunger, but if anything is left, the lady will bring less. This concerns them. The lady comes to deliver. The lady has no English, but the lady's son has come to them, all smiles and his hands in, with a nodded welcome.

They'll climb. Higher and look down, in, the wind slapping. They might sit. Their jackets are thick, like they are, and she will lean there, with his stick up. He might clutch his chest with neither of them laughing, and he would blame nothing.

He has not mentioned his condition.

She never pressed. She'd been a medic.

They'd met in California, talking at the cafe. It seemed silly, then.

But he says now, what's to lose? Is anything really anything?

They will go again, and they will cross the ocean.

They will.

But won't they?

For now, they sit quietly, watching the woman outside, her shovel so seemingly heavy. The wind chimes chime, and it smells like cinnamon toast.

# Pact

## Lydia Copeland

from *The Northville Review*

Sometimes there was snow, and we'd leave water trickling from both faucets. I'd lie on the couch with PBS turned low, listening to the clinking in the sinks and thinking of icicles melting from eaves.

My mother would still be asleep in her room right where we left her, still wearing a coat and gloves. My brother would always carry her to bed, and I'd tuck her in, close the mini-blinds, turn on some white noise. The next morning I'd open her room, raise things, let in the light.

She'd kiss my cheek, say, "Hello sweetheart. Goodbye," and then go back to sleep. For the rest of the day I'd walk around with a sweet whiskey smell where her lips had been.

My brother was tiny. I was tinier. We made a pact to stop eating certain things — cheese, fried chicken, snack food, chocolate. And no more sodas. I was better at the not eating part than he was, but he spent his evenings running and jumping hurdles after class.

Mostly I stayed home after school. I had paint-by-numbers and books on tape. I liked being in my room, and I liked walking around outside looking for birds' nests, fox holes, new growth in the spring. I liked sprinkling our cat food in the snow for the squirrels to find. Our cats were wild, but my brother could coax them into flea collars with cans of tuna.

With so much cold, our windows would fog over, and I'd trace the one in my bedroom with the outline of the river, the mountains and barbed wire fences. A stick figure replica of our land. My scene would fade by the end of the day and reappear every morning like a secret message for me. Go out, it would say, into the world of crosswalks and buildings that white out the stars. Be unflappable, glamorous, tall. Wear nice dresses and speak clearly.

But those things would take years.

# Suspended

## Kyle Minor

from *Brevity*

The locker room walls were painted puke green and lined like a cage with metal hooks, and red mesh equipment bags hung from the hooks like meat. One of the bags was swinging, and I was swinging in it, and Drew McKinnick slapped at it and did his punching, and the janitor got me down.

What did my father say to the principal, and how many times had he said how many things? My boy is not eighty pounds yet. My boy is in the seventh grade. My boy is not a linebacker. Can't you see I love my boy? If you had a boy to love what would you not do?

What did the principal say to my father? Did he say he had a boy and the boy got caught drinking in the tenth grade and he kicked his own boy out of school, same as anybody else? Did he tell my father what he told us once a year when they brought the boys into the gymnasium and left the girls away? *I loved and love my wife, and she is not my ex-wife, not praise Jesus in the eyes of God, despite her running off with the Navy captain, despite it all I wait and wait and one day she will be restored to me. I know it in my heart of faith, I wait as Hosea waited, now let us pray.*

Whatever passed or did not pass between them, this once it did not matter how much money McKinnick's father gave the school, or how many animals he had veterinaried to health, or how many ordinances he had sealed with his mayor's seal. This once I came home beaten and bruised and told my father, "They suspended him for three days."

That night I slept and dreamt of three days free of red ears flicked blood red and slapped until I heard the ocean. The bathroom was mine to piss in, free of fear of footsteps from behind, one hand in my hair and the other on my belt, the painful lifting, then my head beneath the commode water.

That afternoon I skip-stepped to the bus, the Florida sun high and hot, and this once thinking the heat balmy and tropical rather than stalking and oppressive. Then, somewhere between the Route 7 and the Route 8, somebody grabbed me by the collar and slammed me against the black bumper. At first I thought it was him, because it looked like him, same dog teeth, same mocking smile, but bigger somehow, and how had it been kept from me he had an older brother?

"You think you're something," he said, and lifted me until my feet were off the ground. He was as big as my father. "You ever run crying on my brother again, I'll beat you within an inch of your life, you hear me? I wouldn't mind breaking you."

He had me up against the back of the bus, and somewhere somebody had taught him how to do it, and his brother, too. I can see their faces now, but younger, fleshier, their father pressing their bodies to the wall, and then, older, leaner, their sons looking down at their fathers in their fear, learning.

# Laughter Incidence

## Ander Monson

from *Spork*

He could hear occasional laughter through the dark air. He couldn't tell how far away it was, how much air was between the laugher and the listener because at night space opens up, distance begins to flex—perhaps because of the dearth of visual stimuli the mind discerns more from the world around it, catches more of what is thrown constantly at it, all the everything fighting for your attention, and it must decide what is important and what is not, and this becomes more difficult at night, so everything strikes you completely new. There was this guffaw that repeated ten times over the space of an hour, at irregular intervals. He marked this down on graph paper: Laughter Incidence, September 27th, and proceeded to start creating data points. There was also the sound of cases of bottles rattling, likely the result of stacks of beer bottles being transported to a party by several different individuals. Some murmuring occurred. Another laugh—this one went on for several minutes, and then the sound of broken glass. And with that Jeremiah was up. He couldn't sleep again, not that he had tried all that hard to do so for the last several hours, interested as he was in the spontaneous occurrence of sounds happening in the world outside his fourth-floor apartment that overlooked the city.

It was late. Surely teenagers were out having fun, and that would explain the incidence of laughter. He made another tick on the graph and thought with each data point that he would be able to track the engagement of his neighbors and their guests in entertaining activities. This was good enough, some nights, to keep him involved, for him to feel like he was part of society. He didn't go out during the day, causing his neighbors to wonder if he was even there at all and not some poltergeist trudging through the apartment building. He met the girl downstairs, who had quite obviously locked herself out and had to ring the series of doorbells—this was just before noon, and he was the only one home, she said, and he almost didn't let her in, since he had never seen her before either. *Why should I believe you?* he asked—*I've lived here for three years and never seen you once.* This was possibly not quite true. He had seen several of the neighbors surreptitiously through the windows late at night. Not that he went out of his way to spy on the girls who lived here—they were mostly nurses who worked at the hospital less than a mile away, the hospital that was responsible for the airlift chopper service that happened probably three times a night most nights. He wasn't a voyeur or anything like that, but he was interested, and people were interesting, and he had seen some of his neighbors when they did not know they were being watched, and he thought maybe he had seen this girl from behind in a bra one time. Not like he could tell her that, or ask if she ever wore a maroon racerback, so instead he just let her in, said fine, came down to the door and flipped the switch. *Thanks,* she said, *which apartment do you live in?*

*The top floor,* he said, gesturing upwards for no good reason. *Which car is yours?* Because that's the only way he knew most of his neighbors was through glimpses caught at night or by their cars parked out back in the covered lot.

*Gold Probe, I live downstairs on the north side.*

She had said her name too, along with thanks, but he had forgotten it already. His apartment had an excellent little deck. He sat out there at night a lot. He recorded some of these nights on tape to play back later when he couldn't make something out. He did this for no real reason except that he felt the night could use more attention paid to it. Bad things happen then, and you never know what might need documenting later.

He could have overheard a crucial piece of dialogue that might be used later to win an argument, or he might have evidence of some crime, conspiracy or something else, on tape that he could use much later. He did a lot with tape. Ripped vinyl to CD, mostly, cleaned up the sound, did some light remastering. It was lucrative. It was all done through the mail or through his high speed connection to the Internet and by extension the rest of everything. Very occasionally he would consent to talk on the phone, but that was only with the few clients who had earned this through years of contracts. As far as anyone knew, he physically might not have existed. He had disappeared.

He was sort of pale, though he used a sunlamp to give him some of what the medical texts said that everybody needs some of. He just preferred it later, when most of the world had returned to the domestic details of their lives, the casseroles they were concocting (and the smoke that their cooking sometimes resulted in, curling through the air like very tiny eels), their episodes of Jeopardy or All Things Considered played via podcast at their convenience. He wasn't really part of that, he knew. He had given up his role. Had been married, or almost married, twice, to two different girls. Had left one at the altar in front of her and his families and nearly five hundred guests, stood her up as the phrase goes; he had froze, could feel it in his toes in the shoes he was wearing in the rented car on the way there, and he did feel bad about this, but had simply disappeared. No one knew where he had gone. The pressure must have got to him, someone said. Surely he was the victim of foul play, someone else surmised. *I wouldn't have gone through with it either,* the father of the bride said, confidentially, afterwards to his wife, who knew their daughter could certainly be a terror. *But still I would love to kick his ass when I see him again, if we ever do.*

He had given all that up. It was no great loss. The machine of it could have carried on regardless. And it did. The reception went on. Songs were played. Food was consumed. It was a practical conclusion to a failure of a day. *People might as well eat up,* the bride's father said.

*Help us celebrate our loss!* said the mother, before she amended it, *I mean help us celebrate whatever we have left. Forget about the past. Though the open bar has now become a cash bar. Sorry.*

He knew all of this because one of his friends had done a documentary of the wedding, at his request, and posted it on the web a couple days later as a monument to his presumed sadness. It got out when the news media had descended on the story.

He missed it sometimes, the world of humans interacting, but not all that much. He'd go to Wal-Mart or one of the 24-hour FoodUSA supermarkets and talk to the unlucky wackos who worked the night shift if he needed conversation. It wasn't so bad to be gone from it. He was efficient. Set his own hours, obviously. His recordings and his graphs took up a lot of time. And light was so much more pleasurable at night, when it came in smaller doses and illuminated less of each individual story at one time.

# Swanbit

## Terese Svoboda

from *failbetter*

Solely and thus sorely did he row off the disk of the sun that the lake reflected and into the dark of the piling-held dock where many-legged water-denizens and not just water-livers lived, where he lived, when he could. For $54 he rented the boat, the tackle, the winsome boxed flies in inky camouflage, but what he really paid for was the dark under the dock and the water legs with their habit of crawling or clinging to a region that confounded him, where mornings, he reached and pried and sliced open and ate through the variously molluscked and non-molluscked on his own.

He was not mad. He could not get out of his boat without a winch, commercial or otherwise, being legless. The charitable called him cripple but born without, it was not a case of crippled from, but just himself. He towed himself into the best spot under the dock and grasped at the water life, its green shoots as misplaced or misaligned as he, and he became mad.

Starfish, crab, spider but not the minnow he decided— the legless minnow were not fair game. He left minnow alone. Fins were arms and if, while hauling up one of his catches, he tipped the boat too far and overturned, he, in his madness, would hope for the fish to help him swim even better than he with his arms like extra oars, swam. A dolphin with a saddle wasn't what he expected but some fish nudging at his bubble-exhausted middle, nudging for all his pains taken, those many hooks unbent around all those gills. No way could he remount the boat himself if he overturned, he needed at least a leg over.

Birds that knew of his leglessness followed his rowing, or stood off, waiting, or dove at his bait and tried to steal it. He grabbed for them, declaring them armless, the wings useless. In the water with such arms as he had from having no legs, he could grab the birds easily and had, catching quite a few duck, and had eaten them plucked and grilled over an iron pot lid filled with coals. This time, in this fogbound, dark afternoon, he grabbed and caught quite a big bird. Not that he wanted to. The bird had hissed and snapped at him and his six inches of crab bait, had hissed and snapped as if it were going to take the bait right out of the crab pot and sever his line, hissed until he hissed and snapped back. The bird lowered its neck at that, and so did he, while the boat floated closer.

A lot of neck on that bird, a neck that could span the stretch.

The man sprang at the bird, oar and arm. The bird caught the oar blade in its beak and held on, the man levered almost out of the water until the bird, with a twist, tipped the man off his boat where he was perched, legless, in reckless pursuit of its fine stuffing and roasting.

The bird bent double under his arm when he came up for air. Rather, its neck like a lamp post lost its height and its middle went under where its legs landed and his weight centered over. The man rode, he held tight, enough that the life of the bird matched his own in danger and they swam together possessed, toward the boat that the tide was taking an interest in. The swan spoke, wings breaking his grip, its beak leaking hiss, let's swim it said, its big feet flapping.

The swan kicked with vicious complaint and the man bit it then the bird bit the man so hard on the ear he bled. But still they kept ahold, the man more to keep afloat than for dining, the bird in spasms over a catch. When they met a current, both man and bird sank twice, and as soon as they floated over a current-made shoal, the bird, sinking again, gashed at his arm until he let go, cursing and flailing, he let go and chose the shore to swim for. The bird chose elsewhere. A fish perhaps. What fish saw him?

By evening, the boat, dry as boards, made sight of land, the bait sticky-rotten and the second oar dragging in the lock. There was just the worry and tick of fishermen who feared water loss, seeing him in themselves belly down in a crawl from the pushchair he afforded still parked at a beach not infrequently frequented by the fishermen who noticed the boat again, a week after that, the number pried off and scrubbed and painted blank, cutting at their lines with its shiftless float.

Why didn't they look for him? Whoever reports a scrubbed boat is suspected of dealing with thieves. A man with such loneliness repels even the moon's face in water. He could swim, they said. They had seen him.

The swan circles, some say, a certain spot.

# A Short History of Falling

## Pamela Uschuk

from *Terrain.org*

*For Namgial Rinchen*

Sweet Babel of birdsong syncopates
dawn's light as bruised as the hematoma
oozing under the skin of my left knee.
Sudden leaves reshape trees and the delicate longing
of tree frogs pipes snow into a bad memory
old as falling. My knee still aches
from Sunday's tumble on the pallet I didn't see
over the stack of sawn aspen I carried
for the night fire. Unmindful, I tripped
on an iron fence stake cockajar
against the woodpile, this time breaking
my fall with my palm's life line.

My history of falls is unkind. At five, I
plunged through a rotten barn board
all the way from the hay mow
while shafts of numinous straw
whirled like moths on fire
past my Dad shoveling manure.
I smashed into the concrete floor wet
with cow piss near the Holstein's hooves.
Her licorice eyes were big as my fists
as she bawled at me this
first lesson of gravity.

At ten, when I slipped on ice
running for the school bus, I lay
on my back watching my breath
and snow become the ghosts of bare
maple limbs twirling blind white. Not wanting to
move my spine's broken porcelain, I
froze hoping to melt into all
that was pure and cold. When I couldn't
rise, my dad carried me in, cursing
my clumsy and bruised tailbone.

Afterward, falls pocked each year, unpredictable
as a broken clock, until
I crashed in a midnight parking lot,
both hands in my back pockets,
boot catching the cement bumper
turned upside down and painted with tar.

My chin cracked the curb first,
breaking my jaw, then ripping three
ribs from the sternum. What came
from my mouth was garbled
as crow calls, a blood murmur I mistook
for a scream for help. What I remember
are the three good people who walked
around me, not stopping and
the table full of cops I could see
through the restaurant glass, who never shifted
from coffee mugs overlooking
the wounded rug of my body. What I
remember is my lover's face white
as a terrified swan as he lifted me.

Above Mangyu Village, I hiked the thin
trail far above tree line to sunset,

bending to the infinitesimal
in the shape of a plant I could barely see,
petals the size of molecules, its yellow center
smaller than a drop of blood, when the mountain
tilted, and my shoes slid gathering speed
on talus that rattled like oiled marbles of fate.
I could not stop and wondered whether to fly
off the ridge pressed flat so
I wouldn't somersault the thousand feet
to the valley or to sit back on my heels
as if my boots were skis. The last moment
I grabbed the only thing that held
the last rim, a turquoise rock.

The other climbers thought my yelling
a joke, all but the Sherpa who leapt sure
as a mountain goat, Zen master
of shifting stone, and snatched my wrists
to yank me back to the path.
We sat then, breathing for a long time, unwinding
our stories like prayer flags
strung out in Himalayan wind.

How do we ever thank who
or what saves us? Namgial told me to look
at the turquoise rock still clutched in my palm.
*We call that a god's eye*, he said, and there
in one sea-colored facet was etched the eye
almond as Buddha's and open
as if it knew, while above us,
a Himalayan eagle incinerated
before falling to the other side of the world.

# Jimmy and His Father and the Ways about Them
## J.A. Tyler

from >*kill author*

Jimmy, he lives in a town where all the people, they know all the things about one another. Jimmy knows who is taking pills. Jimmy knows who has a spastic back. Jimmy knows that Ms Weather's meatloaf smells good but is powder dry, a fork crumbling it to bits. Jimmy knows these things because he lives in a town like the one he lives in.

And Jimmy, everyone knew his mother was a drunk. Everyone knew that she drank gin on the sides of streets and sucked down bottles with her fingers wrapped on the label, well after all those bars had closed, her throat a gulping calamity.

Jimmy's mother the angel. Jimmy's mother the saint. Jimmy's mother.

And the static that Jimmy sometimes hears in his ears, it is like some kind of reflection, echoing back all the dead moments in his life so far.

There are no streetlights in this town. The neon of a few places casting shadows on the ground, casing the world in colors, otherwise it is dark.

Jimmy sometimes feels like a fish down so low that the light has gone and staying found is like trying to breathe with lips sewn shut. Jimmy's gills going open shut. Jimmy's mouth only sometimes making sounds.

There are a million words that Jimmy will never use. Jimmy watches his shadow crawl.

His father, Jimmy's father, he knows that the sliding door

on their patio is sticky without oil and needs to be fixed. Jimmy's father knows that the newspaper has never stopped coming, that it is making piles on the driveway. Jimmy's father knows what it is like to be a stand of aspens awaiting rain that never comes. Jimmy's father, he hears violins sometimes in the night and he weeps so loud that Jimmy, even when he is deaf, he hears it. And the water collects on the carpet, saturates how they wake in the mornings.

When Jimmy's ears hear, they sometimes hear the words that he doesn't want to use. They sometimes hear his father and a prayer that flutters like bird wings, and then he goes deaf again, sinking down.

Don't go near the water is what Jimmy's mother always said to Jimmy, especially when she saw his rod hung over his shoulder and that look in his eye that was half hook and half bait. Jimmy's mother, she was afraid of the water that surrounded them, so she drank it to fill her belly, to balance out the dryness she felt in her fear.

The river, when it burbles, that is what Jimmy sometimes hears, even when he is listening.

And down the street, where Jimmy goes when his feet are following the road that leads away from the place he lives, down the road there is the sun, coming and going, and Jimmy wishes so many days that he could straddle its surface and punch away, live out on the sky for a day or two, soaking in the blue, forgetting that he is motherless here and his father is going blind with grief.

The violins that his father hears, Jimmy's father, they are part of an orchestra.

Jimmy watches the wind.

Jimmy's father, when the dust runs thick in their house, collects, he hires a woman from town to come over and clean it up. Otherwise they become antiques, Jimmy and his father, living with arms covered in price tags, stickers of orange colored dots, on sale, half off for Jimmy and his father.

But when a woman, like their woman, like the woman that was Jimmy's mother and the woman that was too Jimmy's father's wife, when she is cut in half and the train just keeps going, it is hard to see straight.

Jimmy goes deaf some nights and smiles because his father was in the middle of something slick and thickening and Jimmy didn't want to hear it anyway. Jimmy's father's words are sometimes like weeds that they can't keep out of their garden. Jimmy and his father in a lot of ways have given up. Jimmy and his father are mostly waiting for the end to come around. And everyone in this town knows it, because they live in a town like this, where everyone knows everything, and keeping a cut in half woman hidden is like trying to drape the moon in black cloth. It is there, all the people only have to look.

# One Way to Cook an Eel

## Emily Bromfield

from *Carve Magazine*

### Step 1: Skin and clean the eel. Ensure all scales are removed

She lived in my bathtub. About 80cm in length, speckled mud brown skin, a yellow-white underbelly and pearl black eyes. I found her slapping around in a puddle next to Regents Canal one morning, was only out to buy milk and bacon for breakfast, my Lotto Dream Numbers for that weekend's draw. When I stopped to look at her, bent down right close, she went very still except for a tiny flick of the tail. Should have tossed her back in, but there were these school boys coming up behind me who wouldn't have been kind, who would have used her as a plaything. So I wrapped carrier bags meant for my shopping round both hands, picked her up all soft and warm, fist tight round the mouth and off we went home. I gave her a bit of pipe to sleep in. She fitted perfectly head to tail. When I needed to wash, she went in a blue plastic bucket and both of us slapped about contentedly.

I considered it lucky. Eels are sacred creatures in some parts of the world. In Japan, for example, it's believed they carry the souls of the dead and the heart is a culinary delicacy, swallowed whole, still beating. But Shirley, my wife, told me it was the last straw. She was not sharing a house with an eel. "Todd Ford," she said, "for the last 20 years I have had it up to further than you will know." Then she told me about Alan. He was an operations manager at a biscuit factory. He had prospects, a pension and passions for lots of different things. She was moving in with him.

## Step 2: Cut into two-inch pieces, sprinkle with salt and rest for one hour

We listened to Heart FM in the mornings whilst I brushed my teeth, Gareth John he's a funny man. And Drive Time with Lucio in the afternoon when I fed her a treat, couple of crab sticks or a shrimp. The treats were leftovers from work, Ford's Fishery on the high street, "everything for the body and sole."

I've been in the trade nearly 30 years, took a shine to filleting in home economics at school, much more fun than fairy cakes or pasta bakes. Gutted a plaice when I was 13; sliced its belly, pulled out the organs, the long stringy blood veins and got the carcass so clean it squeaked. At 18 I won the Young British Fish Craft Championship. The crystal bowl and tankard are still on the mantelpiece "First Prize 1984. Congratulations to: Todd Ford." Shirley took nearly everything else with her, stripped the house bare. "Don't argue," she said, "I've only taken what's mine." Alan the biscuit man had waited in his car. I saw him through the curtains, round red face and blonde hair, like a jammy dodger. Shirley kissed me on the cheek on her way out. She smelt of vanilla. There was something new about the way she'd pinned her hair. "I tried Todd," she said and patted me on my chest. Her hand rested on my heart. So she took that too.

That night, I didn't get out the bath. It was the only place I felt safe. The lights dimmed low made my skin look tanned instead of whitey vein blue like under the fluorescent beams at work. My long legs, bony chicken legs Shirley would say, had some definition some muscle not a lot but a bit. The bucket stayed close to the tub. There was no slapping or splashing. When I got out and dried my shrivelled body, she was just under the water wriggling about. I'd gone to bed as the sun came up, lay there calculating costs of a mussel, the smell of vanilla tucked under the duvet.

## Step 3: Soak in cold water for ten minutes, drain and dry

The overall odds of winning a lottery prize are 1 in 54. Euromillions, Thunderball, Lotto or Dream Number, it doesn't matter which. By choosing numbers above 31 the odds are slightly higher because most people choose birthdays or other important days like wedding anniversaries. I play Dream Number and Lotto every week. Once I won £90. I used the money to buy some Japanese chef knives from a magazine, five for £79.99 instead of £199.99. It said they were handmade, hand hammered, by master knife maker Takeo Murata using Yasuki Aogani Blue Steel. I cooked Shirley dinner as soon as they had arrived, a red mullet left over from work. The head came away easy no force needed only a small crunch of bones and a quick snap of the jaw. We sat at the table. It was a special occasion. "Shirley," I said, "you are my soul mate and I love you." She choked on a bone, a small bone I must have missed, and spat out a mouthful of mushed mullet and broccoli.

After the mussel delivery that first afternoon without her I came home and put the knives in a cupboard. It just didn't feel right using them. So I bought two ordinary kitchen knives from the supermarket. I also bought a leather holdall from a magazine, only £12.99 with postage and packing, in case I wanted to go on a mini break. Teletext had some reasonable deals and it would have been good to get some sun, dry up negative thoughts. But I couldn't leave the house. I had responsibilities. So I used my holdall for work to carry my lunchbox, overalls and a newspaper, filling the compartments with cling-filmed treats for feeding time. Every evening when I got in, I went straight to the bathroom and there she was gliding up and down. I had dinner in front of the TV, a microwave meal from a three-for-two deal  and watched a nature programme  or the news before going to bed, her soft ripples sending me to sleep.

## Step 4: Butter a saucepan, season with nutmeg, salt and pepper, and cover with lemon and onions

During an eel's life-cycle they change shape several times. Born in the Sargasso Sea as transparent larvae shaped like leaves, they drift with the currents towards Europe. Once they reach the coastlines they stretch like a sausage and turn into my eel. They can live to 70 years old, a pet for life. But they yearn for home, the tropics' warm waters, and will slither over land if need be to get back, spawn and die. *My Atlas of Fish* told me all this. I liked to lie in the bath and read it, sometimes out loud because the sound of my voice made the house not seem so big.

The vanilla scent began to fade after four months. First it went from under the duvet then it left the cushions on the sofa. After six months it disappeared from the kitchen where it had hung around the sink and by the back door. My regular customers said I was looking better, which I found funny because they only ever saw me in white overalls with guts wiped down the front.

One day the woman from Use Your Loaf, the bakery across the road, came in. I always saw her in the mornings opening up in her blue bakers' coat and meringue-shaped white hat. We were usually the only two people awake, the day still dark, most shops still shut. Sometimes I walked past her close enough to know she wore perfume that smelt of apricots and that she had a broken nose. Once she smiled at me and I could see she had a gap between her front teeth.

She browsed the shellfish and took a piece of mackerel I had put on the counter in a dish. "It's good with horseradish," I said and watched her chew, "or just bake it in the oven in foil." She swallowed and smiled. "You've got mackerel in your teeth," I said.

## Step 5: Cover pan and bake in the oven until eel browns

Her name was Marie. It said so on her name badge. One day instead of bringing ham sandwiches into work I went to Use Your Loaf and bought a cheese and pickle baguette. She made it for me, put extra butter on the bread and wrapped it up tucking the sides under so I wouldn't lose any pickle. "Thank you," I said, "I hate losing pickle." I ate it on the bench in the playground behind the high street. It was the first time I'd taken a real lunch break in two years. It was nice to see the midday sun. After work I went back and bought two éclairs and a cherry bakewell. "Treating myself," I said. She showed me the gap in her teeth again and held her hand out over the counter. There was a bit of icing on her thumb. "I'm Marie," she said. "I know," I said and took her hand, "your name badge says so. Todd Ford." "I know," she said, "your name's on the front of your shop."

I had a bath as the sun went down and nibbled at the cherry bakewell. "It was a good day today," I told the bucket. I had put her on the atlas so she was level with the tub's rim. Her pearl eyes glimmered. According to my *Atlas of Fish*, an eel's pupils enlarge when they return home to reproduce and their smooth skin turns into coppery scales. I photocopied and laminated the diagrams of metamorphosis and blue-tacked them above the taps. "So you can see where you came from," I said when I tipped her back into the bath. She had darted in and out of her pipe and all night the house filled with the sound of water slapping.

## Step 6: Take the eel out and put into a dish with one cup of stock

"If you choose numbers between 32 and 49 your chances of winning are greatly increased," I said, waiting for Marie to finish peppering my cheese and coleslaw bap. She told me she played Lotto too, had done since it started. Sometimes she played Lucky Leprechaun because her family was Irish. "My mother won 500 quid," she said. I had started buying my lunch from her every day. "You're using your loaf," Marie chuckled as she slipped fondant fancies next to baps and baguettes when her boss wasn't looking. In return I gave her some monkfish, a langoustine and a thick slice of smoked salmon.

One day Marie asked if I was married. We were sitting on the playground bench eating tuna rolls. There was a packet of salt and vinegar crisps open. Reaching at the same time our hands had brushed. Her skin was soft and warm. "I was married but my wife left me," I said. "I'm sorry," she said, "that was very personal of me." "That's ok," I said, "I do not mind sharing with you Marie." Two boys had come into the playground and were on the seesaw. It creaked as they pushed hard against the floor to fly high up in the air. As we watched them, Marie slipped her hand through mine, grains of crisp salt tucked between our fingers.

Sorrento's, the Italian restaurant next door, had organised a local traders' dinner and karaoke night. It was the first evening I'd been out since Shirley left. I closed early and went home to have a long soak. We listened to Lucio talking people home on Drive Time, me tapping feet when he played a song I knew, she taking my cue and wriggling in her bucket flicking drops of water onto the bathmat. I had bought a new suit, grey linen two-button fastening, and some Joop! Homme aftershave because the label said it had a classic masculine edge. "You look great," Marie said. "It's nice to see you without a meringue on your head," I said back. She grinned, gap teeth shining, and pressed her hand on my chest. "You should come to mine for dinner," I said, "I would like to cook for you." "I'd like that," she said, her hand still on my chest. She sat next to me at dinner and sang Roy Orbison's "You Got It" with the girls from Use Your Loaf. She looked at me and winked when they sang the chorus, "Anything you want, you got it, anything you need, you got it." I went home with the smell of apricot on my suit.

## Step 7: Bring to a boil then thicken with a tablespoon of butter and flour

Things had got back on track. For the first time in a long time I felt happy. I was living my life again and it was all because of Marie. "You are my lucky star," I told her on a barge trip down the canal, "I was a lonely man but now I'm not." The wind was playing with her hair and at one point blew right across her face so it looked like she had a moustache.

For my birthday, she took me to a Japanese restaurant and I got to meet the chef. He said I had a lovely wife and asked how long we'd been married. "Thirty-three years," I said, "she is the love of my life." He shook my hand and congratulated me, man to man. "That is a good long time," he said, "there must be something very special between you." "There is," I said, "we fit together and that is more important than anything."

When Marie told me about her ex-boyfriend Dean and how he used to sleep with other women, I said I thought he was a bastard as she was something to be treasured. She told me how much she'd loved him though and he hadn't meant to break her heart. "It was a bodily disorder," she said, "he needed to feel universally loved." One day we saw him waiting for a bus. Marie hid behind a wheelie bin. "Just can't bear to see his face," she said. He had a jaw like Sylvester Stallone and wore a t-shirt that showed off his gym body. "I think I should cook for you tonight," I said. Marie looked up at me from her crouching position. "What time?" she said.

## Step 8: Mix three egg yolks with a splash of lemon juice then pour over the fish and serve

Everything was lined up neatly on the kitchen worktop. A chopping board, mixing bowls large and small, and pyrex dishes, one round one square. The Japanese fish knife lay perfectly straight by the chopping board. It was the right occasion to use it again. A fat haddock was on a sheet of shiny wax paper, a pan of potatoes on the hob. I had cleaned the house earlier that day, dusting surfaces, the sofa and chairs. Shirley's photo that sat on the mantelpiece went in a cupboard. The bathroom was disinfected. She thrashed about when I tried to move her to the bucket until I stroked her yellow-white underbelly. "We've got company tonight," I said, "we need to be on our best behaviour."

When it went dark outside I lit candles and put them on the table with a bottle of chilled Soave. The fish knife fit well in my hand. It was like it had been crafted just for me. I slit the haddock carefully, guts out nice and tidy, the long blood veins scraped free. The pan sizzled, lovely hot oil, and as the skin hit heat it crackled.

We waited—her upstairs in the tub, me downstairs in front of the TV. Eamonn Holmes was talking to a Liverpudlian couple in Kenya, the lucky Jet Set winners three weeks in a row. Casualty started; Cyd the technician and Greg the paramedic finally kissed. One of the candles burned out so I lit another. I sat back on the sofa and wondered where Marie could be, she was over an hour late. Tried her phone but the answer machine kept telling me no-one was in. The haddock had toughened, the potatoes wrinkled from too much cooking. I put the Soave back in the fridge and poured myself a whisky and then another. "She's not coming," I said out loud and turned the TV off, "she's probably gone back to him like I knew she would."

From the hallway, a sound of something brushing against stair carpet made me look up from the bottom of my glass. A flash of black pearl shone bright, snaking towards the kitchen. I got up from the sofa and went out into the hallway, and she was at the back door knocking into it again and again. I lunged forward, tripping over myself. She shot away from the door bashing into the table legs so the candles snuffed out in a pool of wax. And I knew what it was, knew what she was trying to do, and there was no way I was going to allow it. "You're not leaving me too. This is your home," I cried. She darted into a gap between the oven and a cupboard and for a moment everything stilled. But then I got down on my knees and pulled her out squirming as, fist tight around the mouth, I stretched her long body on the chopping board. I stroked her underbelly, shushed her calm until she stopped struggling, until she gave in completely and I loosened my grip round the jaw. The fish knife found my hand. And off her head came. There was only a little resistance, a small shudder, a quick crack, pearl eyes dimming, reducing. I slit her belly and let the blood pour out, pushing back pink flesh, and the heart, tiny heart, still beating. I caressed it in the palm of my hand watching the life drain. I slipped it down my throat, felt the throbbing through me as my body curled on the floor. Until I felt the cold of the concrete through the linoleum, smelt vanilla and apricot and the warmth of salt water. From somewhere I heard banging and someone calling my name. But I shut my eyes, saw the sea and heard its calm voice speaking, sun rays burning copper, floating on waves.

# Trouble

## James Scannell McCormick

from *The Barefoot Muse*

Who was asking for you that you've come knocking on my door,
And looking like a single spark in an August of no rain? You're

What follows: There's no easy way to say this, you're the damp crack
In the cellar wall, the shadow on the x-ray, the one last martini before driving back

Home on a slippery night. You've worked your wedding ring
Up over your knuckle and into your pocket (again); you're sliding

Down the bar towards me. Who was asking for you? You're as unwelcome
As a smoke alarm's skirl, a whole side of the body gone suddenly numb,

A midnight phone call, a third straight night without sleep.
You're a bind, a bad way, a pickle, a fix: what I'm in, and deep.

# When I Say Love
## Meredith Martinez

from *Contrary Magazine*

In February, my best friend died in a creek. His mother, driving home from the morgue, stopped at Food Lion and bought frozen turkeys, nine of them, his weight to the pound, burdens she carried, one at a time, straight to the bathroom of her third floor apartment. She unwrapped them carefully, like removing bandages, aware of her rings, her hangnails. Still in her clothes, she kneeled in the tub, gathering the turkeys around her in the shape of his corpse. She whispered to them, hushing their goosebumps, her cheek on a breast, where his shoulder would be. A cold fog rose from them, sweating her hair, her upper lip, how the flu tastes, like vinegar. She slept on her side, dreaming his body, his muddy lungs and freeze-dried hair, breathing with owls, eyes like sugared grapes. She woke choking on juice, shirt stinking, crotch slick from ruined draining poultry. The bird in her arm, limp, headless, pissing bacteria, waved its useless wings at her. She punched and shook it, broke its thighs, tore skin with her teeth. Vomited into its cavity, screaming. When I say love, this is what I mean.

# How I Forget the Shape of Your Mouth When You Are Deep in Thought

## Alison Doernberg

from *Eleven Eleven*

I've taken to keeping my Oakland map on the kitchen table so I can study it while I eat breakfast, as though I am preparing for a test on the quickest way to get from Fruitvale to Grand Avenue. Unfamiliar street names root themselves in my mind and gradually form a cadence: Octavia. Bartlett. Deering. Henrietta.

\*\*\*

Eighteen is the number of extra curtain rings required, in addition to the usual twelve, to hang shower curtains around a claw foot tub. (Three of mine, mismatched.)

\*\*\*

Mason jars have become my water drinking vessels of choice. I have begun to fill the house with them; I also use them to hold pencils and scissors, fistfuls of wildflowers, wispy cotton balls, a spare toothbrush. I arrange the empty ones along the windowsill above the kitchen sink and let them catch the light.

\*\*\*

I bought the bicycle for the fortune. The former owner was an art student who'd been seduced by a fixie and listed the hybrid for sale. Back in Middletown, I rode around her neighborhood to test the brakes and derailleurs, pedaled up a hill, and looked down.

There, taped between the handlebars, was a small, rectangular slip of white paper with red text: Know the right moment.

\*\*\*

These are the reasons why I want to become a regular at the café at the bottom of the hill: Exposed brick. Handwritten brown paper menu. The owner's bird tattoos. Perfectly sized red mugs. Free apricots by the tip jar. The way that, on a chilly morning, even twenty minutes spent sitting outside with a steaming cup of tea that warms both my hands at once feels like a slow exhalation that lasts all day.

\*\*\*

The third drawer below the mixing bowls is full of paint chips in purples and reds. Sometimes I open that drawer by accident when I am looking for the teaspoons, perhaps making the ginger cookies for ice cream sandwiches. The paint chips were part of my Halloween costume this year; I pinned them to my clothes and dressed as Indecision.

\*\*\*

The olive-scented hand lotion smells nothing like olives.

\*\*\*

Lamplit, I open *Unaccustomed Earth* to where my place is held by an envelope made from a topo map (contours unfamiliar, stitched together with blue thread). I've been deliberately prolonging reading the last story for nearly two weeks now, until tonight, because the book is so good I don't want it to end.

***

As a child, I developed the strange habit of not getting out of bed, or closing my eyes to fall asleep, until the digits on the clock added up to nine. This odd routine still crosses my mind on unhurried mornings when I roll over to look at the clock. 6:08. There are three nature settings on this clock, in addition to the usual alarm and radio, and the one I wake to is Ocean. Living so close to the highway now, I am sometimes stirred awake in the middle of the night by the swells of traffic rushing by, and, still half asleep, think that my alarm is going off. 6:12.

# Intercourse

## Robert Olen Butler

from *Redivider*

Lizzie Andrew Borden, 44, murderer, acquitted in 1892

Nance O'Neil, 30, actress

in O'Neil's home, Brindley Farm, Tyngsboro, Massachusetts, 1904

Lizzie

her hands the hands of Lady Macbeth that first time I saw her at
the Colonial in Boston, she stands in a bright spot of light, her
crimson hands flaring delicately before her, her eyes aflame at
the only man in her world because he is a coward, and her vast,
trilling voice fills me A little water clears us of this deed and I
stand for a long while before him as he sleeps in the sitting room
on the mohair sofa in his morning coat, his feet on the floor,
and he is snoring, this man whose name I bear, whose touch I
bear, my Papa, and the stepmother is finished already, upstairs,
and the short-handled ax is light in my hand and I wait upon
myself to decide: he gave away our farm in Swansea to the dead
cow upstairs and he gave away the house on Fourth Street to her
sister, and though to do all that would never have occurred to
him on his own, he could not resist, he is a coward, and now
Lady Macbeth pulls me close: a little of her wetness clears me
of this deed

Nance

from a poisonous heaven I want nothing to do with or from a hell in what may secretly be a just universe, look upon your daughter now, Father, look upon my nakedness and Lizzie Borden's and pound your chest in shame as you did with me trapped in the middle of a packed pew where you placed me so you could cry out my evil to heaven and the congregation She goes off to a life in the theatre and thereafter to an eternity in hell and I tried once more with you, my bag was packed and I was looking beautiful—I could see myself in the foyer mirror and I trembled at myself and wanted you to tremble too—and you cried Get thee behind me but Lizzie would know what to do with you, Father, she would know: your hands are as hard as ax heads, Lizzie, your hands are as hot as blood, your hands have spots upon them, sweet Lizzie, just rub them clean on me

# To a Place Where We Take Flight

**Anne Valente**

from STORY*GLOSSIA*


In my head, it sounds better—in my head, I am Johnny Rotten screaming into a tattered microphone, I am Vince Neil shrieking to a sold-out arena, I am Roger-fucking-Daltrey singing "Magic Bus" at the Monterey Pop Festival, and Chris is my Keith Moon. We play before thousands, a crowd that cheers wildly when Chris at last smashes his drum set and I throw my mike into the throngs, a ripple like a shockwave through their swarm. We sweat beneath stage lights, our skin like oil slicks, and we march off stage as the lights finally dim, as the crowd begins a slow chant no, this can't possibly be the end.

It sounds better, in my head.

But here, in Chris's leaky basement full of house spiders and worn carpeting, we are just two jerks, two nothings with no amps, not even a microphone, only the toy drum set Chris's dad bought him for Christmas last year. We play for no one, not even Chris's awestruck little brother who stayed late at school for origami club, just for the basement's rafters above, where the pipes leak rusty water.

But soon, we will. Not the Belmont Jr. High talent show, not Lila Duldorf's birthday party, not even the Hi-Dive down the street—things we might have once wanted, but now we have no time. Now, we're focused. We have a plan. We will play Moss Regional Hospital, something Chris's dad hooked up two days ago, because he knows a guy on the board of directors.

We will play Moss Regional, in one week. We will play to save her life.

After we practice for an hour, we grab Hi-C and Twizzlers and sit on Chris's front porch, where we were the other day when Chris's dad came home and told us the news. Chris said right there how fucking awesome that was, and I felt like maybe I could kiss Mr. Winchester, but instead I stuffed a WarHead in my mouth and wondered why I couldn't say fuck in front of my own dad.

Though now, the real issue is that he's already given up, just sits and watches the same reruns of "M.A.S.H." and "Three's Company" over and over again, while I bike to the hospital after school, or call mom in her room if I stay at Chris's too late.

"She knows we're doing this, right?" Chris bites the end off a Twizzler and looks at me.

"Sure, man, she knows. I told her last night, when we talked."

"You really think a week is enough time?"

I want to tell him we don't have any goddamn choice, but I hold my tongue and chew on my thumbnail instead.

"Jesus, Mike, don't pull that shit on my porch. If I find one of your fingernails later, I'm going to put it in your Coke when you're not looking."

In fifth grade, I'd saved a bunch of my nails and put them on Chris's pillowcase once, when we were watching *Cujo* and he got up to pee. Just for spite, I bite off my thumbnail and spit it onto the porch stairs.

"Sick, man. Better not leave your Coke alone tomorrow at lunch."

I tell Chris he's a dick, and we sit on the porch until the Twizzlers are gone, until an ant crawls up and carries my thumbnail away.

At home during dinner, dad is quiet. We sit in front of the television, eating microwave dinners while Nick at Nite blares from the screen, an "I Love Lucy" episode featuring Harpo Marx. Dad knows I'll call mom when I'm finished, and I don't know whether he'll choose to talk to her this time, or pretend to wash dishes again, even though we're eating out of cardboard.

"You tell your mother about your little scheme?"

I nod, but dad's eyes don't move from the television. He takes a bite of nuked turkey, and he smiles a little when Lucy hides behind a doorway, afraid to meet Harpo in person.

I know he thinks I'm doing this as therapy—like how music is supposed to heal, to make mom smile, just like pets do for sick people, why resident tabbies live in nursing homes. Chris too, because I said as much, when I told him I wanted to do this. But what I never told him, and what I never can, is that some part of me is doing it for that story she used to tell.

The healing is fine. If nothing else, we'll have that. But why I really want this, what some small part of me still believes, is that when my voice moves across the oncology floor, filtering into her IV bag, her needles, the radiation that permeates her skin, its energy will power the tools she needs to live. And by some strange miracle—but one I can actually imagine, again and again, when I can't fall asleep some nights—the music will make her well, just like it made the ship move and fly away, in the best bedtime story she ever told me.

I don't know what has made me think of the story lately, or why I even believe, in some small corner of my mind, that this will make any goddamn bit of difference. She is sick, and I'm old enough now to stop believing in most things, and dad said last week, after the doctor called and I found him standing in the kitchen, palms resting on the edge of the sink, you know, Mike, your mom might not be around forever.

But I want to believe. Even if I never tell Chris, even if he thinks we're just playing for fun, even if dad watches reruns for the rest of his fucking life. There will still be me, my energy to hers, the last porch light left, like the one she used to leave on when I was out after dark.

I wait awhile to call her, after I've done my pre-algebra homework, and after I know dad has settled into the couch for the primetime lineup, so it won't hurt so much that he doesn't pick up the phone too. They haven't been on bad terms, necessarily, just distant, like maybe he doesn't know what to say to her, or like she's waiting for him to make some impossible move that could make her stay on this earth.

I call directly to her room, since she's been out of surgery for a few days, and the ward nurse will no longer need to mediate our calls, or make sure she's awake. She sounds groggy when she answers, like she's been taking a nap, and she tells me she's just watched "Wheel of Fortune," over a hearty dinner of Ensure.

"How is practice going? How's Chris?"

"You know, good. We can't really play with just singing and drums, though, so I borrowed Mr. Winchester's guitar."

Chris and I had decided the day before that drums and vocals wouldn't be enough, so he'd asked his dad to lend me their family's acoustic. I knew a few chords, from when mom had shown me her old Bob Dylan albums, from when she told me they'd seen him live in 1972, when he was drunk as a skunk, as she'd said, and barely knew the words to his own songs. I'd borrowed her old guitar then, and had learned "Blowin' in the Wind" by playing my own wobbly notes for two days, against the scratch of our turntable's vinyl.

"So you remembered something from our lesson. Still listening to Bob Dylan?" Her voice brightens, and I can hear her smiling. The sound makes me want to cry.

"Nah, mom, I've moved on. You know, Zeppelin, the Pistols. Motley Crue."

"I saw Led Zeppelin once, in college. I almost touched Robert Plant's shoulder, after I pushed my way to the front."

The thought of her pushing anything, of having the strength to elbow through a crowd much less leave her hospital bed, is one I can't think too hard about.

"Mom, do you remember that story?" I blurt it out, a question I hadn't meant to bring up.

Quiet stills her end of the line. "What story, sweet?"

"You know, the story. About the ship."

She's quiet again, and for a second I wonder if breast cancer has stolen her memory too, if the slow spread to her brain has blocked out everything that was once me, if maybe she doesn't even remember dad and that's why he's been so down.

But then she laughs. "The ship in the Sea of Sadness?"

"Yes. The ship in the Sea of Sadness," I say, and something in my chest floods.

"Oh God, Mike, I haven't thought of that in so long. How do you even remember that?" She is laughing still, as if it's the best thing she's heard all week.

"Of course I remember. You used to tell it all the time."

"You know, that was one of your grandmother's stories. Not even mine." She is reeling. Her voice sounds drunk.

"Could you tell me again?"

"What, now?"

In her voice I hear it, that I'm too old for this now, that kids on the cusp of teenhood don't need bedtime stories anymore. If Chris were here he'd say the same thing, only he'd probably punch my shoulder and give me a dead arm, maybe call me a loser. But I tell her yes, yes I want to hear the story, now. So she tells me.

She tells me that once there was a ship that sailed through the sky, a ship powered by the music of one family, a family that played flute and harp and violin and piccolo together. But one day a great storm raged through the clouds, blowing the whole family except the little boy clear away to the other side of the world, and the ship fell to the earth without any music to guide the way. When the boy awoke after the storm, he was alone in a great desert of only sand, on the deck of the abandoned ship, his violin broken beside him. He cried so much that the sand flooded with tears, an ocean from that day known as the Sea of Sadness.

Mom pauses a moment, like maybe she's forgotten the rest. But then she tells me that a great blue heron heard the boy's cries and flew across the Sea of Sadness, landing on the boat's deck where the boy lay weeping. The heron pulled several strands from its own feathers, and strung them across the broken violin, and when the instrument had been repaired, the bird handed it to the boy and flew away. The boy watched the heron take flight, then picked up the violin and played until the abandoned ship roared to life. He played the ship across the Sea of Sadness, the music commanding the boat toward his family. At last he found them, washed upon a sandy bank of deserted beach, and there they at last took flight, the ship at full speed as the family played in unison once more.

She tells the tale with precision, as if no time has passed between the last time she told it while tucking me in, and now, relaying words across telephone wires. She asks, "Is that the one you meant?"

And I tell her yes, mom, that's exactly the one I meant.

I keep a hand over my Coke at lunch, just in case Chris remembers what he said about the fingernails. But he seems too distracted to remember, making plans for our afternoon practice, talking so fast that bits of potato chip fly from his mouth.

"Oh, and I mentioned the show to Lila Duldorf. Just in case she wants to come."

"Jesus, Chris, it's for patients. Do you really think she'll give a shit?"

"I can get her in. You know, VIP passes."

"To a fucking hospital?"

"Hey, man, simmer down. You're not the only one performing."

I look at Chris and see my mistake in not telling him. The show is a spotlight, for him. Nothing more.

"Fine, whatever. Invite her. Woo her with your magic."

Chris crushes a potato chip, drops the crumbs in my Coke.

In science class we talk about kinetic energy, how molecules rotate and vibrate, their electrons bumping into each other until friction causes movement. And for a second I consider this, how sound makes similar vibrations, wavelengths traveling across a room with enough energy to power cities. I scribble a drawing in my notebook, a guitar blaring notes into a stick figure's heart, and shove the figure to the bottom of my bag when the sixth period bell rings.

After school Chris and I are walking across the parking lot, heading past the lined-up school buses toward Chris's house, when Scott Barnstone comes up. He's wearing a giant pair of headphones and his hair hangs down into his face.

"Hey, I hear you guys are playing the hospital."

"Fuck off, Barnstone." Chris has never liked Scott, not since they were in after-school Latchkey together in the fourth grade and Scott spat on him once from the top of the slide.

Scott looks at me. He doesn't like me either. I accidentally clipped him once on a high-sticking penalty during gym class, when I was the goalie and he tried to check me against the net. He'd had a shiner for three days.

"Is it because your mom's got cancer in her tits?"

He grins at me, a line of crooked teeth. Before I can think to say anything, Chris shoves Scott in the chest.

"You kiss your boyfriend with that mouth?" Chris says, and spits on Scott's tattered sneakers. "Go back to your sandbox, Barnstone."

I tell Chris we should go. I pull him toward the baseball fields, which we'll cross to the tree line and Chris's house.

"Whatever, assholes," Scott says. "At least I'll still have a mom after you douchebags are done playing your stupid songs."

Before I fully hear him, I drop my backpack and punch him in the face. His headphones clatter to the pavement, and I stand just long enough to see a line of blood dribble down his chin before Chris pulls me toward the field and we are off, we are running.

When I get home later, the television sits silent and dad stands in the kitchen over a pot of Kraft macaroni and cheese. Two bowls set the table, two tall glasses of milk.

"I thought I'd make us dinner tonight," he says. He looks up from the pot, where he's stirring the noodles and cheese powder, and smiles at me.

I leave my bag in the living room, next to mom's old guitar. Chris and I had planned to practice at least twice more before Saturday, but I'd also gotten out mom's old acoustic and squeezed in some extra prep at home.

"So how was the day?" dad asks when we sit down at the table. He drops two big spoonfuls of fluorescent noodles into my bowl.

"Not great. I punched a kid in the face."

The words feel awkward, as if dad and I don't have that ease between us anymore. Before any of this happened, he took me to the movies for whole afternoons as if he had nothing but time, or when my T-ball coach robbed me of a run, he told me that in his eyes my swing still merited a homer.

"He said something bad about mom," I say.

Dad looks up from his bowl. "You shouldn't punch people."

I expect him to be mad, but he looks more hurt than anything. I take a gulp of milk and ask him about his day instead.

"You know, same-old, same-old. I visited your mother, though. I left work a little early."

What dad does during the day has never really occurred to me, and when I hear him say this, I wonder for the first time if he's done this more than once. I picture him eating a sandwich alone at his desk, driving to the hospital, sitting by mom's bed.

"Mike, there's something we need to talk about."

He sets down his fork and looks at me. His lips are thin, a pencil mark.

"Your mother—well, I talked to her doctor today. And Mike, it just doesn't look good."

He stops talking and holds his breath, and I wonder for a second if maybe he's trying to hold back a burp. But then he looks at me, and I know he's trying not to cry.

"The surgery didn't do any good. And the chemo, well, it's not doing any good either. They say it just keeps spreading."

I've only seen my dad cry once in my life, last year when we buried Sampson, the cat my parents adopted after they got married. We laid him in a shoebox, and dad dug a hole in the backyard. Two tears slid down his nose when he pushed the shovel into the ground.

"I just wanted you to know that," dad says, and I don't know what to say so I just keep eating my macaroni. He's not crying, exactly, but he sits for a few more seconds without moving, then he picks up his fork and we finish the last of our dinner without really talking.

That night I don't call mom, and I don't do my homework. But before bed I set my alarm, to wake up early and gain back the time I've lost by doing nothing all night when I could have been practicing. I take awhile to fall asleep, but when I finally do, it's because I've made myself think of molecules, vibrations, the movement of ships.

On Friday, the night before the show, Chris and I sit on his roof and look out toward the football field. Two teams play a scrimmage game, some peewee league sponsored by our junior high, but we watch the players dart across the field anyway, their helmets gleaming in the field's floodlights.

"Barnstone's face is kind of fucked up." Chris exhales a cloud of Pall Mall smoke, a pack he stole from his dad's sock drawer. It's the second time I've seen him smoke, something he must think rock stars do.

I shrug, and neither of us speaks for awhile. Instead we watch a small crowd cheer on the field's metal risers, and I wonder if those are parents, siblings, moms rooting for their sons.

"You know, I think we're ready." Chris flicks his glowing cigarette off the roof. "You don't have to worry."

I know he's right. We've been practicing all night, not even taking a break for dinner. But now, looking out across the field at the tree line just beginning to brown and fade, I wonder if we're not ready at all, if maybe we never were.

"Your mom's going to be fine," Chris says, the first time I've ever heard him say it. But he avoids my eyes, assures me only because he should.

"How's she doing, man? You never really talk about her."

Chris's face looks strained, as if he wants to say more. But he doesn't, and I tell him she's fine, and we sit again for awhile without talking. Out on the field a whistle blows, and we watch the players huddle in for halftime.

"Do you ever wonder if something totally crazy could happen?" I stare out toward the field, away from Chris.

"What, like Lila suddenly falling in love with me?" Chris laughs. "Sure, man, I wonder all the time."

"No, I mean something ridiculous," I say. "Something totally unreal."

"Playing lead with the Crue? I think about shit like that, sure."

Chris pulls another cigarette from his stolen pack, and my chest suddenly feels heavy. I think of dad, probably sitting in his armchair watching the Friday lineup alone, and I tell Chris I should head home, get some sleep.

Chris stays up on the roof, to finish his cigarette, and maybe watch the start of the second half, though neither of us cares about the game. I bike the five blocks to my house and for the first time the night air feels bitter, like autumn has arrived sooner than I thought.

We arrive at Moss Regional an hour early, but there are patients already seated and waiting, maybe some of mom's friends from her floor. The ward has arranged chairs in a horseshoe pattern, in a small lounge just past the floor's elevators, and my dad helps us set up the tiny drum set, Mr. Winchester's guitar, even a microphone the hospital's chapel let us borrow. Once everything is in place, dad leaves us alone, says he knows we need time to prepare. I watch him head down the hallway toward mom's room. Maybe they need time to prepare too.

"So I don't see Lila," Chris says. The room has started filling up, and I'm glad I don't recognize anyone from school.

"It's for patients, Chris. What did you expect?" Though I don't have to look at him to know we've expected different things. I tell him we can schedule another show, another time, somewhere people will actually want to go. Someplace he can shine, I think, but I stop short of saying that.

Just then I see dad down the hallway, wheeling mom toward us and the lounge. She looks tired, and I know she's too weak now to stand. But for some reason I think of her pushing her way toward Robert Plant, and I think of her laugh when she told me the story again on the phone, and suddenly she looks so pretty. A memory floods me from nowhere, second grade. My Cub Scout leader telling everyone I'm too short to ride horseback on the trail. Mom escorted me to the next meeting, told him I'd do anything I damn well pleased.

"Oh, sweetheart, you look great," she says when they reach us, and I bend down to hug her. Chris hugs her too and she pats his head, like she's trying to absorb the light reflected in his hair.

"You two ready?" she asks, and she smiles extra big, like something in her face might crack if she doesn't.

Chris nods, but then his dad arrives off the elevator and he leaves us, just mom, dad and me. For a second none of us speak. I scan my brain for something to say.

"I can't tell you how much this means to me," mom says. She gestures toward the others gathered in the horseshoe of chairs, as if the show means something to them too, but she doesn't say anything more. Just then the head of the oncology ward waves me over, and mom and dad move to the edge of the horseshoe, waiting for us to start.

Chris and I have prepared three songs, mostly because they're all we know, but also because the hospital told us not to play much more, the patients would need their rest. We move to our makeshift stage, a couple of instruments gathered in a corner, and I stand before the chapel microphone. I cough out an introduction, something stupid that draws a few smiles and blinks. Then I turn back to Chris, and he nods me the signal. We start to play.

We sound rough at first, filtered, the slow strain of Play-doh through clenched fingers. Chris has brought drum brushes, not drumsticks that would drown out my guitar in this small space, and the scratches keep time with my voice, a voice that now sounds cracked to me as I gasp out the first few lines of our opening song. We've agreed on "Patience," my favorite Guns N' Roses ballad, followed by Pink Floyd's "Wish You Were Here"— Chris's pick, and one I've agreed on too. But Chris has let me decide on the last song, one I've chosen just for mom—the Beatles' "Across the Universe." The chords aren't easy, and Chris and I have spent days mastering their progression. But mom has always loved the song, and if I was ever to learn its notes, now was the time.

We falter through the first song, a warm-up at most since our audience doesn't react, and my voice is hoarse but not in the way that Axel Rose might have wanted. My face flushes as we proceed straight into our second song, but when I look up for the first time, I can see mom and dad off to the back. They're both smiling at me. The rest of the small crowd—maybe ten patients, and a few people who look like family members, plus three nurses and the ward director—they all look half-interested at best. But as I stare out over our tiny crowd, their faces suddenly fade into nothing. I know why I'm here. I have little more than a song left to get this done.

My voice rises, maybe not in volume, but in some degree of strength. Chris notices the change, his percussions grow in zeal, and by the second verse our instruments are belting out Pink Floyd together, and I start to imagine what this noise might do. I picture sound waves, floating from my fingers, my voice, Chris's hands. I picture them billowing from this room, down the hall, into mom's room and inside her monitors and tubes. I picture them infiltrating her veins, right here in this room, a surge like a quiet explosion through her brain, her brave heart, her small, pale hands.

And then we are to the last song, and I look up and she is smiling. She is smiling so large, bright tears form and well at the corners of her eyes. Dad is smiling too, like he once did, before everything broke. And that is when maybe I know it has happened—that the world is just like the story said, that for once these notes and chords can inject life straight into our chests, just like the stick figure I drew, just like a ship setting sail toward the sky. I glance back at Chris, just long enough for him to look at me and grin, and for one perfect moment all is right, we are here, we are all alive in this room where sound and waves and molecules oscillate, all beneath the steady rhythm of these drums, my voice, our hearts all pounding as one.

And then it is over. Our last song peals a final cadence of notes, and for a second the room falls silent. But then mom claps first, she claps so loud that she stands to support the movement of her hands, and dad stands too, partly to clap, but also to watch her so she doesn't fall. I see Mr. Winchester to the left of them, and he's clapping and smiling too. Chris and I both take awkward bows, and we smile back at the audience. But our moment is over, leaves as quickly as it came, and the room is just a hospital room, the ward like any other on this earth.

I know what will come. I know the patients will trickle back to their rooms, that Chris will leave with his dad, that when my dad and I pack the equipment back into the van and drive home, he will whisper over to me, his eyes still on the road, you know, Mike. You know she's not going to make it. And I know my mom will pull me aside back in her room, once we've tucked her back into her bed and dad has ventured off to use the men's room, and she'll look at me in a searching way and say, sweet, is that why? Oh, honey, it's just a story. Didn't you know?

But in my head—right now, while we're still standing here—it sounds better.

In my head, I am still singing—even as the energy leaves this room, even as the oncology ward becomes just what it was, ten minutes before we played. In my head, I am still singing, I am playing guitar better than I ever could tonight, maybe I'm even playing the violin, a meaningless difference now.

In my head, she is not in bed hooked up to IVs, she is not so weak she can barely stand, she is nowhere near this wasted floor. She is somewhere else, I don't know where, but she's with me, and she is safe. She is somewhere I can keep her secure, and we are taking flight, up, away from this place, so far away I can no longer see the ground.

# Instructional Ghazal

## David Welch

from *Agni Magazine*

*beginning on a line by Misty Harper*

*1: on lying*

*You will want to make the corners of the mouth
very dark*, so the teeth appear asleep and silent inside the mouth.

*2: on breathing*

Even coming softly the wind rattles the sills.
The windows whistle a song in parting, like the mouth.

*3: on swallowing*

Take only the smallest bodies with your tongue: accept
the muscled rules you must maintain inside the mouth.

*4: on kissing*

I felt your nose like a plum in the dark. Suddenly
I was swimming—unable to breathe or see the mouth.

*5: on tying*

There are three ways you can teethe and three
knots: the shoelace, the noose, and the mouth.

*6: on loving*

If his stomach is the surest path to a man's heart,
you must be sure to take him by the mouth.

*7: on closing*

In spite of tradition, I'm leaving it open:
[place any name you want in my mouth]

# A Baker's Dozen of My Feelings about David Foster Wallace's *Infinite Jest*

## Elissa Bassist

from *The Rumpus*

"Like most North Americans of his generation, Hal tends to know way less about why he feels certain ways about the objects and pursuits he's devoted to than he does about the objects and pursuits themselves. It's hard to say for sure whether this is even exceptionally bad, this tendency." – *Infinite Jest*

\*\*\*

First of all, I didn't even want to write this because who am I to write this?

\*\*\*

Second of all, here is a real conversation that happened:

**Elissa**: What should I do at TheRumpus.net?

**Stephen**: Maybe you can write a book review.

**Elissa**: Okay, but first I need to finish reading *Infinite Jest*.

**Stephen**: Why don't you review that?

**Elissa**: No, I can't review that.

**Stephen**: Why not? We don't believe in timely reviews.

**Elissa**: No, it's not that. I can't just review that book. I'm not a person who is a good enough person to write about David Foster Wallace. There are other people.

**Stephen**: Maybe you should write about your own insecurities about why you're not a person good enough to write about David Foster Wallace.

**Elissa**: Okay.

\*\*\*

Instead of writing about my insecurities, I will write about my feelings, which is just as good/the same. Feelings can never be wrong or misinterpreted as legitimate; they can be generally misinterpreted, which is fine, especially if I'm not being smart or funny enough on the surface of things.

Feeling No. 1: Confidence. I will need this book, and only this book, to study for the GREs.

Feeling No. 2: Fear. I took *Infinite Jest* on a kayaking trip in Colorado. I left it in my car, and when I reached for it afterward, I saw that one-third of the book was soaked in river water. The book is now growing mold on its pages, dark black clouds that keep expanding. I worry that I'm breathing in mold particles when I read (I'm nearsighted, so I have to hold the book very close to my face a.k.a. my nose and mouth). I keep the book at the foot of my bed, so that it's far enough away from me that I don't inhale any minute fungal hyphae while I'm sleeping. I can't buy a new copy because I've solidified a relationship with my current water-damaged copy (also, it's a first edition). Mold is pretty fucking toxic—it even plays a critical part in *Infinite Jest*, when a germophobic mother backs away in terror from her son who ingested hirsute mold of one color that is growing mold of another color. Some critics (a.k.a. Wikipedia) speculate this is a possible cause of the boy's final condition, believing the mold somehow synthesized into a hallucinogenic drug. My fear is real.

Feeling No. 3: Idiocy. I remember seeing *Infinite Jest* for the first time, and judging a book by its cover and length, I thought I'd be clever by noticing it, confronting my ability to read it, and then not read it as a sign of being *over* being able to read it. It just looked long and pretentious for the sake of being long and pretentious. I suggest you don't cultivate the same idiot presumption. Life has taught me that books of substantial length usually offer something substantial.

Feelings No. 4-6: Comprehension, identification, and projection. Reading *IJ* is like forging a spiritual connection with a man who expresses my feelings better than I do. As someone who writes, I've often felt that language is so poor an instrument for communication or expression. I find it unyieldingly difficult to write an honest sentence. DFW exhibits otherwise. George Saunders, in his remarks at David Foster Wallace's memorial service, called Wallace "a wake-up artist." Yes. DFW's words, beyond creating solid smart sentences and solid smart stories, reach this part of you that you thought no one could reach, saying everything you've been wanting to say and hear, everything you've been thinking on your own but haven't been able to share with anyone else. While the whole world lies to you (the media, the politicians, the [insert your own contaminated culprits here]), Wallace tells you the truth. It's as if he comes out of his book and shakes you until you're dizzy, yelling at you all the time, "I GET IT. I GET YOU. YOU ARE NOT ALONE HERE."

Feelings No. 7 & 8: Exhilaration/exhaustion and physical pain/somatic hi-def experience. This book is an exercise in paying attention. To begin, you need a dictionary, preferably the OED. Since countless characters hijack the narrative without warning, I'd recommend keeping a list of monikers to separate the Canadian wheelchair assassins from the recovering/persisting head-cases from the tennis prodigies. Wrist braces aren't a bad idea. A working knowledge of mathematics, chemistry, grammar, physical education, video production, waste management, puppetry, media dissemination, the Twelve Steps, and Canada will go a long way. Finally, a Faulkner-Gaddis-Pynchon-like-patience is necessary, as in butt-in-the-seat-time to power through even what you don't understand, what doesn't seem like English, and what gives you a physical headache; just read the words, and they'll invade some part of you that can absorb and translate and assimilate. Have faith. Persevere. DFW will slap you a couple of times to make you pay attention harder, because you're saying, "I'm laughing too much; I'm crying too much"; you're now facing the challenge of being too emotional to continue reading the book as you're distracted and wiping tears away and recovering. You got a bit off track by engaging with the author as if he were your drinking companion, being all vulnerable and shit, and that's a good thing. You just can't let it get in the way. This book demands your attention, and if you give it, the rewards are unquantifiable. It is possible, as with anything that demands your attention, to glaze over a passage, but you'll go back and read it and see you would have missed everything if you missed those few sentences. It's all essential, and you can't miss a word or a moment without being unbelievably sorry and sad. So read and reread and read again. Eventually you'll do anything for him, Jesus, you now just want to be inside him, because your secrets are now his secrets and his wisdom is now your wisdom, and you praise a

Higher Power that this man existed to tell you everything you ever needed to know.

Feeling No. 9: Mutability. I had to choose carefully to whom to recommend this book. No one who knew me was allowed to hate it. If they hated it, they hated me. Recently I was in a bookstore, and I picked up the book because I wanted to send it to my ex-boyfriend, to say, "Read this, and then you'll know what you're missing by not loving me." I was with a friend, and she wanted to buy it for herself. I didn't have the heart to separate her from the book once she had it in her hands. She deserved this book much more than he did. And then she read it, and she finished it before I did, and she told me, "You getting me to read this book is the best thing you've ever done."

Feeling No. 10: Compassion. In *IJ*, there are no minor characters or incidents. DFW gives every detail respect and every someone a story. He's nice to people and sort of says, "Oh, you failed in that moment? That's a common theme in humanity, and no one can really fault you for that." Not everyone deserves what happens to him/her; we must endure despite other people or circumstance, which is the hardest thing, but the most necessary thing, and actually the only thing, if you think about it, which DFW makes you do, with every word.

Feeling No. 10.5: Admiration. DFW teaches his reader how to be a Student of the Game. The "Game" is tennis, but it's also "Life."

Feeling No. 11: Respect. You give it; you get it. With publishing and media the way it is today (and the way Wallace predicts it will devolve), here is an author and a book that respect their reader, that says, "You get on my level, and I'll get on yours." The words are multi-syllable-d, the language multifarious and poetic, the content often oblique, the characters complex, the font for the endnotes small, and so on. This book is hard to read; it is heavy in every sense of the word; it'll rattle your brain and hurt your wrists. And I appreciate that. But not only that. Good writing offers a portal out of the mundane, out of what you already know, and out of your own boring head. Wallace is incomprehensively imaginative and endlessly inventive, and just to give a taste, I'll mention a few titles listed in the encyclopedic Filmography of James O. Incandenza: "Union of Theoretical Grammarians in Cambridge," "Fun with Teeth," "Kinds of Pain," "'The Medusa v. the Odalisque,'" "The American Century as Seen Through a Brick," "The Cold Majesty of the Numb," etc. When you're holding down a job from 9 a.m. to 6 p.m., you want to read this kind of material, like funny dialogue between competitive junior tennis players or highly uncomfortable sexual situations involving Raquel Welch masks. And the darker end of the spectrum is so dark, like really sick disturbing shit of which your rational, sane, traditional mind could never conceive on its own. You start to feel embarrassed and scandalized and unhinged by what you read, and then you feel embarrassed and scandalized and unhinged by the fact you like it, and embarrassed to have ever been unhinged by it. You want more. You're *into it.* You are, because even though you're just reading *a book*, you feel more alive, vibrant, and vulnerable considering you've just confronted what you'd never have imagined; but you've gotten to the other side of it, the other side of where you were before you read, and that's a better place to be, even if–no, *especially because*–you're more aware.

Feeling No. 12: Infinite Jest. We've entered an era where we've forgotten how to entertain ourselves. In a time when attention and perception have become disconnected, Wallace works to connect human beings with their emotions through the medium of reading. I often have to justify entertainment as more than "wasting time" or "momentarily neglecting my lonely existence."

*IJ* reawakens the art of being a watcher; it's no longer an evil to be alone with yourself, to reclaim solitude as an important activity, one where you confront your subjective experience and face your memories, your feelings, your passions, all of which are reflected at you while you read. The book is not only to be read, it is to be experienced as a life event. The reader has to participate in this book, and in this way, *IJ* is the anti-passivity. Every time I pick up the book, I get something out of it that informs who I am as a person, how I think, how I live, how I'd like to perceive the world. What makes the book "infinite" is what the reader takes out of it, how personal it becomes, how instructive. It's definitive engagement ad infinitum.

Feeling No. 13: Sadness. I feel sad writing this now, knowing my words don't even capture .20148 of how I actually feel about *Infinite Jest*.

\*\*\*

NB: This book is about competitive tennis, addiction, and entertainment. It is set in the not-too-distant future, where time is subsidized (e.g. "Year of the Depend Adult Undergarment") and all the problems of today have gotten worse. But in a really funny way.

# How To

## Aaron Burch

from *Everyday Genius*

Cut from the front of scalp back to the temple. Start where the tip of the widow's peak might be, if you had one, following the hairline. Make sure the blade is sharp to pull through the skin with ease, though be careful to not let it slip in too deep. Holding your forehead down with one hand, pull the skin above it back slow, like peeling the plastic off the top of a container. Tools that may help: tweezers, scalpel, any of a variety of dentistry instruments you may be able to acquire, the tip of the blade itself. Peeled back, the skin may stay on its own or you can hold it in place or, most recommended, pin it back with some kind of clamp, hair pin, binder clip, etc. Retrieve the small piece of metal or plastic or even paper that you've been keeping though you never knew why, and place it against the exposed area. You may need to move it around until in place; when there is a pang of regret or forgetting, you'll know how it fits. Fold the scalp back into place, reattaching as you best see fit. Don't worry about the scarring or healing, it will have already happened.

# Tentacle Mind Report

## Stefani Nellen

from *Conjunctions*

We are here, our tentacles coiled in the pond of Martina's soul, the one untouched by the storm. We see everything. We saw everything. We float here in the cold until her lantern fish mind returns and chases us deeper into the dark. In slow, thudding heartbeats, we pass judgment.

\*\*\*

Martina has been psychotic for some time. She lies on her side in the hospital bed, the soft terry cloth nightgown falling open to reveal her freckled leg. She breathes against her fingertips. Her mother and stepfather lean over her to see whether or not she is awake. They smell soap, fattening chicken salad, and days of sweaty afternoon naps. The parents, tired and frumpy after the long drive from Dresden, build up the courage to touch their daughter.

Martina opens her eyes. Her eyelids are so swollen it looks as if her eyeballs creep from underneath pink pillows. She doesn't bother to pick the hair from her sticky brow. Her mother unpacks a red tote bag with a smiling sunflower in front, a gift from her students. She retrieves red apples, bundles of bananas, and books.

"You know I can't read," Martina slurs.

"Nonsense," her mother says. She hugs her daughter, leaning over the pile of presents.

A day later, they sit in the hospital garden and drink fennel tea from white cups. Martina wears glasses, sweatpants, and a knitted jacket. Her outgrown blonde bob is flattened on one side. Sores bloom between her nose and mouth.

"So, have your friends been visiting?" Martina's mother asks.

Martina shakes her head. "Not yet. Eva might come."

"Eva," her mother says. "That's good." She doesn't believe Eva is going to visit. She is convinced that Eva, whom she has never met, is partially responsible for *this*—her daughter's sickness, the fact that they drove for hours to sit here and drink tea, the doctors' busy steps and indifferent sneers, the glaring sun. Eva and Martina's other spoiled West German friends are responsible for this.

We understand that she thinks that way. To her it is a simple case of comparing the daughter who packed her suitcase and drove off to Heidelberg with the deft enthusiasm of a mountain climber to the daughter who now sits before her. Eva, Tim, Heidelberg with its tan doctors and marble hallways, even the sunlight are part of the alchemist process that changed one into the other.

We, on the other hand, don't assign guilt to a person. We see small actions, unsaid words, a mocking twitch of lips, and a sigh of disgust. These featherweight moments are the units of Martina's destruction.

\*\*\*

The next day, Eva visits.

She arrives in the early afternoon. She has gained weight since she and Martina first met, and wears a pastel green dress that flatters her light tan. But Martina remembers the Eva of two years ago, who wore velvet pants, a dark blue halter top and a matching belt. She walked with long strides, tall and bony, her white shoulders rolling, and her collarbones sharp as blades.

Tim and Eva referred to themselves as brilliant. Martina's memories of this brilliance are a kaleidoscopic cake: a layer of nasal Oscar Wilde quotes, Gauloises Blondes lit with a flourish and passed on to Tim, fingertips brushing his lips. A layer of lean thighs and buttocks, white knuckles, nocturnal bloodshot eyes. A layer of perfect grades and droopy-lidded, shrugging acknowledgment of same.

Martina wishes to cut a piece of this cake. We understand.

Eva walks toward Martina when the nurse at the reception desk stops her and asks to search her purse.

"Why?" Eva asks. Her voice is her weakness. Nasal, yes, but still colored by the vulgar dialect of Mannheim. Her obese family goes on vacation to a campsite in Croatia, and the bathrooms in their house have custom-made extra large bathtubs.

We hope she will reveal this to Martina soon. It will come as a surprise, as the presence of ugliness and ridiculousness in other people's lives often does. Martina still thinks she is alone at the bottom of the pit. We hope Eva will muster the courage to tap her on the shoulder and say, "I know this place." It could happen soon.

The nurse inspects Eva's purse and retrieves a pair of tweezers and a can of coke. "No sharp items on this ward," she says, waving her past.

And Martina and Eva face each other.

***

The seminar room was filled with first-year psychology students, most of them young and still dressing the way they did at school three months ago. Others were older and after careers as accountants, chefs, or homemakers, were ready to learn about the mind. Unfortunately, they would have to learn research methods first. "Basic Concepts of Statistics" was a required class, and the room was so full that people had to sit on the floors and windowsills or lean against the walls.

Yet the chair next to Tim was empty. He placed his arm on the backrest, embracing someone invisible. The gesture kept people away.

Eva entered the room, late as always, angry with herself for oversleeping and necessitating a run to the train station. She studied psychology because she didn't have the guts to apply at art school and be rejected.

Martina entered right behind her, late, too, because she took the wrong bus. Her reasons for studying psychology were as cowardly as Eva's. With her grades, she could have studied medicine, but at the last moment she'd felt terrified by her ambition. She told herself she would help people, like her mother, the teacher. She studied in Heidelberg because students from East Germany were encouraged to study in the West.

Martina and Eva approached the empty chair, pretending not to notice each other. Martina saw a space where she might fit. Eva saw a man's arm opening to her.

We should note that Tim was reserving the empty seat for his almost-girlfriend, a slim, suit-wearing law student. He studied psychology to help her out of her depression, even though he sometimes suspected her of pretending to be depressed so she didn't have to decide among her suitors.

Martina asked in her Saxonian accent, "Is this chair available?"

"Sure." Tim moved his arm from the chair.

Eva asked, "Can I quickly squeeze through? I want to stand over there." She pointed at a free slot of wall behind Tim.

"Sure," Tim said. Eva climbed over the table in front of him and claimed her spot. Martina sat down and lined up her notepad and pens. They were too close together all through the lecture. Eva noticed Martina's gold necklace, her downy neck, and her short fingernails. She noticed Tim's small ears, tender against his coarse locks. Tim and Martina noticed Eva's scent of a fresh shower, the smoking compartment of the Mannheim-Heidelberg train, and perfume.

The trio should never have met. They didn't have good reasons to be in this room. And the trio might have dissolved after the incident. We can't be sure.

We do know that, at the end, the professor suggested the students form study groups of three or four. Martina, Tim, and Eva moved closer together, two of them terrified of having to keep searching and failing to catch the flame.

*** 

We should invest time into evoking Eva's perceptions during the first weeks. She hoped for her friendship with Tim to grow into love. She imagined his broad hands warming hers, his thumbs finding her belly button, his fingers stroking her hips.

And he didn't mind her sharing his bed and stretching next to him in her tight knit dress and her boots. He talked to her about his parents, who loved each other but lived in different cities due to their careers, his dreams of becoming a painter or photographer, his suspicion that he was bi, and his almost-girlfriend. He crossed his arms behind his head so his elbow brushed hers, and stared at the fluorescent tentacles the law student had asked him to pin on his ceiling. Eva stared at the curled up tentacle tips and the suction cups teasing her like moist lips. One day, they whispered, he will leave her for you.

We see all of this, and we empathize with Eva and even Tim, but in the end Martina is the one who sits on a hospital bed all day with her legs dangling over the grey linoleum floor. The walls sweat. She sweats. Fat food oozes through her intestines. She feels it push forward and out. She needs to be supervised by an intern at all times and everywhere, because she tried to cut her wrists with the paper scissors from the behavioral therapy room and then walked up to the nurse exposing her wounds as if to say, "See here, I found a beautiful butterfly."

To us, who creep through time intertwined with each other and sustained by thought, Eva's desire doesn't measure up to the terror of slipping away. Where would we fall?

*\*\**

Martina's first sign of weakness—or our first glimpse through the crack at the light of her mind—happened shortly after her meeting with Tim and Eva. And it did happen after a sequence of the small gestures we talked about. Had her mother been there, she might have told her not to meet these people again. But her mother was in Dresden, bragging about Martina's new life in the West. And she would have been wrong to point at Tim and Eva, because she would have ignored the assault wrought by the city of Heidelberg, which had bombarded Martina with deadly pellets of beauty and softened the wall between the light and us.

Martina lived in an attic apartment that was little more than a triangular shelter from the wind. The room held a mattress, a suitcase, and a portable stove with two hot plates. She shared a bathroom and a larger kitchen with the Polish girls staying on the same floor. She could see the sky through a window in the roof, but the window didn't close properly so she had to sleep in a sleeping bag. A cosmetic mirror stood propped on top of her suitcase, next to a heap of makeup, pencils, and brushes, most of them the same as her mother's. She didn't feel at home with makeup; applying it reminded her of preparing for a costume party. But looking at Eva and others, she yearned for that extra line around her eyes, and for blush on pallid days.

The trio went to Martina's place only once. It happened soon after they had formed their statistics study group, and before they had become familiar enough with each other to be friends.

They walked through Heidelberg in the early dark of November, Martina leading. She wore her mother's knitted cap with the green stripes. Tim and Eva wore black coats.

Heidelberg bewildered Martina. She couldn't see why lunch had to consist of grilled strips of chicken breast on radicchio salad with capers and orange dressing; or why there had to be a special shop exclusively for Christmas paraphernalia, open year round with a red locomotive circling a pile of presents in a fake frosted window. Other shops offered silk scarves, "Student's Kiss" pralines, fashion, art, incense, bikes, board games... Every second building was a historic landmark, forever unalterable and dramatically lit at night; the city was populated with stern statues illuminated from below and tourist plaques touting the city's history. And there were the real neighborhoods with filling stations and supermarkets and pharmacies, but even here she felt oppressed by a sense of luxury. Heidelberg was so pretty, and it had largely escaped bombing in the Second World War. Its beauty had the smugness of invulnerability.

Martina's apartment was in one of the few ugly houses. They climbed four flights of stairs and walked down the hallway, which smelled of heated-up canned meat. Martina let them in, realizing how small her place was. Eva and Tim were too tall to stand up, so they crouched, looking for a place to sit with the exaggerated craning of the necks appropriate for surveying a vast plain. There was only a rectangle of carpet.

And as she saw her friends' diligent but consternated attempts to deal with the smallness of her life, Martina's perception did its first hiccup and became sharper, but also strange, as if someone had secretly injected her with LSD. During this moment, Eva and Tim changed into tall reptilian creatures, hairless, lidless, and cold. They shifted forward, nostrils sniffing. They grew bigger, twisting around each other, until there was no more room in the apartment. Pulsing flesh enwrapped Martina, pleasant at first, then painful. Martina's mind hiccupped again and Tim and Eva changed back. Tim and Eva looked at each other and, as one, sat on the mattress.

"Are you hungry?" Martina asked in a shaky voice. She still felt scales rubbing her cheeks, and part of her had lost its grip and was falling, crumbling off as she spoke.

"One hungers," Eva said.

Tim laughed in appreciation. "One thirsts." He took off his coat, still sitting down. "And one coats too much."

Eva took off her coat, too, and they leaned back on their elbows on a blanket of black wool and grey lining, lazy, waiting for entertainment.

Martina opened her suitcase, where she kept many snack-sized bags of crispy chocolate bits. The stash was meant to last all semester, but Martina brought two handfuls to the bed, squatted down, and offered them to her guests.

Tim picked up one of the golden brown bags. He turned it around and read, "Yummy Crunchy Chocolate Bitsies."

"Cool, are these from the East?" Eva asked.

"From my parents," Martina said. "My father knows someone who works at the factory. They're outtakes. The packaging is wrong." She lifted a bag, which clung together in an odd shape.

Tim tore open the bag, picked out a single chocolate bit, and popped it in his mouth.

Martina observed his lips as he chewed. She knew that West Germans joked about the bizarre inferiority of East German food and only sampled it so they could tell their friends how pathetic it was. Seven years after the reunification, there was a market for genuine GDR articles. Ossi-jewelry, -pickles, -dinnerware, -pop music, and -sweets were apparently both amusing and historically significant.

Eva reached for the bag and had some chocolate bits, and Tim had another one, too.

"This is fun," they said.

Martina was relieved. On the one hand we find this pathetic, on the other hand understandable, considering that her guests were reptiles in disguise and had to be placated.

Martina offered them Club menthol cigarettes, another East German gem. Tim lit three at once and passed one each to Martina and Eva. Oscar Wilde had passed cigarettes like this to his companions, so Eva termed this gesture of sharing cigarettes "to oscàr."

***

Tim and Eva liked to do the statistics assignments the night before they were due. Martina had never spent an entire night without sleep. The first morning at Tim's place was magical, with the fog lifting outside, and the sunlight creeping through the naked branches. Tim opened the window and let the heat and stink of the night escape. Martina's eye sockets itched. She was hungry and sick at once, and her face felt like a rubber mask. She stood close to the window and let her cheeks soak up the air.

This was the time when computers were new and slightly suspicious. Their statistics professor had insisted on printed-out or typewritten homework, causing drama among the many students who still wrote papers in longhand. Tim owned a desktop computer and a printer, presents from his parents.

Martina observed her friends and tried to understand.

They ate spaghetti at three a.m.

Tim and Eva skimmed the books—*Research Methods for Social Sciences*, *Statistics*, *Linear Statistics*, and *The Logic of Hypothesis Testing*—and seemed to find them funny. They threw possible answers and solutions at each other, always lying on the bed, feet up on the wall or on the windowsill or over the pillow. One of them would volunteer to type, and another would summarize the answer in a pompous, mocking style brimming with deliberately false Latin plurals and fake references to textbooks that didn't exist. Much snickering ensued, and Tim brewed coffee.

Martina's stomach ached and gurgled from the spaghetti, but she drank her cup of coffee, even though it made her sicker. She wanted to sleep and hoped for signs of exhaustion: did the bags under Tim's eyes darken, did Eva slur? Yes to both, but they went on, faces gleaming, Eva's pimples peeking though her foundation. It didn't matter. Mind over matter. A priori, de profundis, Oscar, oscàr, only three more hours to go. Ha.

Tim and Eva worked on one document, and once this was done, they made a new copy of it and made changes so it looked like original work. They had to do this because the professor insisted on receiving original work from each student, even though they were studying in groups. They oscàred more cigarettes. Martina sat on the only armchair, churning inside, feeling like a geyser about to erupt. She was part of this, but she couldn't follow. Tim and Eva's conversation didn't make sense to her. So she listened closely to them and wrote everything down in stenography, which her mother had taught her so she could take more extensive lecture notes. And when it was her turn to alter the document into "her" submission, she inserted all of her notes. Some of them said the same thing, others hardly made sense, but she couldn't bring herself to leave anything out. She opened Eva and Tim's documents and copied everything she didn't already have into hers.

It was as if the extra insulation of more words would cover up the gaping failure she knew was hidden underneath. It took her hours to complete her assignments. She tried to hurry, but there was always more to add. Martina became scared. She had been a good student. She had skipped a class. She'd won awards. Now she copied gibberish, and it worked (they scored the highest grades in the class), and she didn't understand why.

\*\*\*

Tim and Eva started to dress in a similar style, both wearing black coats and silk shirts. Trying to keep up, Martina ran out of money. Uncountable cups of coffee all over town, slabs of pizza, fresh lilies, French breakfast at the Café Rossi, movies, clubs, and now new clothes burned away her monthly stipend. She ladled out more chocolate bits, which she brought from her weekend visits home, and more cigarettes, and hoped it would count as a contribution.

\*\*\*

Tim and Eva were done with the last assignment. The semester was almost over. They lay down on Tim's bed, next to each other as always, she on her belly, he on his back. They didn't touch. Eva looked like a snake curled against a rock. One of the plastic tentacles came loose from the ceiling and fell on Eva's face. She left it there, reaching for the tip with her tongue. Tim laughed.

Martina turned to the computer screen. The text waited to be manipulated by her. The letters swelled and shrunk in sync with the thuds in her head, which could have been her heartbeat, except her heartbeat was a thin red thread jerking at the rim of her perception. Her hands felt like claws. She could only use her middle fingers to type. Using the other fingers nauseated her. So she pecked words into the existing text.

Her mother's voice called out to her in the tone she used when she wanted to be heard over the noise of schoolchildren: not loud so much as chiseled, every syllable unmistakable.

"Go to bed," her mother said.

"I have to finish this," Martina said. Her standard answer. Getting work done in time was a priority at home.

"Nonsense," her mother said.

Martina pecked. Each peck was accompanied by a

pneumatic hiss and one syllable: Non-sense, non-sense, non-sense. It wasn't her mother's voice anymore but a message from the machine telling her to stop. So she did. The silence stunned her.

"You done yet?" Eva asked. Martina turned on the swivel chair. Her friends were tired and white faced, flat on the bed with only their heads raised. The tentacle stuck to the side of Eva's face.

Martina realized they wanted her to finish. She was too slow. So she turned around and continued pecking. Eva and Tim started talking again, something about the subtle homoeroticism of something. Could they be talking about the statistics professor and his research assistant? Martina took deep breaths to drown them out, but it didn't help; the words lodged themselves between the ones she wanted to peck into the document.

The estimator of the population mean $\mu$ is the nonsense mean of the sampling tender glances distribution of nonsense $\mu$. Repeated platonic empirical nonsense samples decrease the variance of the puckering lips and nonsense make me go moan on the table sampling that's crude distribution, because the standard deviation $s$ as in Allen Ginsberg decreases as $N$ increases. Nonsense.

Tim gave a sharp, howling laugh. It startled Martina. She kicked her knee forward and hit the computer's reset button. Everything disappeared. This was the time before autosave.

Martina and Tim writhed in slow motion, disentangling from a daze. They almost giggled, but their faces remained white and rigid.

"Did you do a save?" Tim asked.

"What?" Martina said. Her throat burned. Her friends got up and walked toward her, stretching. She remembered Eva and Tim changing into reptiles and wondered whether they would do it again.

"Ha ha," Tim said. "You just destroyed your work." His face cracked. A vein appeared on his brow as he continued laughing.

Eva rubbed her eyes and yawned. "It's about time we leave anyway. It's almost five. Let's have breakfast and hand in our stuff at eight."

"What will I do now?" Martina asked.

Tim and Eva staggered through the room, bumping into furniture. Eva put on her boots and tried to tie the laces.

"I still have to finish my assignment," Martina said. Her stomach clenched. She hated her friends and their stupid habit of working at night, and the stupid machine that lost a text simply because she'd hit a button. She hated Heidelberg and psychology.

She should have said: I can't do this anymore. I will leave.

And they should have said: Yes, leave. We bear you no ill will. Sometimes coincidence strikes up harmful friendships, such is life. Go save yourself. You're tired, your skin is breaking out, you're having this rim of tears around your eyes, and we don't dare talk to you because you might cry. And at the same time, you're so solid and literal and slow, and you copy us, and it bores us. Go.

Instead, everyone was too tired to be honest. Tim let her stay at his place and type up her notes again.

If we judged them based on this moment, we would have to judge them equally.

***

During the second semester, Martina got used to Heidelberg. She moved into a student apartment in Dossenheim with five other people. Her room had two bunk beds, one of them obstructing the window, but she felt encased, suspended.

Eva and Martina still met with Tim, even though they weren't a study group anymore. At first, they arrived at the same time, but as the semester continued, Martina would arrive at Tim's and find Eva already there, dressed up in a tight dress, legs crossed. Recent words not meant for anyone else weighed down the air, and Martina was afraid to stand between them.

Some days Eva smiled, while Tim scratched his head and searched his shelves for a CD. Sometimes, she winced as if sustaining a cut in a hidden place. She thinned out like a reed whipped around by a storm. She became so thin her stomach looked hollow.

Tim drove home most weekends, then on Thursdays, then from Thursday to Monday. One day, he walked down the corridor of the university library and the pointlessness of studying psychology, of all things, struck him. He wanted to bang his head against something, so he jumped up and hit the sign saying "Art." He dyed all his clothes blue and often laughed the way he had laughed when Martina had hit the reset button.

Toward the end of the second semester, he calmed down. He bought a camera. One afternoon, he visited Martina and asked if he could photograph her. He wanted to apply to art schools and needed a portfolio.

Martina and he sat down on the student house patio. The sun was out, and they had a couple of beers. Martina had never been alone with Tim before, and felt guilty thinking of Eva, but at the same time tipsy and seductive.

"You're more photogenic than a bowl of fresh fruit," Tim said.

On the photos, Martina's skin looked creamy. She raised a glass of bubbly gold at the camera and grinned like a child planning some mischief.

***

Tim moved away after the second semester of psychology, and Eva went to Madrid on an Erasmus scholarship.

We think this illustrates their good instincts. Some entanglements can best be solved by leaving them alone. Even poisonous vines shrivel without sun and water.

We want to live, too. We are not all bad. We will retreat without a fight once sanity acknowledges us. Meanwhile, we have much to give.

The cracks grew. We could see outside. She could sense us.

With Tim and Eva gone, the bookends keeping Martina's life together disappeared. She slept in, dug her heels into the mattress, and moaned with the pleasure of not having to negotiate Eva and Tim's stares or the late nights or the tugging expectations. And while she did this, life accumulated as a distant wave. The yellowing leaves, the blue-and-white pedal boats on the river and their mossy smell, the marinated olives served at the French bistro in Neuenheim, the kettle-corn smell of the cinemas, and the high-pitched hiss of the streetcars coasting on intersecting rails on the Bismarckplatz; the spicy tea rimmed with brown sugar at the café Art, the bikes' bells jingling as the cyclists drove up the uneven streets, and the fireworks during the castle illumination (the castle itself bloodred like a horror toy): the entire city became a wave of sensation that rose higher and higher until it crashed into Martina's mind and dissolved it into swirls of sand and shells and flesh and washed us free.

At first she didn't understand what was wrong. Life had grown fat and loud. Everyone she met filled her with raw longing. Her roommates brought a string of friends and lovers to the apartment. Martina fell for the perfect silver sphere dancing on the tongue of a Turkish girl and got a tongue piercing of her own, sucking down the taste of metal as she tried to fall asleep.

She bought printed dresses, let her hair grow long and braided it, and gave herself away to so many kisses, hands, and thrusts. She gorged on details: textures of hair, taste of spittle, and an accent. She copied and took notes the same way she'd done with Eva and Tim, only faster, more. Like an invisible woman, she needed to roll herself in paint to remain human.

\*\*\*

Martina sat in the library to study. She opened the book on test theory. She needed to prepare for the intermediate exams. It was a quiet day, unlike the others before. The wave of life had surged back leaving a surface like a glass marble. Nothing was left except the crack of the book when she opened the pages, and the white flat tree pulp.

She started to read, and couldn't. She knew the symbols on the page were letters, but she couldn't recognize them. She opened another book and found the same thing. The marble surface tilted and she started sliding down.

She tried to stay calm by muttering a syncopated syllable under her breath, something like now-now-now, asking to remain sane only until the next now, and the next. She picked up a pen and printed her name across the book's first page. Her hand remembered the shape of the letters, but she didn't recognize them.

Her palms turned cold. She sweated, felt sick. Through the window, she searched for something, anything to read. She didn't see anything. She slid faster, hot now—except for her hands—as hot as her breath and her cheeks as she ran downstairs, outside, looking for the street signs. She couldn't read them. Now she laughed.

And we laughed. Free at last. We took a long heaving breath, and the air and light tasted like fire. Our tentacles strained upwards, waved, clapped, claimed her mind, and fell crashing down again. We are not strong enough to ravage, not strong enough to destroy. We are gentle and full of longing for life, real life. We can only claim a moment at a time. But we linger. We float in the dark.

***

Martina drove home to Dresden. She tore out the piercing as she was driving, digging into her tongue until she swallowed gobs of blood. Her mother turned white when she saw her.

"See," Martina lisped. "I got rid of it."

They drove to the emergency room. The doctor assured them that tongue tissue heals fast. In the early morning they were back home. Martina's tongue puckered despite the painkillers when her mother finally embraced her.

Martina remembered the synthetic knit fabric of her mother's blue pullover, the sensible lemon smell, and the soft rolls spilling from the bra underneath. She remembered the sunflower wallpaper, the thin walls, and the soft noises from the neighbors. She cried. She wanted to touch her mother, submerge herself into the broad back, the long earlobes carrying fake sapphire earrings, the fuzz over her lips, the large, harmless breasts.

Her mother prepared goulash. She carved the meat, ground the pepper, and hurried from cabinet to cabinet. Martina followed her, unable to bear more than a step between her and her mother. And she talked.

"And I forgot to hand in my forms for the stipend and now I'm out of cash but the car needs inspection and I can't work because that costs me my stipend and I have to prepare for the exam except I can't read I tried everything I borrowed summaries I took out the books from the library I made copies I covered the pages so I could read one line at a time I tried to read to myself I asked Alex to read to me and he says I'm crazy and Mel is in Greece and the deadline to sign up for the exam is in a month and I have to pass because otherwise I'll lose my stipend..."

Her mother turned around and put her hands on Martina's shoulders.

"You can't read?" she asked.

Martina nodded. Her glasses were dirty.

"All right," her mother said. "Everyone has problems preparing for exams. There are all kinds of tricks. Remember what you did at school? You went to the library each morning before breakfast."

Martina's mind lurched at the memory. She had been eighteen. There had been fatigue, clear-cut and honest fatigue. Her table in the library had been smooth and golden brown. She had opened the book, and leaned on her elbows and digested the words one by one. She had been tired but solid. Afterwards, she'd walked home, the knowledge a firm parcel in her mind. She yearned for this time, the morning smell and the smell of library books, old and new at the same time.

"What happened?" her mother asked.

"I got a new computer," Martina said. "It's broken. I need money, but I can't work..."

"No," her mother said. "What happened? With you?"

"I want to come home," Martina blubbered. "I want to be your daughter again."

When it was almost morning, Martina's mother and her stepfather went to bed. Martina sat down in front of the bedroom door, trying not to disturb them, but she couldn't stand to be alone out there in the hallway, so she opened the bedroom door and snuck in. She wanted to sit at the foot of the bed, but Martina's mother noticed. She got up, took her daughter's arm, and dragged her out of the room. She wore a cotton nightgown with narrow straps that slid off her shoulders. Her stepfather pulled the sheet up to his chest before turning on his side, facing away.

"I can't read," Martina said, her voice a tired monotone. "I can't do anything, my tongue hurts, I'm too fat..."

"You can't be in our bedroom all night. You can't be in here."

Martina froze. She still hadn't cleaned her glasses. She reached for her mother's naked arm. "You feel good," she said.

Her mother squirmed away, almost crying now. "Get out. You need to go to sleep."

Martina stroked her mother's arm, cupped her breast with an expression of wonder. Her mother slapped her hand away. She pushed her out of the room by her right shoulder. "Stay out." She shut the bedroom door.

Martina leaned against the door. Inside, she heard stifled sobs. Steps approached the door. The doorknob shook. The lock clicked. Martina sucked her thumb and bit down on her fingernail. Her tongue puckered against her palate. She went into the kitchen, picked up her car keys from the key bowl and left. Her suitcase was still in the trunk.

No, she wasn't a coward. She wasn't irrational. She stood in the dark, her car key in the door, and waited. Mist that wasn't quite rain settled on her skin and calmed down the hot pain in her tongue. She took a deep breath. As she stood in the night, she looked at the rows of dark houses on the side of the street, and the single dim light in her parents' bedroom. She thought of herself in the car as a comet that would burn a trail back to Heidelberg, and she hoped there would be something left of her when she arrived.

What we admire her for, even if it means we have to return to the dark, is that she thought of Eva and Tim. Not with the mixture of envy and craving and incomprehension she was used to, but with detachment. She saw them as fellow comets, eaten by their own fire elsewhere. And when she thought of Eva, she saw another lonely woman, one she could turn to for help now that her mother couldn't give it.

***

Back in Heidelberg, Martina heard that Eva had returned from Madrid and moved into a carriage house in the garden of a villa in Handschuhsheim. The villa belonged to a commune of eighty-year-old therapists who liked to have students around.

The carriage house looked like an exhibit, freshly painted in red and beige. A dirt path went from the main gate to the staircase that led up to the door. Next to the staircase was the door to the bathroom. A heart was carved into the wood.

Martina sat down on the stairs, embracing her shins. Earlier in the day, she had tried to drink warm oil so she could vomit out some of her weight. It hadn't helped. Nothing helped anymore. That was why she had come here.

Eva pushed open the main gate. She had to struggle against the iron bars. The gate fell shut behind her as she walked up the path. She looked fuller. Her hips jiggled underneath her crinkled short dress. She carried a stack of books. Martina figured she must be almost done with her intermediate exams.

When she saw Martina, she stopped.

"Hello there," Eva said from afar. They hadn't spoken in a while. Life had hurled them down different roads.

"Hi," Martina said in her young voice. "Can I come in?"

The single room wasn't as large as it looked from the outside, but the open windows let in the sunlight and green from the garden. The tips of ivy peeked inside the windows, too, as if branches cradled the room.

"Do you want some tea?" Eva asked, putting the books down on the coffee table.

"I think that sounds nice," Martina said.

Eva busied herself in the kitchenette. "So, are you doing your exams after all?"

Martina smiled. Everyone pretended that she functioned. She was like a spider, small and defenseless and so crushable, but she terrified people.

"No," she said. "I can't."

Eva brought back two cups of tea. She and Martina sat down on the secondhand couch. The pillow sagged and they spilled some tea and giggled, like old times.

"I'm not feeling too well," Martina said.

It took Eva a while to comprehend this. Martina expected her to dodge the remark, label it as a normal complaint, a thing that could be fixed, but she didn't.

"How bad are you?" she asked.

"I didn't sleep for weeks," Martina said. "I stayed with people, but they all ask me to leave. And they're right. It's not correct to enter someone's bedroom when they want to be alone."

Eva put down her teacup, rubbing her neck. "Maybe you should get some help."

Martina drank the tea Eva made. Peppermint tea, good for her stomach. She remembered the old Eva, a stick of skin and pimples, and how small she had looked next to Tim. She remembered their long statistics nights together. The taste of coffee and spaghetti still lingered in Martina's throat, but Eva had changed. She now lived in a world of peppermint and ivy. She had disentangled herself from the plastic tentacles at the ceiling. Martina wanted to follow her, but she was afraid she'd be pushed out once more. And maybe she shouldn't follow anyone, anyway.

She opened her purse and took out an orange sheet of paper. She had taken it off the pin board in the institute hallway. She thought she recognized the color: emergency contact information for students in need of psychiatric help.

"Could you call them for me, please?" she asked.

Eva picked up the sheet and looked at it for a long time.

"You said you couldn't read."

"No, I can't." Martina held up the orange paper. She saw a neat string of symbols and a jolly drawing of a phone.

"Please help me," Martina said. "You're the only one I could think of."

***

Eva and Martina sit opposite each other in the hospital lobby.

"Yesterday I tried to write," Martina says. "They didn't like it."

"Why not?" Eva asks.

Martina stares past her.

"Why not?" Eva asks again.

Martina leans over. Her face lights up. "I made chits with your phone number and wanted to smuggle them into visitor's handbags so they'd find them and call you."

Eva nods, pretending this sounds like a reasonable plan. Inside, she cries, Nonsense.

"But I realized this wasn't right," Martina says, her face still bright. "So I tore them into shreds and mixed the shreds in my salad. A nurse saw it. No more writing."

Eva nods again, then stops. "Wait. This was a stupid thing to do."

Martina blinks. "What?"

"Who mixes paper shreds into their salad?"

Martina ponders this. A faint smile forms on her lips. "You're right," she says.

She dozes off. Eva takes a book from her purse and starts to read.

Martina wakes up again a little later and doesn't say anything for a long while.

"You look beautiful," she finally says. "I want to look beautiful, too."

Eva's impulse is to say, you will. But the truth is, she doesn't know.

They don't speak anymore. It's an awkward, tough business, visiting Martina, but Eva promises she'll stop by again.

"I would like that," Martina says.

When Eva leaves, she passes a small woman who walks as if she'd prefer to run and who carries a red tote bag with a sunflower printed on it. They step to the same side of the hallway in an attempt to make space for each other and brush shoulders with muttered excuses. It will take only a small variation in timing for them to meet.

We hope they will be kind to each other, and kind to us.

***

We can't be destroyed. We don't destroy.

We are here, our tentacles coiled in the deepest pond of Martina's soul, the one untouched by the storm. We see everything. We saw everything. We float here in the cold until her lantern fish mind returns and chases us deeper into the dark. We burn with the anger of Martina's mother stifling her sobs in the pillow, cursing herself for pushing her daughter out of the door. We ache with Eva lying next to Tim under a canopy of plastic tentacles. We laugh with Tim photographing Martina on a golden afternoon. We hold Martina while she bangs against the doors, and we won't let go until one of them opens. In slow, thudding heartbeats, we pass judgment.

# Me and Theodore are trapped in the trunk of the car with rags in our mouths and tape around our wrists and ankles, please let us out.

## Mary Hamilton

from *SmokeLong Quarterly*

I built a bridge and named it Samuel. I built a bridge out of tongue depressors and cotton swabs stolen from my doctor's office. I built a bridge out of paper gowns and syringes stolen from my doctor's office. I built a bridge out of soap dispensers and air hoses stolen from my doctor's office. It took me seven years to build my bridge. I visited eighteen doctors. I stole from eighteen doctors. I waited in eighteen exam rooms. I looked through eighteen sets of drawers and cabinets. I had a sore throat. I had an ear infection. I stepped on a rusty nail. I stubbed my toe. I broke my arm. Influenza. Yeast infection. Shingles. Lyme Disease. Breast lump. Strep throat. Poison Ivy. Hair loss. Swollen tongue. Glaucoma. Concussion. Herpes. Hangnail.

I built a bridge and used it to cross. I built a bridge and used it as shelter during storm. I built a bridge and skated in ice and snow. I made my ice skates out of razor blades and rubber bands stolen from my doctor. I cut my nails and made a mirror. I grew my hair and made a rope. I cut my hand and made a river to run under. I cut my hair and made a mattress, a shirt, a rug to shake and beat over the railing.

I built a bridge for strong and sturdy.

I built a bridge and named it Doris.

Not done. I needed a tree. I needed a road. I needed a car to move me faster. To make me crash. To throw me free. I followed my doctor home. I chased his Honda. I put a flag on his bumper so I could see it from far off. I kept my distance. I followed my doctor. I followed my doctor home. I waited outside his house. I waited for him to sleep. I waited for him to eat dinner. Do the dishes. Read a magazine. Jerk off. I waited for him to take a shower. To watch the talk shows. I waited for him to sleep. For him to R.E.M. For him to toss and turn. To dream of children. To dream of pre-pubescents fighting a war using elephants and camels instead of horses. Waited for him to dream of children firing guns and throwing grenades and building bombs. I waited for him to snore.

I stood in the moonlight.

I hung from a streetlight.

I broke down his door.

I rearranged his furniture. I made an omelet for my hunter. I washed my clothes. I tore the curtains and made a dress. I made shoes from the door handles and earrings from the soap. I made a garden salad from paint chips and used batteries.

I found his room I said his name, Doctor. I moved closer and said his name louder, Doctor. I moved to the bed and said his name louder again, Doctor Doctor. He rolled over. He pulled his knees to his chest. He nuzzled his pillow. I moved to his bedside. I sat next to him. I kissed his forehead. I stole pieces of his hair. A corner from his blanket. His right slipper. His four front teeth.

I found his attic. I found his workshop. I unlocked the door and I found a model airplane. The size of my upper half. Wingspan my wingspan. I found an airplane made of skin samples and hair. Blood cells and Petri dishes. Propellers made of charts and hair roots. Wings of x-rays and phlegm. I found maps made of bed trays and goggles made from rubber bands.

I took the plane to the roof.

I made the plane fly.

# Great White

## Julie Platt

from *Gold Wake Press*

In the highest of three stacked attics, I find a paperback *Jaws*
with a safety pin through its first twenty pages, sealing off
a scene where a man slides his hands up a woman's
sandy suit and she, a little drunk, leads him down
to screw in the water. I replace the pin and return
to help my grandmother sew, cutting squares of sky blue
crepe for throw pillows. *Careful—there's not much left.*
*That's from your mother's bridesmaids' dresses, and this here*
*is the one I wore.* I want to cut up the white dress too,
for the lace. *No, we have to keep it nice*—the same answer
for why I cannot wind her clocks or make tiny pies
from green potatoes and her elegant
dough. But later that evening, she lets me strip
to undershirt and panties while she lifts
her own daughter's bridal gown from its shallow box.
Mother's satin pump sits prim as a pearl-handled
gravy boat. I can't crush my heel in. The skirts curl
away from my ankles. My shoulders strain against
the ancient stitching. In all the pictures, my mother
shoots up through this gown like a stalk, filling it out
like wet white corn, a glossy inner glove of sweat. *Stand up*
*straight. Let me get my camera.* But I want to carry violets.
But I bleed. But I put my toe clean through the skirt hem.
In my grandmother's version of things, the story begins
when the monster tears through the first limb,
starts a fire in the crabapple orchard and returns
with arms full of brambles, panties stuck with grass, no shoes.

# Karner Blue Butterfly Hunt

## Julie Platt

from *Gold Wake Press*

Some narcotic wavelength breeds
backward through the pigment. Seconds,
then the siege. They struggle
to disedge their shine against
the grass, and thrash to powder.
Smearing hands with this must shear
the common from the hours—
otherwise, it would be greed.
Last night, I dreamt of passage:
a rough midwife in a land
of barren women. No one
spoke of what I was, or scorned
my forceless, distant gifts. Coarse
cotton draped our dull commerce
and we halved a dish of figs.

# Samuel L. Jackson Is Not a Good Name for a Rabbit

## Elizabeth Ellen

from *Wigleaf*

I made it my goal in life to be pretty for you so that when we met you would want to put your mouth on mine and fill my head with your bullshit ideas. I had worked out a life for us in the form of a blue-collar family sitcom, complete with a gay son and a Goth daughter and weekly misunderstandings based on the stupid things you said, and at the end of every episode I forgave you and it felt like you learned something though probably you didn't and just said you did so the credits could roll.

Then when we finally met you told me you didn't like pretty girls and the words you were saying didn't make any sense to me like they weren't really English. I asked you to clarify and you said you liked ordinary girls instead; girls with sallow skin and tattoos of insects on the backs of their necks. The girl you were with when we met — Anastasia — had cellulite on her thighs and acne between her shoulder blades and I visualized you sitting on her back popping those zits all night long. There were some really good-sized ones and I figured it would take a long time. I had a clarifier/toner combo pack on the counter in my bathroom. There was nothing whatsoever interesting about my back.

I didn't know how I was going to fill my nights without our sitcom family so I went to the pound, which is where I'd heard lonely people went to pass the time. I'd planned on getting a dog but none of the dogs looked lonely enough so I got a seventeen-pound rabbit named Larry instead because Larry looked sufficiently melancholy. It said in Larry's papers that his previous owners had given him up due to an out-of-state move and I promised Larry right then and there that if I ever moved I'd take him with me because I'm not an asshole like that.

I'm an asshole in many other ways, of course. For instance, I have really bad road rage. If you cut in front of me in the fast lane on the freeway I'll ride your ass a hundred miles until you get the fuck over. One time I rode this chick's ass half an hour and then when I got to my exit I flipped her off. It felt good flipping her off for about a second, like I'd really gotten one over on her, but then she crossed three lanes and got off the exit behind me and that didn't feel as good. I had to drive twice the speed limit and run a few red lights to lose her and I don't even smoke anymore so it's not like I could light up a cigarette after or anything.

The other night I made a sketch of you riding a camel and showed it to Larry. Admittedly, Larry doesn't have a wide range of facial expressions. He pretty much had the same expression on his face staring at the sketch of you on the camel as he does when he watches me take a piss or masturbate or eat low-carb pretzels. Which is to say, it's hard to tell what the hell that rabbit is thinking sometimes.

I bet if I stopped exfoliating and got a tattoo of a mosquito or a cicada on the back of my neck and wore my hair in a ponytail every time I went to the grocery store or movies until you noticed, you'd leave Anastasia and move in with me but then you'd want to change Larry's name to something funny like Mr. Wiggles or Samuel L. Jackson, which is another reason I'm glad it didn't work out between us. Samuel L. Jackson is a stupid fucking name for a rabbit.

# After I Blew Through My Hysterectomy

## Kendra Kopelke

from *The Potomac*

After I blew through my hysterectomy, I
should not have been surprised by the baby
dreams that were released in me, like dozens
of helium balloons, nor how the gold finch's
disappearance into the dark green patch of garden
saddened me with its quick graceful exit. It was
a summer spent on the other side
of the operating table, taking in the view and I
came to know more where I stood, and
what to listen for, and I made two piles,
what was here and what was gone, then
watched them overlap. The old Cape Cod
shipwrecks that rise up every year,
under a full moon, I could see them, just at the
edge of the horizon, the Whydah, the Jason, the Portland,
my eyes level with the outside's outside, its periphery,
where things linger and circle back, where
feeling takes real shape. Nature, says Thoreau,
knows what to pay attention to, and ignores the train whistle.
Before I headed north, my father gave me a long warm hug
and I let him, let him hold on,
past the standard Kopelke hug time,
because he needed to transmit a message to me,
and maybe I could risk it all again. I have missed him.
Surgery isn't the magic moment I make it out to be,

you certainly know I am making everything up,
but not the part about being cut open,
when the skin becomes more astute,
and doesn't take itself for granted, and
the insides, well,
it will be awhile before they can tell
me what they felt about what they saw.

# Father

## Brian Evenson

from *Wag's Revue*

Nights, we kept father confined to his room by draping the walls with black velvet curtains to hide the door—which in his sleep-addled state he did not entirely remember existed—and by hanging the drawing of the girl on the window. He would get up, not even half-awake, grope around in the dark until he found the flashlight, and then make for the window. When he caught sight of the girl's image, he would give a shriek. Then we would come and turn on the light to find him tangled in the curtains. We calmed him—sometimes vodka was enough, sometimes we had to resort to tranquilizers, sometimes there was nothing for it but to beat him with sticks until he lost consciousness.

In the morning, father was always his old, arrogant self: blunt, cheerfully deranged, in command of even the minute comings and goings of the house, his domain. He ordered us about our tasks and, when dissatisfied, jeered at us or fixed upon us his reproachful and imperious eye or sentenced us to a few hours' confinement in the darkened cellar.

But at night, everything was different for him. How we had had the foresight to draw the girl's portrait before her disappearance we did not know. But we knew we couldn't have done without it.

# Caves

## Matthew Simmons

*from Lamination Colony*

**one**

This man only dated caves. It was, like, a fetish or something.

He used the internet and travel magazines, outdoor magazines, etc., to meet caves. He went online and found websites that helped him meet caves to date.

It worked out pretty well for him, sometimes. Usually.

Sometimes.

**two**

This man who only dated caves would—when he found an online listing for a cave he thought he'd like—send them a short, introductory email. He'd tell them all about himself—about his wants and needs, and his desires, and stuff like that.

He was always very honest about what kind of a person he was when he would write to the caves and tell them things. He was always himself. You know, he never fronted like he was something he was not.

He was real with the caves.

They seemed to appreciate that about him, he thought.

**three**

This was 2013, this time when the man was still just out there dating and had not yet met a cave who he really wanted to settle down with.

On the radio that year was nothing that really spoke to the man who only dated caves. None of the popular singer-songwriters of the day really seemed to "get him."

They all got something, though. Just not him.

He wanted to use music to make himself feel better. He wanted music to help—but it didn't. It really didn't. Not new music, anyway. No one from his contemporary time could help him.

Older stuff, sometimes.

**four**

The man who only dated caves would ride his bicycle to work every day. All the cars hovered high above the ground in 2013—like a sci-fi film!— so the streets belonged to the bicyclists.

He rode his bike to work, and dinged the bell every time he saw a fellow rider. The other rider would ding back, and the man felt good about things because of it.

The other rider dinged. The other rider recognized that the man was a fellow bike rider. They had this one very significant thing in common.

**five**

When the man got to work, he would walk by another man who was sitting on the stoop selling copies of his Xeroxed book of poetry and a CD of his very own reggae music.

The reggae man would ask the man who only dated caves if he wanted to buy some poetry or some reggae, and he always said no thank you.

He always tried to say it in a very pleasant way. But the reggae man always got mad and said: why don't you support the arts?

The man who only dated caves *did* support the arts.

He really did.

Don't think less of him.

**six**

The man who only dated caves didn't tell people about his cave thing. He thought his friends and coworkers would be alarmed by it if they knew.

A lot of times, people are intolerant of those who are different. Like, say, if they are covered in a thin layer of red hair, or they have been born with no sweat glands (a REAL problem!), or they have a harelip, or they are only attracted sexually to naturally occurring cavities in the sides of mountains that are big enough for a man to enter.

This could've been a real problem for him, work-wise. Career-wise.

So he kept it to himself.

**seven**

But sometimes, oh sometimes the man who only dated caves would fall in love, and his coworkers would notice, and they would say something.

Gosh, you sure seem up today, they'd say.

Sure I am, he'd say. Sure I am.

What's the deal with that, they'd say.

Coffee, he'd say. Coffee.

**eight**

When the man who only dated caves was asked to describe his body type? On those online dating forms?

He'd say medium build.

He could've stood to lose a pound or two. Even what with all the bike riding to and from work, sure. Sure. He could've lost, say, ten pounds, and looked a little better.

But what the hell. He felt medium.

So he put medium.

**nine**

Sometimes when he went on a date, he'd bring flowers. Sometimes he'd bring a little gift of some other type. He'd bring, maybe, a mixed CD of songs he liked.

He'd make the CD at home on his computer when he was thinking about the date. He'd try to imagine the likes and dislikes of the cave he was going to date, and try to guess what songs they would like.

(None of the songs, you know, spoke to him. But they spoke to *them*.)

You know what would happen? He'd bring the CD to the date, and they'd play it during the date, and the sound would reverberate off the walls of the cave in a really pleasant way, more often than not.

**ten**

The man who only dated caves lost his entire family in a very, very tragic car fire.

Except for his mom.

And his dad.

And his brother.

And twin sisters.

Really, then, the man who only dated caves lost a middling, four-year old hovering Buick (they were newer then, and not quite perfected) with 97,000 miles on it in a very, very tragic car fire.

Nonetheless, he took it surprisingly hard.

**eleven**

This guy, this man who only dated caves, lived in an apartment in a building where the wall facing the street was made entirely of glass. From down there, it looked to passersby like a slightly bigger version of the set of the Hollywood Squares.

The man who only dated caves kept his shades drawn, but his neighbors always kept them open. They like to do things so that everyone in the street could see them.

To his neighbors, it was sort of like the opposite of television.

**twelve**

For the record and in no particular order:

Stompbottom, Marengo, Culverson Creek, Whigpistle, Friars Hole, Banes Spring, Kings Saltpeter, Raccoon Mountain, Great

Onyx, Onego Millstream -Roaring Creek , Windy River, Janus Pit System, Buckeye Creek, Long Hollow, Anvil, and Dunbar Caves

—fucking broke his fucking heart.

**/intermission/**

That thing I said earlier, about him having some sort of cave "fetish?" I'd like to take that back, or amend it, or something.

Looking through all of this, I'm realizing that it was in no way a fetish. It was real.

It was a real, real thing that he had for caves, a real desperate, beautiful, and emotional connection that he made.

I suppose a fetish is real, yes, and a connection of a kind. But not like this.

This wasn't a kink, or just something that got him off, or a hobby, or an affectation, or any of that stuff.

This was just who he was.

Sorry for the interruption. It won't happen again. Let's get back to it.

**thirteen**

He liked the song that went:

I don't want to set the world on fire
I just want to start
a flame in your heart

And he liked to listen to the song in the morning when he was half asleep. It made him dream.

He would dream that he was deep in a cave, striking flint,

starting a fire, watching the little bits of flame flicker, shadows and flickers on the cave wall.

He was sometimes embarrassed by how literal his subconscious mind took things.

**fourteen**

The lies he told himself to make himself feel better were usually about the following things: his appearance, including assertions about his weight; his possibilities for career advancement, and the way such advancement would positively affect his mood; the cleanliness of his apartment, in particular the bathroom where he kept the cat box; his ability to remain relevant and aware about popular culture even when taking into account his advancing age; his sexual proclivities, and the way that, even though they were out of the mainstream, they were a normal part of the spectrum of human sexual behavior; the fact that he was very definitely going to be happy any day now.

The odds that he would believe those lies: not so good.

**fifteen**

He did a lot of house-sitting. He was trustworthy, and people often asked him to watch their homes when they were away.

He was good at it.

He also stole something from every house he stayed at. He stole a toothbrush, usually. Just a single toothbrush. A single, used toothbrush.

People thought they had brought the toothbrush with them, and left it behind at their hotels. And left it behind at the cabin in the woods where they stayed. And left it behind at the home of one of their relatives.

But, no. He had them.

If you went into his apartment and opened his medicine cabinet, you would find dozens of toothbrushes.

He never used them. He just kept them as mementos.

**sixteen**

He bought a little toy piano at a thrift store. The keys made a sound like the ringing of a bell.

He played little songs.

He sat out on the step in front of his house and played little songs. People would stop and listen.

They would stop and listen, and sometimes say nice things. And sometimes they would walk by without even looking at him.

He liked the walk-bys best.

**seventeen**

He met a girl, this man who only dated caves. A nice girl, too. But nothing.

They went out, the two of them, to have dinner at a local Italian restaurant. The man ordered a ravioli dish that had little bits of smoked duck and peas in the sauce.

The nice girl ordered a chicken dish of some sort—one without any pasta—and two bottles of wine.

The man watched as the nice girl drank one and a half bottles of wine. When she finished the first bottle, she laughed into her hand and ordered the second.

He liked the way she laughed into her hand after a bottle of wine, so he thought maybe they could go out again. As friends.

But he knew it couldn't work on any other level. He hoped she understood.

**eighteen**

He enjoyed an overcast climate. When it was sunny out, and everything was bright, it always looked to him like the world's edges were way too sharp.

The world, all sharp-edged, seemed dangerously unreal and strange, and he was made quite uncomfortable by it.

But he refused—he flat out refused—to buy himself a pair of sunglasses so as to take the edge off the world.

Instead, he simply let himself feel strange, and feel uncomfortable, and feel like he was in some sort of danger.

A cave of indeterminate age called to him from a photo in a magazine.

**nineteen**

The indeterminate age sang to him. It *sang* to him, for all the world. It *sang* to him.

So he traveled a very long way, and he found the cave, and he built a little lean-to next to it, and he lived there.

This was South America, so he adopted a South American boy, and named the boy Allen.

He and Allen cared for and tended to the cave.

**twenty**

The man died of heart trouble quite suddenly. Allen left the cave, and the lean-to, and he moved north to Chicago, Illinois.

In Chicago, he washed dishes at a place, and worked out-bound telemarketing at another. At the second place, he read from a script, and got hung up on for hours on end.

And he wrote poems about his dad. And he photocopied them into small books that he sold on the street, sitting on a building's stoop.

**twenty-one**

End.

# Premises for an Action Plan

## Scott Garson

*from American Short Fiction*

**1.**

Spencer Bray's picture was not among the pictures of faces the cops had me look at. The cops, as of a quarter past ten last night, knew nothing of Spencer Bray. Or they just weren't considering him as a person who might perpetrate a hold-up of the Boone Street Gas 'n Go. Five eleven, six foot, I said to the cops. Beefy. Black hair. All true information. Color? What? I said. Race, they said. White, I said. (True.)

Features? Eyes? Nose? Lips?

I don't know, I was scared, I was the one getting robbed. I did my best not to look up.

All true! The cops will not be able to say, Rory Jeffery, we know that you lied.

**2.**

Pumping gas outside as the money was taken: W Voss, who was questioned too.

She may not have had a good angle. She was close but may not have been looking at us when Spencer Bray clapped his small firearm down, holding it to the counter like a mouse, and lifted his ski mask—which was mustard-colored, as I reported, and ribbed—to scratch at his face.

She may not have seen him, or recognized him as

himself—the kid who had cheerfully terrorized us on the grounds of Wright Elementary.

Then again she might have. And if she did, she'd have given the cops his name.

She's that kind of person. She's never not paying attention in AP Economics. That's why she can be looked at.

**3.**

And if she did give the cops his name and offer the fact that she and Spencer and I had attended the same elementary, the cops might wish to talk further.

If that were the case, would they dial my cell? Do cops call people on their cell phones?

They'd use the home number.

And who would pick up?

**4.**

Therefore I can't be sure that by doing nothing I'm doing all that I can to prevent trouble with the cops, and trouble with M and D, who still don't know what happened last month—how our Buick was backed into a Self-Service Island at the Boone Street Gas 'n Go on a super-cold night when I failed to push the button for rear defrost, and how, after that, I was able to forge a deal with the owner to work off the damage. (Knowledge of this would have to precede any sympathy I might get for being robbed.)

**5.**

Neither is there any clear action to take to *reduce* the risk of trouble with the cops and trouble with M and D.

**6.**

Therefore trouble of these two kinds should not be the primary concern.

**7.**

Do I know you? Spencer Bray asked. And I shook my head in the slightest possible way, not wanting to move. I know you. Wait.

And I wasn't looking at him but could feel his mirth coming in waves.

Wait. Hang on.

I peeked at his hand on the gun on the counter. I waited with all of my might.

One scenario: recognition never comes to Spencer Bray. He forgets about thinking he knew me. Recognition never comes to W Voss, either, so his name is not given to the cops, and the cops do not find him. Result: I'm home free.

Another scenario: recognition does come to Spencer Bray. He wakes in a bed in the house of one of those uncles or cousins he always stayed with, and sits up, and says, as the dust motes spin in the sunlight, *Rory Jeffery*. And he puts on his parka—red, as I reported. And puts his gun in its right-hand pocket. And finds me. And kills me. Shoots me right through my tetanus-shot scar, which is just where he once put the pocket-knife blade on the grounds of Wright Elementary. The bullet glances the humerus, slips through the rib cage and explodes my heart.

Goodbye life. Goodbye W Voss.

**8.**

Or this: recognition does come to Spencer Bray in a bed on the north side of town, but he stays calm, regarding me—correctly, I guess—as one of the kids he subdued for good a long time ago, on the grade-school playgrounds.

But recognition then comes to W Voss, too (if it hasn't already), and she tells the cops, who she trusts from watching high-rated shows like *Law & Order*.

Everyone watches them. Can W be faulted for this?

In that one pair of jeans she has, in that tiny green shirt, as she paints her toenails, maybe, she watches the shows and trusts the cops and gives them the name, *Spencer Bray*. And they go to his house, or the house where his parents live. As I've indicated, though, he's never there!

So the cops don't get him. But he learns, through the family grapevine, that the cops are after him now, and he blinks his eyes and guesses he must have been wrong about me being permanently subdued. And he gets the red parka, the small gun. And kills me.

That flat pink color, the toenails would be. Bubble gum. She applies it innocently, without asking what others might think about it. Because she likes it. She likes that color.

**9.**

Or how about this: he awakes in that bed on the north side of town and says to himself, *Whitney Voss*. Those syllables slide into place as he remembers the girl he saw standing by Pump #3 as he was leaving with the money I gave him.

He gets the red parka. The gun.

**10.**

I scrape the Buick's tire sides into the curb and sprint to her doorway.

Rory.

Whitney.

Listen.

But I'm out of breath.

And she waits without feeling infringed upon by this visit from this guy who's not much more than an acquaintance. The day may seem uneventful enough, but she's sensitive. Right away she's able to see we've been joined in the weather of crisis.

Or I take the left onto W's street, and as I do I pass Spencer on the sidewalk, in his parka, on foot.

Rory.

Whitney.

I reach for her hand, close mine around hers. There's no time to explain.

## 11.

RE: delayed recognition, though: how likely?

I recognized Spencer Bray. That's firm.

Spencer Bray didn't recognize me.

W Voss did or didn't recognize him. But if she did, wouldn't the cops have called here already—if just to have me look at more pictures?

The day is quiet. In the yard, snow is melting away. I'm looking at sopping brown leaves.

Rory? M calls.

Yes.

Rory?

*Yes.*

Would you take out the trash?

## 12.

What's likely: W Voss, at Pump #3, didn't recognize Spencer Bray. It was darker out there, after all.

What's likely: Spencer Bray will forget about us—me and W Voss. By the time the cops start looking for him—if they do—he won't even remember our faces.

Will the cops catch him?

They could. It's possible.

He could buy everyone tokens at the Southroads Arcade, say it's on the Boone Street Gas 'n Go. He might do that.

We'd be called to testify, me and W Voss. And then he'd remember. *Rory Jeffery*, he'd think to himself. *Rory Jeffery. Whitney Voss.*

And how long could they keep him in custody anyway? He's only sixteen years old.

Concerns of this kind—are they not serious? Do they not compel me to quit typing, right now? To stand from this lightweight office chair? Cross the floor of the walk-in basement?

They do.

Cross the floor. Get my cell phone. Flip up the screen. Press in W's number. Touch the cold glass of the doors as I wait. Examine the tree limbs, the power lines, the tiny sparkling crusts of snow out there by the chain-link fence.

# If You See Buddha On The Road, Kill Him

## Barbara Yien

from *Emprise Review*

Brush strokes stingy as Mao's schematic
pictogram for love: black eyes, bare ribs, no heart.

What I thought was calligraphy. The scrolls I filled,
the dictums: No slack. No suet. No shopworn silk.

Later, even the script seemed wrong, even
the instrument (too soft, too singsong). I switched

to razors, wire, flint. I burned the sacraments.
Peonies, azalea, sweet-scented osmanthus—I beheaded

them all. Years passed. I brittled,
I flensed! Then a hole in my chest opened

like a flowering koan: You have misunderstood,
you will return to this life as a beetle.

# Proxy

## Emma J. Lannie

*from >kill author*

I do the kissing only very occasionally. I am okay with it, but sometimes it just complicates things. For the most part, it is just about the touching, the skin-on-skin way of it. There's nothing special I need to do. It just happens the way it happens, and I move about accordingly.

Sometimes, I get to be inside my head, and do all the personal thinking that I like. They can't tell that I'm not being who they want me to be. And I think about how swimming feels, and about how many hours are left of the day. I don't think about the heat coming from their hands, or the smell of onion, or cabbage or cigarettes. I don't think about the warm wet sometimes. Or the up-close throw of it, being pressed together like that, by words.

I started out as a hugger. I would stand close and reach my arm over a shoulder. It was only one arm, at the start. And then it progressed to two, that kind of full-body bear thing. And that was what they wanted most. For hours sometimes. They would stand and not let go, held in my arms, and I would get out of my body and race around outside, waiting for the sound of an ending.

I wear all grey, like skin when the heart stops. Even the mask is grey, and while it only hides the top of my face, it seems to suck out the colour from the bottom half as well. The bottom half is kept uncovered because of lips. Lips are part of what can be utilised. They hardly ever are, though. It's a very rare person that wants the Proxy kissing his or her lover. Sometimes it just happens anyway, and when it does, I always try to be as still as possible, as not-there as I can be.

Tonight, it's the man with the lover in Canada. He misses her more than he lets her know. He is all jokes and funnies when she's online. Through my earpiece she directs me to pat his arm, tells me to let my fingers curl over his shoulder. I hold the pose while she tells him it'll be okay, that it won't be too long now, and then she tells me to move my hand to his neck, to let my thumb rest against his jaw, stroking softly. He closes his eyes and it's her. He says I love you. He says it too quiet for her to hear it in Canada.

The man with the lover in Canada has a blue corduroy sofa. Sometimes when I sit on it I dig my nails into the ridges and let them travel all the way to the edge. With my free hand. My other hand is usually in his, our fingers interlocked, leaving a space between our palms the size of an egg. A small egg. I think about that space, hoping his lover has it filled with all the things they are going to do. It is a pocket in the closeness of two bodies. Breathing space. A plan. Or anticipation. There is another space in Canada just like it. And it's the same space. That's how this works.

With his free hand he types instructions for his Proxy. I don't look at the screen, but I know that in Canada, the Proxy's thumb is tracing circles across the quiet veins of the man's lover's wrist. She tells me to rest my head against his shoulder. I can smell him there, the nervousness and the excitement. His tee shirt is the scent of summer. My grey face presses against it. My mouth, open, breathes a hot circle and I let my tongue out to taste the fabric for just a second. She didn't tell me to do that. I close my mouth, glad of the mask and of not being anyone. His thumb is still against my wrist. I have a heartbeat there. It's quick, but I don't know what he thinks it means.

I listen carefully for more instructions. A lot of what

I do is about breathing. Taking a breath before executing a movement, holding a breath waiting for the next thing to happen. Or breathing in how they're feeling. Up close, skin throws out secrets. Like now, his skin is saying I Miss Being Touched. I know that's an easy one, it's the whole purpose of me, really, but it doesn't make it any less true. There are subtle changes to this. Like when his lover tells me to rest my hand on his back, and I do, but I rest it high, so that my fingers brush his neck. The missing goes away. The missing becomes a closed-eyed shiver of something different. The hairs on his skin rise up, prickle, and he sits quiet, doesn't type, just lowers his head, breathes in and out, and in and out again.

The man's lover in Canada tells him she has to go. They say their I love you's and she instructs me to leave. The man types the same instruction to his Proxy in Canada. I remove my earpiece. He closes his laptop lid.

My hand is still on his back. He still has hold of my other hand. I don't feel like I can move. I should be walking down the corridor. I should be on my way home. The blue corduroy sofa is underneath us both. It supports us. But I am not me. I'm not anyone. And I shouldn't be on the sofa any more.

He won't let go, though. Sometimes it gets like this. It's easy to see why. There's a thin line and we, as Proxys, walk it. I have a bracelet I can press. I will be safe in no time at all. But I'm not going to press the bracelet. I'm going to keep my hands where they are.

I have no idea what is happening in Canada.

We sit like this for a long time, staring at each other's hands. The skin on my hands is not grey. They're the only part of me that can tell him anything. The skin on his neck is hot. I lift one finger off at a time, until it's only my palm that is resting there. Without the voice in my ear, actions become awkward. There is no flow and no justification. It's easy when the choice is made by someone else. Even if I don't obey exactly, what happens is still not quite down to me.

There eventually comes a point where we break our grip, and I use this as a means of leaving. I don't say anything. I just raise my hand in a gesture of goodbye and he matches it. The corridor is long and full of too many chances to turn back. I slap my feet against the concrete and quickly leave it behind.

She says, We need to talk, from her computer in Canada. And then she tells me to rest my head on his shoulder. I try to stare out of the window. I try to think about the sea. The man with the lover in Canada presses his hand into the small of my back. Then he types something with his other hand, and I think in Canada the same thing happens, but I can't be sure. He fans out his fingers and I feel his hand not as a certain thing, but as a variable, as a thing that can change. I steady myself, placing my hand on his hip. He doesn't know that she didn't say to do that. He doesn't know that her only instruction so far has been Rest Head On Shoulder. We are caught up in the beginnings of a slow dance. My feet are not grey. They have a life of their own. After a lot of talking, her voice says It's over, I'm sorry. Then her instruction comes telling me to pat his back, to let him hug if he wants to. The man with the ex-lover in Canada lurches into my embrace. He holds me tight. I hear my own breathing in the space where she doesn't type. I'm stuck in my skin, waiting for the next move. He breaks from the hug and types something, hits the enter key hard. Then he comes back to me, his body slamming itself around mine, arms strong and inflexible.

My earpiece is quiet. All the sound has been sucked out of the world. He kisses me and it feels like a car crash. Something you know you shouldn't enjoy, but you can't help it.

He types something else. He is letting her know what he is doing now, with me. He lies me down on the blue corduroy sofa. All he knows of me is in my lips and my hands. But it's enough. He kisses me again, and this time, I'm there. Even before he shuts the laptop, even before I pull out the earpiece.

# Pop Star Dead at 22

## Dave Housley

from *Wigleaf*

Do you know what it's like when Myspace tells you they have to pull your profile because you're getting too much traffic? When Spencer Pratt friends you on Facebook? And then the next day, Brody Jenner? I mean *they* are friending *you*. You know what that's like? I do, bro. It's fucking awesome.

And then all of the sudden, the bottom just drops out? Dude. One minute you're cruising down the street, waiting for a callback from the people at Best Week Ever. The next, you're reading the headline on TMZ — Pop Star Dead at 22.

Now everything else is going to be after, and before is going to be the good times, like those 80's drug movies where everything is awesome and funny and bubbly soundtrack until somebody's nose starts bleeding, and then it's all rehab, narcs, and power ballads, everybody crying and getting too skinny and sad and ugly.

I remember before — that night, when we were getting ready to go out and I was like, I don't know if I should wear the Calvin Klein boxer briefs or the Hugo Boss tighty-whiteys, and something in my gut said tighty-whitey, dude. And I didn't think much about it until way later, after her people came over and told us to go into the private room, and our crew is hanging with her crew and we're all looking at each other going, Dude, I can't believe this either, but trying to be cool about it, too, like this happens to us all the time. And she's like, Let's go skinny dipping! And I'm like, Sure! And later on, when we're by the pool, and I'm trying to catch a glimpse and her people are taking away my cell, she's all, I really like a man in tighty whiteys. And I laughed and felt kind of like a tool, you know, because she is her and I'm like just some random dude at the bar, right? And she was like, Seriously, I really do.

That's how she was, though. Old fashioned. Honest. Like, I believe she really did like a dude in tighty whiteys, and not many chicks will tell you that and really mean it.

She was different.

People say they could see it coming and maybe that's the case if you weren't actually there. If you were, like, you know, so far away from her that you could sit up there in your glass tower, you might say, I, dude in glass tower, can totally see it happening: this pop star, who we all love like the sexy girl next door you want to not just hook up with but maybe actually cunnilingate in a loving fashion — that's how clean and nice and wholesomely sexy she was — she's heading for a Heath Ledger and she's heading there fast.

People might say all we shared was that one night but they don't understand. They didn't really know her. Not like me. Like I told Perez, I don't kiss and tell, but let's just say that yes, we were intimate, and that yeah, there's a real good chance we were going to be in love.

Did you know I texted her the night she died? She was pronounced at midnight, and I texted at like ten. I wonder if she got it, but there's no way I can know. I think about that a lot, whether it would have made a difference.

I picture her there, just before — maybe she's wearing a dress, kind of frilly, a little old fashioned, a little southern, not the kind of thing that's going to ride up while she gets out of a limo. Maybe she's not wearing any makeup and yeah, maybe she has a few zits, like a real girl, but prettier. Her hair is still a little wet from the shower and she's sitting there in her hotel room, way up on top of the LA hills, and maybe she's thinking about me — that one guy, the normal one, tighty-whitey guy who went skinny dipping and made out and shared a few laughs, a Marlboro Menthol or two, the guy who maybe reminds her of all the guys back home who she never got a chance to date — the not bad guys, the ones who would have been normal and nice and treated her good, who maybe would have taken her out for an ice cream sundae, a trip to the movies, a real date. A nice one.

I picture her there with her legs tucked under her, twirling a piece of hair and thinking about how did a nice girl like her even get into in a place like this and does anybody understand at all, and maybe she's wondering what happened to that one guy who seemed like maybe he could, like maybe he did understand.

I wonder if she ever got my text. Here's something I never told anybody before — not even *People*. You don't even have to mention my name, not if you don't want to. That's how serious I am about all this.

That last text, it said "Howz it goin gurl?" So maybe that's what her last text said: Howz it goin, gurl? Think about that: her last text. That shit should be in the Smithsonian.

When I sent it, I meant so much more. I meant this means so much to me. I meant I have finally arrived. I meant every day of delivering pizzas and folding t-shirts and working out and trying new things with my hair until it was just fucking right was all worth it. I meant thank you.

I wonder if she got it. I wonder if she understood.

What do you think?

Anyway, like I said before, you can use it if you want to.

## Translations of "My Refrigerator Light Makes Its Way Toward You" Into the 34 Languages Spoken in the Many Woods of Grief

**Lucas Farrell**

from *alice blue*

> *"If man was indeed born when the first animal wept, then it should be clear enough why I have been dying to drown."*
> —River of Life

If it weren't for my refrigerator light
I'd acknowledge the incandescence of the bird in my refrigerator,
the one I understand to be a regular bird, just a regular old bird
without a head.

...

I'm afraid God thinks I'm his telephone voice.

...

I'm afraid God thinks I'm his nose in profile.

...

I'm afraid if God saw me, he would very nearly recognize me.
Lost as he'd be in my many woods of grief.

...

Don't touch my things,

he would want to say—

so say it.

...

Welcome to the three-star
hotel of my mind.

...

Like anyone else,
I quote the many woods of grief.

...

For instance, the moon here is divided into thirds.

...

The moon is a love triangle dropped in a flour bin
(its white cloud outpour incorrigible, soft).

...

Months come and go as if bearing
fresh trout for supper.

...

You, me, our awesome appliances.

...

I'd like to use that toothbrush, please,
the one with your face attached to it.

…


In the orchard of beloved green apples,
there is a relinquishing of the city-body, the city-self.


…


My refrigerator light is one weir in the River.


…


Like the first kiss of a stranger's elbow
in the backseat of your mother's fears,
wait for it (my refrigerator light)
to brush up against you.


…


You whose seawater floods my acoustic guitar.


…


In the same way bees dodge raindrops in the night
given their capacity for discerning particular
shades of black, I've spent
a lifetime searching for the blackest film frame
in the People's History of Drive-In (from 1933 to the Present),
exploring every public archive
in the many woods of grief.


…

This country of *I know what you left unsaid.*

…

As my refrigerator light makes its way toward you.

…

The musk of careful interaction in the limelight of uncertainty
rustles through the leaves. In the many woods of grief.

…

The dial-tone.
Which is the equivalent of
God's unfamiliarity
with aspects of himself.

…

All that is clear is that everyone around here drinks.
So as to employ the vocabulary of the birds we've hunted to extinction
in the many woods of grief.

…

I am fortunate in that I happen to be
a pretty good-looking dead thing.

…

For instance, I could never imagine what it
must feel like to be asphalt in its infancy.

...

When the doctor asked me to have a little faith,
I told her to expose her right breast
so I'd have something to press my unholy against.

...

That's a line should be FedExed to the many woods of grief.

...

Your words are the house lights coming on
after a double-bill screening
in a theatre I was led to ungently by the wrist—
the words whose sole effect
is in reaffirming how real this world we live in
must be to live in.

...

No one is ever so alone as in the moment he asks for
the check and, instead, receives an incandescent bird
where the dinner mint should be.

...

This is not a precise enough translation
of what I was unable to tell you
the night you became something other
than moonlight in a drawer.

...

I want to and do believe in bird and in you

# One Day All Your Teeth Will Be Mine

## Sasha Fletcher

from *Gigantic*

Outside the windows were trees and in front of the windows were plants and on the windows were blinds. The plants were buried in dirt up to their necks. I will bury you up to your neck she said. I said But where. She said The Bathtub. But then I said You'd have to clean the bathtub. Or bathe in the sink. Nothing she said Would make me happier. Except this she said. One day I will possess your teeth and they will be in my mouth and my teeth will be in yours and I will dance very slowly and you won't even know I'm dancing at all. I will keep very good care of your teeth. I told her I once walked out the backyard and down several blocks and ended up in a house and when I opened the door all my teeth were nailed to the wall in the shape of my mouth. I put them back in my mouth. It took all day I said. I imagine it would she told me.

# The Sky as John Saw It the Night Kate Sparkled
## Molly Gaudry
from *ABJECTIVE*

The sky rolled up and fell through the hole in Kate's roof and bounced from her forehead and floated to the floor, upon which it made a crinkly sound as it brushed the hem of her bed skirt. As it brushed the hem of her bed skirt, she sat up and said, "Who's there?"

"Who's there?" she said. She said it one more time, then got out of bed and found the rolled up sky hiding behind a plant stand holding ivy. Behind the plant stand holding ivy, she bent, and the rolled up sky trembled when she picked it up. She picked it apart and it resisted when she tried to unroll it. She tried to unroll it and it sighed. It sighed wide open and the stars exploded in her face.

John was long gone by then but he had a telescope trained on Kate's attic, and he saw the whole thing happen, and as it happened he screamed.

Kate turned and looked out the window but couldn't see.

By the time John rowed to her window and climbed through, Kate was nothing but a pile of sparkling.

He swept her into the flattened sky and rolled it up. He rolled it up and climbed back through the window the way he'd come, but he slipped getting his footing in the rowboat, and the rowboat tottered and the rolled up sky unraveled and Kate's remains fell upside-down into the empty space above in which the moon and the sun played hide-and-go-seek. *Seek and ye shall find*, John's mother used to say. John's mother used to say, *You're such a good boy, Jackie. You're such a tall, strong, dark, handsome young man, Jackie. You're all I have in this world, Jackie.*

His mother's recent death had not prepared him for Kate's. Kate's remains in the rolled up sky in his hands had been hot, and the rain had sizzled, and the rolled up sky in his hands had sogged heavy like corn starch mixed with water. *Look Mother, it's running.* It wasn't running. It was solid. It was a solid liquid, running, not running, heavy, sogging mess in his hands, and his mother had said, *Just look at what you've done, Jackie, you've ruined my best rug.* The rug was red and black. Kate's hair was red. His mother's was black. The moon is red like Kate's hair was red, the sun is black like his mother's rug was red and black, but the red and black rug wasn't really ruined and Kate's not really dead: "Who's there?"

# From: Chorus from the Land of Grownups
## Donora Hillard

from *Night Train*

She staples her plaid skirt shut. The buttons shot off, she says. I want to ask whose glitter press-on nails I found beneath a desk, whose clot of blood I smeared with my shoe in the girls' bathroom. I visited it a few days later. It had dried and flaked, as if scratched by someone's fingernail.

There's a lesson on how to sit properly going on in the cafeteria. (Don't straddle.) There's also a Student Council meeting about ways to get the boys to stop chewing tobacco and masturbating in the lavatory between classes. They've been writing on the walls with themselves.

# This Is Not to Say

## Amy Lee Scott

from *Brevity*

> *"So many feelings fit between two heartbeats*
> *So many objects can be held in our two hands*
> *Don't be surprised we can't describe the world*
> *And just address things tenderly by name."*
> —*Zbigniew Herbert*

This was supposed to be about the dirt that flies up in puffs between bare feet when the bees are buzzing all a-thrill, their noses deep and delighted in flat Cokes that sit out for too long while kids splash in the creek, browned legs stemming from cut-off shorts and browned arms hallooing, glinting like sun-spackled trout. This was supposed to be about the bits of white skin that peek out from beneath bathing suit straps or T-shirt collars. About sunlight that puckers bright, about edges that haze as the nights draw long, deep breaths. This was supposed to be about tangerines—how tangerines tangerine. It was even supposed to be about my grandmother's guacamole—pluck four avocados from her tree, dice them up with no sense of symmetry, stir the whole green mess with a pint of sour cream, a good smash of garlic, and the squeezings of one lime (not too green, mind you, picked from the leafy lower branches).

Or maybe it was supposed to be about the way water condensates beneath sweating glasses, or the arc of a bow swooning at a cello's strings, or the Sanskrit assortment of roots snaking out from the hillside—the same roots to which we as moss-footed children lassoed jump ropes to and propelled down the hill, propelled through deep caches of dried leaves while our toes dipped below the crumpled surface into mulch. Or maybe it was just supposed to be a remark on the lean shadows streetlamps bandy about as kids circle the block on bikes with spokes thrumming at clothes-pinned baseball cards. About when the thrumming slows and the Charley horses unknot, when the jump ropes unravel and the roots unearth. Because that's when the oaks started falling, one by one, felled by the weight of their own leafy heads. And shortly thereafter the birds got into the nets we laced around our fruit trees so that the only peaches left were pecked at and angry.

Or maybe it was about something entirely different: the unfolding of ironed laundry. The grout going black between bathroom tiles. The casting of kites into a thunder-capped sky. The last of the summer fireflies drifting in the grass. But never mind the "supposed to." This is not about (was never about) Dvořák —no, not about kneecaps—nor the clasping and unclasping of his limbs with mine.

# Ghosts and Monsters

## Angi Becker Stevens

from STORYGLOSSIA

"Hey, did you bring your Swiss Army knife?" I ask Justin while we're unpacking our shit in the cabin. "Because I was thinking we might need a Phillips screwdriver and a wood rasp when we go canoeing."

"Fuck you," he says, which I know means of course the knife is in his bag. I'm always making fun of the stupid thing, one of those Swiss Army knives that's like three inches thick and has about seventy-three different tools inside. Like we're really roughing it up here and you never know when you're going to need a little bitty pair of pliers or a magnifying glass. Neither of us were ever Boy Scouts, we wouldn't even know what plants would kill us if we were lost in the woods. We'd last about an hour. But you give the kid a Swiss Army knife and he thinks he's some kind of real outdoorsman.

Justin's family owns this huge chunk of land that used to be a scout camp like forty or fifty years ago. They fixed up the big main lodge like a regular house with a TV and a stereo and a pimped out kitchen and everything. They bulldozed most of the little cabins because they were pretty much falling apart, but they kept a few and did the necessary repairs, and Justin and I sleep out in one of those while we're up here and his asshole brother Kurt sleeps in another one and their dad stays in the lodge. We still have campfires and shit and cook out on a camp stove every now and then just for the whole camping experience or whatever, but most of the time being at camp is more like being at a hotel. Justin's dad loves to cook. There are like mountains of scrambled eggs and pancakes or waffles or French toast made from scratch every morning by the time we even stumble into the lodge half asleep.

We tell our moms and my sisters that we really live off the land up there, like we go out and kill our own food.

After we get our stuff out of the car and into the cabin, we go out by the fire pit, where Kurt's getting ready to split wood. He's got his shirt off and he's already sunburned even though summer doesn't even technically start for like two more days. Kurt with an ax is a scary fucking thing. Justin and I stand behind him going "swing, batterbatterbatterbatter," because we want him to mess up and hit the edge of the wood and send it spiraling off the stump. But he ignores us and holds the ax in one hand; his arm swings back and arcs forward and the wood splits clean in half so fast it looks like the log saw the ax coming and just divided.

"That could be your heads," Kurt says, and we stand there quiet after that, both thinking of the ax coming down dead center in our skulls.

I wouldn't go anywhere near Kurt if I really believed he'd smash my head in, but he's the kind of guy you believe could turn into an ax murderer, under the right circumstances. Whatever the hell the right circumstances for that might be.

I started coming up here with the Parkers the year my twin sisters turned one and I was almost six, which I guess makes eight years now. My other sister was born a year after that. My sisters are getting a lot less obnoxious the older they get, but I still look forward to "guys' week" like crazy, even if I do wish Mr. Parker would quit calling it something so lame. I like being somewhere without Barbies and ponies and pink frilly shit everywhere I look for one week out of the year, but the best part is probably that there's nothing like a week with Kurt to make me appreciate not having a brother of my own. My sisters always seem great for like a month after I get home.

I'm sure every older brother on the planet can be a real dick sometimes, but Kurt is seriously crazy. Crazy like, no one can seem to find the right kind of pills to make him any less crazy. And when he flips out and smashes shit up or beats the hell out of Justin, Justin gets yelled at for setting him off, which to me seems about the same as blaming some kid who got his leg blown off playing in an old, unmarked minefield. Justin always says he wishes they'd just lock him up already, and I know he means it.

Most of the time, Justin just goes right on being a little pain in Kurt's ass and trying to push his buttons anyway. But sometimes I can tell he's really genuinely afraid, like he'd feel a hell of a lot safer without his brother around.

I've known Justin pretty much forever, and he's a tough kid. But lately he's been starting to freak my shit out, to tell you the truth. Sometimes I think I can see Kurt in him. All last season, he got carded in almost every soccer game, and Coach kept threatening to bench him for good if he couldn't calm the hell down. And then last month he got suspended from school for three days because he beat the shit out of some kid in the locker room. We didn't have phys ed the same hour so I wasn't there, but what I heard was that it wasn't like a normal fight. What I heard was that Justin just went psycho, like he would have killed the kid with his bare hands if he could have. No one even knows what made him go off. He won't even tell me.

Mostly, though, what freaks me out is that he just looks like there's something in him that's about to crack, like he's about to just split wide open. He makes me think about volcanoes, the way they can just sit there looking perfectly harmless for like a thousand years before all the shit comes spewing out and there's no time left to run.

That first night, Mr. Parker and Kurt both go to bed pretty early, and just Justin and me are still sitting out by the fire pit. He keeps poking at what's left of the fire with a stick even though it's almost burned out and the night is warm enough without a fire, anyway. Justin seems like he wants to sit out here all night, but if he doesn't at least start talking about something soon, he can sit out here by himself. He knocks a hunk of charred wood loose with the stick, flattens the ashes until they aren't shaped like anything anymore.

"Do you want to come back to the cabin?" I ask him. "Or should I leave you out here alone with the ghosts and monsters?" That gets him to at least snicker a little bit. Every year, Kurt tries to tell us these bullshit scary stories up at the camp. I don't even think he expects us to believe them anymore, at this point he tells his stories out of habit. Some of what he's told us is actually true. The camp really did close down back in the 1960s after scouts disappeared from the place two years in a row. We believed that when we were like six, and then a couple years later we were old enough to think Kurt was full of it. But when Justin finally asked his dad, we found out for sure that the part about the kids vanishing was the truth. We've looked up old newspaper articles and everything, about how they searched for weeks with scent hounds and these kids' parents stayed at the camp all that time, waiting for them to just come wandering back. I guess when the first kids went missing, the people in charge of the scouts were like, whatever. Could happen anywhere. But when the same thing happened again the next year, they shut the place down and the whole camp sat vacant for a few years before Justin's grandpa bought it. Two boys disappeared the first year, and then two the next, and no trace of any of the four of them were ever found.

Sometimes Kurt tries to tell us ghost stories about the boys and sometimes he tries to tell us about the monster that ate them and how this beast is going to come back for fresh blood, but neither me or Justin have ever heard anything up here at night except for owls and rats and Kurt making stupid noises outside the windows.

Our guess is as good as anyone's, but we figure the same thing everyone else figures, that some whackjob took those kids, probably kids that snuck off to the woods to get stoned or something, and after the camp closed he probably moved on to somewhere else, and he's probably long dead by now. Kurt always goes, "how would some whackjob take two kids at once?" and we always go, "okay then, maybe it was two whackjobs." I mean, what the hell makes more sense? A pair of psychopaths, or a bona-fide monster? I'll tell you which one I think is less of a leap of faith.

"I can take my chances with the ghosts and monsters," Justin says after a few minutes. He's still looking into the ashes.

"I forgot," I say, "you've got that anti-ghost raygun on your Swiss Army knife . . ." I wait, but he doesn't smack me in the head or even tell me to fuck off, just sits there poking around with his stupid stick.

"Go on back if you want," he says. "I'm just going to sit out here for a while."

"Okay," I say, but I don't go. We're still sitting out there when the fire is all the way out, and even for a while longer after that, until none of the wood is even glowing anymore.

The third day we're up there is boiling hot, like 90 degrees and humid as hell. So we go down to the lake, which is really more of an overgrown pond, but a lake sounds like a more impressive thing to have all to ourselves. Part of the lake has a little beach with sand and everything, but mostly there's grass right up to the edge of the water. There's even a tree close enough by to tie a rope to, so we can swing out over the lake and let go and drop in. Justin and I launch ourselves off more or less from the ground, but Kurt climbs up into the tree, stands way the hell out on the branch with the rope and flies off. Watching him, we always hope one of these days he won't let go of the rope, will swing back and smack into the tree instead.

We run to the end of the little dock and cannonball off, and then Kurt comes crashing in almost on top of us. He makes me nervous in the water. When he dunks us, he always holds us under just a few seconds too long.

"Hey fucktard," Kurt says to Justin, "you forgot to take your shirt off."

"You forgot to finish evolving," Justin says back, and I try not to laugh, hoping to stay out of the crossfire. Justin climbs up onto the dock and stands there dripping.

"Moron," Kurt says. "What, are you getting a gut?"

"I don't want to look like a fucking flamingo like you," Justin says, and he jumps back in. They leave each other alone for a bit and we're just swimming, treading water. Kurt is climbing the tree and jumping out of it over and over again, and we're just trying to stay out of his way. Justin can't leave well enough alone, though. Eventually he gets back up on shore, and then Kurt's on top of him right away, smacking the front of his soaked t-shirt.

"Are you getting a little belly?" Kurt asks, slapping his stomach. He hits Justin's chest like bongo drums. "Are you getting tits?" Which is just too ridiculous to even be an insult, Justin is lanky as hell. I feel like I should do something, but there's really no point in putting my ass on the line. "I bet your back's all covered in zits," Kurt says. And Justin goes: "Not as many as your face." And I brace myself for the thud as Kurt tackles Justin and they hit the ground. Kurt's trying to wrestle Justin's shirt off, but Justin gets on his feet somehow, and they stand there face to face for a minute like these dumb animals ready to pounce on each other. I stick my head underwater. I can hear yelling when I'm down there, but the words are all murky and mumbled and far away. I turn and swim down further and their voices fade more and more the deeper I go, but then my lungs are burning and I have to turn back around. I break the surface just in time to see Justin haul off and punch Kurt right in the stomach.

Defending yourself against Kurt is one thing, but throwing the first punch is like an honest to god death wish. And I'm scrambling all frantically up out of the water and Kurt's got that maniac look in his eyes, and before I can even get close to the two of them, he's landed a punch that spins Justin's head around, that picks him right up off the ground. And I'm trying to figure out what the hell to do, how I can possibly stop anything without getting my own ass kicked or without running off to Mr. Parker like some kind of little pussy, when all of a sudden Mr. Parker comes jogging up without me having to do anything at all.

"Kurt," he shouts, just once, sharp, the way someone calls off a dog. And Kurt stops just short of kicking Justin where he lies on the ground. "You two knock it off," Mr. Parker says, and he's got this look on his face that he has a lot these days, like he's wondering how the hell a totally normal guy like him managed to spawn these lunatics. "Kurt, why don't you just get out of here for a while?" he says. "Cool down. Take the truck and go pick up some groceries." Kurt spits on the ground next to Justin's head, turns and walks away, muttering under his breath. Justin's still just lying there, looking up, blinking, like he still hasn't quite figured out how he ended up horizontal. "You okay?" His dad asks.

"I'm fine," he says.

"You've got to know when to back off, champ," his dad says. That's all he says, and he turns around and walks off toward the lodge.

I go over to Justin and hold out my hand. He grabs it and I pull him up.

"Champ," he says. He laughs.

"Your face is going to be about seven colors tomorrow," I tell him. "That's going to be one hell of a black eye."

"Not the first," he says. "Won't be the last." The whole left side of his face is puffing up and there's dirt and sand all stuck to his soaked shirt. He looks like something that just crawled out from the bottom of a swamp.

We go back to the lodge and spend the afternoon lying around on the couches watching TV while Justin holds a bag of frozen peas on his face. To tell you the truth, I hate swimming anyway. I always just feel like I'm trying not to drown.


Later on in the evening we're back in our cabin, avoiding Kurt even though dinner was fine and more or less peaceful. Justin keeps poking around at his face and wincing.

"At least your stupid eye isn't swollen shut," I tell him.

"Peas are good for something," he says.

"What the hell were you thinking punching him? He's like three times your size and five times as crazy."

"What, are you my dad?" he asks.

"No, I'm not your dad. But there's a difference between not tiptoeing around someone all the time, and punching them in the fucking stomach. Jesus Christ."

"He just pisses me off sometimes," he says, which is obvious, who wouldn't get pissed off at Kurt sometimes, most of the time? But still. Justin's lucky a black eye is all he's got.

"Well maybe sometimes you've got to, I don't know, go kick a tree or something." I sit down on my bunk, the one on the bottom. "Someone's going to kill you eventually if you go around throwing punches every time you get pissed off."

"Whatever," he says. "I can handle it." He stands there looking down at me. "Want to know why I couldn't take my shirt off in the lake?" And I sort of shrug, because the truth is I don't really know if I give a shit or not. I can tell just by how he asked that this is one of his big mysteries, which probably means it's something lame. But he doesn't actually care if I want to know or not, because he's already pulling his T-shirt off over his head, tossing it on to my bunk next to me.

The word "LOSER" is carved in, like, two-inch tall letters across his chest, along his collarbone.

"Who the hell did that to you?" I say, jumping up, like now I'm the one ready to fight.

"I did," he says, and he's got this sort of disappointed look on his face, like I'm supposed to be all impressed. But I don't think he's cool, or deep, or any other thing he wants me to think. I'm just standing there thinking, you're going to carve something into your chest and you can't even think of anything better than loser?

"Oh," I say, "did you use the douchebag-carving blade on your knife for that?"

"Yeah," he says, "that's the sharpest one."

"You're an asshole," I say.

And he goes, "that's the point, Einstein."

And I'm pissed off that I can't even insult him because he just fucking agrees with me. "I hope it scars," I tell him. "I hope you're stuck with 'loser' on your stupid chest for the rest of your life."

"Yeah," he says. "However long that is." He snatches his shirt back up and pulls it on, and even the way he does that is all jerky and frustrated.

"Can't you just stop being such a drama queen?" I say, like I'm personally offended, which I guess I kind of am. "This shit isn't cool," I say. "It doesn't make you cool."

"I'm not trying to be cool," he says. "You know, I'd rather not feel fucked in the head, if I had a choice."

We just stand there then, looking each other straight in the eye, and I'm trying to decide whether or not I believe him. I never know anymore how serious I'm supposed to take him, how much is for show. I'd rather think this is all some kind of act, this look-how-messed-up-I-am, pay-attention-to-me bullshit. But that kid he beat the hell out of probably didn't think he was acting. Those dumbass letters carved into his chest must have bled like the real thing.

"Forget it," he says. "I should have known you wouldn't understand."

When he walks out of the cabin, the door slams behind him so hard it bounces back open, bangs against the frame twice before staying still.

I wait around probably longer than I should before I go after him, and even when I do go I still don't really want to, but I feel like I don't exactly have much of a choice. It's not like I've got all these other friends around I can hang out with instead of him, or like there's someone else I can crash with out here in the middle of fucking nowhere. To be honest, I'm actually starting to worry when I can't find him right away, but the last place I think to look is out on the edge of the lake, and that's where he is. He's sitting there on the dock hugging his legs to his chest, with his chin on his knees.

Last summer, a dog got hit by a car on the road out behind my house. He was okay, the dog. He belonged to a neighbor, we found out, and he had a broken leg that healed up fine in a couple months. But when the car hit him, I heard him yelping and ran back to try to help. And when I reached down for him, that dog snapped at me so fast I thought he was going to take my hand off. You could tell he was a nice dog, though, I mean the look in his eyes wasn't that evil, mean-dog look. I could see he was just hurt, and scared, and kind of pissed off all at the same time, the confusing sort of pissed off where you'll lunge at anyone just because they're there. That dog is what I think about when Justin looks up at me standing there, with that same hurt animal look on his face.

"Hey," I say. He looks away from me, wiping his eyes on

his arm. I just stand there for a minute and then his back starts to shake and he buries his face in his knees, crying like a girl. I don't know what I'm supposed to do, what he wants from me, what he needs. "What the hell is the matter with you?" I ask.

He mumbles something I can't understand into his knees, and I say "what?" and he looks up at me and goes "I said, I don't know what the hell is the matter with me." And then he puts his head back down, but he isn't crying so hard anymore. I sit down next to him, because I don't know what else to do with myself but stay there and wait. The sun is going down by then and the water is all orange, like something on fire. Like lava. I picture it slowly oozing up onto the shore, bubbling up over us, leaving behind ashes in the shape of me and Justin just sitting there next to each other, stuck, until the wind blows and we scatter just like that, like we were nothing.

"The lake looks pretty sweet," I say finally, and he looks up but doesn't say anything.

"I don't know what's the matter with me," he says again after a few minutes, only he doesn't sound pissed off anymore, just scared and kind of sad. I should say something, anything, tell him that everything will be okay, that he should talk to someone who can maybe do something, his parents or a shrink. I should ask him what he needs me to do. I should tell him that I'll do whatever the hell it is, anything, absolutely anything. But I don't say those things, I don't say anything at all. I just squeeze his shoulder like I've seen men do, and pretend I really think that's enough.

The sky is close to black when we walk back to the camp, and Mr. Parker is getting the fire going. I don't feel like doing anything but going to bed, but I sit out there with the three of them, not really listening while they talk. What I'm doing mostly is looking up at the stars, and thinking how clear they are up here. I'm thinking how the stars are supposed to be good for so many things if you know how to read them, how sailors used to chart courses by them. But to me they're just like Braille, random dots I could stare at forever without any kind of meaning coming clear.

After Mr. Parker heads back to the lodge, Kurt is real quiet, sort of eerie quiet, just putting out the fire without comment. And then just as we're about to walk off to our cabin, he grabs Justin's arm and goes "hey, you guys hold up a sec." And he sounds real serious, so we wait.

"Listen," Kurt says. "I know I always tell you guys stories up here, okay? But listen to this. When I was in town earlier today, I heard these old guys talking. And fucking animals are disappearing around here again."

"Again?" Justin says, his one eyebrow raised, all skeptical like he should be.

"Like they did back before those kids disappeared," Kurt hisses, which I'm sure was part of his story one year or another, but I don't remember that part. "It's happening again. A fucking horse disappeared the other day."

"Horses can run away," I say.

"They found blood," Kurt says. "Just blood."

"Sure," Justin goes. "Whatever."

"Aren't we getting a little old for this?" I say.

Kurt, fucking Kurt, he actually looks like we hurt his feelings. "Look," he goes, "I'm just trying to look out for you guys. I'm just trying to be nice for once. I mean, you're right, you're not little kids anymore. We're more like buddies now, right?"

Justin laughs, this real sarcastic cackling sound. "Right," he goes. "We're buddies. Pals. Fuck you, Kurt."

Kurt's got this almost panic-stricken look on his face by now. "Okay," he goes, "I'm sorry I was such a spaz earlier, I'm sorry about your stupid face, but I'm serious. I know I sound like the asshole who cried wolf, right? So fine, ignore me if you want. I'm just saying, I think something is out there. And I'd sleep in the main house if I were you tonight."

"Sure," I say. "We'll get right on that."

"We'll keep our nightlights on," Justin says.

"Screw you guys," Kurt says, as we walk away. "Don't say I didn't fucking warn you."

Getting ready for bed, I think I feel just about as exhausted as I ever have in my life. I've got that drained out feeling that comes after a day outside in the water, in the sun, and I guess maybe Justin is wearing me out, too.

"Let me see your stupid chest again," I say. He's got every reason to think I'm just looking to give him shit, but he pulls his shirt off over his head anyway. By the light of the dim little camp lantern, the letters look black. I reach out and trace my fingertip over the L. The skin there is still puffy.

"How long ago did you do that?" I ask him.

"Couple weeks or so," he says.

"Didn't it hurt?" I ask, pressing my finger a little harder into the L.

"Well yeah," he shrugs. "It hurt like a bitch. That was the point." He goes to scratch the back of his neck, and when his left arm is raised up like that, I can see what I didn't see before, all the slashes high up on the inside of his bicep, dozens of lines all close together, some of them fresh and some of them old, so old they've already faded to faint pink. He sees me looking and rushes to pull his shirt back on. And we're still looking each other in the eye, and what I really want to say is stop, Justin, for fuck's sake just stop. Please. But all I do is turn out the light.

"Can you believe that asshole back there?" Justin asks, when we're lying there in our bunks. "I'm just trying to do something nice," he says, in a whiny voice. "What a prick."

"Kurt's a prick," I say. "What else is new?"

"He was sure laying it on thick," Justin says. "How long do you think it'll be before he shows up here trying to freak us out?"

"I give him a half hour, tops," I say.

"Horse blood," Justin says. "What an ass."

We're both quiet then, and I'm doing that thing where I'm still wide awake but I'm afraid he's asleep so I don't want to talk, and he's probably up there doing the same thing. I'm thinking about reaching my foot up and poking the bottom of his mattress to see if he just lies there or jumps up and tells me to knock it off, but I don't really feel like it. There's not really anything in particular I can think to say to him right now anyway.

"My parents are getting divorced," he says, in the dark, out of nowhere. I just lie there for a minute not knowing what to say.

"That sucks," I say eventually.

And then he goes "My dad's been fucking Ms Franklin." Like this is just some kind of side note, that his dad has been doing our English teacher.

"Bullshit," I say. Ms Franklin is young, way younger than our parents, and she's pretty enough, I guess, but mousey and quiet and afraid of all of us. She's not, like, the kind of woman you think goes around sleeping with older, married men.

"Swear to God," he says, and I know he doesn't even believe in God but I let it go.

"How do you know?" I ask him.

He swings around, hangs forward, looking at me from the top bunk. And he goes: "I'm the one who busted them. In bed."

And I go: "No way. You're so full of shit. When?"

"Like three months ago. But my mom just got suspicious and I finally broke down and told her like a couple weeks ago. I feel like a rat, but he's the one who fucked up. He wants to keep dating her, I guess. I guess he's been banging her for a while, way before I found out."

And I say: "And you never told me?" I can't believe we sat there through three months of English class without him telling me he's seen our teacher naked, with his own dad. He just shrugs, as much as he can shrug while he's hanging upside down.

"I didn't tell anyone."

"That's fucked up," I say, and I'm not really sure if I mean him not telling me, or the whole situation. And I know this isn't all of what's been wrong with Justin these past months, but it sure as hell can't have helped matters any.

He's still hanging there upside down, his face starting to turn blotchy. I feel like he's waiting for something from me. Like he's always waiting for something.

"Who are you going to live with?" I ask. I'm thinking about how, if, this is going to change things for me.

"Whoever Kurt doesn't live with," he says.

That's right when the scraping starts on the outside of the cabin.

"Speak of the devil," I say.

"Kurt, knock it off," Justin yells. We're quiet for a minute or two, and the noises don't stop. There's a clawing sound, and I swear there's some kind of slobbering, snarling noise going on, too. He swings around again, hops down out of the bunk.

"Fuck off, Kurt," he says, louder. "We know it's you." And I know I'm being totally stupid, but I'm starting to think, what if it's not Kurt? And apparently Justin's starting to think the same thing, because he goes over to his backpack and rummages around inside and pulls out his stupid Swiss Army knife.

"You gonna jab the corkscrew in his eyes?" I ask. "Go after him with the plastic toothpick?"

"Bite me," he says. "Listen to that." He hears what I hear: the wet, rumbling un-human noise under the scratching and the banging. He folds the long blade out. He barks directions at me, like I've been waiting for him to do. "Scoot your ass over," he says, and I do. He gets into the bottom bunk next to me, pulls the blanket up to our chins. "Just hold still," he says. "Hold totally still." He lies on his side, facing the door, his hand clenching the red knife handle on the pillow. I can't tell if the quivering I feel is him shaking, or me, or both of us. I'm so close behind him I can see my breath rustling the hair on the back of his head. The bed is like being in an oven: the blanket is too heavy, the night is too warm, our bodies are too close. But I'm not going to move.

When I see his hand relax on the knife, I know he's asleep. I reach my arm around him. I put my hand on the knife, too. One of us has to be ready.

Justin could sleep through a goddamn earthquake.

Me, I'll lie here awake all night, holding still. I'll lie here in a pool of my own sweat, with my arms going all tingly and numb. I'll still be lying here awake when the wood starts to splinter and the walls implode and everything, everything gets torn right the fuck open.

# The Reckoning

## Leigh Stein

from *The Scrambler*

Am I the only one in this who hopes it gets worse?
For us at least, the adolescents, the ones
who will still be here in fifty years, possibly
jobless, but possibly not. I say worse
because maybe then my friends and I
can buy a farm, or an island with an abandoned asylum,
if we pool all the money we've saved from working
the jobs we never told our parents about. Not knowing
what else to do, the history books will say,
some young people moved to the country, bought
livestock they made the mistake of naming, spent
their days taking turns in the hammock,
and grew illegal drugs until they ran out of food.
For the first time in history, an entire generation
was completely unprepared for absolutely anything.
But oh how the stars will show themselves
to be such miracles that we will comment nightly
upon their arrival, reciting the constellations
we learned in a tent set in our elementary school
gymnasium, back when we were still impressed
with parachute games. Andromeda, Aquarius,
Aries, Orion. In the darkness, one of us will
clandestinely reach for another. Someone
will disrupt the silence to remark on its totality,
and in the morning we'll find that he's left

with his rucksack and two jars of peanut butter
in search of the noise of yesterday. We'll lose more
this way, to nostalgia, than famine or disillusionment.
There won't be anything left to be disillusioned about.
During our first winter, we will come to understand
why our ancestors knew so many ways to eat an apple.
In spring, whoever owns the tandem bicycle
will hold monopoly over our amusement. Historians
will see that in the aftermath of the crash
the birth rate dropped, we used currency for decoupage,
and had to learn to play acoustic instruments by candlelight;
that all the childless women went out and renamed the land—
Oak Tree Stands Alone, Kristen Loses Her Wedding Ring,
Christmas Tree Farm Gone Wild, Pedestrian Turnpike,
The Night the Trouble Started, Two Hills Give Us Pause—
because we couldn't name our children, because we wanted
to be remembered as cartographers of the new earth.

# Attending the Tasting

## Sarah J. Sloat

from *The Literary Bohemian*

*Maison Fandang Merlot*
Unbuttons the tongue. The bouquet includes the calls of wild animals, far off, fur bristling with an electric zip of rubies. Fruit falls from the trees. Violets tremble at the edge of the glass. Accompany with a plump cigar and anything by Balzac. Best served by the goblet.

*Daux Semillon*
This white is a saint of long silence, ponderous with quince and lanolin. Uncorked, dollops of fog slip from the bottle, flavors tinging the lips with blonde sugar. Cool at first, but turn the lights down a little: a flame is kindling in the robin's throat.

*Chateau Bonmot Syrah*
This Syrah enters the mouth like an intruder and bursts into song. Aged in caves, it's developed a muscular bloom. The chief note is of toast slathered with jam. The high proof makes this a popular choice for slumming, even if it's just around the back yard. Pairs well with game and all shades of red lipstick.

*Rabellais Sauvignon Blanc*
A profound, complex white, barren of trickery. It has a linear acidity that hones focus. On the back palate, the rinse goes down with the sob of a solo cello, then trails into a gripping finish. The nose breathes lichen and tin with an undertone of mango, bringing this wine zen spaciousness and balance.

*Veuve Seiden Brut*

And what is champagne? Woodwinds played outdoors. The feather quilt on the clothesline. Champagne is the rain-trickled taxi that ferries the bride across town. Not the body but the mind. Not the crown but the tiara. Not the prayer but the hallelujah.

# Journey (Aigues-Mortes)

## Sue Standing

from *The Literary Bohemian*

Outside history, outside the word hoard,
we met near the wild dunes and the cyclops
of the lighthouse, among mounds of salt
evaporated from the flat pans of the étangs.

Centuries ago, at the tower of Constance,
such salt was poured over the bodies
piled on bodies, to preserve them,
heretic, until they could be buried.

Everywhere we went, we left a residue.
For years, we walked the ley lines
of neolithic menhirs, Viking passage tombs,
Roman walls that cut the width of England.

Now, at the center of this perfect grid
of ramparts, I plaster over the past
with borrowed tools, efface the room
in which we ate and slept and loved.

# Nostrum

## Michelle Reale

from *BluePrintReview*

Her mother whispers a promise: that if she is a good, good girl, she will be baptized. They will plug her nose and tip her back into the lake. It's all she can think about, the cool release that water, in any form, might bring. *It takes only a few seconds, and everything will change,* her mother had told her, brushing her daughter's bangs to the side in her gentle way. Her lurking father had heard and raged. He put his big fist through the wall, adding to the collection of cracks and falling plaster. He did not believe in redemption and wouldn't let anyone else, either. He grabs the little girl and heads for the door. His wife grabs at his t-shirt, but it's no use. The daughter waves to her as she hangs over her father's shoulders, caveman style. The mother, resigned, blows her a kiss, then sits down on the curb to wait.

She calls to her father. She sees him look in the rearview mirror, crinkle his eyebrows a bit, then gaze back to the road. She lies down on the back seat, closes her eyes, wills herself to stifle a moan. When the car slows down, she thinks that they might be home, or close to it and she waits for her father to say *Up and out!* like he usually does. Instead he leans across the front seat and gives the door a push. A girl flops down on the seat, blows the smoke from her cigarette out sideways. Her eyes are rimmed in black and her feet are dirty and bare. *You won't get very far without shoes,* the father says, with a catch in his throat. *You'd be surprised,* is what she says, her voice flat and devoid of all emotion. She ignores the small girl in the back seat.

He has that far away look while he drives. The station wagon, a rescued relic from a buddy who desperately needed money, travels at 75 mph down the highway. His daughter sits in the back, twirling the seatbelt around her arm, the sweat making a slow crawl down the sides of her sticky face. She'd like an ice cream or something cold to drink. Dark clouds hang low, and she'd like to snag one with her fingernail. If she could pierce a cloud she would. She'd tilt her face up to the sky and feel the cold rush of water on her face. The air draws a tight hot curtain around them that shimmers. The girl they've picked up smokes, picks at her toes, sleeps, fiddles with the radio, closes her eyes and occasionally startles.

When the daughter wakes she cannot remember where she is. The seat belt is under, not around her and she remembers the long ride in the car. Her mouth is dry and she can hear the whoosh of cars coming close, and then going far away. When her father and the girl return to the car, they seem different. Her father turns around, reaching for his daughter, gives her cheek a hard pinch, then a playful slap. The girl in the front seat dares to look for the first time. A sad and dirty face stares back. She asks the little girl in a small voice *how old are you?* The daughter's tongue is so dry, but she answers the question with a question: *Do we know you?*

When they stop at a gas station the father bellows, *Up and out!* The girl with the dirty bare feet goes into the mini-mart. The father follows her and quickly returns with two cold and sweating bottles of water. He hands one to his daughter and pours the other over her head. The shock of cold has her gasping for a few seconds, but then she beams with relief. He lifts her by the arm and tosses her into the back seat.

Before making the turn back onto the highway, the little girl turns around to see the girl coming out of the mini-mart lighting a cigarette, hopping around on the hot asphalt, landing on one foot and then the other.

*No one can save you, remember that,* he tells his daughter in his strange and distracted way, stabbing the thick air with a fat finger. *You can do what you want, just be prepared to pay the consequences,* he tells her while pounding out a furious beat on the steering wheel.

The day has been a long one and she wants her mother now. She aches to feel that soft cool cheek against her own and hear her mother's voice telling her of all the good things possible, if you only believe, but she feels different now.

She needs to hear all of the stories again, because she has already forgotten the most important parts. Maybe it was because of the constant thirst. Or the heat. Someday she'd like to find the girl they'd left behind. She'd tell her a few things. Buy some shoes. Quit smoking. Don't take rides from strangers. *Try not to be afraid.*

# Letter Written on a Paper Crane

## Dave Rowley

from *The Literary Bohemian*

Dear Person,
The world is worsening.

This bird has been carefully crafted
from the last sheet of paper
in my notebook. She cannot fly.

I know this, but am relying on wind
and good luck, hoping she will be carried
toward people who can help. Clouds live

between me and the horizon, and the streets
are too quiet. Did something happen? Warm birds

are rare here, they fell from the trees weeks ago.
I'm sending my paper crane in search of life, though
I doubt you can come. Please care

for the bird even though she cannot sing.
To compensate for this I sang while making her—
each crease contains one song. If you come,

you will know when you find me; my house
has a light on. Please bring paper.

# Now, Right Now

## Jennifer Pieroni

from *Wigleaf*

I stopped at the door of the East Entrance of the mall, finishing my cigarette. The sensation of smoking in this heavy heat was so specific, a feeling of smoking you would never get without the humidity, and every time it happened I was acutely aware of it. It's happening now, right now, I would think.

Gavin waited for me inside. He'd never smoked and never would, but he drank and drove, a habit I didn't have.

Inside, the air conditioning cooled my sweat immediately.

We went to the arcade and found some kids we knew, not from our town, kids we knew just from being at the mall.

Gavin and I had our pictures taken again in the photo booth. I showed off the finished print to a few of the girls.

One of them said, "Wait, your ears aren't pierced."

I wasn't very tolerant of pain. I had bad periods and none of the medicine worked. I had migraines, too.

The girl working at The Earring Hut had me sign a waiver. "Just put that you were born in 1978," she said.

I signed the form and sat in the gray pleather chair. "Pick out a pair," she said.

"You help," I said to Gavin.

"There aren't any hoops," Gavin said to the girl.

But I couldn't have hoops for at least thirty days, until the holes healed. The girls who had come along helped me pick the pair of sterling silver dots.

The girl brought the gun to my face, she hovered by my

ears. I listened for a motor or for the device to cock, like a real gun. "Try not to jerk your head," she said as the first needle cut through. "I said don't move," she said, reaching for a compress and an ice cube.

The pain had caused me to tear, the tips of my fingers to tingle. The ice killed. I saw the spots of blood on the compress.

"I don't want to do the other," I said.

"You don't?" the woman asked.

"You have to have follow through," Gavin said. "Just do it."

"No, I really don't," I said. "I'm not doing it." I reached up to my pierced ear and pulled out the stud she'd slid in. "I'm sorry," I said, taking off down the mall.

I passed some stores and the food court, my ear throbbing hard, and ducked into the candy store. I reached up to check if my ear was still bloody. It was.

The girl behind the register nodded at me.

I grabbed a bag and spooned jelly beans in. I grabbed another bag and spooned mints in.

Gavin found me. He slid his arm around my waist.

"I can't picture you ever giving birth," he said.

I grabbed another bag and spooned gumballs in. At the register, I told the girl that he was paying. He didn't hesitate to open his wallet, slide her the cash, and take the slip for me.

# The Taste of Mangoes

## Jie Li

from *Cerise Press*

In August 1968, a visiting minister from Pakistan gave Chairman Mao a basket of mangoes as a token of the friendship between the two states. The Chairman, who was very particular about what he ate, did not care for the taste of mangoes, so he sent them to the worker-peasant Mao Zedong Thought propaganda team. The workers, flattered and overwhelmed by the Chairman's love, preserved the mangoes in formaldehyde and revered them as sacred relics. Thousands from around the country made pilgrimages to the mangoes, and the mangoes, accompanied by drums, gongs, and banners, went on tours in various cities where they were placed under glass cases and watched over by security guards. When they started to decompose, thousands of replicas were made out of wax, and millions of propaganda posters were painted and disseminated, so that everybody, even toddlers with split pants, knew what a mango looked like, but almost nobody knew what it tasted like.

Two decades later, in 1988, Uncle New Sea came back from Hainan Island with a bottle of mangoes. Uncle New Sea was the big shot of the family, always at the tip of the new wave. Out of everybody we knew, he was the first to wear a Western suit, first to buy a color television, first to ride in a chauffeured car or fly in an airplane. From his plane ride he brought us children plastic forks and knives and butter and cheese wrapped inside shiny aluminum paper. He got to stay for three weeks in a state guest house in the city center, for free since he had government connections. During his stay we all went to his clean, white-tiled bathroom to take private showers and to use the flushing toilet. Uncle New Sea had been to Japan and ranted until his saliva ran dry about the huge apples and pears as large as baby's heads and as perfect as wax fruits we painted in school. We listened incredulously, chewing our small apples and pears bored through by worms.

For the sake of preservation, the mangoes, brilliant as tropical fish, were already pared and cut into slices that came in a large, sealed bottle of salt water. As Second Uncle unwound the cap, we children gathered around the table, knelt on our chairs, and propped ourselves up with our arms. Everyone was given just one slice, perhaps a sixth of a mango, and told not to spill the juices on our clothes because the stain would be permanent. My piece was sour and bitter, and its fibers stuck between my teeth. I looked around and saw that my grandparents and my cousins all had the same awkward look on their faces, but as Uncle New Sea talked on and on about how exorbitant and high-class mangoes were, we all finished our slices, hoping to acculturate our tongues to a modern, expensive, foreign taste.

It was the era of Three-in-One Nescafé Coffee (which, aside from Coca Cola, was all that Uncle New Sea said he drank) and of "Melt in Your Mouth, Not in Your Hand" M&Ms, ten times as expensive as Chinese chocolate, which soon tasted to us like cement. For my ninth birthday my little aunt took me out to Kentucky Fried Chicken. The newly opened restaurant was on the most prominent street in Shanghai, and I dressed up in my best clothes. The girls behind the counter wore red-and-white-checkered shirts and a matching paper hat. The place was clean, empty, and well lit, and it was the first and last time that chicken tasted so good.

In the summer of 2000, I returned to Shanghai after a decade's stay in the United States. Before I left for China, Grandma blurted into the phone: "You don't have to bring anything. Everything you have in America, we have here." Nevertheless, I brought some toys and stationery for my young cousins, recalling how much I treasured even the fluorescent wrapping paper of a color eraser in my childhood, but of course my cousins were not in the least interested in my singing teddy bear or glow-in-the-dark stars. My grandparents proudly showed me a supermarket the size of a shopping mall right in their neighborhood, yet in the bounty of its aisles, my little cousin, whose childhood was defined by her gluttony, could not pick out a single item she wanted to eat.

That summer, there was a great harvest of mangoes and they became the cheapest fruit on the market, leading toward the ruin of several counties in the tropical south that converted all of its land to mango orchards. Finally, the mangoes made famous by the Chairman really entered worker households. Grandma bought so many mangoes that our stomachs revolted against their saccharine, medicinal taste. In the end, only Grandma, seared with the hunger of her childhood and the doctrine that no food should go to waste, sat by the table and bit into one mango after the other, patiently, dogmatically, as though demolishing the idols of a century.

# Geomancy

## F. Daniel Rzicznek

from *Guernica*

The feathered saints of evening flit
down through the wooded hills to construe
salads of hailstones and leaf-wreckage,
the thunder having sped east-northeast
toward open water after leaving nothing
altered in the major features below.
The angle of river can always guide
a dumb soul or two to welcoming fields
where struggling plantlings yearn
for breath to sweep their leaves, enter
a rough, black portal at the thin roots.
A young crop of beans: stationary
ferry to a strange, coppery existence.
A good dog can scout this scent for miles
over mountain fog and village cookfires.
The wind is a color she can deduce
a million intimations from, unflinchingly.
The same wind comes to the saints, as if
they were abandoned boats on a wide bay
when the clouds pass and the chop slows
to a pulse, the shore a long mouth
that hasn't shifted expression in years.
All things that find a death there take
an invisible token of that freshwater pout:

a bone is dragged into pines and oak,
an organ ends up sailing around in the rain,
the rest is dissected there on the sands.
High song in high branches—a sane
nothing that will happen until it ends.

# Sounds of Silence

## Nanette Rayman Rivera

from *carte blanche*

> *"Hello darkness my old friend,*
> *I've come to talk with you again"*
> *—Simon and Garfunkel*

I watch him smiling to himself as we eat our first married meal together. McDonald's. He has some light in his eyes now, his hair is combed back into his ponytail, and when he looks at me, his face turns a pale shade of pink. I love that in a man.

I think I've made a mistake, I'm jittery and can't eat except for the French fries. I married a schizophrenic with droopy brown eyes and incisor cheekbones, a 5'7" Puerto Rican man with butter lips and buttery under-biceps, a belly that I bounce on and a habit of grabbing my breasts, smiling and saying, perky boobies. Look at you, he says, taking my face into both his cracked-skin hands, where the knuckles are raw and red from sleeping in the castle. You are dewy. Your skin is even more beautiful. You're glowing like a jack o lantern.

Don't talk to me like that, Jose, that kind of talk won't change what you did. What he did was not tell me. Not really or fully or what's true. Wouldn't tell me when he left his life behind.

He's crying. Right there in McDonald's, loud sobs blending in with the loud gangs of kids that should be in school, with the single mothers and their triple strollers.

My new husband is crying and flurries today and he's up and running into it, ketchup-faced, not wearing his parka, and the snow's swirling around in cones, like tornados, twisting over the empty streets until they whip against Jose, and I'm not getting up, not running to him, a little revenge of mine, and I think: crazy Puerto Rican man doesn't know how to act. And I'm thinking, oh no, what if he runs away for good, where will that leave me?

Then I'm looking through the window, shaking so much I think someone will think I'm the untamed one, and that's when Jose, in some crazy wild search for his right mind, falls on the snow like a clown. That's when some people dressed like Eskimos stop and pick him up and before I know, they're in here with me, asking, Are you his wife, he says he loves you, but he's afraid. And I think of that movie with Linda Fiorentino and Bill Pullman where she rips off his money and becomes Wendy in a cow town, and as she's running away, Pullman says: You better run! Well, Jose, You better be afraid. I married you but I can't cope. Every minute I think you'll be off, and see—look at you— every minute I think of what could have been in my life. Damn it. I was runner-up in Miss Massachusetts. I had a scholarship to Trinity Repertory Conservatory. I had everyone stare at me when I walked down the street—hey, pretty, whatcha doin', hey chickie—wanna come with me? Hey sweetheart—how come you're not in pictures? And I am not from this low life.

Then I'm saying, tell him, go ahead, tell him to come in. It's all ok. Then I see them go out to him, take his hand, bring him to me. I see a snowy shadow of a man—looks like a petrified snowman—people pointing and saying he's so scared he shook out of his own skin and take him, you, woman, wife, take him, be kind. And so I'm kind. And so I hide my throat-closing love inside. I mean to make him pay. I mean to be mean. For now.

To worry about snow is to be snow, bound; and snow's where I got married and this picture of him running like a cartoon and his sad-happy eyes is like a canvas I can write anything I want. An open prairie. I wish he'd stop flailing his hands, wish he'd place them on me, at least. I haven't known him in his private dimension where he wants me to follow, not like this.

Stop it, baby—Jose. Stop. You want that doorman to call someone to take you away?

He hangs his head low. He lifts it to say I love you Nanette, more than all the galaxies. To think about snow will take more time than any woman has left. Like all the robins in spring, not enough for this woman.

\*\*\*

I married a schizophrenic man to fly. Right out of that homeless shelter on Beaver Street, the one tucked so low and in between Duane Reade and the Sanitation Department you'd hardly notice it even with its burgundy door. It was sleeping on pavement moments that uncorked me. One night of that and I dropped in to the drop-in center. That's what they're calling them now. Two days homeless and he put his hand in mine. He's all tornado and moan. He's hearing voices and I wipe sweat off his temples. I want to grab my hand back, he's a street guy, a *vaquero*, a younger guy, a *muchacho malo*. I don't. I keep my hand there and he steals indiscriminately from my future. He walks me to the river, his flamboyant face in mine. Come, baby, come! And I know he could render me like the insides of a clam, but I come. And I eat the ice cream he buys me and I let him take me down, down by the river, to the Japanese Garden, through tangled trees and big purple flowers, through the sunflowers with long green necks. They swerve through me like he will and I know this is one way to be fed.

The next night we didn't sleep there, we slept in Battery Park, told them we needed some air. You have to tell them; you're a number on a lined notebook sheet, they want money from the state. Your name, your body is cash. The third month we escaped from there. We began as butterflies but when the State comes, and it comes for all the homeless people, with their rules and their humiliations, we ejaculated with truck-driver mouths, we gouged like x-actos ripping cross curtains and we planned and we got a license and we got married.

We got away from the uneducated social workers who told me this: Get your lips off of him, girl. And they told him that: You ain't got no beautiful mind, you crazy.

I'm thinking this is my wedding day. And where to go now? Married and it's like a new country, even newer than homeless land. I'm remembering pictures and TV clips of girls and women being pulled from rivers, it's always rivers, and here we are, a few blocks from the beginning of water. See, since I couldn't find work for so long and since I got evicted from that women's residence, I got no feeling for anything, and I'm tired of the skull-capped boys and men trying to cop a feel, and the women with six pocketbooks trying to cut me up in the shower.

I need him. Still—at the corner of my mind there is me in my mind-pictures: glamorous, Audrey Hepburn dress and pumps, a cigarette holder, me in cool jeans and a flowy top, me in a white lace sundress at the beach, me on the cover of a magazine, me walking through roses on a grand stage after the best performance of my life, me as Alma, Phaedra, Lady. Me as me. I carry these pictures with me still, like they are real, mementos in my pocketbook that don't wither or crack, that just get more razor-sharp, clear as windexed windows and more dangerous until the schism between what is today and what is in my mind-corner causes permanent dissociation.

Baby, baby, Nanette, he's crying. He's soaked, he's mine. Nanette, I'm sorry. Don't leave me. Where should we go now? And so I take him in my arms, stroke his drenched hair, his ponytail I used to love that I want to cut off.

When the real love, the real connection came: it came first as the aura of love, Broadway stained whiter than chalk. Then when it came to me fully it was the bottom of my belly bottomed out and only Jose could fill it up. And there too was the sound of tires whirring and a scary silence, the sound of no people and snow, tapping loudly on the street creating a canvas, a painting and we, two lone married figures huddled and walking to the subway, where my nerves were stretched taut and I realized yes, I do need you, Jose, I do want you. You are my only thing in life. This life I never dreamed could be so surreal. And a subway to the infamous hell of EAU. The Emergency Assistance Unit in the Bronx.

\*\*\*

Signed in, we sit on a low bench among a thousand screaming kids, their mothers too pooped, or too stupid to try to quiet them. The air is saturated with sweat, baby's diapers being changed, overflowing toilets, stinky snacks I never heard of. Some of them stare at me, where's your babies? their eyes say. Some of them sneer at me and I sneer right back. And of course they back down. I don't care if they don't. I almost want them to start something. Maybe a brawl, an incident will call in the media. Then I can tell my wild story. But they do back down. Must be the disgust-glow in my eyes. Must be they can tell I'm no longer afraid, that I know I don't belong here, so hey, you and you, don't mess with me, 'kay? This is their world, their ritual, and I am only a honkie, again, maybe a spy. The hall is littered with bodies, the cops, or rent-a-cops, who knows, pointing fingers at drooling, snoring faces. Get up get up; get out of the hall. Find somewhere else to go. Voices garbled and rock-concert-decibled over the loud-speaker, belting out names, places to report to, papers to fill out. A mini-series could fill the reams of paper we have already filled out. That I've filled out. For a reason never to be revealed, and God forbid you ask, the woman is head-of-household. This means the woman is burdened with all the paperwork, all the aggravation, the husband just signs his name, here, there, and over here. And because my identification still holds my maiden name, I'm seat-belted into eternity as Nanette Rayman, not Nanette Rivera.

They strip your dignity. They strip your name.

This is my wedding night. I can still feel your hands pulling me naked. I can still hear you brimming in my ear.

This place, this noise is forever. It's a measure of time, dissemination; it's a string of hornet-stings that harden to agony. Forever hovering. I sit on the low bench, Jose outside smoking. We can't smoke at the same time because if they call us and we don't answer together, we're logged-out. That's homeless-welfare-big-brother-speak for kicked out. Gotcha. You have to start over. They say to us: Pay attintion, or yull git logged out. They have the power to name things. Hours are years in this homeless module.

My forehead beads with sweat. Pain centers in my right eye like a chainsaw, dribbles into my teeth like medicine, burning an IV drip, like iambs of electricity. The chairs and the people have orange coronas around them and words are really dancing alphabet letters that make no words. I forget why we came here. Why I live. Jose drifts toward the bench like smoke. He says, What is it, what hurts? Is he trying to be facetious or trying to be a sweet husband? I don't know. Imagine being so dissociated, you imagine tales of rot when your husband is sweet to you.

A stinking man stands in a pool of water bubbling with blood, like a lollipop going down the drain. There are tough women, like crocodiles lunging from the rash of bodies to tear the daylight from anyone who looks half-way normal and pretty; one tries to sit down next to me, her legs and arms sticking out of her hot pink hootchie clothes like a handful of matches, her stench like a reptile. Jose tells her to Beat it. Get lost.

Like my long-ago self, I wish for a star or a button to push, anything to magic me away to a decent life, to a life with people afraid of crack, disgusted by noise, and terrified of where I am sitting, right now. Or a button to vaporize me into no-thing-ness.

Jose leans in to kiss me. He whispers, I love you, baby, I love you. We sit together on a low bench, M&Ms and gummy bears stuck to the wood; dolls and hard pieces of toy trucks hurling through the air. We sit together, Jose hearing voices, me nauseated and blinded by a type A migraine. We plan our future before sunrise, and cast our blotted images at Bronx's feet.

Voices, noise over me, under me, beside me. A deaf person could hear them. The thing I notice most, will remember most, is the noise. Everywhere in the system. As if people on welfare, homeless people, and all generic degenerates need noise to breathe. You could fill Shea Stadium with middle-class people with jobs, and have it be the last game of the World Series, and still, the noise wouldn't be as loud as these people sprawled all over the floor at EAU.

A woman over there, right across from me, yawps and bellows and squeals until her lips burn rubber. I see white teeth, slash of tube-top, jeans splitting down the ass. I think: She wants to combust. She whoops again, tossing her melon-tits into faces. Her words popping like guns, that voice zigzagging along the long room, across benches and benches and benches, into my cranium, my blood vessels, my migraine.

Days of this. Twenty four seven. Our marriage feeling like bondage. Jose is crying, fingers twitching. Can't take it can't take it can't take it, he says. His mind has its own shape like a dress clothes-pinned to a line, unable to move with it all.

Men hacking green phlegm and bleeding from noses and armpits. Children with faces of grown women, lined and pitted, wonder why their mothers refuse to answer. Children cursing, talking trash, wait for fathers who won't be back to save them. Women thin as dental floss. Women fat as two-car garages. They all flop around gulping Cheetos and Popeyes Chicken, gallons of grape soda. We don't have money for that. We don't have children. That's the trick. Have babies—have money. They swell and swell. They chew til their eyes roll and then they topple over, farting and belching and smacking their lips and their children.

It's foul. I want to take a bath, put a mask over my

nose. Plug up my ears. Acres of bodies with no impulse control. Mouths spewing words, any words to keep themselves alive. No one can stop them. Bodies chomping and bleeding and snorting.

Now they bring us in grade-school fashion, lined up neatly, to the basement kitchen. There are rows and rows of cheap tables and chairs, and along one wall those restaurant-style barrel grey cylinders pouring out milk. Boys and girls lift the spigot and milk flies all over the counter, lays in pools of white everywhere. Not one mother scolds. They are too tired or too who-cares. There are loud words and louder screams that don't stop. There are emotional moments, and statements made in the fire of all these anxious moments, in the heat of this eternity: When the fuck are we gonna get outta here, man? One droopy-faced guy with a droopier dirty hat slobbers jam all over himself. Will ya shut the kids up, already? His sleek-haired wife shakes her head, humungous fake gold earrings dancing, and clicks her teeth. She does that almost-belly-dancer thing with her neck and glares right at his droopiness. Why'd we have 'em anyway, huh? Huh? Tell me lover. Tell me fucker. Each word louder and meaner.

I sit at our table and force myself to swallow a few times. Nerves make me gag and when I can't swallow I feel I'm drowning. Hard to eat with all our stuff with us, under us, between my legs. Never be foolish enough to leave your things anywhere. Gone like a dress on a clothesline during a windstorm. Gone.

Runny eggs, fake orange juice, the noise, the people, the kids, the stink of milk all around, bacon and white toast, all glowed like apparitions. Eat something, baby. Jose's voice a massage, a whisper, yet far, far away, feebly piercing the migraine aura jackhammering my head. You can sleep on the benches. I'll listen for our name; promise, baby. They bring out tiny cartons of real orange juice. A delicate hint of normal. Doesn't last long. They're all locomotives, steaming through each other and

Jose tries to get at least one o.j., but he's shoved into the milk dispensers and he's crying and he's saying I'm schizophrenic, the people, the people, and I see his mouth moving, and can't hear him anymore, but his lips are saying, Nanette, come, Nanette, help and I rush over and an obese woman knocks my ear like a boxer and I'm crying and the stress and the pain and I want to kill these animals. These professional homeless with their scruffy babies and their boom boxes and appliances and plaid laundry bags and their big fat mouths and their fat hands on my ears. Only the ones who know about the system would know to bring all this stuff. And no one helps Jose, not one worker, even though he looks crazy now. And no one says a word about the fatso who almost took my ear off.

The room is spinning or is it me and the air is gone and the stench and I just sit right down on the floor. Jose makes his way over to me. Let's go upstairs. I'm using the crazy card. Telling them to make it faster for us; I can't take it. Can't. He's pulling me up, pulling my hand like a little boy. Baby, come, are you alright? The smell of baby's vomit. … God knows how I will last … who will save us now … Eggs melting in my mouth with that metallic migraine taste … I let him pull me and I stand up alarmed, the pounding in my head bigger now, reinforced like pelvic exam forceps, and that howling storm of fluorescent light.

\*\*\*

Upstairs Jose knocks on the social worker's door. I didn't even know there was one. Jose has radar for anyone he can kind of con, anyone who will listen to his schizophrenic woes. He knows that he's got nothing to lose. And sometimes it works, he says. I look out over the sea of bodies, the fog rising from too much heat and too much flesh. I look out over them as if I am on a beach, and for miles and miles there are big sea creatures dying on the sand and I am not part of them, I am an observer.

Dissociate again. It works for awhile. The sweat down my back, between my breasts dries deliciously. But the noise is worse than the planes flying low over Balboa Park. It is an entity, the main occupant of this place; it is everywhere, it leaks continuously as from chambers where gas is trapped and ignited. I am tired of rearranging our bags. My back hurts and I can't open my jaw.

Without warning, the social worker's door swings open. She looks half-way normal. Please, miss, please, I must speak with you … you see I'm a schizophrenic, please let me in your office where the noise is gone. Please let me tell you what I have to tell you. I never thought she'd let us in, but she shoos us in fast and slams the door before any of the fauna could push past us.

She's kind, this woman, she really feels for Jose. He exaggerates his sick mannerisms. Fingers twitching, eyes scrunching, a rocking back and forth and voila– she lets us sit in her office for two hours of peace. No noise, no smells. This is the Roman Coliseum, Jose says to her. The babies are falling out of walls. They're dying and dead. They're too many and too many colors, green, some. This woman looks like she knows what he means. She looks like she knows Jose is hallucinating. And I'm sure he is. It's just that he doesn't hesitate for a moment to use it. And why should he?

This is war.

What she doesn't do is tell us we have to stay awake all night. Jose and I sleep on touching benches. No room for two bodies on one. Our bodies, our homes. We melded and his long hair smelled of cigarettes and stress. For one tiny moment he cupped my breast. Our wedding night. His palms were hot on my face. He opened to me and with me and we slept too deep. With his unbrushed tongue—I couldn't find his toothbrush— he traced my ear and then my face. It was sweet and candy-tasting from all the candy we bought across the street to keep us silenced. In a room decades away I hear my father tell me I'm pretty, that pretty girls are lucky in America.

***

In the morning, at the barred cage the workers stand behind, cages like prison-visiting cells, we are told we have to start all over again. We've been logged out. That's how they get you. Government as game show. I lost my head. Then I'm falling somewhere, rage-blind, no seatbelts, no logic, nothing to reign me in. I see my hands rip the metal bars and snap her neck, her haughty expression, her jiggly body flying into tiny scraps. Then the snotty girl is telling me again, like she's teaching me a hard geometry lesson, that I am the head of the household, not Jose, because in this world that's the way it is. The woman's the head. And being the head, I was supposed to stay awake all night waiting for them to call our names. And being the head, I lost my head, again, crying and stamping my foot like a little girl. The caged girl snorted, smiled her ha-ha smile and handed up the long forms to start again.

Can't you just use the same form? I make that face I make when I'm near lowlifes trying to cage me. A sneer with my mouth and a smell into the air like something stinks. This is stupid, why do I have to fill it out again, when you have it right in your hand? Jose is banging on the ledge. Yeah, what is your problem? I'm sick you know. Schizo. I smile because he's using it, playing them like they're playing us. You rock, baby.

She said OK, she looked a little green, like she knew he could go ballistic and she'd be hurt. She knew. And Jose and me, we smiled our own ha-ha smile. On the second night we get a voucher to line up at midnight to be bussed to a sterile prison-like motel for the remaining hours until dawn. Jose and me. We stand outside. Wind blows through our coats. Air washes us. We're getting clean, as clean as we can be right now.

# The Girl Needs to Be Kissed

## Christine Schutt

*from Blackbird*

Ned wrote BOIL on his hand, but he forgot to look at his hand. Why was Isabel making excuses for her husband? Ned was late; he got to the restaurant after dinner but in time for dessert. Did he order eight-layer or eight-year-old cake? Was there such a thing as eight layers? The cake was striped with cream filling—that much Isabel saw, and she saw the greedy way Ned ate, very fast and self-deserving. He didn't cut off the shelf of frosting to save for last. Cake was cake; he would have another piece if he felt like it, and he felt like it—and he did! Amazing! Ned ordered a second drink, and not long after, a third. He was talking about Stahl and all the big-shot, lit-man Stahl had done for him with *Lime House Stories* when the waiter brought Clive his brandy. Isabel held out her hand for it. May I? she asked. Just a sip?

Outside the restaurant, when Clive crossed the street for a taxi, Isabel wondered just how tall he was.

Six-four at least, Ned said.

Ned was five-eleven; she was five-four and so was her mother—more or less—and Ned's mother, how tall was she?

Pet was very tiny; five-one, and that was stretching it. She hated the fact of her size. One of her theories was that women over five-ten never get into trouble but hold their own and go to good colleges.

Ned's near and sour breath appalled her.

Do you mind if I open a window?

The driver was on the phone speaking in a furious

language, and she was glad to get out of the cab while she could, away from the close, coarse—too mortal—smells, his and her own.

If a street had seasons, White Street was early spring, too colorless, hardly sentimental, no budded touches, nothing risen but March, secular . . . evaluated by possessions and they, Isabel and Ned, had possessions. In the White Street loft the oven hood shone holy, but the rest of the space was dark, and when Ned knocked his hand against the wall for more light, Isabel moved out from under it to the kitchen sink and ran cold water over her wrists. Too much wine, she said, and felt the water's sting.

The next day, charmed, everything looked new to her. Isabel had hoped for this much, also the cessation of hunger. Relief not to be hungry at all but rather pleasantly distracted by the body's other parts. Nipples, for example, hers prickled, and she touched herself and leaned into the corner of her desk, and she played—the way she remembered as a kid, skipping little words over the placid future: ram, cat, slut, cunt. At work on the corner of her desk—if Clive were only a woman was a thought.

Clive had kissed her at the Chester-Harris wedding, had pulled her up against the old club's coffered wall in a gesture to save her from the press of the tuxedo crowd when his intention was to kiss her—and he did. You look like a girl who needs to be kissed, he said, and Clive kissed her again, and when he found out she was married, he was no less amorous. You led me on, he said.

Did I?

Real excitement at a wedding at last!

\*\*\*

After lunch—skipped—Isabel stood in the long window at the magazine's offices and looked at her reflection: pretty, when not distorted, much as she would hope to look when being nasty to Ned. Waste of time to be mean, surely, but when had she ever been wise? She had kissed another man, not her husband, at a wedding, which was not a big deal, except that she had kissed this same man again, with clearer intentions, last night, and these plans did not include Ned. She was disappointed when Ned arrived, but she liked this phone call.

You forget I'm at work, Ned.

Was he trimming his nails as he talked to her, she wondered, and then, off the phone, what had they said or agreed on? She couldn't remember, so distracted was she first by her reflection and now by the hot spots in the making high inside her legs. Once home, she chugged down her pants and saw hives. Just when the possibility of being seen again had presented itself, these hot, dime-size pustules—pink, ugly, itchy—had come out high on the inside of her legs. Fuck. Fuck me.

The hives shamed her and she scratched them until they popped, like blisters, with warm blistery water inside. She felt ugly. Felt even uglier later, when Ned, not for the first time, sat on the edge of the bed and said, You're going to have to be the initiator.

O, so bring out the three-prong speculum, the ratchet mouth gag, the dittle kit, the forceps.

\*\*\*

*You look like a girl who needs to be kissed.*

She was that girl; she admitted it freely!

But Clive Harris did not call, and Ned had called to say he'd be late. So was it any wonder she got sick? Here again were the near-dead, weird days when she lived as in a closet in her migraine hell: her bed, a box of rags; her heart, a corner, spooky.

Sometimes Ned crossed the room; then the room emptied of people and she shut her eyes and saw a trillion pink dots—flashes of colors that made it look pinkish inside, which was also the inside of her brain, not the clay, gray, ridged outside, but inside with alleyways in all directions. If she thought too long on it, Isabel felt sick but when she opened her eyes, she felt sicker.

***

Clive? The curtains in the bedroom were drawn, and she was speaking softly from her bed.

Isabel?

My God, this phone is heavy.

Isabel, he began, but she had to hang up, and when the phone began to ring again, she pulled out the cord.

***

There was weather outside and she asked Ned to describe it.

Milky sunshine, he said.

What?

That's what I heard on the radio this morning.

My skull, Isabel said, it feels vacuumed.

*Good-bye, so long, I'll see you, I'm off.*

If she were to ask him to stay, she believes he would. Ned? she calls out, and again until she is sure he is gone.

This time—but what time was that?—she answered the phone and listened to Clive's gentleness. He asked about Ned.

Oh, come over, come over and look me over the way you did. If only she knew what to say. The phone was in her hand. Was that all? Would that be all? Now when her body was ringing, why weren't they making plans for the future?

***

The actress used her hands to convey Mary Tyrone's suffering. My heart goes out to Jamie. He's the sufferer; Edmund can write and has this thing with his mother.

After the play, Ned gave Isabel his handkerchief, and she used it and said, Oh, that was sad, that was stunning, that was terrible. Families. Oh, god! Her ankle twisted and she almost fell but he caught her up.

You okay?

Hardly.

# Ground Truth

## Claudia Emerson

from *Valparaiso Poetry Review*


My brother's funeral over, the dark-clothed
    congregation clots the church doors, a lingering

aftermath moving into flat light.
    The sky low and swollen, a storm siren

begins sounding long, expansive notes, evenly
    measured, so loud the pauses in between

ring with aftersound. Used to it, no one here appears
    alarmed, and the church ladies, gravely industrious,

stream into his house bearing platters
    of fried chicken, devilled eggs, casseroles—

colorful, layered creations—congealed salads
    with fruit suspended inside.  All of it sand.

The muted television is tuned to the weather,
    a small area of warning now upgraded

to watch, the words streaming across the bottom
    of the screen calling conditions perfect, this town,

this house disappeared beneath the map's isolated
    lesion, its red edges uneven, unmoving.

The forecasters rely they say on spotters,
    those who confirm what the radar cannot—

what they call ground truth; until then
    no one knows anything for certain

beyond this inward watching.  People mill
    around balancing heavy plates, the room

humming, an airless, crowded hive. Their mouths are full.
    They have no wings. I have come here too late,

his body gone, already ash. Its body
    could be forming now, tightening from cloud

to the gyre that will consume its path, all of it
    a becoming—spiraling a wall of dust,

mud, sand, and water; with dispassion taking up
    into itself the fence line, a barn—the house

beside them spared with the same dispassion. Or this,
    more likely now: siren silenced, the winds

diminishing, the light, afternoon's concession
    to another dusk—severe, more common truth.

# Arizona's Lonely

## Rachel Yoder

from *Necessary Fiction*

### 1. Loosely Based on Us

When we were in writing school, Violet and I decided one of the fiction writers had the biggest dick, and the poets who wrote about love would be best at going down.

I said the ones who wrote about soup rain and mouths that looked like blackboards would be best at dirty talk, and that's when Violet said, "Donald would fuck you with Emily Dickinson — *hope is a subtle glutton, baby* — or else say something about how he was going to stick tabasco up your ass."

"I don't even want to know what he'd do with *doom's electric moccasin*," I said, blowing smoke out my nose, and she said, "Oh Jesus, I would."

I told her I had told Donald that what was said of Sartre sounded like him, how *he seduced and conquered young girls by explaining their souls to them*. "And all he said was, 'Jackie, I'll Sartre all over your face.'"

"He must have been drunk," Violet said, laughing a little and putting her feet up on the coffee table. "That's not even original."

"Did you know Sartre adopted his mistress as his daughter?" I asked. "Did you know Beauvoir didn't get jack shit?" We sat in silence, considering this. Violet pushed empty beer cans around with her painted toes, and I looked out the window, thinking about how I was alone.

"What's this have to do with Donald?" Violet asked.

"Donald likes Asian teenagers," I said. "That's what this all has to do with him." That's when we decided two out of three nonfiction writers were movie rentals — *take them home for a few nights before returning*, Violet said — and that it was too hot to be sitting inside, so we went outside and set up her old lawn chairs on the front lawn, what I always called her *front dirt space* since there wasn't any grass, just Sonoran desert.

"If the tide came in and swept us out to sea in our lawn chairs, we'd be a Tony Hoagland poem," I said.

"Jesus, wouldn't that just do it," Violet said, sipping from a can. We watched the orange streetlights come on, and sweated without knowing it. I thought about how I didn't want to fall asleep that night, and how I hadn't been in love for what seemed like my whole life.

After a while Violet said, "I do like this cheap beer, Jacks. I do like this cheap beer in these lawn chairs," then, "Tell me something," since we'd both been thinking for a long time.

"Ok," I said, "I have these dreams about Chip."

"Oh, God," she said, since Chip was our professor. "He's about seventy."

"I can't help it," I said, putting one hand over my eyes and stretching my beer toward the sky, which had grown dark and purple. "Black lace panties and blow jobs," I said, "in his fucking office." I started laughing.

"You've got to be kidding," Violet said, laughing too, and we just sat there for what seemed like forever, laughing so hard.

"I need help. Seriously," I said, still laughing, but thinking I might cry soon because I felt alone and loveless and, quite frankly, a little goddamn sorry for myself.

We couldn't see much from our lawn chairs that night, just the white concrete bleachers at the University, the boxes of houses and apartment buildings, the asphalt and power lines running away from us, out of Tucson, to the strange mountains in the distance.

Violet's hair was done-up curly, and she had on her red lipstick and polka-dot high heels even though it was just a Tuesday and we were drinking cheap beer in her front dirt space in a town I liked to call Hell's Waiting Room. Violet shifted in her seat to cross her long legs, then gave me a wink as she sipped her beer. She gawked at the stars and sighed, the most contented sound I'd heard in years.

Pretty soon we'd both be gone from there, from school, from the hot city I hated. That was the truth. That's what I needed to remember. We'd all be gone so soon.

## 2. On Human Happiness

I knew the problem was that I was lonely, but I didn't know what to do about it. Graduate school had ended, and it was time to move, from Tucson to Prescott. Nearly everyone had already left, but Charles was still around, and he said, Yeah, sure, he'd drive the U-Haul. It's not like he had anything better to do.

We weren't the closest of friends, me and Charles. He was reserved, pale and good with computers, one of those guys who required sunscreen and hand sanitizer. And it was July in Tucson, melt-your-brain hot, so I was surprised when he agreed to help.

I hadn't seen the place where I was going to live in Prescott, but my friends owned it and had given it to me cheap. It was a double-wide trailer named Boulder's Edge with a wraparound porch, piles of boulders, a view of Granite Mountain. Charles discovered a path leading to a shack strewn with old tools. We both liked the pencil sharpener inside, screwed to the wall. In the trailer, I pointed out the knocker on the bathroom door, and outside, Charles rang the bell positioned on a twenty-foot pole. It made a giant ding dong.

We unloaded the heavy stuff that afternoon, then all the boxes blocking in the box spring and mattress, which we finally heaved to the bedroom. After that we were so hot and tired we couldn't stand it, so Charles had a shower, then me.

I took him to dinner at the place downtown where they made beer in big, stainless steel vats. At dinner he told me how he had read about a study on human happiness. In the study, he said, the researchers had people estimate how happy they'd be after, say, a really good meal. The people always predicted that they'd be incredibly happy, but inevitably they vastly overestimated their future satisfaction. (That's how Charles talked, *vastly overestimated their future satisfaction*.) The only thing the researchers found that could make people truly happy, Charles said, was other people.

On the first night at Boulder's Edge, I slept on the living room floor in a sleeping bag, and Charles slept in my bed. After he left, I didn't change the sheets.

I found his crumpled t-shirt under my bed a few days later. It was inside-out, and I pulled the hem through the neck hole and then held it in front of me by the shoulders. I decided to smell it. Detergent and sweat, but not in a bad way.

That afternoon I washed it along with my clothes. Ever since then it's been folded on the shelf under my bedroom window. This has happened a couple of times: I forget about it, but then the breeze moves the long curtain that hangs over that shelf, and I see the shirt, folded neatly, as if it belongs there. I still haven't told Charles he left it. I plan to keep it indefinitely.

### 3. What to Write Down

Libby told me about this punk guy she fell in love with in Minnesota. She tried to bake some bread and it didn't rise — I mean, it didn't rise at all, is what Libby said, holding her thumb and forefinger an inch apart — and he still ate it and said it was good.

It wasn't good, Libby said. It *was not* good.

And later, late at night, he called her and said he was coming over. In bed, when he asked if she wanted to snuggle, she blurted *no* even though she meant yes. They spent the rest of the night lying next to each other, trying not to touch.

Then he decided to hop a train to San Diego — hobo-style, Libby said, no ticket, no nothing — and on his last night in town they exchanged coats. He got her ice fisherman's coat, and she got his watching baseball/drinking beer jacket. He said he'd wait for her in Prescott, Arizona, and she said she didn't think the train ran through that town.

She said she's still waiting for him. (We were standing on a corner in Prescott, Arizona, outside the Thai place.) She slapped her hands over her eyes and yelled WHY WAS SHE SO DENSE? — not because she was waiting, but because she had to wait, because of her *nos* and theories about train routes — and I laughed because that was the only thing I knew to do.

*That fucker*, she said, hands resting on the top of her head, and grinning, beaming, even though I could tell she would have preferred something less emotional. *I'm still waiting for that fucker.*

The only thing she's heard from him is that the coat she gave him has been warm, is keeping him warm. This was through a friend of a friend of a friend. She said she doesn't even have an e-mail address for him. She said he's somewhere in a boxcar, or on a veggie bus, you know, one of those bio-diesel things, she said, full of real anarchists and punks and hippies.

I told her I thought it was the most romantic story I'd heard in years, and that she needed to go home and write down all she learned so that she'd know the next time, know how *no* really means *yes* (even though this is the opposite of everything we've been taught), and know how if a punk guy wants to eat your unleavened bread or snuggle or swap coats or wait for you in Prescott, Arizona, how all this also means *yes*.

She said yeah, but he left on that train and *I'm* always the one who leaves, that's how I like it.

She said, *No one's ever left me before in my life*, and I said, write that down.

For God's sake, write that down, too.

# Segue

## Lisa Zaran

from *Juked*

Suppose a bridge.  Then another
a few hundred feet from the first,
then another and another, bridge
after bridge, all crossing the same river
with no bridge more sturdy or outstanding
than the other.

Now suppose a man in the prime of his life,
another man, elderly as a grandfather, and
a boy of twelve.  Suppose a crippled man
or one whose mind is in riot all needing
to cross the river.

Suppose each bridge has a moving floor
or optional seats or wheelchairs pushed by
stronger men with nothing to do but go back
and forth pushing the sick and unable to the other side.

Suppose no burden, no eye for an eye,
no segregation, no unsteady plank or missing
rail, no tattered rope or tangled knot.
I could go on.

Suppose a bridge.  A frail man in his hospital bed.
A strong man behind him.  Below, the river.

# Glory

## Cami Park

from *Staccato*

A woman's hair is her crowning glory, my grandmother always said. Brush it every night, one hundred strokes.

She also once told me she felt like she was drowning. We had been doing the dishes together in silence, her freckled hands wrist-deep in suds. I placed the plate I'd been drying in the rack and leaned over the sink on tiptoe to look out the window at the star-speckled sky. Searched for the Milky Way, scanned for the moon.

# Baby Love

## Sara Levine

from *Necessary Fiction*

I had a baby.

"Why'd you have to have a baby?" Denny wanted to know. "There are so many babies on this block already. You know this neighborhood's really changing. First the Starbucks and then we got a Gap."

\*\*\*

I had a baby.

"I *heard* you had a baby," Ellen said. "Mina Denelsky also had a baby. Ginger Stanhope had a baby. Sue Rodriguez is pregnant with twins." She paused to slug her sugar-free vanilla skim latte. "Alan Cage's wife had a baby in August. Jenny Richardson had triplets. And here's a shocker, you know the Trachtlers? Expecting number five."

I pulled off the blanket I'd draped over my stroller, where plastered in sleep, the baby lay, one eye leaking fluid, his face a wrinkled turnip on a platter.

"Jesus fucking Christ," she said. "You certainly did have a baby. You did. Fucking Jesus Christ."

\*\*\*

Once home I handed my husband the baby. First I had the baby, and then I handed my husband the baby I had had. Can you follow me, time-wise?

"Everybody is having babies," I said. "Ellen Webler in Starbucks told me. Johnny, it's so weird. Like that time all the people we knew were down at one time with the flu."

Johnny jiggled the baby. "What were you doing in Starbucks?"

"You're not listening. All these people having babies, Johnny, and we didn't even know. We hadn't *heard* they had babies, too."

"Remember when you bought a car and wanted to know, like an errand from God, how your Volkswagen measured up? Cars, trucks, hybrids, minivans! Even after we bought, you saw the world disproportionately as roadway, forgetting our city's dependable, low-cost, environmentally sound though stinky means of public transportation." Johnny smiled fondly. "People refine the world according to their present capacities."

Since the baby I'd had trouble following conversations that weren't about me, and sometimes ones that were. My eyes dimmed. "What are you saying? I was a car bore, now I'm a *baby* bore?"

"No, no, no, no, no!" He spoke in the high-pitched wibbly-wobbly tone with which we talked to the baby.

\*\*\*

I had a baby and sent friends and relations digital pictures of my baby. Roughly two to three hundred digital pictures. Each digital picture a 400 kilobyte .jpg file which my 56K modem took two to four minutes to transfer. People downloaded two to three hundred pictures of my baby and wrote back. "What an adorable baby!" "I believe it is against the law to be such an adorable baby." People wrote letters to the editor. They phoned the media.

SHE HAD A BABY.
(The headline read.)

"We had a baby," my husband said.

"Oh quit feeling so goddamned sorry for yourself," I said.

\*\*\*

I had a baby.

The Mortons came over to meet the baby.

This was a big deal. We were letting the Mortons meet the baby. Even though the Mortons were guests, the baby was the guest of honor. We took the Mortons' coats, hugged the top parts of their persons, and tiptoed them into the baby's room.

"Boy, does it smell in here!" said David Morton. "Like someone took a dookie!"

My husband, I assume shocked beyond speech, stepped back hard against the wall. Our perfect baby, with his short habit of living, lay whiffling in the crib, a miraculous compression of human nature, cute and amazing and wondrous, capable of evolving into anything, permitting us to gaze on him in repose. And all the Mortons could do was sniff the air?

"One day," I said, "he'll be able to go down the hall like you, David, and shit in the toilet all by himself. Will that impress you? He'll be able to shit in the toilet and wipe his own ass while the rest of us have coffee and pretend not to hear."

"Oh," my husband, who had recovered, said faintly. "Would anyone *like* coffee?"

\*\*\*

I had a baby and I was pushing the stroller and wearing a backpack diaper bag. Laden. Slowly. Listening to my husband talk but thinking only of where I could get my next sugar or caffeine fix. As we came to the intersection, the traffic light turned orange. "Quick!" My husband stepped gamely off the curb.

"Quick?" I said. "There is no quickness in me left."

To remedy the lack of personal energy, I took six p.m. walks my husband called exercise, about which name I had sturdy doubts. A five dollar bill crumpled into my pocket for donuts, an unwillingness to pick up the pace beyond an elephantine circus march, the baby frequently mewing for tiny adjustments of blanket, hat, and sock, I never labored less for exercise, nor felt more tired failing to break a sweat.

But oh, the women, the slackly guarded women, cruising with babies through the summer dusk! Before the baby, I walked the city in silence. Now I spied Young Mother and, like an octopus scenting chemical along the ocean's current, drew close.

How old is your baby? Live in the neighborhood? Doing a play group? Sign up for Wiggle Worms? Baby sleeping through the night?

Scraps with telephone numbers collected in my diaper bag.

Megan from Uptown, baby Jane.

Julie from Lakeview, baby Cooper.

Liza from Andersonville, baby Maya.

"Pick-ups," I told Johnny. "Not even one night stands. On the street I hunger for connection. Once I'm home, I never call."

"Maybe you and these women have something in common."

"I had a baby!" I shouted. "For cripes sake. You think their experience can touch this?"

***

I had a baby. More and more, the baby exhibited a personality neither wholly pliable nor designed to reflect the fact that life, as his mother orchestrated it, was perfection itself. Time, which helps to coordinate an infant's limbs, did not spare him, and from the lump in the bedclothes he grew into a small, active, battering person. His achievements left us breathless and a little self-conscious about our own relatively faint capacities for growth.

"Wasn't it yesterday he just wiggled on the sofa?" said Johnny. "I mean for hours, while we watched a DVD?"

"Sunrise, sunset," I said cynically but felt, in my solar

plexus, what he meant, especially as the baby stumbled across the room, pulling my hoary hairs out of a brush and throwing them at the cat for sport.

"I get Ma'amed more than Missed," I said.

"Well, no one can stay a baby forever."

"Ba ba ba," said the baby.

"Let's not *rush* him," I said.

But as I hauled the baby to parks, libraries, garden centers, rummage sales, swimming pools, sandboxes, airports, and anywhere with an escalator to kill an hour or two, I observed that the baby, with his jouncy pounds and self-feeding hands, no longer struck others as something I had obviously, and with enormous effort, expelled from my body—an effort about which, let it be said, the world can in no way be too reverent.

People called him boy, kid, little man, though to me the baby was Pumpkin and Bunny and Kernel and Babycake.

One morning the baby looked up from the sticky floor where he sat spooning almond butter from a jar and said, "I am not your Babycake," and I wondered: should I stop thinking: I had a baby? Maybe the baby was no longer something I had had. It was true he had learned to speak, clever animal, and I no longer conspired against his very wakefulness. I read him stories for fifty minutes and he hollered me back three more times to ask one more thing, and then after I had trained myself to associate bedtime with elaborate tricks and popish ceremonies, he changed again; he began to go bed with jarring ease. "No stories," he warned.

No stories?

I closed the door, listened for my summons, and heard nothing. Stood in the hallway dizzy, as if I'd stepped off a treadmill and my exhausted legs still wanted to run. Don't ask me to tell you what I was feeling. I had a baby. For my feelings substitute the emptiness of a rain barrel, its wood drying out, its metal staves creaking; an unbidden, arid silence after two years of learning to hold the rain.

# A Companion Text to *Modernity and Self-Identity* by Anthony Giddens

## Angela Woodward

from STORYGLOSSIA

*1. Of key importance here is the emergence of the 'pure relationship' as prototypical of the new spheres of personal life.*

Typically, a relationship comprises three things. At first the first thing rises in front of you, a volcano, an ox, it fills your eyes, overwhelms you, cancer, your mother, your lost job, Isabel—the one thing stamps its feet on the mat, knocking the door down, bellowing in the hall, announcing, "I'm here, the one thing."

Over its shoulder is always—Giddens confirms this—the second thing. A swallow, a collar, maybe something as small as a hyphen. But in any case, the opposite, the other hand, the alternative. With these two things, you can walk, like on stilts, left, right, left, right. You move forward smoothly, with balance. How capable you are. You were so worried. Now with these two things, the world is at last complete. The male, the female. The dark, the light. The eyelid, the blazing orb.

For a few days, I was at peace. Then I woke just like I used to, only hours after falling asleep, and pulled the curtain aside. Clouds whited out half the sky, and in the other portion, the stars seemed about to retract into their lairs. I was still sick, and even after the operation, I would be sick some more. The third thing, which I had hoped would be the spiritual one, crawled out of the blankets. A mist, a gas, the ineffable, it coiled around me, whispering something incomprehensible into my hair.

*2. 'Futures' are organized reflexively in the present in terms of the chronic flow of knowledge into the environments about which such knowledge was developed.*

Later that week the doctor asked me what I was so morose about. It could quite easily be cut out, my malingerancy. No, not a malignancy. Had I gotten such an elemental thing wrong? "You'll be out of the hospital in twenty-three hours," he said, leaving me to wonder if the bill kicked up a notch when the fateful twenty-four was breached. But even my skepticism was a symptom. "You'll be in your garden pulling weeds in three days," he said. "You'll go out to eat with your family." A little pain when I coughed or laughed, that was all. And after? I said. This question too was part of the disease. His lasers would eradicate all my doubt and separation.

On the drive home, I noticed the leatheriness of the unrelieved orchestra music pouring out of the radio. I couldn't imagine how everyone else stayed so skillfully in their lane, when the other lane was occupied by gigantic cranes swinging their laden beaks over our heads, only a row of lighted stakes keeping them to their side. Yet we rolled along in ours, the city planners having carried out their project well, so that during construction half the street remained open.

*3. Trust is specifically related to absence in time and space, as well as to ignorance.*

You'd think this has to do with a lover or a thief, but in fact Giddens refers to the dissolution of clear categories. For example, I turned the television on after the children had gone to their father's. An old man with a twisted neck shouted at another with a long beard—perhaps they were castaways or revolutionaries, ensconced in an elaborately decaying mountain shack. Their world was wood, cursing, and an old file cabinet.

No women livened the story for at least half an hour. I started picking the crumbs off the rug, then went upstairs and dusted the mirrors. I returned in time to witness a wedding, on another continent or 50 years in the past. Maybe it was just my state that evening, that I made no attempt to sort this out, but was all the while thinking other thoughts, that chronic flow, perpetual outgassing of concern for the things I have little control over.

What he showed me on the X-ray was galactic, a cluster surrounded by mysterious dark matter. The light spots, he said, were troublesome. I nodded, as if I could possibly concur, when I had no training in diagnostics, in radiology, or in anything to do with sickness, disease. We looked gravely at each other, as if we understood each other, me with my calcifications, he with his burdensome responsibilities. He allowed me to put my fingers on the edges of the film, giving me a tangential relation to my very innermost being.

*4. Such an example is one which demonstrates . . . the risks of driving, and thereby serves temporarily to pull apart the protective cocoon.*

For a long time I took Giddens' admonitions about the "reflexive project" of the self as a peculiar kind of wording. I mean not even words, but "wording." He had a cool, gray way of laying down his prose, like so many cleanly cut iron rods. Only if seen from above would the pattern generate into a bar code for some object of desire not yet invented. Something like that—in any case, pure abstraction. So reading him was not even ingestion, not contractual, as in give and take. My aesthetic appreciation had a glow to it, a lunar luminescence, which I ascribed totally to Giddens, not to my reaction to him.

The boys in the library gave me a lot of difficulty. They set their chocolate milk and donuts by the computer, sprayed their deodorant on in front of everyone, having no sense of what was properly private, i.e. grooming. I had to ask the smaller one to go outside to make his phone call, as he was not capable of talking in a soft tone. As I said this, he told me he liked my bracelet, and asked me where it came from. I said my mother had given it to me. "I'd like to meet your mother," he said, not knowing that she was in Arizona, and then dead. I contemplated calling a staff meeting to discuss whether we could force the boys to leave. They were behaving to the best of their ability, which had more limits on it than most. Then all of Giddens, which I had misunderstood for months, rolled out at me—the dread of being held together only with provisional struts. The color or flavor of "modernity" became suddenly palpable: a windswept, orphaned emptiness backing onto an exhilarating freedom.

*5. A creative involvement with others and with the object-world is almost certainly a fundamental component of psychological satisfaction and the discovery of 'moral meaning.'*

I left work early, ascribing some weakness to my "condition," so I could read some more. Giddens at that point seemed to be speaking directly to me. It was hard to meet his gaze, he was so earnest, but I left my fingers in his, looking down at our entwinement. I was so afraid of dying during the surgery that I contemplated killing myself first, cutting my throat before the anaesthetist could get hold of me. Giddens understood that my need for certainty trumped even the animal will to survive.

"I know," he said, "I understand." Whereas before he had fascinated me, amused me, now it appeared he had written his whole book so that I could finally make sense of myself. He asked me if I wanted him to be quiet now, and I said no. I fell asleep, then woke again, to his continual murmuring.

# Selections from *Sucker Jane*
## Sean Kilpatrick
from *Spork*

Similarly Rented Womb Stank

Touching outside involves less god. The river where I drown
for thirty miles every night, huddled zigzag between fists in
an ugly tickle, crowds of men seen pummeling slant from the
bank, where my sockets ruckus pure money with the ancestors
of whatever sex destroys me, chewing sediment toward China,
hunkering through methods that heighten the land, disappeared
splash by splash, an epilepsy of hue so tight I skip myself sore
around spunk buoyancies. *My absenteeism is symptomatic of
my being there.* In the stasis my blood refrains; combing the
skin above until fire. Every nanosecond fluctuates overlapping
hatreds so immense—and then little glances happen and I want
to get married, someone pets me and I reconsider procreation,
someone stands up and I want to slit their ballsac, shivers when
I brush their hair, I want to bunch off all their skin and roll
around in it, gives me some laconic refusal and I want to prove
the world is flat, but not really. I call my period back from
limbo, back from starvation, whisper the egg out of hiding and
it sits up purring without nuisance of gravity, thighs spider
webbing, black months reverse. The gush heats my esophagus,
revolving downward, traceable on the glow of my birth marks,
stains that mean put me back in, my ribs box the revolving
cramp and I flap my arms to help inch belly upside down,
dilated red, lips parting reflexively, sprinkling a baby no one

might be cruel enough to raise. Better in town square, or on the floors of schools disassembled by movement. I am a parasite and I miss my host. I miss not having been born yet. Their unzipped pants taste of gas. They roll me in the balled hide of a screaming animal. The drool I hover with reflects me. Horsefly stung cataracts slapped down, scooting terror, sees the grass mashed fuck to soup and me humping on it: ass and folds. Folds chasing folds shiver off, muscular system exposed, shiny fat, wrapped in our own flay and squirting dermis, whining louder with each mouthful, blood dizzy and wedged maggots feed each shivering hunk, rowed through the plaster with torn placement, our doggy blanket drying slowly. All tomorrow I sneeze Flintstones Vitamins wrapped in fur. My wrecked circulation, so many veins the light, now blue, chaws inside a mother sound fainting forward.

Baby Bitch

"Your baby bitch weakness is never as cute an unreasonable defense as you think, especially when you're off speed. If your tricks rather called you ugly, instead of letting you, in false modesty, say it first, they would then adorn you beyond your tiny comprehension, and you'd have to fill your own cunt with substance." He placed my wounds like a petty savior, closing one eye, staring down the still unfolding prim and slick haltered tucks of where I land. He's sucked my clit in a thought bubble all day. Now sweat lamps our torsos, public slime, conducted chafing. He slaps an extension cord through my come. "At some point we'll miss each other, lick the wall socket." I leak ounces of water I've eaten for the last week. He stirs, punches his tongue up my ass, cooing me close to an almost throb, floating inside gooey suction, his fingers v-shaped, compressing my clit, stuck out, elastic. Wound around thick calibration, I contract and lock tight enough for him to slam pathways. Our hips ache rhythm, my legs thrown, an afterthought. We bake through so much friction the house leans. I plug my hand into my mouth and shrink, organs choking into a suffocated spasm around his cock. We let go, pulse, vision loss, screaming in our skins, his tip audibly whacking my cervix like a rewound car accident. Our hearts tamper fabulous congruities. Body language is the one form of communication I keep finding myself trapped in and liking, so saying hi is hard. I quietly become a man under the sheets. I slip into cumy boxers and do hot dog rotations, make the sheets rise like something's there, extend my good confidence to the world, focus on the limitations of my length and how to hide. Because he stretches out my undersized panties, folded into them like an after-sex magic show, I assume his genitalia, no longer accomplishing that grotesque male bounce and flap, are inch by inch retracting into egg sac. I'll have his musk by the time he's awake. He'll cream himself flowery and miss my big holy penetration. My fucking him leaves an imprint, an echo of cock he reverberates in girly sing-song. He contains my puddle, flutters around, dripping me. The physical memory lasts longer than he cares to think. He is sore and angry for being sore and mocks my enormous protuberance under red sore sheets, pretending to be me before on to the next breeching, which occurs in possibly five minutes. I finish ogling transvestite me, with my Rocky Horror hands, though I disagree with leather, unless it is in my mouth. I show Canada my tits. I live in a Japanese closet. I sneeze Algerian sperm. I log online and talk about dead dogs. I make phone calls and text messages and type in the instant message hatebox. I tap a telegraph on the small of my back, spread my legs around a smoke signal, take cell phone pictures, send them to a girl who tongues my ass, a boy with gout, a child with clap, a transvestite who takes notes, people in Hong Kong circle jerking in the middle of a crowded street, posted on the blog with pubic hair font. A guy from Sacramento is crying on my voicemail. I film my feet for someone in Kansas, toes wrinkling hello. I attend a webcam orgy, choking myself with my bra. I laugh asking if father catches feast in my diaphragm. He died in childbirth. Literally, he's negative seven years old. His prick looks like a coat hanger. Boything from Colorado wants to watch me piss on cam. Girlcreature from school asks what drugs her boyfriend stuffed me with. LSD suppositories and I got pyrotechnic groin trauma. So he shampooed your cunt for CNN? Acronyms are hot. I'll punch your clit later. LOL. I type upside down in the hatebox, legs over the chair top like white feathers that hate themselves. I invented wingspan. I'm typing I fucked your mom over and over to my own screen name. I answer my cell and continue an online conversation mid-sentence. The television is loud enough to upset my stomach. I hold music to my ear and type with one finger and yell "What!" into the phone while performing on cam, taking another picture, switching the lights on and off with my toe.


Graveyard


I hump the graveyard so bodies fizz. Their stains grow inside me. Exhaling into the corpse dirt above each grave, a lick of something molded dry inside my thought. I kill the hot end of a cigarette on my nipple, leaving white scars dividing the pink like a second nipple failing to begin. In a minute the world can turn your crucifixion runny. My scraped tits bobbling clay, retarded putty sucked by all. I want to get my gang rape on. Fill up a small closet with my blood. Comb it out of me, enough to paint a house. I'm too far up my own rashes to hear. My genitalia need constant sensory information. It's how I can tell where I'm going half the time. I miss the ex who smoked my vulva like a bong. He spent a lot of time down there with a flashlight, being religious. That kind of spatial misconception is common amongst the devoted. For instance, when I'm five years old, I fall down trying to grab the moon. I want to use it to shave my legs. I miss a version of the future invented for my sorry inclusion. The particular slapped-tall ostrich pounce these fuckers ritualize. I am too far splayed again by hands.

# Fifteen Unrelated Stories Titled "The Man Inside Her Pillowcase"

**Brandi Wells**

from *Keyhole*

1.

She doesn't know there is a man inside her pillowcase. At night, she is drowning him. Her drool seeps through the pillowcase and covers him, drenches him. It is overwhelming. He's tried sleeping in a raincoat and scuba mask, but the moisture always finds a way in. It clogs his ears and clings to his eyelashes. He doesn't open his mouth to speak or eat, fearing the saliva will roll down his throat and choke him. He is so quiet, the man inside her pillowcase.

2.

The man inside her pillowcase likes to be between her legs. He feels safe there. She tucks him in every night and he nestles against her crotch, damp and warm.

3.

While she sleeps, the man inside her pillowcase gnaws at her. Eats bits of her hair and freckles. Each morning she wakes and is a little less herself than the day before. She spends all her time looking for things she can't remember, lists she never made, and people she never knew.

4.

The man is trapped inside her pillowcase. He thought he could escape, but then she put the pillow sham on and he couldn't find a way out. After a bit, the pillow sham made him feel more comfortable, like she was the kind of girl that would piss with the bathroom door open and drink beers with him on Sunday.

5.

The man inside her pillowcase has not always lived inside her pillowcase. He once lived in a baseball, a cooler, a DVD player, a dictionary, a package of bubble wrap and a can of tuna fish. He cannot stand the smell of tuna fish.

6.

The man inside her pillowcase is not quite a man. Legally, HE is still a SHE. But she has the paperwork for a legal name change in her glove box. And she just started hormone therapy. The name she picked for herself was "John," so she would blend in.

7.

The man inside her pillowcase has been submitting stories to the *Paris Review* once a year, since he was nine years old. The rejection letter he receives each year hasn't changed. One time there was a footprint on the envelope.

8.

The man inside her pillowcase has trouble sleeping at night because his nipple piercings are infected and every time she rolls over, it rubs his chest raw, till bleeding. He holds his hands over his chest, but bleeds through the pillowcase anyway.

9.

The man inside her pillowcase has no upper body strength. Instead he spends all his time running laps around her pillow and stretching his calves. He worries about shin splints.

10.

The man inside her pillowcase applied to law school and got into North Eastern Ohio with full tuition and fee waivers. He plans to buy a house and give his cat away.

11.

The man inside her pillow keeps her awake at night, practicing "da stanky leg," a dance he never feels comfortable doing at the urban club he frequents on Saturday nights. He can't bend and twist his leg like the other guys.

12.

The man inside her pillowcase refuses to come out because he is ashamed of the crown tattoo he got on the back of his neck. He just thought it looked cool. He had no idea it was a gang symbol for the Latin Kings.

13.

She is in love with the man inside her pillowcase. At night, after her boyfriend falls asleep, she whispers into her pillowcase. She breathes heavy and rubs her tongue across it.

14.

The man inside her pillowcase is unsure about their relationship. He doesn't want to move west with her and he doesn't want to break up. "Can't we just see what happens?" he asks.

15.

One morning she wakes to find the man inside her pillowcase is dead. She isn't surprised. She knows if she hadn't suffocated him, he would have smothered her.

# Crystal Castles

## Matthew Kirkpatrick

from *Action Yes*

Baby Jessica waddles across the
autumn lawn. Cool gusts blow
across the overgrown grass like
thick waves of water. Pulled
down by the undertow. Sucked
into an old hole. Stretches
her baby-fat arms across the
circumference of the narrow
forgotten well and hangs.
Dangles feet above the cold
earth below; dirt crumbling
around her downy body down
into darkness. Wind blowing
through hair wisps. Cold soil
around her waist. Something
heavy dragging her down.

Ever since being struck by
lightning:
She has no recollection of
lightning.

Remembers playing in a tangle
of electrical cords behind the
television and stereo pawing
at plugs like bristle blocks

The Mole lounges horizontal
on the couch in his
subterranean living room
thumbing the Atari control
about to best his best Crystal
Castles score. The lights
flicker and the Atari resets.

Whiskers twitch.

What he remembers is waking
in a bundle of blankets on the
floor, making coffee, eating
a bowl of dirt, checking out
Today for a while. After
he figures out what to do
with the glasses resting
on his belly, he rummages
around his hole, finds poems
unfinished in a bundle

squished precariously together.
She would remember the stereo
blasting something adults called
Journey and her parents on the
couch rocking out with Fritos
falling from their mouths and
Pabsts. Remembers a dull jolt
like being punched in the chest
and smoke and an attempt at
amateur CPR despite her still
beating heart.

What she remembers: waking
up in a bundle of blankets on
the floor her body and mind no
longer bulbous and opaque, her
childhood cured by inadvertent
amateur electroshock.

When the darkness lightened
and her parents bent over her
body saying you were struck
by lightning something like
lightning, she felt something,
blacked out and static, hurt but
bitter and wise.

Hanging above the well she
imagines the bottom full of
better Barbies and tea parties
and worms and a basket of
batteries for all her dead robot
toys. She can feel herself aging

beneath his pillow, a rad
Atari, dishes to do, and like
many of us pieces together
from the shit lying around
his apartment what he is
supposed to do with his day.

This is a poem the mole
wrote about

Love:
The thing comes
of itself

(Look up
to see
the cat & the squirrel,
the one
torn, a red thing,
& the other
somehow immaculate

Lonely Mole.

The mole gags at worms so
eats dirt sandwiches, dirt with
fries, dirt spread over toast
with strawberry jelly, hot dirt,
cold dirt. For protein, he eats
dirt. This makes cleaning
dishes easy. The mole eats

there at the rim, hear her
future in the darkness: first
date, middle school dances,
and the cold clawing and many
marriages, to images of an
accident, being held in front of
cheering and cheering, warmth,
cameras, marriage to the hole,
marriage to an ex-con. She will
miss them all unconscious in
darknesses.

Like being struck by lightning
she does not remember
the second lightning strike
(drowned in neighbor's pool)
being hit by a car (dropped)
falling down stairs (hit by car)
burnt in car accident (forgotten
in backyard, struck by
lightning.) Accidents somehow
perfect.

Tired of hanging and trusting
that somebody will save
her again and enjoying the
warmth radiating from the
well hole below her cold
feet she sighs and succumbs
sliding down the narrow
tunnel, her baby body though
toughened from so much
electrocution

a bowl of dirt ignoring his
twitching whiskers.

When The Mole moved in he
painted the place red, pink,
black, yellow to remind him
not to eat the walls of his
house.

The Mole can't ignore the
whiskering and investigates.
He stands at the edge of the
old well and sniffs.

Floodlights above fill the dark
hole.
He hears them calling
from above, distant sounds
bouncing down the tunnel.

He sees a small girl.
They stare at each other.

The Mole is startled to hear
such a small girl speak,
doesn't understand how she
knows his name. Frail and
pale, smudges of black across
her almost white cheeks. She
shakes, from shock, perhaps
– he can't tell if she fell down
the old hole, or climbed
down, though her claws were
very short so he assumed
a fall. Would she require

roots and wire scrape her skin
and insect arms reaching out
of the darkness their claws
clawing

at her newish skin
rot down here, decompose,
compost.

Throw olive pits and eggshells
and banana peels and coffee
grounds down on top of her
and her body will return to
dirt. Let something take root
and grow in the decay.

Baby Jessica is surprised by
the colors of dirt. Deep red,
pink, black, yellow like layers
of birthday cakes.

Baby Jessica senses something
in the darkness in front of
her.

Floodlights from above fill
the dark hole. She hears
them calling her name above,
distant sounds bouncing
down the tunnel.

She sees a mole.
They stare at each other.

medical attention? How
would the Mole get her out
of there? What of the bright
lights, the calling? What does
she eat?
He scurries back into his den
and turns off the television,
then scurries to return.
"Hi little girl."
"I'm a mole."
The Mole extends
his hand
is cold and claws and fur and
he knows this
shaken his hand before, never
a talking Mole
never a beautiful baby girl

The Mole could help her,
wrap her in blankets, feed her
dirt. He has heard about little
girls falling down wells before
and knows that it could
take days to rescue her – the
danger of the well collapsing
around her.
The lights above are bright
and he can hear her name
"Baby Jessica! Baby Jessica
down in the well!"

He leads her into his den and
wraps
A blanket around her. Offers
her the Atari controller.
"Crystal Castles!"

"Hello Mole."

"Where did you go?"

"Hello Mole."
"I'm Baby Jessica."
Baby Jessica is afraid to take

makes her nervous – no
human has ever extended a
hand, never

fallen down a hole, lost and
cold she has
nobody but to trust

She finds the Mole handsome,
debonair for an underground
creature.

The lights above are bright
and she can hear her name
"Baby Jessica! Baby Jessica
down in the well!"

The Mole leads her

She loses on the first level and
he's disappointed at her lack
of hand-eye coordination.
He's been practicing for years,
though and doesn't hold it
against her, puts the joystick
on the coffee table and offers
her a handful of dirt.
He thinks maybe she doesn't
know what to do with dirt.
He shows her shoving dirt
into his little mole mouth and
when she doesn't understand
he drops mouths of wet dirt
from his mouth into hers,
drops the mud onto her lips
and massages her necks so she
can swallow.

He can tell she doesn't like
the taste of the dirt and
disappointed – he doesn't
know what to offer guests  -
he wraps the blanket around
her tight and reads a poem to
her:
"This one is called For No
Clear Reason. I am pretty sure
I wrote this one."

While he reads the Mole
wonders if he didn't actually
write this one. He can't
remember writing any of
them, but each day intends to
write but plays Crystal Castles

and lets him wrap a blanket
around her and takes the
joystick in her hand despite
knowing its function,
she lacks the hand-eye
coordination required for
video games and loses on the
first level.


She thanks him for the dirt
and doesn't know what to do
with it.

She watches him eating the
dirt and believes that he
intends for her to eat it and
she doesn't want to be rude,
but before she can push a
handful into her mouth.


Are moles like birds dropping
food into the mouths of their
young? She opens her mouth
and accepts the chewed dirt
and swallows with as much
enthusiasm as she can muster.


She listens as he reads:
I dreamt last night
the fright was over, that
the dust came, and then
water,
and women and men,
together

all day – how else could he
be so good? He wakes up the
next day not remembering
writing any poems, and
yet with a stack of poems
scattered around his hole.
Because he can't remember
anything, can't remember
reading, he assumes he has
written them, thinks maybe
he has written every word
in every book stacked in his
den. Rewards himself with a
day of Crystal Castles. Rarely
with audience, he is suddenly
embarrassed that he may be
reading work not written by
the Mole and yet presented as
the Mole's own. He will begin
to take careful notes.
He Blushes.
He gathers up the pile of
papers on the table and takes
them to the kitchen where
he drops them into the trash
where tomorrow he will
find them and wonder why
he would throw out such
precious words and remove
them and read them and put
them on the desk to work
on tomorrow after a game of
Crystal Castles and maybe
a little tea. He didn't write
these, he thinks. He means
to write it down on a post-it

again, and all was quiet
in the dim moon's light.

A paean of such patience—
laughing, laughing at me,
and the days extend over
the earth's great cover,
grass, trees, and flower-
ing season, for no clear
reason.

"That was beautiful, Mole."

"Mole! I'm cold."

He packs newspaper beneath
logs in the fireplace and
pushes her in her chair closer
to the fire.

A whistle whistles.

the mug to her lips. She sips,
the spice and citrus hot in her
mouth and

and put it on the refrigerator,
and start some new poems
right away but hears Jessica in
the living room say

He wraps her in another
blanket.

He puts a kettle for tea on the
stove.

He drops a teabag into a
wide ceramic mug and when
the water has cooled a bit he
pours the water slowly over
the teabag and takes her the
steaming mug.
Too frail to lift the mug
herself, he holds

She begins to fall asleep. He
pulls a claw soft across her
cheek and sniffs her lips with
his.

The next day the Mole
wakes and makes the usual
discoveries – he has Crystal
Castles! He finds a stack of
poems which he assumes he
has written in the trash and
wonders why he would have
thrown them away the day
before. He retrieves them
and spreads them out on the

"Good morning, Mole."

"Remember me I'm Baby
Jessica I fell down the well
and you found me and read
poems to me and fed me dirt
and made tea and kept me
warm?"

she drinks another mug of
tea andeats the watery broth
happy to have something in
her stomach besides tea and
dirt and he shows her

she agrees that it's beautiful,
lovely work, so intricate.
They wrap themselves
the fire
above, the lights
they hear them shouting her
name
bottom of a forgotten well
pressed together, their cheeks
hand

Baby Jessica in the hole
forty hours with the mole
creweling and cooking and
eating and forgetting and
playing Crystal Castles
together.

coffee table and sits down
to write but decides to try
his hand at Crystal Castles
and sees the girl curled up
in front of the fire and is
startled.

"Excuse me, little girl?"
"How do you know my
name?"

The Mole didn't remember,
but he decided it must be
true because Baby Jessica
was beautiful and sweet and
curled on his couch.
He makes her tea and
he finds a can of soup that
had fallen years ago down the
well and she

how to play Crystal Castles
and shows her the embroidery
work he keeps finding and
together
they wrap themselves and
watch
hear the commotion
shining down on them like
spotlights, hear her name as if
they were listening at the end
of a cardboard tube their ears
pressed together their cheeks
in hand

it's impossible he made it,

he says, without thumbs,
even though it is just that
he doesn't remember making
it, usually before bed he
sits down to try his hand at
embroidery in imitation of
the beautiful pieces collected
around his apartment and
finds that he is really good at
it, finishes a small piece each
night before succumbing to
sleep, waking in the morning
forgetting how it got there,
rediscovering his talent for
needlecraft and poems
The Mole considers asking
Baby Jessica to be his
subterranean bride, but can't
help but feel like a pervert for
thinking about an eighteen
month old baby bride, but
when the Mole sits down to
do the math, he's got about
36 months total to live and is
now around 22 months or so
(he doesn't keep good track.)
So if the average adult lives
to be 76 or so, then Baby
Jessica is 38 in Mole Years.
The Mole, in human years, is
around 45. Acceptable range.

Baby Jessica is rescued from
the den by claws that drill
down through the earth,
widening the eight-inch wide
hole she had fallen into. As
she rises she looks down at
the sleeping Mole and longs
for him. As she enters the
light of the cameras and
lookers-on she, too, forgets.

She will become a
photograph.

Baby Jessica will:
Say she remembers nothing,
say she has no recollection
of falling down the well and
meeting a mole and eating
dirt and drinking tea and
falling down the well again
sixteen months later and
meeting a mole and eating
dirt and drinking tea and
falling down the well again
a year later, eating dirt
and meeting the mole and
drinking tea and sleeping in
and playing Crystal Castles
and falling down the well
again, and again, and only
when she can no longer fall
down the

The Mole lounges horizontal
on the couch in his
subterranean living room
thumbing the Atari control
about to best his best Crystal
Castles score. The lights
flicker and the Atari resets.

This is a poem the mole wrote
about Love:
The thing comes
somehow immaculate

What he remembers is waking
in a bundle of blankets on the
floor, making coffee, eating a
bowl of dirt.

Cold in the hole the Mole
looks up, light shining into
the well, and imagines for a
moment the glimpse of a girl.

What he will remember
is waking in a bundle of
blankets on the floor, making
coffee, eating a bowl of dirt.
Cold in the hole the Mole will
look up, light shining into
the well, and imagine for a
moment the glimpse of

*Note: The Mole did not write the poems in Crystal Castles. They were written by Robert Creeley.*

# Cube

## Amelia Gray

from *Spork*

The children who found the cube shrieked over it as children do. The adults couldn't be pulled away from the picnic at first, and assumed that the children had found a shedded snakeskin or a gopher hole. Only when the Rogers kid touched the iron cube and burned his hand did the parents come running, attracted by the screams.

It was a massive monolith, wider than it was tall and taller than anyone could reach, wavering like an oasis in the heat. The Rogers kid wept bitterly, his hand already swelling with a blister.

Nobody knew what to make of the thing. It was too big to have been carted in on a pickup truck. It would be too large for the open bed of an eighteen-wheeler, and even then there were no tire marks in the area, no damaged vegetation and not even a road nearby wide enough for a load that size. It was if the block had been cast in its spot and destined to remain. And then there was the issue of the inscription.

They didn't notice it at first, between the screaming Rogers kid, his mother's wailing panic to hustle him back to camp for ice, and the pandemonium of parents finding their own children and clasping them to their chests and lifting them up at once. The object in question itself received little scrutiny. Only when the mothers walked their children back to camp for calamine lotion and jelly beans did the rest of the adults notice the printed text, sized no larger than a half inch, on the shady side of the block:

## EVERYTHING MUST EVENTUALLY SINK.

The words caused an uncomfortable stir among the gathered crowd.

"What about Noah's Ark?" asked one man in the silence.

"After the Flood, the Ark was lost in the sand."

"What about buoys?"

"Given time and water retention," said a woman who worked in a laboratory, "a buoy will sink like the rest."

This was disconcerting news. Everyone stood around a while, thinking.

"What about an indestructable balloon?"

"Such a contraption does not exist, and is therefore not a thing."

"A floating bird, such as a swan?"

"It will die and then sink," the first man said, annoyed.

One man made to rest against the iron cube and stepped back, grimacing in pain at the surface heat.

"A glass bubble, then."

The laboratory woman shook her head. "The glass would eventually erode, as would polymer, plastic, wood, and ceramic. We are talking thousands of years, but of course it would happen."

The group was becoming visibly nervous. One young man recalled a flood in his hometown that brought all the watertight caskets bobbing out of the earth, rising triumphantly out of the water like breeching whales. The water eventually found its way though the leak-proof seals and the caskets sank again.

Another man recalled a mother from the city who drove her car into a pond, her children still strapped to their seats.

A man and a woman walked to camp and returned shortly with a cooler of beer. The gathered crowd commenced to drinking, forming a half-circle around the cube. They agreed that many things would eventually sink:

A credit card
A potato (peeled)
A baby stroller
A canoe
A pickle jar full of helium
A rattan deck chair
A matress made of NASA foam

They even agreed on alternate theories: everything that sunk could rise again, for example. One of the men splashed a few ounces of beer on the iron surface as a gesture of respect. The place where the beer touched cooled down and the man leaned on the cube. It didn't budge.

The men and women grew drunk and their claims more grandiose (a skyscraper, an orchard, a city of mermaids). Eventually, the mothers came to lead them back to camp but they didn't want to go, eliciting words from the mothers, who had been stuck with the children and each other all afternoon and were ready for the silence of their respective cars. Back at camp, they were throwing leftover food into the pond. Ducks paddled up to eat the bread crumbs and slices of meat and the children clapped. The Rogers kid stayed on his mother's lap, picking jelly beans from her hand. A pair of siblings threw an entire loaf of bread into the water and watched it disappear.

'     The mothers didn't talk much, preoccupied with children or ducks. As they sat, some thought about the children, and some thought about everything eventually sinking, but most thought of the long drive ahead, the end of the weekend, and the days after that.

# Wife to Magrite

## Krystal Languell

from *DIAGRAM*

Let me be the man
with the bag over my head
kissing the bag over
your head, your head
also under a bag. Let my
burlap lips graze your
burlap face, my canvas
tongue snag your sand-
paper cheek. Let me be
the man in the painting.
Cock your neck, chin tilt
while I stand. Bend to.
Let me be the man, leaning
over you. Over your head,
over your gagged mouth—
my man's face in a bag
over you, your head
in a bag.

# You wouldn't believe Me if I told You, but Me and Theodore built a time machine

## Mary Hamilton

from *NOÖ Journal*

Before the wood rotted. Before the elms suffocated and starved. Before the looters stole our hubcaps and copper wire and cabinet doors and doorknobs and canned food and toilet seats. Before the sky got low and touched the ground and the neighborhood got small and fragile and the storms came through and tore trees apart and threw them onto houses and garages and split cars in half and pulled away the swamp grass and cat-tails and roof shingles, and rope swings, we spent our days in play.

We acted out cops and robbers in the neighbor's yard. Our neighbor was this old woman with hands like Saran Wrap encased electric wires and smashed grapes. She sat on her back porch swing and watched us run in zigzags between the cottonwood trees and lawn furniture. And when the cottonwood bloomed all the fuzz got in our hair and eyes and covered the screens on windows and doors. The cotton was like a million dead dandelions had been turned into wishes and we ran through it like Mounties through a blizzard. And when it got hot, the cotton stuck to our skin and sweat and made red rashes, it made us burn. On these, the hottest days, the old woman neighbor poured us full glasses of sour lemonade. The kind that is almost as clear as water until you put the big chunks of lemon in the glass and spoon in plenty of sugar when you drink it. Even so, our lips puckered and our eyes closed and we tried very hard to smile and say "Thank you."

He played cop and I played robber and he shot me dead

nine times out of ten. When it was my turn to die, I would stumble around the entire yard, my hands clutching my chest. I'd hobble left, I'd hobble right. I'd settle into a wicker chair and then I'd gasp and rise again all suddenlike. I'd stumble some more, bumping into trees and a bird bath, slumping over the porch railing and exhaling a final, willowing, singing, gagging breath. But that tenth time, when I would be the one to make the fatal shot, he would just drop to the ground, splayed out like some kind of fallen bird and the old woman neighbor would clap the soft pads of her hands together and cheer.

Sometimes I would have dreams about the games we'd play. In the dreams, he cheated. He stole my lemonade and stepped on my gun and I woke up very angry. Sometimes he would show up at the front door of our house the next morning, all decked out in his fringed white vest with sheriff badge and big white hat and matching white cowboy boots with plastic spurs, having walked four blocks in the complete outfit, and I would stand behind my mother while she told him I wasn't feeling well and I saw him look around her hip to see me standing there, my gun aimed at the curious wrinkle that had formed like a bull's eye between his eyes.

It is true, that sometimes after playing cops and robbers, the old woman neighbor would invite us in to wash the cotton off our hands and faces and necks and arms and it is also true that I once took a tiny little seashell from a dish on the back of the toilet. It is certainly true that he made me return the shell to the old woman neighbor. He held my elbow like he was a real cop and I was a real robber while we stood on her front stoop and my head hung low and the old woman neighbor took the seashell and put it in her apron pocket and went back inside her house and closed the screen door, and all the bits of cotton caught in the mesh of the screen shivered in the wind that got pulled up and turned around and told us a branch-breaking, flood-making, basement-hiding kind of storm was coming our way.

I am a bullet and I am very fast. I make a sound. I make a spark. I cut through metal, air, I burn fabric, I shred skin, I splinter bone, I settle into the muscle that makes the heart. Not quite inside, but close enough to do serious harm. Close enough to slow the pumping of blood. Not enough damage to make a spill of red, but just enough to create a kind of plug to the natural order of things. Just close enough to make everything stop. An involuntary and violent action that is just enough to make it all my fault.

# Games Are Not About Monsters

## Christine Hartzler

from *Fiction Writers Review*

## 1. Video games aren't about monsters, even when they are.

In a role-play game, or RPG, gameplay consists largely of traveling and fighting battles. Traveling, like the "free and easy wandering" of the *Chang tzu*, isn't as easy as one might think—surviving monster attacks is usually the order of the day. Even so, traveling is one of my favorite things about RPGs because an RPG is a lengthy journey in a (hopefully) immersive world. My favorite game, *Shadow of the Colossus,* is difficult to place in a single game genre, but it's more RPG than anything else. You wander an expansive landscape, soaking up the aesthetic splendor, gathering information, and eventually, finding and fighting colossal monsters. Monster-killing is central to the game, and yet this game is no more about monster-killing than gardening is about slaughtering aphids or *Ender's Game* is about killing Buggers.

What sets *Shadow of the Colossus* apart from other RPGs is its successful elevation of monster-killing to near-spiritual levels. Monster-killing becomes, like Shiva's austerities in the mountain cave, complex and meaningful. Most games require frequent monster fights as you travel, which creates a constant low level of anxiety. *Shadow of the Colossus* compresses this anxiety into 16 terrifying and epic boss battles. All monster-killing is inextricably linked to a game's quest, which gives that violence a feeling of greater purpose. A quest is a concept to which we, almost because of the archaic resonance of the word alone, attribute the capacity for meaning. So the tasks that make up a quest, such as monster-killing as you travel, can start to share in that aura of significance as you play. This is powerful in *Shadow of the Colossus* but also present in games jam-packed with minor monsters.

I've probably killed thousands of beasts. I'll spend 100 hours completing a game primarily consisting of monster fights. I'll do this, and if a game is good, I'm as clean as a whistle at the end, not drenched in psychic gore or remorse. Monster-killing is a practical reality of most games; it's best not to worry about or relish it too much. With monster-killing, as with practicing yoga postures, it helps to remember what it's all for. It's part of a quest for something meaningful, but monster-killing also relates to what, in RPGs, is often the main in-game activity: developing your character. Typically, higher levels of important characteristics, skills, and so forth will accrue to your character as you complete battles. Your character (you) becomes a more multi-faceted, capable, and efficient being. Let's call this self-cultivation via monster-killing. In my experience, games that lack self-cultivation feel a bit one-dimensional; I recently played *Ms. Pac-Man* (the super-speed kind, of course) and felt once again the frustration of playing a character that does not evolve.

So, monster-killing has to mean more than survival and more than self-cultivation and more than entertainment. For a game story to have legs, monsters must be able to be seen as signifying something, and killing them must also signify something. Monster-killing need not be as deeply transformative as a hypersigil; it's more simple than that. The organizing moral principles of a game world often boil down to something desperately obvious: black-and-white, good and evil. This isn't bad in itself because a good game, like a good book, then takes the player into a more familiar ambiguity. Good and bad become less easily separated and less relevant, in fact, the longer you travel. It's sad when a game uses ambiguity itself to create interest, shifting the ground beneath our feet so frequently that we become bored and don't even care when the true enemy is revealed to be our best friend. The trick is to create, in the gamer, a commitment to a point of view, whatever its morality—dramatic plot twists are never quite as devastating as they're meant to be (unless the gamer or reader just hasn't paid attention, which I admit can happen—my failure to anticipate the ending of *Ender's Game* is a good example). No, I'd go for creating a creeping sense of doom, a teetering feeling, a worry— that's how to get people. Never is this more elegantly done than in *Shadow of the Colossus*. The narrative is only ever suggested, but the gamer is completely committed to the events, even as your understanding of what is really going on gradually shifts and grows.

## 2. Choices.

In *Shadow of the Colossus*, you play a man alone in the Cursed Lands. Only a hint of context is given, no explanation for his arrival there with a dead woman in his arms. The man is essentially nameless, since we don't learn it until the end. There are decrepit buildings throughout the Cursed Lands, clearly built by people now absent. The present occupants of the area are mostly lizards, turtles, fish, birds, and 16 Colossi, monsters that remain dormant until the man tracks them down and starts a fight. Each fight is absurd, terrifying in scale, a pesky fly of a man against a lumbering animated tower or a giant armored horse, until a glowing glyph is located somewhere on the Colossus and a sword thrust into it. Ribbons of black stream out of the monster and into the man after each kill.

They seem to replace the light in the man, and his skin takes on ever-darkening tattoos that suggest, as they do on the Colossi, that something's *in there*. What does all this mean?

No official explanation has been made, but here's one idea: he doesn't realize it at first, but he doesn't hesitate once he does realize—he's sacrificing himself to bring his girl back to life. He's trading his soul bit by bit for monster souls. The monster souls are actually smaller pieces of one larger entity, which, fully reunited in the man's body at the end, ousts his soul.

So perhaps *Shadow of the Colossus* is, ultimately, a game about becoming a monster and setting evil free. All along, the man has been taking orders from a voice that emanates from a god-mouth in the roof of a crumbling temple filled with 16 Colossus idols. It could be humiliating to be such a toady, to be used so, but if it is, then we're all a little pathetic, a bit tragic for our refusal to admit that we always serve something. In the end, the man appears to have agreed to trade his soul for his girl's. She opens her eyes as he is finally subsumed. The interesting question is, *At what point did the man agree to the trade? Did he just think all he had to do was take down a few monsters and he'd get his girl back? Did he know that he was reconstituting a force that would destroy him?* You never get the sense that the man is gleeful or macho or even confident as he battles the Colossi; this is no *God of War*. If he isn't informed about the particulars of his task, at the very least I think his sobriety suggests that he knows something serious is at hand.

Overall, *Shadow of the Colossus* is a remarkably neutral game, and I enjoy the freedom to speculate about the story and the man's state of mind. In *Cooling Time: An American Poetry Vigil,* C.D. Wright calls poetry a way of respecting the white space. That's exactly how I love poetry and how I love *Shadow of the Colossus*. I feel invited to participate in forming the meaning of this game. The game has room for my experience of it. Perhaps this is why the prospect of a film version of *Shadow of the Colossus* terrifies me. I dread being told with such emphatic finality what the game is "really" about. There is another writer who has already said what I mean here: in *Weight,* Jeanette

Winterson calls herself a writer "who believes in the power of story telling for its mythic and not its explanatory qualities." The white space is where things are not explained and the reader or gamer is allowed in.

Honestly, most games do a poor job of respecting the white space. RPGs often give you either a distinctly "good" or "evil" character to play. In some RPGs, however, such as *Oblivion: The Elder Scrolls* and *Fable 2*, you can cultivate yourself in either direction. Americans, it turns out, prefer to play good characters. I toyed with murder in both games and had no stomach for it. (I guess that makes me an exemplary American.) That killing in video games can become objectionable could be either a feature of the high realism of many of today's games or the possibility that we are now living in some kind of meta world, where everything is cleaner and less tangible than ever before and mostly originates in our minds. This is like living in a story. Today's tenet is that killing is bad even in games. This is because we live in our heads so much, everything we do and value sometimes seems more abstract than ever before. We do not live in a real world anymore and war is too real for our refined palates. Our moral context therefore lets us object to play killing. At least, this is one way of seeing it. I find it interesting that at some points in time, it appears that a taste or talent for killing did not automatically disqualify a person from society. Knights did the dirty work to protect the more refined aspects of civilization, as embodied by the Ladies. This is the story, anyway. But Knights weren't considered bad if they had to kill a beast or a beastly person—the Knights' work was in service of the good and there was no moral quandary. But I think these stories live on and grab us today not because of their historical or literary merits but because we are fascinated by permitted murdering. Playing video games, then, becomes an exorcism of sorts—or a Tantric practice of excess meant to cure the obsession.

## 3. Hunting and not hunting.

Monster-killing is different, though. It's funny how you can know yourself to be mostly, if not just ethnically, a pacifist—being raised by Mennonite-raised parents—and you then find yourself *hunting*. It's digital hunting, but hunting nonetheless. There isn't any blood, but there are grunts and sighs and other intriguing sound effects (praises to the sound engineers) as the beasts give up the ghosts and whatever treasure they carry. I'd argue that the realism of many games is what makes it so easy for observing non-gamers to connect real-world violence with game-violence and skip right over the critical thinking part. Was this a problem in the era of *Jungle Pit* and *Space Invaders?* No, I don't recall anyone suggesting I not shoot at the alien-piloted ships encroaching on my personal space. (Now that was true exigency! That was do-or-die.) But just because I have to fight several vicious floating fish, mutated dinosaurs, and some Berserkers as I cross a desert in *Final Fantasy 12* doesn't mean I'm a killer. Someone once asked me, "Don't you feel bad killing all those beautiful creatures?" It's my pleasure to inform you that not only do I not feel bad, I enjoy it. I'm getting paid and collecting mad loot.

Yet, monster killing isn't what any game or story is about. For me, *Halo 3* is not so much about hacking through an endless onslaught of aliens and Flood; it's almost entirely about the novelty, fun, and challenge of playing with a partner (I find the enemies' comments hilarious, too—something about their tone). *Shadow of the Colossus* is not so much about finding and fighting large beasts. While I did spend most of the game feeling terrified, I've got some sweet memories, too. The Cursed Lands are vast and still. A small breeze blows. Sunlight is dappled under the trees, brilliant over the oceans, and it turns the crumbling stone shrines and plazas a soft platinum. A melancholy music plays during battles; otherwise, it's mostly environmental sounds: water, wind, Agro's hooves on the ground. I can hear these now. But what stays with me the most is the image of the woman's body lying in the temple, diffusing the sun with her white dress, the doves shifting around her, the man and his horse simply watching. A few feet from an aisle of menacing Colossus idols, the tender scene becomes sublime. Without the weight of words, it speaks of the frailty of the living, the uncertainty of our tasks, and the ache of love. It is mythic. It moves me.

## 4. The Path and the Glimpse.

But even in a gorgeous world, monsters are not just a distraction from these emotional treats. They are not just for killing either. Monsters could be the Path itself, the path to the end of suffering, a path worth walking on, that gives sense of direction and purpose to life. A holy man tries to walk toward God, away from the world. Other holy men try to help others find the path. Sometimes I wonder if I think by completing tasks I'll be enlightened. Sometimes I look at the end of my various efforts for a face shining behind the veil and I wonder if I'm conflating worship and task-completion. I'm knocking and knocking at the door, completing side-quests, collecting Nirnroots, rolling a katamari out of fireflies... Who waits on the other side of these doors? Does he even want what I am bringing to him? Is it even good?

    I know a physicist who would chuckle at my dilemma. This man goes from A to B. Granted, his B is fusion energy, a true "creative sort" kind of vision, and the path between his A and B is far from dull. The important thing for him is to get there. Going from A to B—having a clear question and methodically answering it—in the rest of life oftentimes is dull. There is no room for wondering or wandering and asking what about C? When I think about what it is that makes playing RPGs interesting to me, it's not the A to B. That, in fact, is what makes them *boring*. There are no real stakes involved. If there were real stakes, a real possibility of closing an *Oblivion gate* and preserving humanity to flail poignantly another day, I might value basic A-to-B a bit more. I might reject my own formulation of monster-fighting as self-cultivation and call it critical training. But I prefer to live and play in worlds where self-cultivation, the cultivation of life, and the search for something divine are respected options. Consider: in our world, gardeners are usually respected and admired. They may cultivate the most arcane or common of life forms. They may grow things in apparent disarray or in the strictest regiments. In truth, they spend more time spreading silica to lacerate slugs' soft bodies, unleashing plagues of ladybugs upon the aphids, and drowning Japanese beetles in jars of soapy water than anyone ever knows. But no one would diminish gardeners' work as mere beetle-killing.

Ask why not and someone might say, "Because gardens are beautiful." Ah, beauty. The ultimate excuse and the ultimate end goal. The trump card. Beauty is God. Sometimes people will use God as a trump card, but that's just too obvious. God is unknowable. God is barely perceivable. Beauty is often attributed to God. What people who invoke either are really trying to do, I suspect, is indicate that something beyond us has been Glimpsed.

Can monster-killing cause a Glimpse? Perhaps. The figure of the Death-seeker is a warrior who does his warrior duty, but more than anything hopes to be killed himself one day, never is, battles on, and inadvertently becomes a better warrior, better than everyone else, his skills ascend beyond known levels, and to those who worship that sort of skill he gives the Glimpse. They call his killing beautiful, they call it God-given. For him, monster-killing was to be his path out of here, but like some kind of bitter Bodhisattva, his field of compassion is the field of blood and blade. The Death-seeker is like Arjuna. He does not want to fight, but God says Fighting is Your Duty, it is your duty to fight because that action keeps the world in balance. The hero Beowulf also has a duty to fight. The poem *Beowulf* is not about battling horrendous monsters—it's about keeping the world going, about following a code of behavior upon which life depends and derives its structure, its meaning, and its perpetuity. Without a hero to keep monsters away from the good people, all would be chaos and death. Power protects the people, and, as in Seamus Heaney's translation of *Beowulf,* "Behavior that's admired/is the path to power among people everywhere."

## 5. The qualities of a monster.

Which brings me to *Ender's Game,* by Orson Scott Card, and the question of what a monster really *is.* Like the monsters of *Beowulf,* the Buggers are known to be remorseless, inhuman outsiders with whom humans cannot communicate. When you can't communicate with something, the obvious course is to fight it, right? So humans and Buggers fight. The book is the story of Ender, a super-sensitive, super-intelligent child trained from age six to lead Earth's armies against the Buggers. Throughout the entire book, Ender is kept busy trying to survive against a wide range of more immediate threats to his survival—his violent brother, his unforgiving training program, his loneliness and isolation, his terror about becoming a monster himself. Always a new enemy for poor Ender. He is kept so busy trying keep his head on straight that he never has a minute to question the assumption driving everything—that the Buggers are monsters—and the first time I read the book I was so tangled in Ender's daily life that the story's denouement practically gutted me. To learn that the child-genius battle commander Ender has been tricked into wiping out the Bugger race, and to witness his grief and remorse as he learns the truth about the Buggers—it was just too much. Turns out the Buggers were, more or less, everything a monster should be—hideous, aggressive, and incomprehensible—except an actual threat to humanity. From the beginning, Ender's reward for protecting humanity from the Buggers would be freedom from terror, as well as honor and glory, but in the end, in return for killing the Buggers, Ender is not free and is not honored. Ender is used, as the man in *Shadow of the Colossus* is, by a powerful and detail-withholding force.

Withholding details—in other words, failing to communicate well—is a sign of a monster. Those who use the child Ender are monstrous in their treatment of him, whatever their motivation. The Dormin, as the disembodied power in *Shadow of the Colossus* calls itself, speaks cryptically in a strange language; even without form, a more disturbing monster I've seldom encountered. I wish game designers would remember that giving monsters casual speech sort of neuters them. A monster is not for chitchat. A boss monster bloviating on its plans to kill you is comedic, not scary. Better to make the bosses unforthcoming, otherworldly, and alien. Especially since so many games promote the value of self-cultivation. In the game, your goal is to cultivate yourself into the ultimate of what you are (human, elf, whatever), the fullest expression of your potential, and why shouldn't this include communication skills? Sometimes it does: the Speechcraft skill in *Oblivion* perfectly fills this need. The more pleasantly and effectively you can communicate with townspeople, the higher your Speechcraft level. Among the many typical skills your character must develop, including weapon and armor skills, fighting skills, strength, endurance, magic, etc., Speechcraft is what truly separates you from thugs and monsters.

Self-cultivation is the process of becoming good at things. It is also the process of becoming "good" in the game's moral universe. All of us like being good, or at least knowing how to be bad. But let's put that aside. There are some terribly beautiful games out there, and they really aren't about good and bad, self-cultivation, or monster-killing. They offer a way to transcend necessity and ambition: deep appreciation, which is deep observation, a meditative state. A game can be played like this—*Shadow of the Colossus* allows it, but few others do, in my experience. I admit I indulge myself in this way of playing. I look for it. A game so perfectly rendered and self-contained, that requires so little compromise from my imagination—maybe it's just me, but just being *in* this kind of game world is itself the desired outcome. It's the good result, as the surgeons say. It's the end of yoga practice, as the yogis say, when you don't have to practice anymore because you have achieved enlightenment and now you can just lounge in the temple garden and leave the monster-killing to the noobs.

## 6. Postscript.

That, in part, is what monsters are for. Of course, monsters mostly just want to kill you. So there's great risk. But isn't there always? With great risk we are born. With great risk we love. With great risk we read books, listen to music, and play video games. It would seem that we cannot help but run around naked everywhere with our hearts hanging out. And then there are those monsters we fling ourselves against over and over until we get better, know more, can put our legs behind our head, or die. We need game monsters, since sometimes life's monsters are just too arbitrary, too, well, monstrous; it matters to be able to accomplish something, even if only in a game. That could be why we invent our gods, couldn't it? So we can suffer a little less.

# How I Became a Ghost

## Leslie Harrison

from *Memorious*

It was all about objects, their objections
expressed through a certain solidity.

My house for example still moves
through me, moves me.
When I tried to reverse the process
I kept dropping things, kept finding myself
in the basement.

Windows became more than
usually problematic.
I wanted to break them
which didn't work, though for awhile

I had more success with the lake.

The phone worked for a long time
though when I answered
often nobody was there.

Bats crashed into me at night,
but then didn't anymore.

The rings vanished from my hand,
the pond.

I stopped feeling the wind.

One day the closets were empty.

Another day the mirrors were.

# John Henry's Tracks

## Matthew Glenwood

from *DIAGRAM*

> *"John Henry was a mighty man,*
> *Born with a ten-pound hammer in his hand."*
> —*"John Henry"**

Some dirt-diggers in the Holy Land claimed to have found the bones of Jesus and his family. Jesus' son, too. We'll probably never know for sure if those were the holy bones or not. That kind of news could prove ungentle to dreamers. Like finding the remains of Amelia Earhart under her front porch steps, or the skeleton of a baby bird beneath its nest. We would hope for a wider arc to the hero's journey than bones at the starting point. It could be called bad news if Jesus, the alleged foreman of Heaven, left bones behind. News that says *nobody's going very far.*

But it wouldn't be the whole truth. There is somewhere to go.

We can go sell our plasma for fifty American dollars a week.

The journey to the Biolife Plasma Center in Marquette, Michigan came easy for me. I just had to follow an abandoned train track for a few blocks. The track met the edge of the woods along the shore of Lake Superior; rabbit, chipmunk and deer crisscrossed it as beasties would any ready made trail, for there were no tracks left on that line. The rattle of my mountain bike startled ducks from the shallow waters of the ditch alongside. In winter, the flat, open space doubled as a cross country ski trail. You might say everything ran on that track except for rails.

The region, too poor to have a reason to run its trains, pulled up many of its train tracks, and commerce that way moved at the speed of wild grass. The poverty of the Upper

Peninsula of Michigan is probably why the plasma company came to the Upper Peninsula of Michigan. That and the local college students, the reliably poor. As any farmer with a bad back could tell you, the easiest of tall crops to harvest is one that stoops to meet the hand of the harvester.

At the plasma center, technicians tap into the natural resource of your veins. The process takes, at most, a couple hours, and you're paid for it. It's easy money, and couldn't come much easier; all you have to do is exist. The plasma company calls itself a "donation center" but really it is a selling center. Poor people coming to sell the one possession they unquestionably own: the materials of their being. Take away those materials and the world would have no more poor.

Our folk songs say that John Henry could drive steel harder and faster than any man. The job of a steel driver was to pound holes in rock by hammering a long metal drill held and rotated by another man known as a *shaker*. Dynamite was then dropped into those holes—tunnels blasted into mountain stone. Steel driving was done for the mean benefit of the train companies laying track across the nation. In other versions of the song, steel driving was intermixed with pounding spike into the rail lines.

One day a salesman brought a new steam-driven drill to the line. John Henry, fearing for his job and for the jobs of his fellow rail workers, challenged the machine to a contest. John Henry declared to his captain:

> *Lord, a man aint nothin' but a man*
> *But before I let that steam-drill beat me down*
> *I'm gonna die with a hammer in my hand*

John Henry won. But after beating the machine, he suffered a heart attack and died. That's to say, he could do no more work for the train company.

Like Jesus, no one can prove the John Henry of legend. Some stories say he was an ex-slave working for the Chesapeake and Ohio Railway during the Reconstruction days of the South, following the Civil War. People disagree on where, and if, the events of the song took place. One man thinks the contest of hammers happened in Talcott, West Virginia. But everybody knows that you've got to bite the coins that come out of Talcott.

About twenty years ago, a man in my hometown got caught in one of the big machines of the mining company. A rock crusher, if I remember right. He was the father of a classmate. I ought to have attended the funeral, but didn't. In those high school days I was discovering the books of the American Transcendentalists: Whitman, Emerson, Thoreau. "Transcendentalism" was a big word to me at the time. The idea of it is that you can ride your porch swing to the truth of all flowers. The notion sounds sound to me, still. But, being young, I felt as if I had inherited a mansion up in the blue air; as if everything wrong were, with an idea, suddenly right.

The daughter of the killed miner, my classmate, needed some consoling, but I was too shy, too awkward at social graces, to be one of the people to give it. I had no consoling to give. Her father was a good man of Finnish descent; he left behind a large family. The family had a new lesson to learn about the worst of all possible outcomes. As for me, I had my books which said spirit dances with matter.

Much of my life has passed since those books. Those Yankee writers of old are truer to me now than when I was young, and it's likely that I need them more now. But an idea isn't much true unless we are willing to wear its dirt. A frog of ugly sits at the center of true, and his appetite is Void.

Rather than the gift of a mansion in the sky, transcendence now seems to me a lifetime of lonely carpentry. Carpentry on a house nobody can see. And that house won't shelter from the rain, but make us wetter. Those who ply this trade might not finish even the front steps before the cold evening comes on, before the closing whistle blows. Maybe no one completes the house called *Idealism*—built, as it is, on the foundation that is the suffering of the world. The hammer is usually abandoned with much work left to do; it hums only a little while with the vibrations of the last nail driven, until stillness takes it.

Had the good miner's death happened today, I would've gone to the funeral. The fact about our portion of transcendence is that some of us get flattened in rock crushers. The fact is that there is blood on the machine.

And in the machine.

Sometimes the crashing waves of Lake Superior, powered by strong winds, sounded like a train through my apartment window. But, in the city of Marquette, the only real locomotion taking place was the centrifugal force of the Autoapheresis-C machine (made by the Baxter Corporation) separating plasma from blood. The word "apheresis" is Greek for "take away".

In an introduction to the work song *Take this Hammer*, folk singer Leadbelly explains the shouts of *hah!* that pepper the verses, "Every time the men say 'hah!' the hammer falls."

> *Take this hammer*
> *Hah*
> *And carry it to the captain*
> *Hah!*
> *Take this hammer*
> *Hah!*
> *And carry it to the captain*
> *Hah!*
> *You tell him I'm gone*
> *Hah!*
> *You tell him I'm gone*

Gone to donate plasma. This is how it works. You are made comfortable on a long, curved couch of smooth leather—a kind of psychiatrist's couch where nobody cares about your mind.

*Hah!*

At your side is the machine, the Autoapheresis-C. It looks harmless enough, a white box of plastic on wheels with dangling tubing. It is sanitary as a saint's glove.

*Hah!*

A friendly worker, clad in hospital scrubs, sterilizes your arm with a cool swab and slides a needle in your vein. You are connected to the Autoapheresis-C.

*Hah!*

First the collection phase. Your blood, sucked up a tube to a little spinning chamber of clear plastic, slips out of you with the speed of a snake on the run, staining the tube's transparency as it goes. Some of your inside is now outside.

*Hah!*

A chemical thinner is added to keep the blood from clotting. The spinning separates the plasma from your blood, as substances of differing densities are wont to do in a centrifuge.

*Hah!*

The plasma drips into the collection bag. The plasma is yellow, like foggy urine (for women taking the birth control pill, it's a pale green, like swamp water). You watch your plasma gather in the bag, a few drips at a time.

*Hah!*

Second, the return phase. Your red blood cells are returned to you through the same tube in which they were collected. Some of the outside is now your inside. Steps one and two are repeated.

*Hah!*

It's like that. Throughout the donation process, the Autoapheresis-C communicates by beeping. It tells the technicians when there are problems, such as low vein pressure.

The donation center is riddled with these beeping sounds, like the metallic-bright chirping of birds on a machine planet. Once enough plasma been harvested, the machine beeps to signify the end of the donation process—the brassy, four-note heralding of a king—*da-da-da-DAH!*— a worker comes with a heat gun and cauterizes the collection bag severed and sealed.

The Autoapheresis-C then pumps a saline solution into your bloodstream to aid in rehydration.

When this is done, the needle is pulled from your arm. You are no longer connected to the Autoaphoresis-C. Consider yourself siphoned. Your donated bag of plasma is labeled, put on a tray with other bags, turned to ice in a freezer.

Once or twice a week, the plasma-ice cargo is loaded in volume onto a truck and delivered to medical companies. Businesses whose executives are themselves likely too wealthy to need to donate plasma.

*Hah!*

After donating, I returned home on the same train track I arrived by, a tight gauze wrap over the new hole in my arm, and new American dollars in my wallet.

> *If he asks you*
> *Hah!*
> *Was I running*
> *Hah!*
> *If he asks you*
> *Hah!*
> *Was I running*
> *Hah!*
> *You tell him I was flying*
> *Hah!*
> *You tell him I was flying!*
> *—Leadbelly, "Take This Hammer"*

A donor doesn't have much to do while the Autoapheresis-C frets at its machinations, but there is one task to perform. The donor is asked to pay attention to a strip of traffic lights on the side of the Autoapheresis-C; it tells how well the collection phase is going, how fast the blood is flowing.

Red means *not well.*

Yellow means *could be better.*

Green means *all is well.*

The donor is asked to make a fist and pump it if the colors fall from green to yellow or red. This increases blood flow.

It can't be a surprise, that in this society we are informed by lights when to stop and go.

According to a reporter on National Public Radio, long into the rebuilding of New Orleans after the devastation of Hurricane Katrina in 2005, even the simple act of driving a car was fraught with risk. Without working stoplights, four-way stops were a matter of guessing three other drivers' minds. But maybe this is true not just for a flood-ruined city. Maybe there are no traffic lights blinking anywhere with the kind certainty good citizens would like. Maybe the hesitance of a New Orleans driver at a four-way stop shows how it always is for the poor, who are asked to pledge allegiance to a gamble.

When surge water from Hurricane Katrina overloaded the levees of New Orleans, it took the lives of the excluded. People with nothing having it taken away. During those early crisis days, the nation with its flag flying on the moon couldn't deliver a bottle of water to a woman standing on her rooftop.

Where was government? The corpses of the poor spiraled down the flood streets, while those with the American dollars to pay for their escape told their survivor stories from neighboring states. The plumb-line division between the rich and poor—as divided as dry is from wet—tells what kind of country America has become, is becoming.

Two countries.

*John Henry's liddle mother*
*Was all dressed in red,*
*She jumped in bed, covered up her head,*
*Said I didn't know my boy was dead,*
*Said I didn't know my boy was dead.*
—*"John Henry"*

This is not to say that the poor are without means of providing for themselves. At the plasma center in Marquette, a donor is allowed to give plasma twice a week. The first time you donate, you get twenty American dollars. But if you come back within two days (it can't be the next day, the body needs time to generate more plasma), you get thirty. Maybe the poor can't "pull themselves up by their bootstraps" as the phrase goes—cheap bootstraps break—but they can bleed their boots for American money.

Corporate executives now earn four-hundred and fifty times what the average worker earns. Translated to plasma money: whereas the average plasma donor can earn up to $50 for two donations a week, a C.E.O. would be right to expect $22,500 for their two days at the plasma center, though their plasma drips the same.

I would as soon trust a corporate-driven democracy to care for the needs of its poor as I would trust in the pity of venom. Considering the fever of the profit motive in our nation, and seeing how slow the government was to react in New Orleans, the surest way to save that city would have been to contract-out the first responders—allow companies to charge poor people for their rescue. This would be done, no doubt, on credit—a kind of indentured servitude for being allowed to live. Profit-seeking sometimes moves with a speed kin enough to justice. But maybe it's not a government's task to come between the poor and their right to die unaided.

*Government will be our rock,* is the promise of all the

regulation we accept into our lives, but at the time it is needed most, government occasionally gets a headache and blurred vision, has to go lie down. It might need a few days to get itself together. Fail to pay your income tax and you will feel the full focus of government, in the shine of badge and the shine of gun, as if you were the most important person within its borders; begin to drown, on the streets of your hometown, and government reaches at you with ghost hands in the tardy dark, and you are one among too many.

This offends the idea of sound contract. Citizens are not allowed to fail their government, but they are allowed to be failed by it. That's a devil's deal. But poverty itself, best defined as a lack of options, is a devil's deal. John Henry, as an ex-slave, was free not to work on the railroad line if he chose not to, but he couldn't choose not to, because he was directed by the overseer of having no other choice. Call it freedom, if you like. That brand of freedom is spit on a handshake without the handshake.

Where is government? Not in stormy New Orleans. Over fifteen-hundred lives lost to the flood. Government may be somewhere, but not in stormy New Orleans. In stormy New Orleans, government was gone, gone, gone.

> *They took John Henry to the White House,*
> *And buried him in the san',*
> *And every locomotive come roarin' by,*
> *Says there lays that steel drivin' man,*
> *Says there lays that steel drivin' man.*
> *—"John Henry"*

I once scheduled a plasma donation too early in the morning. My heart rate was beneath the company's minimum requirement. I was feeling peaceful at the time; one of those unshakable good moods. The girl in charge of my screening said she would give me a chance to test again after I had a few minutes to wake up. This was encouraging news. While waiting, I walked to the restroom and did jumping jacks, push-ups. I imagined chaotic, violent scenes, adventure scenarios requiring fight-or-flight responses. I made my mind a nightmare, and this worked swimmingly. My heart rate rose and I was allowed to donate that day.

I raised my heart rate on behalf of the machine, the Autoapheresis-C, but John Henry's heart rate rose against his machine, the steam-drill. I let a needle pierce me for American dollars, which required my reclining on a leather couch; he drove a kind of needle into rock for principle, which required his death by exhaustion.

I readily admit that I lost my contest with the Autoapheresis-C, because I never contested it.

For us moderns, the contest to keep up with the machines is a daily event. It could be said that technology has raised our heart rates by allowing us weaker hearts; we now do less work but we are less at rest. Machines have made us more immobile in our busyness. Sitting in one place has become our hard day's work, not because the labor is difficult, but because it is hard to give up the freedoms of the body, the joy of movement for which our muscles and skeletons were built. We walk faster than we used to, but not as far. We do many things at one time, we are more specialized, but we are barely defined; the lines that outline us flicker unclear.

In the early days of the steam-driven locomotive, trains moved at around twenty-five miles-per-hour. Slow enough to stop along their routes for fishermen, and berry pickers, and hunters, to exit into the wild and follow their hearts' pleasure into ambling afternoons. It made no matter where they got off the train, they could always hop back on when it made its return trip.

In our time—as bullet trains scream speeds of over three-hundred and fifty miles per hour—the train doesn't stop for ripe berries.

Are we better people for having a faster train? The sheen of technology tells us so. We are better people if moving faster is better. But the life choices within the minds of passengers throughout time always move at the same rate, that is, at the speed of timeless. A caveman, the first of gentlemen, might have moved slower (the pace of slouching is nothing to brag about, for sure) but if his choices were truer, he may have outpaced the astronauts. It might be that his integrity broke the sound barrier, even as his slogging feet begrudged the bog. He traveled as far as a man could with the least technology. He walked so far he became us. And the easier we make our travel, the less we hear in his walking blues something of our own.

Now it's all new. The new trains are made to hover upon a magnetic field. At speed, they don't even touch the ground that they cross. If John Henry were to swing a metallic hammer on a magnetized track, he'd only swing it once.

Some say the year in which John Henry beat the steam-drill was 1872. There wouldn't be much point in John Henry challenging a drill to a contest now. Steam-drills have made way for industrial lasers. To compete in our day, John Henry would have to swing hammer faster than a ray of light could burn, which, currently, is approximately one hundred feet of rock an hour. Against such a machine there is no competing. Whereas it once took the strongest man around to fight against the machine, in our time only a man weak in his reasoning thinks it can be fought. This is progress.

> *The steam drill started at half past six,*
> *John Henry started the same time.*
> *John Henry struck bottom at half past eight,*
> *And the steam drill didn't bottom till nine,*
> *Oh, the steam drill didn't bottom till nine.*
> *—"John Henry"*

A mild controversy slipped into the media about an internet search engine's satellite images of New Orleans after Hurricane Katrina, or the lack thereof. The images continued to show a New Orleans before the devastation occurred. Some people alleged that not to show New Orleans in all its ruin was an attempt to hide the truth.

The satellite images of the category three hurricane as it crossed to the American coastline are stunning. With technology, we now have the power to watch an entire city drown.

What a satellite sees, I can't say, though many are the images which tell what it records. This star's-eye view is no doubt an upper-rung moment in our species' long ladder climb out of monkey. So very high, our machines. But there remains the question of what we do with the view.

Recently, an observatory was nearly destroyed in a California wildfire. We humans have a telescope that sees back into Time and shows us the fiery beginning of the Universe, but that great magnifier overshoots and overlooks the flames threatening—in present time—at its own observatory door, and so is lacking in the bi-focal. The weakest lens would have shown the encroaching fire clearer than one so very good. What is the Big Bang to me while my toes are roasting? As if simply to see is everything.

It means something, that John Henry named his hammer Lucy. His labor, his tools, were close enough to his heart to remain in his hand.

> *John Henry's woman, Lucy—*
> *Dress she wore was blue;*
> *Eyes like stars an' teeth lak-a marble stone,*
> *An' John Henry named his hammah "Lucy" too,—*
> *Lawd,—Lawd—*
> *John Henry named his hammah "Lucy" too.*
> *—"John Henry"*

I wonder if the makers of satellites name them "Lucy." It wouldn't mean much for me to name a satellite "Lucy," as my hands have never touched one. But a satellite knows me, if it wishes. I don't think I could see a satellite in orbit as well as it could show me my own face. If I happen to notice a satellite passing in the night sky, it might be technology, it might be a shooting star, it might be a messenger of the gods of old. No matter what that object in the sky is, it's the same as a train in the distance to me—one I am late in catching.

The tools we use today can go adrift in our hands. They don't always extend us, as a hammer does. They sometimes disappear from us.

Mississippi John Hurt said that John Henry could drive spike faster than any man because he swung two hammers, one for each hand. But John Henry's hammers are up there—high—spinning in near-zero gravity; the question is, who down here has the strength to grab them back?

> John Henry went to the tunnel
> And they put him in lead to drive,
> The rock was so tall and John Henry so small
> That he laid down his hammah and he cried,
> That he laid down his hammah and he cried.
> — "John Henry"

Sometimes during donation the Autoapheresis-C would make a peculiar beep, an alarm, and the machine came to a halt. A worker would come to my station, press a button, and reassure me that it was "just an air bubble" that had found its way into my extracted blood. The Autoapheresis-C would then destroy the bubble and return to its churn-work on my blood. If the machine didn't catch it—if an air bubble was put back into my bloodstream, and reached my heart—I could be donating all my plasma, in one sitting, to the undertaker. This "just an air bubble" popped up as much as three times in a single visit. At such moments, my life depended upon the Autoapheresis-C not making an error.

Sure the risk was small. But so was my reason for being there. Had I died, it would have been for nothing.

Not for nothing, Biolife Plasma Services would have you believe. On their radio advertisement, the plasma company calls for heroes on a regular basis. *Help save a life today*, they say. And it's true. Without a doubt, donating plasma is for the greater good. It saves lives. Plasma can't be duplicated in a laboratory. When plasma is needed, nothing but plasma will do.

And yet Biolife is a business that requires the existence of poverty in order to turn a profit. It trades in the bodies of the poor to achieve its earnings. If you doubt this, ask yourself why there are no plasma donation centers located on gated streets with hilltop mansions.

In the defense of the buying and selling of vital body fluids, compensating donors would be unnecessary if enough people donated out of the kindness of their hearts. The fault, then, is not in the greed of the needle, but in the stinginess of the vein. Outright kindness, however, rarely marries well with profit.

It is true, without the incentive of American dollars, I would not have donated plasma nearly so often, maybe not at all. I made a lot of American dollars at the Biolife Plasma Center. What, you ask, did I use my plasma money for?

Rent, groceries.

Scar tissue is likely for long-term donors. One man donated his plasma so often he had a hole in his arm that wouldn't seal. You could say what the poor also sell is the integrity of their skin. I have a divot on my arm from being pierced so often with the needle. The mark shows no sign of disappearing, even years after I stopped donating. I am branded.

Plasmapheresis may be mostly harmless, as the company would tell you, but the body isn't made to assembly-line-out its parts. To donate plasma is to temporarily weaken your immune system, so what the poor are also selling is a little bit of resistance to disease. For some donors, strains upon the body are more immediate. One woman collapsed in a local Wal-Mart soon after her visit to Biolife Plasma Services.

I saw a woman faint while donating. In the aisle across from me, a college girl, merry enough, in sneakers and sweatpants. Suddenly her eyes rolled, she blinked, she slumped over— way over—nearly fell off her seat. Technicians rushed to her aid. The on-duty nurse was called.

"Wake up, John Henry! John Henry, wake up!...John Henry, wake up!" they said in something just short of a shout, patting her cheek (though I doubt, in my poor memory, that her name was "John").

She woke up. She wasn't out very long. Groggily, she asked what happened, then vomited into the trashcan.

To those upper-middle-class moms and dads who gleefully sell their plasma, or the retired who gleefully sell their plasma, or college students who gleefully sell their plasma—who use the American dollars earned to meet car payments, or build a Christmas savings, or buy beer and a pizza—I have only these words: November doesn't rain on a fish.

To those whose life may have been saved by the plasma from out of my very own bloodstream, I'm glad for you, abstractly—but I didn't do it for you. *Well, what on Earth did you do it for, if not for me?* you ask.

Rent, groceries.

*John Henry was on the mountain,*
*The mountain was so high,*
*He called to his pretty liddle wife,*
*Said Ah kin almos' touch the sky,*
*Said Ah kin almos' touch the sky.*
—*"John Henry"*

## WEALTH ENDED DEMOCRACY

That's what my sign said, as I joined the crowd of protestors outside the Superior Dome in 2004. We rallied against President George W. Bush making a rare stop at the Upper Peninsula on his re-election campaign. He slid into town on schedule like a goose on a slant of mud. He came to make his goddamn argument. I'm not sure what we were protesting, exactly—except him, his war, his policies, his rise to office, and probably his shoes.

We protestors were put in what was called a "free-speech zone"—a section cordoned off with police tape, as assigned by the very authorities we were demonstrating against. It wasn't really a free-speech zone, but a *go-stand-in-that-corner* zone. Local prison guards were on the scene to assist with crowd control.

Still, we weren't much removed. We stood face to face with the people waiting in line to see the President speak.

A man in the Presidential line saw my sign and scoffed. He looked robust, kempt, in his late twenties. His black hair was styled reasonably short, as my brown hair fell unreasonably long.

"*How* has wealth ended democracy?" he asked.

I had no fast answer. The words of my sign were three, easy to write in permanent marker (though they still came out crooked). My answer to him was a smile and a shrug. I had no real argument with him.

This was my first protest, after all. I only expected to stand. I didn't expect to be button-holed on my stance.
But he was right to ask. I should've been able to say what I felt, or I shouldn't have been there. This didn't make my sign untrue. But it made me a questionable holder of a sign.

Nearby in the crowd, a girl who seemed about ten years old was protesting, too. She was much more vocal than I was (meaning, she actually said something)—sometimes yelling slogans at the people standing in the Presidential queue. Her voice had gone hoarse with shouting.

Her parents, standing a step behind her, looked like professional protestors. They had what could be called that protestor-savvy. They were proud of their munchkin, it seemed, sometimes joining in, following her lead.

*No blood for oil!* she shouted.

*No blood for oil!* her parents shouted, too.

Interesting, I thought. Apparently protest can be inherited, like a grandmother's ring.

Other children were demonstrating, too. Children opposed to the death of Iraqis and American soldiers overseas, though death, to a child, is likely no more real than the drawing of a derailed train.

The longer I listened to her hammering out phrases of outrage, the more it seemed to me that she should not have been there, either. At least, not there in that way. She was like me, voicing an opinion she probably could not explain, if pressed. Though not a fair comparison (she was short, and I was not)—there ought to be truth within the protestor to equal the cause.

John Henry was equal to his chosen cause. He was so equal, he matched it with his life. John Henry didn't win the contest of hammers because he was right. John Henry won the contest of hammers because he was true.

Someone might have asked the wee protestor, "What really matters to you in this world?"

And if her answer was honest, it might be, "I don't know yet."

Maybe, given the time to think, free from the bias of her parents, the girl might have chosen to stand in line to see the President. Her freedom to do so would be worthy of defense.

I left the protest that day less sure of the free-speech ground I had been assigned to stand on. This is not to say that one should have to be perfected before fighting injustice. But, when the battle comes, if one is only half-present, it is little different than not being there.

This extends. Sources tell me that it is bad to not care about the downtrodden.

Downtrodden. Say that word and prisoners bake you a custard. Heaven's rickety gates creeeaaaak open with all the glamour of a Vaudeville backstage shooting, when you say that word. Downtrodden, downtrodden. There's nothing that shouldn't be done for the downtrodden. Gather all the buttercups in the world in one be-glimmer-dazzled petal pile, and leave a note atop it that says *These are for the downtrodden.* An astronaut launching from Earth, on the verge of achieving escape velocity atop a towering cone of fire and smoke should— stop—mid-air—and come back to the ground and...care for the downtrodden. It means nothing to be *up*trodden. Forget it. Uptrodden will get you no favors around here. If you find yourself uptrodden, then you'd better have wet tears in your eyes for the downtrodden, or you are lower than you might be, and not nearly low enough.

Why should we care for the poor? Because the poor, like baby birds, *cheep cheep* loudly for the good worms? *You are cheap, cheap for not giving us some!* Poverty has always carried a begging bowl, and there appears to be no natural law that says the rich should fill it. In Nature, baby birds that fall out of the nest are often left to die. And sometimes their stronger siblings block them from food, to the point of starvation.

If I choose to let you die from want, brother, sister, I wonder who would stop me? The cattle-whip of platitudes that tells me wealth is wrong, and makes me shrug and shrink when it's snapped overhead by anyone who happens to pick it up? Snap it at me, if you wish. Even a mean law to make me feed you would not stop my mean heart, which rolls all over the downtrodden like a flaming boulder, and treads them down more.

*Now the straw boss came to John Henry*
*He cried, "This tunnel is caving in!"*
*John Henry just laughed at the straw boss and said,*
*"That's nothing but my hammer sucking wind,*
*Lawd, Lawdy,*
*That ain't nothing but my hammer sucking wind."*
*— "John Henry"*

If I were a John Henry, I wouldn't have let that Autoapheresis-C machine suck me up. I wouldn't have sold my plasma for American dollars. Maybe, on a good day, I would've given it to my brothers and sisters for free. If I were a John Henry, I would've driven steel against the Autoapheresis-C, and spat at the American-dollars-idea to push selling my body as an option in my poverty.

But I'm not a John Henry. That work continues. I'm trying to lay enough track within myself to make an uninterrupted line possible between the two coasts of my loves and hates, but there's no telling how far that steel will reach, what mountains block the crossing. Maybe there isn't as much time to finish as I had hoped. Maybe, for delays, that track will never be complete.

As he was dying, John Henry said:

*"Captain, I've hammered my insides in two,*
*Lord, I've hammered my insides in two."*

We sing John Henry's song, and keep singing it, because he was a hero. John Henry died defending an idea in his brothers' and sisters' name. And what of that? I imagine the crowd that watched John Henry drive steel that day, watched him win over that machine, watched him lay his hammer down and collapse in the dust—I imagine they hung their heads in sorrow, for a time—a good, long time...and then went to the bar for a cold beer. The steam-drill he conquered was likely ready for work the next day, if not the next moment. The company still had track to put down. And the poor returned to the routine of their poor lives. In versions of the song, John Henry's lover Polly Ann picks up his hammer after he falls, and she then drives steel like a man—but we are left to infer why. Though my heart would like to believe she swung that hammer for love of her fallen man, love is a track where every train runs on time, and I can't make such a schedule. It might be safer to say that she did it because she needed groceries. Heroes of tomorrow, take note: if you make your heart explode for invisible principles, the results may be invisible.

So was that railroad track worth John Henry's dying? In the song, John Henry knew full well, even as a child, that "this hammer'll be the death of me." To him, fighting the machine was a battle worth all his effort, and all his effort meant his dying. Maybe what is needed in our society now is to stand like John Henry did. That's a heavy hammer to swing; heavier than fourteen pounds, for sure. Still, my hands tell me that a good idea is a hammer worth swinging. And any hammer worth swinging is the only one worth swinging, even if we are driving invisible spike.

I don't believe that John Henry died so the trains could run. Why hammer a golden spike into a railroad track that carries mainly coal? The fretting weighs more than the freight. It was probably more important to him that a human built the track than a train could chug the length of the continent. The aim of his labor was purer, prouder than steam power; more deeply driven. I think John Henry, born a steel driving man, was laying a different track entirely; an invisible one.

> *White man saw John Henry's*
> *Steel a-goin' down;*
> *White Man says,—"That man's a mighty man,*
> *But he'll weaken when th' hardes' rock is foun',—*
> *Lawd,—Lawd,—*
> *He'll weaken when th' hardes' rock is foun'."*
> *—"John Henry"*

What if we lived in a world where religion, philosophy, government, technology, social justice, were not enough to get us through? As false as they were true? Not support, in their last, tested strains, but shackle? When our beliefs fail us, what would we have for a foundation upon which to stand and say *here!*—say, like John Henry, *here and no more!* What if there was no John Henry, never was and never could be—what would be left?

Our plasma.

*This is the hammer that killed John Henry*
*But it won't kill me, no, it won't kill me.*
—*Mississippi John Hurt, "Spike Driver Blues"*

* *Most of the John Henry lyrics were taken from this marvelous website source, and apparently gathered by a man named Guy Johnson:*
http://www.ibiblio.org/john_henry/early.html

# I Feel Better, And So Can You

## Matt Hart

from *H_NGM_N*

After the flood, I walked up to a cloud,
then down some stairs into a fire. There
I came face to face with the following:
a mammoth (wooly), a snapper (red),
and a naval commander in the field.
"All words I like," I volunteered, so found myself
consumed by a uniform, its meaning indeterminate,
its policies unsettled. "If only I had been consumed
by a unicorn instead," I thought—though
judging from the quotation marks
I may have said it out loud… Anyway,
there I was holding a fish
and being asked by the fire (the very one
I walked into) how to cook it.
"You put your right foot in…" I began.
Then a blizzard blew up—a real violation of decorum
trapped inside an even realer violation of decorum.
"What do you have to say for yourself?"
demanded the commander. I hiccupped trying
to giggle, but it came out a sloth, sleeping in a tree
with no opinion whatsoever. That's when I thought
of the word wallpaper—another word I like.
I said it out loud, "wallpaper" and the fire liked it too,
though the sloth, as usual, was indifferent.
The poor red snapper was gasping for air.

"Can somebody get this snapper some water!"
I snapped. "On the double," said the commander
in a rather predictable turn of events.
By this time the fire was licking the fish
and the mammoth was totally wallpaper.
When I looked up from my typewriter
the levee was breaking, and I walked
into a legendary sympathy.

# Family

## Jensen Beach

from *Necessary Fiction*

Someone suggested swimming and someone else said that in this weather all we need is another incident. Someone recalled that there was an expression that perfectly explained this very moment. Someone said that yes they remembered it, lightning doesn't strike twice, and someone else said that as a matter of fact that's happened to a friend. Someone said that no one believed this story the first time and why should they all believe it now. Someone said that they'd read an article on the Internet about this topic and someone else said that, well then of course it's true. Someone suggested that everyone just calm down immediately. Someone began to walk away and someone reached out an arm to stop someone. Someone turned and said that they begged someone's pardon, but could they please release their grip. Someone struggled to hold on until someone else suggested that maybe lunch should be served, which turned the subject to food, which as usual had a calming effect. Someone prepared lunch and someone else set the table. Someone opened a bottle of wine and someone else accused someone of drinking too much. Someone lifted a phone to call someone about this and someone said, could you please put the phone down, lunch is served. Someone sat near the kitchen so as to fetch items from the stove and to refill serving dishes as necessary. Someone made a comment about someone's cooking and someone else found this indulgent, and someone else found it simply untrue. Someone said that it was raining now. Someone left the table and then the house until someone was in the yard and looking up at the rain, and the storm was large and billowing in the distance and the rain was still light above the house and in the yard as it rained on someone there. Someone pointed to the approaching storm and someone else remarked at how dark it had suddenly become. Someone said that someone had better be careful out there and someone else pointed to the clouds, now thick and black and seeming in some way to breathe if such a thing is possible, and the rain fell in enormous drops and someone started to run for cover. Someone saw a flash of lightning and someone else said that, yes we all saw it. Someone no longer appeared to be in the yard and someone remarked upon this change and someone else looked intently and rapidly at every part of the yard visible from behind the large window, which was now streaked with water. Someone else ran to the kitchen for a similar, but slightly enlarged, view of the yard. Someone sat still and hoped that someone was uninjured and someone else attempted to determine the likelihood of real life violating our most tested truths in this way, and as someone sat and considered this question someone seemed to recall that the expression someone had previously mentioned further qualified the circumstances of two lightning strikes with location. Someone said out loud that this was a variable someone had very foolishly forgotten and someone else said that that was no big surprise. Someone else said, what do mean by that? Someone said that as a family we're always forgetting important details, and someone else said, do you mean forgetting or ignoring? Someone said to look out the window and someone else did, where they saw that someone was now lying on the grass near the house in a wet heap of someone. Someone said, did it happen? Someone said that it had and someone else said that it hadn't, and they all gathered there before the window in the kitchen through which they had all looked so many times but never together like this, and they looked for some evidence of the event they feared most, and they looked in every direction but could not see the past because time doesn't move in that direction, and so they looked for a long while and nobody saw anything at all.

# Photo Opportunities for a Dislocated Elbow

## Stokely Klasovsky

from *Jellyfish*


I lean on a lamppost, as if in an old painting:
A Drunk on Broadway, 1905.
Not a vacuous type of man:
A son of steel workers and shipbuilders,
A son of knuckles and pipe wrenches.

The corpse is kitchen clutter,
its glass bottles eyeless
with savage angles
that promote decay, float mold,
and witness tragic hands of Solitaire.

Blame the architects my fingers know,
sick with powders,
sore from tracking patterns in static
and acting out battering rams
of juvenilia; operate, cloud a house:
The smoky air, the sleep of dogs.

"Habit-forming" manifests
as a theatre in yards of unraveled socks,
sick days that wander like zombies,
The blur over the face of a witness.

A wishful sculptor sleeps here,
picturing a surface scalded and lunar,

distended like galaxies; a body between
wood and lead.

The scissor-trim of acid trips
cradles words with white.

The history of apartments
drifts in address books
with the names of women
whose memories become
burn victims thimbled in gauze.

# Field Notes

## August Tarrier

from *DIAGRAM*

No. 26: Sandy blond hair, in his twenties, with a red baseball cap. Grinned when I took out my notebook.

No. 131: Very tall. Jean jacket and grey sweatshirt. Stopped to chat briefly. *I'm married, doll.*

No. 79: In his sixties, wearing oxfords and a three-piece suit—no tie. Tipped a straw bowler. Frowned at me when I asked to see his hands, when I asked the color of his eyes.

No. 17: Big beer belly. Wore a button: *Lose weight now—ask me how.*

No. 82: Red-faced with a big mustache. *What's this all about?*

No. 101: Hairy fingers clutching a plaid wool coat. *Jesus loves you, daughter.*

No. 79 is back. Brought me a cup of coffee. Sits in the parking lot in his car.

No. 33: Scraggly beard and red hair. Laughed when I asked where he was on the night of September 23rd. *I gotta ask my wife!*

No. 64: Mid-forties. Didn't walk toward the factory, but went out to the street. Had a cocker spaniel on a leash. Let me pet her. *Isn't she soft?*

No. 145: Baseball cap that said "Toto's." Asked about my

notepad. Gave me a dollar.

No. 79 is back. Nice face, balding. Brought me flowers.

No. 16: Dirty nails, plaid pants and a parka. *Get a job.*

No. 65: Shaved head, one blue vein throbbing on his left temple. *Let me see your titties.*

No. 79 approaches me and asks why I stand at the factory gates at the edge of the parking lot. I look into his puzzled grey eyes and I tell him that I am waiting for someone. He has brought me flowers again, daisies, and he holds them tightly in his clean, soft hands. I ask him a question and he frowns, turns away from me. Asking helps me remember, even a few fleeting seconds— moments of fading in and back out again. *Was it you?*

It wasn't. It wasn't No. 79, but maybe it was. I keep asking. When I ask I remember black barbed branches swaying in the wind. I remember the final rays of sun on the windows of the factory, so many windows, some blazing, some already black.

Imagine a girl, slender, with long, dark hair, two eyes, blue, wearing a short green dress and strappy shoes, a girl with hard, white teeth, crunching ice cubes in a bar. Not square four-sided cubes, but round lozenges. And she smiled at the Chipped One.

My fingers gripped the handle of a car door as I lay on the back seat. *Get out,* he said.

I turned to see the factory huge in the moonlight, its black windows gaping. I remember the green fronds down by the river. The fronds brushed my arms as we trod on marshy ground.

He left bruises blooming dark and ominous across my thigh.

I, underneath, I, underwater, I came floating up, scuttling, sloshing, pulled by the underwater tug, still I came floating up into silver foam.

There was a witness, according to Captain Sergeant, someone who made a report but refused to give his name. He said only that he worked at the factory. What did he see? He saw a body in a body of water, he saw a body bobbing amid bubbles, in slick water, in the gentle but insistent surge.

Men's hands are worth noting. One had a broken finger—the other one. I remember how it stuck out at an odd angle as he held his drink. And their eyes—watch where their eyes go when they're talking to you. The Chipped One, the one who smiled at me, his eyes were made of millions of icy blue slivers. The left eye floated, unmoored, in its blue orbit, like a wobbly planet. These things I have not forgotten.

A partly submerged tire, a clear glass bottle broken at the neck, an overturned shopping cart, mired. Beneath the aqueduct, the pilings rose above me and moss edged between layers of stone. A blue-green patina of algae bloomed in the seams.

I remember rolling, turning, a gentle, lilting turning, a slow waking.

I told Captain Sergeant about crunching my ice and sipping my drink, and the numbing, swooping blankness. I told him about being carried to the car, my eyes open and then shut. I told him there were two. I told him I remember holding the glass of vodka—and then the next thing was crouching under the chain-link fence. And the river.

My shoes are in my hands.

No. 79 sits in the parking lot in his car. He tells me it is a 1965 Buick Goldstar. He invites me to sit in the passenger seat, to rest. He looks out toward the horizon. *Bless this land,* he says. His eyes are a deep, velvety grey-blue and when he talks they drift and shimmer somewhere far off and he doesn't look at me at all. He tells me he used to play the clarinet in a Salvation Army band and wore a *jacket with gold braid.* He tells me that when he was a boy his father wore *a fedora with a black grosgrain band. My dear,* he says to me, *allow me to drive you home.* Were you the witness, I ask, but he says no. He never saw a body in a body of water, he's never been past the chain-link fence. I have a lot more work to do, I am not done with any of them yet.

This is what's left of that night: one green dress, packaged on a shelf in the office of Captain Sergeant. One glass bottle broken at the neck. A green-foil wrapper imprinted with the word *Andes.* The little shiny green square was plastered to my neck, the shattered glass bottle was what I grasped in my hand. My dress is evidence now, my fish-scaled, moldering dress, reeking of chemicals, silver-green, a meadow green grassy dress, a blasted Easter basket, woven with fronds and threadbare threads. It is the dress I died in and the one in which I lived again.

Each day I stand in the parking lot with the factory behind me. I walk past blocks and blocks of empty lots and chain-link fences and warehouses to get here. I am the girl in the blasted green dress, with long, streaming hair, and dripping eyes. I still know how to smile and that is what they really want. I still know how to dream and even now my dreams are my own. I do not dream of the wavering mouths of fishes, of being buoyed up on the bumpy backs of frogs, of slimy silver eels, of the webbed feet of mallards. I do not dream of the beaks of terns plucking brackish streaks of green from my hair.

The Chipped One brought me to this lot. He and the other one carried me past the factory windows and through the chain-link fence, down to the rushing, silver river. I remember his eyes, made of a million chips of blue light, I remember his chipped front tooth, his chipped, bitten fingers.

I am the silver river girl, the dripping, drowning girl, the one who did not die.

*I like bodies,* he said.

Imagine being held in water, covered with spume, spinning

green and not dying. Imagine sleeping on dark silt beds, floating on currents, spinning deep and rising on black, cold waves. The witness, perhaps he knows how that could be, how I survived that night.

I saw windows, hundreds, thousands, perfect quadrangles, silver-white in the moonlight. As I ebbed and flowed in the dark waters, the factory was still, but when I awoke it had resumed its roaring, pumping discharge and the wind ruffled the silver water and the smoke and mist rose on the river.

I lay partly on the bank and partly in the water and the mist rose and rolled over me. I looked up at black branches against a silver sky as I lay there with the water still lapping at my left arm and left leg. Birds alighted in the branches and then took wing. A clear glass bottle lay in the sand by my right hand, so close that I could almost reach out and touch the broken neck of the bottle, and then I could—my fingers reached out and grasped the clear glass.

Captain Sergeant, he of the long, thin hands, hands too delicate to be those of a captain or a sergeant, he of the muddy brown eyes that never wavered—except once. He told me that the river had no name, and he raised an eyebrow and folded his long, thin hands when I told him I did not know the name of the Chipped One. And then his eyes drifted far away from me when he spoke of bloodstains and semen, and they traveled back again, to rest on me, on my face, as he told me my dress had been brined, with me in it, and that it therefore offered no secrets, only oily river water and smoke. *You're one lucky lady,* he told me.

I told Captain Sergeant it was dark and I was kneeling in the river muck, then standing, then falling again. I told him that the factory loomed behind wire fencing, that blood trickled from my knee and wrist and that the fence was broken, twisted. I told him that I was gasping and retching and being alive. He looked right at me and he didn't say anything. Then he told me that he would need to keep my dress. He said there was a witness, someone who saw but did not give his name. *That's lucky, too*, he said.

No. 79 sits in the parking lot of the factory in his Buick Goldstar, his hands folded on his stomach. He invites me to sit in the passenger seat. He tells me that he's retired now, but that he parked in this lot every day for 22 years. He turns his kindly grey eyes to me, but then he looks out again and his eyes change, they get clear and chilly, and I wonder what he has seen, what he knows. I want to remind him of the swirling eddies of the river and all it contains, but I don't because then his eyes come back, they get cloudy with concern and his brows are like black hillocks looming over the grey.

I keep asking my questions and taking my notes and so far I have ruled out Nos. 26, 48, 55, 63, 76, 91, 92, 103, 106, and 112. Asking keeps me windy inside, like the *golden prairie* that No. 79 tells me about, like the soft, green pastures rolling out to the blue horizon, like *papa's white shirts on the clothesline*, like the way his heart soared *to see my mama standing there*.

The Chipped One, his hands were like wild birds fluttering in all the crevices of my being. I tell that to No. 79 but he shows no sign of recognition. If he stumbled upon that scene, maybe he would never tell. But I keep asking. As long as I keep asking, then I do not dream of huge stone pilings made of schist soaring above me. I do not dream of bloody chain-links and wrecked, spindly trees; I do not dream of smelting sparks and embers and bonfires.

Each day now I sit with No. 79 in the Buick. He tells me his name is Henry William Gastemeyer, but I don't call him that. I don't call him anything. *I'm sound as a clock*, he says, and thumps the steering wheel. He tells me that he remembers every word his mother ever said to him. I tell him that I need a witness, that I need someone who can remember what he saw. I tell him that I am collecting slivers and shards and strands.

I remember sounds, ones I'd been hearing all along—birds, far-off traffic, the laplaplap of the river.

What I know is that in the deeper place of the river, there are soft white fronds, long grey eels, catfish with whiskers floating on the currents, clumps of moss and tangled river weeds. Over all this, a sweet gray smoke holds sway, a rising chemical mist hovers over the water and burns the lungs.

I've stopped asking No. 79 any more questions because asking makes him quiet and I want to keep him talking, I want to rest in the vast, windy grey of his eyes, I want to hear about how the plow churned up *newly turned earth*, how the *swallows swooped out of the trees* and how his heart soared *to see my mama standing there.* He brought her *fistfuls of Michaelmas daisies* and *Queen Anne's Lace,* and she put them into the pockets of her calico apron, stalks and stems and dirt still clinging to the roots. *She shooed me away,* he says. But he stayed and she turned back to him and drew him to her. *Land's sake,* she said and drew him closer.

*Was it you*? I ask him, and he nods. But when I ask him what he saw, he just shakes his head. I tell him, Imagine the body of a girl bumping along in the undertow. She is bathed in silt, her hair streaked with algae, and she breathes in vapors and mists. She rises radiant from a slurry of isotopes and polymers, she rises toward the oxygen, she staggers up into silt and loam, her hair rank and steaming, rivulets of flotsam coursing from her dress, oozing from every orifice.

I stand at the entrance to the parking lot, by the factory, in a different dress, my hair lank and unwashed. I have been steeped in deep waters, nudged by the gentle mouths of eels, grazed by the underbellies of frogs, mired in the soft, sodden muck of rotten leaves. The silver slurry of no-name river left its imprint on me: my breath comes a little harder now, my eyes are the cool, watery eyes of a not-drowned girl, my fingers tremble now, sometimes I can't feel my feet at all, my spine rattles, my skin is translucent.

No. 79 walks me partway to the river. We get almost all the way there. He is gallant and gentlemanly, offers me his arm. As we walk, I tell him that I need a witness. He doesn't say anything, but he turns to me, up close, and his eyes are narrow, his brows hunkered down over them. I urge him on, thinking that if we get there, he'll give himself away, he'll tell everything he knows. I tell myself to breathe as deeply as if these were my last breaths. No. 79 looks everywhere but at me; he stares at the pewter sky smoldering before us. And there is the river, just as it was. He turns back.

No. 79 has asked to see my notes, and I turn over the 86 pristine pages. He scans them before handing them back. I tell him that these are my notes of that night, the night for which there is no evidence, nothing that is not steeped in chemical brine. I tell him that these are the minutes of that night, from which minutes and hours and more are missing, and I wait. He stares straight ahead.

No. 79 parks the car amid the fronds, by the fence, and I get out. He stays behind the wheel, and when I look back the car seems to hover there amid the fronds, silver in the gloaming. He opens the door and gets out, he stands with the door open and calls to me. *You mustn't cross*, he tells me, and points to the No Admittance sign by the fence. I tell him that I need to get to the river. *It's not much of a river, miss,* he says.

I remember the glittery mosaic of the Chipped One's eyes, even in darkness. The factory was at my back and I was on my knees in sand. Something came out of my mouth—a throaty slur before swooping back into darkness. Then I remember morning and the sun heating up the high grass. I remember birdsong.

I am not afraid. I know the way back in through the twisted links of the fence. I know the way the trees lean out over the river. I know the river's shallows and its depths, I know where it forks, I know where its bottom rises up, I know where a slender body can float and shimmer in those waters, I know how to stop breathing and then breathe again.

I don't know how I slept in those waters, how I swam, or scuttled, or breathed with water breath, how I made my way. Perhaps I parted the reeds, navigated the eddies and sloughs, and rode the quickening currents all night long. I took what the river gave me, I breathed in flakes of soot and ash, I inhaled one bright bubble at a time, and I lived.

Captain Sergeant held some papers in his thin, white hands and read aloud and shook his head. *You're one lucky lady,* he told me.

I lead No. 79 past plastic bags and discarded syringes, under the blue-green pilings. He scans the horizon, as he always does. Then he looks down when he realizes he has splashed into the water. He backs away as the water engulfs his shoes. He offers me his arm. *I'd like to walk you home*, he says.

*I take note of your tears*, he says. He steps away from the water and stumbles on the stubby, stony bank. But then he turns and comes back toward me. He stares at me, his eyes dark pinholes. I don't move. Do you remember a girl like me, I ask him, only silver-green and waterlogged and streaked with dirt and tears? Do you remember a girl spinning and drowning and rising again? He doesn't answer. I keep one foot on the bank and one in the water. He turns, tips his hat, and moves back toward shore. He won't try to stop me.

The trees lean over the water, spreading their splintered branches, the birds sing their uneven song, the waters slap against the schist, leaving a scummy rime, a sparrow stalks the shore, spreading its metallic wings, a cold wind crests on the rugged, silver waves. All things that settle here, in these waters, on these banks—prepare to bear witness to a shivering, riven, surfacing girl.

# Where the Glazed Girls Go

## Kasandra Snow Duthie

from *The Summerset Review*

After the butter princess wins her title, the other glazed girls who were sculpted and born from a ninety-pound block leave the fairgrounds too. They go to foster care. Butter flows slower than blood. When you eye butter-flesh closely, you can see its transparency. Faint ripples of mustard seed pollinate her shape as a butter girl walks.

Glazed specimens, dollop-breasts, shiny teeth, and grins as wide as the sky, are softer and less protected than regular Minnesota girls. They're odd. These girls will begin a sentence melodically, the way a harpist plays, but as the thought continues, their tone turns deep—the sound a ewe makes when hustling her lamb close, from a hum inside her throat. A glazed girl is the sadness a country songwriter laughs about before he weeps. I know the way dairy girls act. I know both sorts. I've lived among the real girls, and I was a friend of a glazed girl named Wyn who died. The state fair is the ultimate gathering place for us farm kids. We come from families who teach us to control a heifer with a stick before we can read.

Unlike us, the glazed girl is fragile and weak, her soul and body parts born piece by piece from a chisel. Each year, the real dairy princess poses to be sculpted from butter in a temperature-controlled observation room, tiara on her head, parka worn over her pink dress. Created to look like the fair's real dairy princesses, the ruined butter copies fail. When a glazed girl forms, something goes wrong in her enzyme construction.

Her DNA is not like our own. She has bad genes and runny chemical compounds. Heartless want grows this cold block of butter into a damaged waif whenever a Frankenstein sculptor works her business. Then, when she arrives, the curdled baby girl rises from a hideous dark place, crying all feral and sheepish, and singing. And if she sings long enough to survive, the glazed baby immediately becomes a yellow pad of gypsy waste to us all.

The first time I saw a glazed girl I shunned her because I had learned the butters were known to be diseased and violent. That day, my friends and I had been playing underneath a mailbox on a dirt road. The tiny yellow Vaseline-faced girl walked over and poked a stick at the ants we'd corralled in our fortress of dirt. We shunned her for a while, saying *get out of here* and *go*. We said *your momma is dead*. We said *we're going home to eat cake and play with all our money and dolls*. We told the glazed girl she was unwanted, but we saw in her eyes she'd already known that her whole life. It made us sad for a minute, so we buried all the ants we'd gathered until they smothered underneath our shoes.

\*\*\*

In high school, something beyond that yellow-pollen dust followed my friend Wyn around. Rumor said she once walked to school on a sub-zero Minnesota day, bare-chested, waist-up naked. I took a sculpture class with her. None of my good friends were there, so talking to Wyn in art class seemed safe. Ms Feroy made us do unbelievably trivial things with clay. She played Judy Collins and Buffy Sainte-Marie for mood music. One thing I remember her making us do was pour white plaster into milk cartons. After it dried, we peeled away the carton, revealing a chalky brick. I whittled and sanded, but my art stayed coffin-shaped and plain. Wyn smashed her brick in two and chiseled the most marvelous replica of what I believed to be a poolside snack shack.

"Hey," I said. "I would never think to make a snack shack out of plaster. What are those little oblong things?" Poking her short yellow finger on the table, Wyn dabbed up plaster shavings and debris. She wore her hair back the way those Robert Palmer girls did in the music video, a sleek, sleek ponytail. Hair the color of a chicken foot.

Wyn covered her sculpture in burlap, and looked at me the way a goat spies a person in the distance with one eye—still and frozen, but aware. "I saw your ugly, manure sculpture. No help for it. And, I must say, your stupid friends suck a lot of wang."

"Not too much," I said. Then I thought about my allegiances and muttered, "No, they don't even suck wang at all."

"Mmm," Wyn grunted, rubbing grit off her fingers. She glowered at her burlap-covered shack. "This is no snack shack. It's a buttered corn stand. Those things you pointed at are not oblongs. They're wine coolers."

After that, Wyn took leave from Ms Feroy's class for a week. We moved on to coil pots, prepping them with glaze for the fire. When Wyn came back, she smelled like canned pumpkin, and her gold lion eyes sat deeper in her yellow face. I asked her where she'd been and she said, "Milking. It's in my blood." I didn't know what she meant, but when I started to ask again, she walked away.

"Feroy," Wyn said, clomping toward the art room boom box. "Play that Charlie Daniels Band." Ms Feroy said she wasn't familiar with Charlie Daniels. "Sure you are, Feroy," Wyn said. "It's that fast fiddle song about the devil the carnies play when you walk past the Zipper ride. At the fair." People laughed. Wyn didn't care.

Once fired, my clay pot turned the color of an old soggy tube-sock. After the kiln, Wyn's vase reflected mirrors of moving halo light the way her skin often did. She kept to herself after the class critique when nobody would admit to admiring her art even though it was masterful. Ms Feroy said that Wyn should pursue her talent as a sculptor. Wyn shrugged, telling Ms Feroy that she wanted to become a 4-H leader and a County Extension officer instead. "County Extension officers know about the land," Wyn said. "Art is a dream I won't have time for."

The next week our class started to work on clay busts. Ms Feroy asked each of us to choose an inspirational person to be our muse. I selected my friend Becky Norwick because she was sexually active; this made her street-wise and great. Most of the boys chose guitarists or sports stars. Wyn asked Ms Feroy if she could use someone she had never met. We sculpted our busts for a week before we revealed them to the class for critique. My finished bust looked unromantically fat, and noseless and chinless, instead of loved and voluptuous. Wyn had formed a giant fried pickle on a stick, a face frozen in a murderous scream.

\*\*\*

We all knew glazed girls ended up in foster care, motherless and unwanted. People told stories about Wyn. She lived in a house full of kids and had to eat lutefisk and oyster stew every day. Foster kids like Wyn had to drink powdered milk instead of the kind that comes from cows. And her transient "siblings" tried to molest her. That's why she had to padlock her basement bedroom door. Wyn had to be locked in that basement all the time. Once she tried to scrape her way out, her fingernails cat-scratching the floor. She came to school, bandages covering her yellow scabby fingers full of mustardy mucous blood. Wyn's foster mother weighed more than a cow. She made Wyn wash the younger foster kids' soiled underwear with a wire brush and soap made of lard. It couldn't be proven, but people knew Wyn's foster mom once shook a baby glazed girl so hard she died of brain rattle.

These were lies, of course. High school girls tell lies. They use what they know to invent fear and shameful things they won't understand until they grow old. Or they tell a convincing modern day folk story about a pied piper and his rats. Only this time, the piper is the town hockey hero named Sven, who drives a rusty Ford Bronco. The girls follow him around. They belong to his thick hands. They become entranced and lean into his wintergreen chewing tobacco breath. They lie about how magical he is. Or, for example, a girl tells her friends something quite stupid. They believe her. Now, why, for instance, does a girl invent a psychotic dwarf she once saw masturbating on an old mattress in her neighbor's basement? She invents this story because she likes being afraid of old pipes and darkness. She likes the idea of fear and suffering, but only hypothetically.

After Wyn sculpted the creepy pickle face on a stick, I had no choice but to ignore her forever. She had opened some freaky fear in that pickle face, displaying it proudly to the high school world. My friends and I only spoke of the heinous and wicked when we could invent ways to pass judgment on others. This was something we saw our mothers do. Our mothers weren't gossips. No, *they were actually just shedding light on what was already common knowledge.* We teens hadn't yet honed our mothers' subtle talk-of-the-town skills. We sought drama. Our teenage pain and confusion became what we said we saw in people like Wyn. My friends and I drenched each other with stories about shaken babies and orphan glazed girls without identities.

After the term ended, I didn't see Wyn very often. She started dating a guy who sported a thin moustache and wore big black boots. People said he gave Wyn crabs, and then they forgot about Wyn entirely. The guy didn't go to our school. He looked old and singed, way too heavy metal. Sometimes Wyn and I would nod at one another when we passed in the hall. That was about it. During the winter, Wyn walked to the old guy's Chevy pickup near where the smokers stood when they could stand the cold long enough to smoke. Even in winter, she wore nothing more than a jean jacket or one of those windbreakers with all the useless zippers. I never understood how her gaunt yellow body could stand the cold and wind. It was as though Wyn lived to be bravely frozen and oblivious, standing around smiling in the gray brutal tundra of our winters.

About a year after art class ended, I met Wyn's mother while I shopped with mine at the dime store. They knew each other through church group. Wyn had never lived in foster care. She had been adopted as a three-day-old butter baby by this woman named Carma. Wyn's adoptive father was named Jim. The Gustafsons worked as accountants in the strip mall in an office they shared. When my mom introduced me that day, I told Wyn's mother I thought her daughter was a good artist. But when Carma left my mother and me, I whispered that Wyn was having sex with a pedophile dope-dealer.

*** 

What happened is, Wyn died. A few years after we graduated, we learned the news she'd been in a car wreck somewhere near Owatonna. It's funny how people become close to grieving even when the sadness isn't theirs to own. Large devastation, say one hundred thousand people dying in India or somewhere, is hard to consider. Pretending to know one small tragedy is easy. We trace small patterns then, in a glazed and melted life like Wyn's.

Posthumous Wyn reminded us girls of driving around in some old car. You look down to the left and there's this black raggedy scar running through the driver side mirror. Our own cracked faces reflect our distortion, allowing space, and trees, and somebody passing behind us. I remember so many people saying Wyn was the funniest glazed girl. As if they knew a multitude of butter girls. I remember someone saying how they once parked in the woods with Wyn, and drank blueberry milkshakes and talked about the stars. After her death, Wyn's short life became famous because we wanted a new fable. Everyone knew her suddenly. *Ha ha ha,* we said, I remember Wyn doing the Hustle in a barn loft, her hair matching the color of the hay.

Wyn was a borrowed child; her adoptive mother told me this years after she died. I saw her mother in the grocery, and I confessed I hadn't been close to Wyn. But she sure did march to her own drum, I said. I smiled the stupid way you do when you know you should stop talking. Wyn's mom looked off toward the dairy aisle. "We adopted her when she was tiny," she said. "But you know, even when Wyn was very young, she was reckless." Then Carma's face puckered. She looked at me as if prescribing some sentence or judgment. "We were aware of it," she said, wringing her hands on the grocery cart.

\*\*\*

I saw Wyn one time in the summer between junior and senior year. She sat on the back of some guy's motorcycle. One of those beat-up Yamahas. I waited behind them at a stop sign on a dirt road. I remember all the soy fields and the way the sky seemed thin and white blue. I knew it was her, on the back of the bike. I saw shiny harvest cornstalk skin, and the pollen haloed all around her. For a moment she turned back at me with some kind of hindsight intuition. And she smiled. Then she turned to look ahead. Her life was just now beginning: full throttle force, eight-hundred-octane fierce, faster than the Zipper ride could spin, faster than Charlie Daniels could ever play that fiddle.

# Tricks

## Thomas Cooper

from *Keyhole*

By the time Sis was fifteen the doctors started calling her problem a gift. Sure, a gift, my parents and I said and suppressed our bitter smiles because the doctors never had to put up with her constant tricks, the card games, the disappearing coins, the magic hat routines. They weren't the ones who found her in the front yard behind a folding card table strewn with shim shells and half dollars as the neighborhood punks threw pinecones and chanted retard, retard, retard.

Sometimes I lost patience with Sis as the years went on, as she grew old enough to be called a spinster and the doctors started calling the gift Asperger's syndrome. Take that time I tried to break the news of Mom's death as Dad muttered and drank Stoli in the kitchen. At first Sis seemed to understand, pursing her lips solemnly, but then she started pulling colored handkerchiefs from my ears, a look of zealous concentration on her face. "I'm trying to have an adult conversation here," I said, shaking her by the shoulders.

Later that night Sis made Dad's antique fob watch disappear, the last anniversary gift he ever received from Mom. She seemed oblivious when Dad and I got down on our hands and knees and searched behind the bookcases, underneath the couch, inside the plant pots. "I don't know how I'm going to handle her alone," Dad said with his face in his hands once Sis went up to bed. We never did end up finding that goddamn watch.

Then there was that Christmas Eve right before my divorce. The family now reduced to three, we watched a Tony Danza holiday movie as we unwrapped our thermal underwear and socks. Dad was plastered so I tried to confide in Sis about my wife leaving, and for a second there was a flicker of sympathy in her eyes. Then she withdrew playing cards from her robe pocket. "Pick a card," she said, "any card." Afterward I went to the bathroom and turned on the faucet so no one would hear my weeping.

But now, the day of Dad's funeral is the final straw. After the burial family and friends are gathered in the living room, sharing remembrances and piling paper plates with Swedish meatballs and potato chips. A cousin smells strongly of model airplane glue. Someone else is insisting that he met Dad during the Tet Offensive, which is impossible. Meanwhile I watch Sis in the corner with her cards, cocktail sauce smeared around her mouth.

She holds her balled-up hands out in front of me. "Right or left," she says.

"Sis," I say, teeth clenched. "Please."

"Right or left," she says.

I want to slap some sense into this fifty-year-old woman, tell her this is no time for her tricks, but I would never dare. Instead I pick a hand. Sis unfurls her fingers and shows me the antique fob watch. For a second it doesn't even feel like everything has changed.

# Ideally Learnt French For Eavesdroppers
## Brian Baldi
from *Matchbook*

The presidents are lonely. The presidents are
self-absorbing. The presidents want to use the guichet
automatique, but cannot be unfrozen until I tag them.
This is hard on their tendons.

> Oeuf? says the waitress.
> Oeuf, say the presidents.
> Frozen until tagged otherwise, I say.

Forty-three blue jays visit the presidents in the
hair sections of their heads. Some sections are
smaller than other sections. Other sections are
basically not even sections. The presidents are all
reluctant hosts.

> Oeuf? says the waitress.
> Oeuf, say the presidents.
> No cameral oeufs, I say.

The presidents make come-hither looks at the guichet
automatique. I know they want to give it their codes.
The presidents want to touch the guichet automatique
and choose the right language. They want to be
thanked for their transaction. They want to hear the
spinning drums.

Oeuf? says the waitress.
Oeuf, say the presidents.
Nope, I say.

The presidents oh man the scenario and the sun, but
remain untagged. Waitresses become the definition of
spinning around, and the guichet automatique becomes
the definition of historically being there, and all
that can be heard is oeuf, oeuf, oeuf, yet the
presidents will never be tagged, and will never push
the sides of their forks down upon yellow
midsections. I smoke about it for twenty minutes.
Okay, all day. I smoke about it with the fur traders.

# When a Furnace Is All that Remains

## Steven J. McDermott

from *Necessary Fiction*

### 1

From the bus stop I walk up the gravel service road. All of the puddles are frozen over with thin windowpane ice and I amuse myself by stomping through the sheets of crystal. They break with a sharp crunch and a whoosh as the air escapes around my boot. No puddles in the potholes beneath the ice. It's as if all the liquid has drawn upward out of the hole to create the icy lid. I crunch eighty-three before reaching the parking lot. No vehicles. The fairways and greens are bleached with frost. I unlock the clubhouse door and enter. The chill in the room, nearly as frigid as outside, means the furnace has shut down, means for the third time in a week I've turned down the thermostat too low.

### 2

Fifth sign of trouble: The head professional at the club, my boss, after the last time I caused the furnace to go out, said: "Three strikes and you're out, kid. I don't mind giving you a chance, but when you screw up like that and it costs me a service call—that's a couple hundred bucks. Don't let it happen again."

### 3

Must relight the furnace before the boss arrives so I go into the storeroom, pull back the rug, and lift the trap door out of the floor. I climb down the four rungs of the ladder, crouch and duck walk under the joists until I reach the furnace. The pilot light is out. A box of wooden matches is on top of the beam. I sit cross-legged in front of the furnace with my back against a support pillar. I flip open the safety shut-off, strike the match, let it burn a second or two, then turn on the gas. I thrust the match into the pilot light and avert my face waiting for ignition. Nothing. I blow out the match and turn off the nozzle. Sniff. No gas. That's never happened before. I'm hoping the tank is empty because that wouldn't be my fault.

## 4

Fourth sign of trouble: After sixty days in juvie and eight weeks of weekend community service at the food bank, I still have a year of probation ahead of me—provided I stay employed.

## 5

The propane tank is out on the edge of the driving range, thirty yards or so from the clubhouse. When I get there, the light blue paint of the 500-gallon tank is glazed with a sheen of frost. A pipe exits one end of the tank and connects to the regulator. Another pipe leaves the regulator and goes into the ground and feeds the furnace. The fuel gauge, also coated with ice, is on the pipe between the tank and the regulator. I brush away the ice. Three-quarters full. The regulator must have frozen shut, cutting off the gas flow. An ice-crusted sticker on the side of the tank says: "Flammable, keep open flames fifty feet away." I consider my options. Hot water is the obvious solution but then I remember that the hot water heater is gas, too.

## 6

Third sign of trouble: The public defender said: "The DA has a hard-on for you now. You've gotten thirty days twice. Car prowl. House break-in. Now busted in a pharmacy. You're progressing down a path and he aims to stop you before you go any further."

## 7

Hot piss seems the answer. I unzip and start peeing on the regulator. Steam rises and frost melts off the galvanized metal as the urine runs down the pipe to the frozen grass. A strong whiff of urea stings my nostrils as my bladder empties. I lean close and shake the last drops onto the regulator. I return to the furnace, light the match and turn on the gas. Nothing.

## 8

Second sign of trouble: The burglar alarm didn't sound. Why? Two police officers waited inside the pharmacy with guns drawn.

## 9

I'm thinking fire. Head to the propane tank with the box of matches. I'm not totally sure this is a smart thing to do. There's that flammable sign. But I figure a fire isn't going to burn through the tank, or the pipe, or the regulator, is it? No way. And if the tank had a leak I'd smell it, right? I scrounge twigs and sticks, build up a pile beneath the regulator, then push the stack flat. Better to keep the fire small, never allow the flames to reach the regulator—which is two feet off the ground—just let the rising heat do the work. I strike a match, watch it burn a few seconds above the twigs, then shake the match out. I squat there, look over at the clubhouse, the frost on the roof and windows. I light another and hold the match under a branchlet, which curls with flame. I add twigs, make a six-inch high fire. I touch the bottom of the regulator. Chilly. I build the fire higher, until the flames are licking within a few inches of the regulator. Keep adding twigs, careful to not let the fire get out of control. Melting ice drips from the metal into the fire, where it hisses and spits. I let the fire burn for a couple of minutes and then feel the regulator. Toasty.

## 10

First sign of trouble: The pharmacy door Sonia was supposed to leave open was locked. I sliced an eight-inch gash in my arm reaching through the broken glass to unlatch the door.

## 11

I stomp the fire out and return to the clubhouse, sit cross-legged in front of the pilot light and the six tubes of the burner. I light the match, turn the valve, hear the gas, let it flow for a few seconds, then insert the match. The tubes ignite one after the other, whump whump whump whump whump whump. I snap my head back, bumping against the pillar as the blue flame flashes, gushes towards my face, then sucks back into the tubes, where it flickers, glows. My nostrils twitch with the smell of burnt hair and I twist the singed ends between my fingers. The pilot light burns steady. I wait for the furnace's fan to switch on and then I scramble out from under the floorboards.

# Headlong for that Fair Target

## Eleanor Wilner

from *Cerise Press*

> *The traveller owns the grateful sense*
> *Of sweetness near, he knows not whence...*
> — *John Greenleaf Whittier, from "Snow-Bound"*

You might have said our aim was bad,
     for we had spent years chasing it — that
*sweetness near*, the target that kept moving
     with the years, borne away on wings,
or in the open freight cars that rattled
     through the night across vast sweeps
of plain, or sealed in envelopes sent
     by courier from Vladivostok to Minsk —

we tracked it in the packs of mules
     making their slow way up the tortuous
paths of the Himalayas, or glimpsed
     on a backroad in Mississippi, then
lost around a bend — despite our expert aim,
     like a mirage, it always moved
before us, always just beyond, no one
     knew quite where it might be found —

and so we traveled on, read almanacs,
     picked up lingua francas, practiced our aim,
visited psychics, mystics; racked our brains,
     riffled through racks and racks of
clothes, of magazines, guide books, schedules
     for the island ferries, encyclopedias;

pursued it through the chartless ways, the Metro
       of D.C., and the sewers of *Paris*, among
the living and the dead; it led us to frontiers,
       to the opening of the Panama Canal,
the discovery of snail warfare in the margins
       of monastic manuscripts, the zero
that could hold an empty place, the neutron bomb,
       the seedless tangerine.
                    Some thought it
could be found in a dream of used-to-be — for Freud,
       it was his mama's knee; for Orpheus, Eurydice;
for Yeats, full moon that mixed its silver with
       Byzantine gold domes; for the *philosophes* —
time-whitened porticos of reason, poised high
       above the marketplace; for all the weary
workers, abundant Eden with its frolicking
       naked pair... oh, where was the fair
target to be found? this strange ground-zero
       of desire, concentric circles, widening out
from a central lure, the jewel in the dragon's lair...


       But look! the weather-vane is turning in
the wind — its arrow, *this* time, points the way.
       You can feel it in the air, beneficent and beckoning,
and look! a light that's bobbing up ahead, though
       strangely, it glows red, is swinging like a lantern
in the dark, the way trains used to look when they had
       passed, their smoke still hanging in the air, the light
           on their caboose a vanishing point of red.

# Penumbra

## David McLendon

from *Everyday Genius*

The wires inserted beneath the skin during the cinching and draining allow me to position the limbs of each body perpendicular to the ground. This accommodates the shadows that move across the outside wall of my room. The shadows are each cast from the trees at the brake of the garden. Before I purify the bodies, I sit for a time and watch. Later I will braid the hair from where it falls and cut each braid from the hank of its root. The garments I will burn after unpocketing any overlooked possessions. I will scalpel each face from its undercarriage and mark the feet of each body with my colors. I will carry or drag or swaddle each body into the garden for its final ungristling. These are my duties. These are my evening chores. But for now I allow myself this small and peaceful time. Here the breeze off the water is lively year round. The darkness allows the moon a weak but sufficient light. The shadows of unmoving hands and feet are made to interact with the moving shadows of the trees. This overlapping of stillness and motion lobs up images of climbing and swimming and dancing. Something drops from the trees and the shadows are made to lift. The trees are not enough. There are people I still love, whom I no longer recall.

# Flashlight Tag

## Kyle Booten

from *storySouth*

My black shirt
inside out
I trip in
the wet ditch
but keep
going past
the tree
Jenny and
Matt humped
for money
past the
trampoline
where we dared
them
 and
 I hide
in a bush and
am quiet but
I hear your
 breath and
see your
lantern
I cower
in the drainage
pipe beneath
the street

but you know
this place
so I make
for the school
dumpsters
but you
are always
there rotting
I stow
myself be-
low deck on
Charon's
zombie barge
and you are
the coin
 and the
transcendent
dead I
fly back to
my warm
house (which
is really
 cheating b/c
houses are off-
limits)
reach into the
refrigerator
and how
much sweeter
milk tastes
when I am
a fugitive but
of course
you are what

makes it sweet
Everybody
has gone
home With
my night
vision I
see only
you I wish
you'd yield
but it's not
in your nature
now is
it You look
frozen but
are faster
than I am
Moon
of my
Hour
who must
chase me

though never
in your
real form

# A Sigh is Just a Sigh

## Sean Lovelace

from *Wigleaf*

### My Wife

claimed no one ever said "Play it again, Sam" in the movie *Casablanca*.

I told her no way that was true. No way are all these people going around, quoting that line, cherishing that line, claiming that line as theirs—and then it never existed at all.

"Look it up," she said flatly, and returned to the Scrabble board.

### Ingrid Bergman

told me she'd sleep with any man who desired. And there had been plenty. She slept with the majority of her costars on every film, most of the directors, several costume designers, and once, for kicks, a sound-effects editor—"helps me get into the role," she argued. It didn't bother her at all. It was like taking a walk, "like reading from a script," she said.

I was tempted. Oh god, I was tempted. Things like that don't just fall into your lap, and, honestly, my blood thrummed with the possibility. To put it plainly, it had been a while. But no, I told her, I just couldn't.

She said, "You ever seen a Nordic woman naked? Skin like fresh milk..."

She said, "I'm more flexible than I might appear, I'll tell you that."

She said, "Are you jesting? Marriage? That's just the art of saying no."

She said, "Do you mind if I smoke? Do you mind if I place this cigarette between my moist lips, and set it on fire?"

I told her actually I did mind. No tobacco smoke in the house, please.

She popped open her Zippo, lit, and inhaled. Blew a thin tunnel-cloud into my ceiling fan. Said, "Well then, come over here and stop me."

\*\*\*

Later that evening my wife said she smelled something in the house. Those exact words: "I-smell-something."

"Ok," I said, and walked outside, to winterize the lawn.


## The Doorbell

rang. I suffer some strange phobia concerning visitors to the front door, so whispered up to the peephole: a tall man, in a dull gray military uniform, cap, belt, holster, what appeared to be a pistol.

"Choose!" he said loudly. "You must choose: a trick, or a treat."

I stood in silence, holding my breath.

"Attention! I am selling *National Geographic* subscription, and decorative candles. For a youth group. What kind of man would deny himself a glimpse at a larger world, and an instrument to light the way?"

He shifted in the warming sunlight, took off his cap, scratched his head. In the bedroom, the droning of water, my wife showering. She was running late for a business trip to Fort Wayne, Indiana.

The man re-rang the doorbell, and stood there, blinking. His voice cracking a bit, he said, "Please open this door. I found your little dog. Your little dog was running free, over the hills and the roadways. Now I return him, so you can rope or chain him to your home, whatever is your pleasure. He will wag his tail. Don't you want to see him wag his tail, and call him happy?"

Strange, how time can bend and stretch. Minutes into hours, and so on. The shower stopped, and a toilet flushed.

"Oh, you!" the man said, his face reddening. His hand dropped to his holster, and my pulse kicked up. But then he paused, and shouted, "Oh you of very bad faith!"

Like a child, he made a face at the doorway, a scrunched-up scowl, then turned on his heels, marched up the street, and was gone.


## Humphrey Bogart

woke fully clothed in the guest room and complained about my futon: "Got a metal bar running down the middle. Hurts my back."

Actually, my futon frame was made of cedar. And had eight inches of mattress foam. The industry standard is six inches. I paid extra. I didn't tell him any of this. I just said, "You want some Pop-Tarts or something?"

He gave me this look. "You see this face?" he said. "How do I get by with this face? Looks like a potato."

I suggested many found his face handsome, in a rugged way.

He coughed, a dry rasping, and dug in his shirt pocket for a pack of Chesterfields. He said, "You don't know squat, do you? But thanks for the bunk. My wife is crazy. She'll be home right now with a knife, or a gun. She has one. But a man needs to face what he's made for himself, kid. I hope you're learning something here. I hope you're watching."

I was watching. He lit a cigarette, and I said nothing. A siren rose and fell in the distance. Or maybe the howl of a neighbor's dog. Bogart rocked himself up from the futon, and stood wincing. Rubbed his left knee and said, "Ever had your kneecap broken?"

I said I hadn't.

"Well, you will, one day. Sure as the rain. And you'll touch that place your whole life."


# I

rolled the garbage out on a Tuesday evening. A gigantic moon: silver and crackling. The bin caught the curb-edge and toppled over. Overfull as usual: Bisquick, a bag of stale croutons, empty bottles of Zinfandel; and a coffee maker. We bought a new coffee maker, one with pause-and-serve, and I had no idea what to do with the old one. I was thinking how—

"Pssst," a shadow said, from behind a shrubbery. A young woman stepped out, scrawny, pale and sweating. She was barefoot and wore a tattered dress.

"What the hell?" I said.

She held up a red duffel bag and hissed, "I've got them. I have the papers."

*The papers....*

The porch light kicked on; the garage door screeched open, and my wife appeared in the streetlight's pale wash.

"What's all this?" she said, squinting at the ground, the soda cans and coffee filters. Then up, at the woman. "And who is she? What's that she's holding?"

I stood there. Felt the dew between my toes. Searched

my mind for words, phrases, some rising soliloquy. Looked to the young woman, the duffel bag. Then to my wife, past her, to the blank face of the house. Looming window-eyes. I could hear crickets sawing in the grass—or the first stirrings of music, notes twinkling.

"Well," I said. "It goes like this…."

And in rolled the fog.

# Pregnant with Peanut Butter

## Michael Czyzniejewski

from *SmokeLong Quarterly*

was how Agnes described the sandwich. I'd asked her how much peanut butter she'd put on and that was her answer, like the bread was with child. Like it glowed.

"To make it count," she said.

I'd never eaten peanut butter. One sliver of one peanut would kill me. The amount of peanut butter wouldn't matter— you either die or you don't.

\*\*\*

I met Agnes at the pharmacy. She was the pharmacist. Every three months, my epinephrine injectors expired and I had to reload. I'd bought dozens, keeping two on my person and one in my house at all times.

"You've never gone into shock?" she said.

"Once, as a baby," I said. "I don't remember it."

"Fascinating," she said, sliding my debit card through the slot. "Come over tonight."

No woman had ever propositioned me. It had been years since I'd been on a date.

"Eight o'clock," she said, looking behind me to the next guy in line.

"Where do you live?" I asked.

"See you at 8."

Agnes was beyond what I considered my range. She looked like an actress playing a pharmacist in a movie. Her white coat seemed something the store made her wear, cover for her short skirts and plunging tops.

"Eight," she repeated as I walked away.

***

At 7, Agnes pulled into the parking lot of my complex. Then I recognized her car, her. She lived in the condo next door, was also the sexy neighbor. She entertained a lot, mostly men. I didn't make the connection, not in three years, not without the white coat.

I spied out the peephole. As Agnes walked by, she mouthed 8, and made for her door. I had to shower. I had a date. With Agnes, the neighbor pharmacist.

***

The sandwich was on the kitchen counter when Agnes let me in. I took a step back, as if it were a growling dog. I could be in the same room with it, as long as I didn't touch it. But still. I'd read about a guy in Michigan who walked into a grocery store, a store that sold peanuts in bins located on the back wall, a hundred yards away. The dust in the air was enough to do it. He died on the express lane conveyor. I'm not that sensitive.

"I've delayed this," she said. "Since you live next door."

"Delayed what?" I asked.

Agnes dimmed the lights, finished a glass of wine. "Did you bring your shots?"

I carried my shots like I carried my wallet and keys. "I can come back when you're done eating."

"Follow me," she said.

By the time I got to the bedroom, Agnes had undressed. The sandwich from the kitchen counter loomed on the credenza next to the bed.

That's when Agnes told me what we were going to do.

\*\*\*

The timing would be crucial, Agnes explained. First, she'd fuck me. Nothing weird, nothing violent, though I could make requests. At the cusp of my climax, she'd feed me the sandwich. As my throat closed, as my skin hived, I'd cum, the most magnificent, powerful, immaculate ejaculate of my life. Then she'd poke me with the shot and I'd be fine.

"I've always wondered if this would work," she said.

That's when I asked how much peanut butter she'd put on, when she used the word pregnant. She had nothing to lose and I could very well die.

"You should be on top," I said.

\*\*\*

When I was 9, I was abducted. On the way to school, there was this house with a million trees, a million bushes in front. One morning, some guy pulled me into the cover. I thought it was a kid from down the street, this bigger kid who was our paperboy and liked to torment me. But it was a strange guy wearing a wrestling mask. He put duct tape around my mouth and hands and carried me to the driveway where his red van was parked. We drove all day, stopping once for gas and once for McDonald's. When he reached his destination, it was dark and the tape on my mouth had come off.

"Why didn't you scream?" the guy asked.

I shrugged. I was an agreeable kid.

He led me to a shed behind a house in the woods. Later, I became much more scared of that shed than I was when it was happening. When I was 9, I didn't know what kidnappers did to kids in sheds in the woods.

It never got that far. Inside the shed, the guy's brother and dad were working on something, a table maybe, doing things that should be done in sheds, sanding and pounding.

"Marvin, what the hell?" the brother said.

"You just got out," the dad said.

The dad went to the house to call the police and the brother smacked Marvin across the head. Marvin undid my tape and cried, apologizing. I was home the next day, my parents never letting me go anywhere alone again until I was 17. My mom insists this is why I haven't married. I'm 39. I think I'm over it.

***

"I thought it would work," Agnes said. "Like with a noose."

Three empty epinephrine vials were next to me on the bed, along with my apartment key. I wiped sweat off my body with a pillow, catching my breath.

"It got stuck to the roof of my mouth," I said. "I thought that was a myth."

Agnes took the plate with the sandwich and disappeared. I dressed and followed.

"Up for a movie?" I said. "Dinner?"

Agnes was still nude, smoking, staring out her window. The TV was on the news.

"I liked the first part of it. Before the sandwich."

"You'll be back in tomorrow, for replacements," she said.

"First thing."

"First thing," she said. "I work at 4."

# Requiem for the Orchard

## Oliver de la Paz

from *Guernica*

1.

The hours there, the spindled limbs and husks
          of dead insects. The powders and the unguent
smells. What's left, now, of the orchards?
          What shape and hammer? What clang of apples?
What crease of brown paper sacks with greasy sandwiches?
          What salt burned into the brim of my cap?
What spines? What limb-aches from paintbrush
          handles? What white acrylics spattered on green
and dense humidity of dew from grass?
          Where lies the fruit trees and the hardy stock?
Where lies the open acre where we broke bottles
          with pellet guns during break? Where we shot
feral cats and rabbits? Where no animal was safe
          from the ferocity of boy?

2.

What's left now? The dumb hours of early risings,
          the laying down of metal irrigation pipe. Hush-a-bye
of sprinkler heads. We'd cinch the joints up, thread to thread
          and we'd take dabs of stolen chewing tobacco. We'd tamp it
down into the pink edges of our cheeks as we'd launch
          dirt clods at each other and hum to the prop-plane's
low pass over tree line. Bell-sounds, the thwack of aluminum

on rock kept time. And so did the horizon, browning
from pesticides. So did our skins, browning in the bare acres.
 We were keeping pace with a dying river, the water pressure,
weak with each new fitting. We were keeping pace with our shit job,
 how we each knew we were getting ripped off and how the filthy
dollars we'd wad into our pockets couldn't buy us a fuller river, time,
 or the deep meaning of zinc powder on chapped hands.

3.

What shape and what hammer held our breaths
 in the storehouse where the migrant workers hid their liquor?
Where holsters hung from coat hooks on the landowner's door
 and where we moped, still shining despite our growing declension.
Vapor-bloom of apples crushed against the forklift's tire
 cooked our senses and we'd dare each other
to steal the pistols for quick target practice. We'd stack
 mealy cores on top of each other, squint and pull the trigger
back and laugh as arms jerked from recoil.
 We'd pick off rabbits and birds, and though the owner knew
what we had done he'd drink black coffee with bourbon,
 laugh, and shake off the radio static with a wave. Later
in our houses, our hands would arc to the tender and luminous
 memory of firing a round and the twitch of a body's last kick.

4.

What crease of brown paper sacks? What amplitudes, our hunger
 to be men? What cheese sandwiches and noon times
sick from soda and too hard running? Our hands were
 the real language and we hit each other with closed fists
just to unhinge the details. This was a nowhere place.
 Miserable lunches and shit pay left us scuffling between
rows playing the tripping game or slapping down hard
 on each other's backs, leaving red palm-shaped welts.

We were fuses, amped on caffeine and the urgency of youth—
        and the orchard was hallowed ground. Like everything
we did was righteous and holy. Where the void was
        nowhere and everywhere and where our brown skins, dappled
with paint and insect bites were as pastoral as the understory
        which held all things in its cold radiance.

5.

And what salt? What hard cake on the hat brims? Our sweat
        gummed up the works, made us thick and slow-witted
in the early summer haze as we moped and stooped, painting
        row upon row of spindly trees, from the full-leafed
to the saplings. Our arms were heavy and our hands
        ached from carrying the gallon paint cans. We'd spill
a little here and there to lighten our steps. Moving was such
        theater. Acres blazed in the late afternoon.
Chemicals dusted our caps and mixed with our body mineral—
        white crystals and yellow film. We'd cough into our sleeves
and drink well water from our thermoses. And we'd pour
        the rest of it into our caps, letting it run down
our lengths, letting it mix with the mud, oil, and dust of ourselves,
        cold, decisive, and purely from the earth.

6.

What spines and what handles? The thin stripes of paint
        dried to bone on the boughs. The arc of our backs
curved. We were fingers bent on triggers—giddy
        and the trees would break beneath our savagery.
What we didn't kill, we'd break. Whole afternoons of breaking
        left us breathless and wet. The sweet tang of chewing tobacco
curled into our lips and we'd press the stuff and spit
        brown gobs at each other, until we were sick from the chase.
The bee boxes at the edge of the orchard were home

to our dares and we'd bet tins of chew on who'd do
the most damage with baseball bat to a bee box while suffering
the fewest stings.

     It was stupid and we knew it. And despite all
discretion, we charged,
our lips stinging from cinnamon while the open air
     hummed, impossible and kinetic.

7.

Where lies the open acre and all limns? Where the shade
     and what edges? What serrated blades and what cuts?
Where are we, leather-skinned, a spindle of nerves
     and frayed edges? What spare parts are we now
who have gone to the orchard and outlasted
     the sun and the good boots? The once tongued
salt from a tooth-cut wound scars now. The scars
     the deep-ruts of tree root where the earth's worn away.
And now, what? Salt? The memory of youth? The long
     hours of hands holding trembling hands? And what of
the hard
breaths and the crack of a bullet against a trunk. Leave it
     to memory and memory's unmaking. Leave it
to the sun's hot sear and the haze-induced recollections. Leave it
     to the hours and the hours and the hours.

8.

What then of the orchards? What then
     of the tree limbs, dark and heavy with fruit? What of
the stolen
pistol and the animal deaths suffered in the heavy sun? And
what of
     our masks, the resonant pitch of our throats as we'd cry
fair or foul with each blow from a fist? What of the orchards

where we grew long as the bramble and just as jagged?
Where our hearts kept pace with the sprinkler heads' *chk chk chk*?

Where the gauzy horizon was like a belt cinched around
our waists, keeping us together despite our youth?

What of our youth? What then, of our youth?
Of the cheap indiscretions with a stolen flask,

and a glance at skin magazines? Where we earned
quick dollars
doing nothing except being boys, learning without
comprehension,

the difficult industry of men?

# ex libris

## Kristiana Colón

from *Our Stories*

The tube lights flickered on. You were about to bite my cheek and stopped. We rustled against Collins and Dawson, the musk of shuffled pages settling to a hush. A shabby grad fingered the spines of nihilists two aisles over and I mouthed stop before the words could hatch in your throat. You leaned into the collar of my coat and mumbled something husky. The slow drag of an undergrad's Uggs through Hegel was no deterrent. You wanted to make love in the bookstacks and I loved that you wanted to make love in the bookstacks, though I probably would have said fuck. We neither had papers nor powerpoints looming and two a.m. bookstacks are pitch black and empty till the clack of Nine West stilettos cuts down PS1190 to PS3320 and even then the tube lights burst on like an isolated and noncommittal rainstorm and dissolve back to blackness once footsteps recede. And we knew the dull yellow painted metal of the second shelf would be cold against my bare buttocks and we argued over the significance of which aisle to do it in but we agreed without speaking to avoid anything sentimental, ruling out Shakespeare and Nelson Mandela, Morrison and Plath. A wet and open spasm dislodged the biography of de Sade and it coptered to the marble with a splat. You sat against a stack and invited me to your lap. I climbed and rocked and watched your head loll back to paperbacks that collapsed into a neighboring aisle. The stacks were never mopped or swept and their floors powdered us with dust. You lifted me into a mid-air buck, my denim dangling from my ankle like an orphan. We choked our thrill and tensed for footsteps. We blushed.

Thursday I went for sufis and mystics and the biography of Abd al-Malik. You were there in the aisle, with a sweater and glasses, and your hair perfectly combed.

# Maybe Visionary Sermon

## Ander Monson

from *CEIIA's Round Trip*

Tube lights flickered on. You were about to bite my cheek and
Okay. Expecting a savior but getting a sailor,
a salutation, a salami, and a couple dozen sales,
I regret everything I asked for and neglected to.
Something needs to save me from the glory flurry
of holiday benedictions greased so that they slip onto &
into everything, to buy a bunch of shit for our children
and our awe-inspiring pets. I am surprised to find
that, as it turns out, I want my personal Jesus to be Jesus,
and Christ, I am ashamed. On fire with it: pinpricks of guilt
everywhere, swelling on my body like hives.

A week after the holiday,
I am surrounded by a chattering cluster of asses. In the locker room
naked men stand and talk to me, their penises pendulums. It is weird
& hard not to think of Poe. And porn. And then Lorena Bobbitt. You see
the way my mind works. You can view pictures of his severed dinghy
online. I don't like Jesus or Johnny Cash. I distrust
rings, fire, and bushes, loaves and fishes, bars and bread.
No snow for weeks and in text I will not reveal myself.

I am not open
as a jar, heart surgery, or door. My neighborhood's windows
teem with unattractive naked bodies—I could use some grace here,
big forever X. I walk by them at night, every night, on patrol.
Spines of desiccated pines

dot the curbs, and I am asked
by the city to come up with a creative use for them.

I hope
for some evidence of full lives to come to me by telephone
at night, or by motor home at noon, or with cutlasses at dawn,
to my eyes via a variety of voyeurcams on the web,
conduit to another simulacrum of a life that could
be mine, they say, for less than a penny a day.

Each day is
a sieve through which almost anything could slip.
What I want for Xmas this year is X

Is intersection,
is new big sexy dream of rood, is towering powerline crosses
receding into horizon, as if they were marching robots
and we were on TV, helplessly, and had only the one slim
chance,
(If we were in Wyoming we could see another dozen miles
Before the light gives itself away to the next zone of smoke,
to the stroke that still separates your grandfather from his language.
If we were in the bright flat line of Wyoming

we would be being
or being beaten, being gloriously lonely, or being on our way
to anywhere but here.)

So I don't get anything at all,
no religion, Furby, Constantinople, headless driver in a ditch.
Thus it must be in me.  I rub myself to open.

I am wound
like twine into a colossal ball.  I touch myself like I would a wound.
The epidermis splits and inside is all light and starry sky.
It's hard to say what I should conclude about this.

# Ashes to Undermine the Smell

## Josh Maday

from *Lamination Colony*

Father is draped over the windows: what is left of him, dried and stiff and burgundy-brown: somewhat wrinkled and dirty, bleeding and caked with soul.

No, this was an accident. It should be soil. Soil, parched and small and something to be washed away at night. Just soil.

Flies. Smell of rot: meat untouched for days, spoiled in the heat, swarming swimming with maggots:

the air becomes a plastic bag over his head.
the house a festering womb

His head ached. No sleep. Prey to the blinding white heat.

[many mouths]: gutless wonder

Something is incubating inside the house.

It is always night. The sun does not know that it has already burned out.

*Now the blood shall be a sign for you on the houses . . . and when I see the blood, I will pass over you; and the plague shall not be on you to destroy you when I strike the land . . .*

Mother has hung sheets smeared with Father's blood over the windows to keep out the demons and the sun. The evil spirits must respect blood authority. But the flies still get in. They are hungry. Always hungry.

It is always night inside the house.

She will see a fly slide through the air, a spot darker than the dark. She will follow with her eyes as the fly lands among those already feasting on the bloodstained sheets. She will scream. She will call for

He walked through the house, swatting flies with a newspaper,
        all afternoon, for days,
          old rolled up newspaper, yellow and leathery,
          in the everlasting night of the living room.

The flies kept coming.

hungry for more

Many Mouths:

Mother sat in the chair while he stalked the flies.
        Take advantage of the darkness.
        He moved slowly in on the fly, limp yellow whip poised until inches away the flies fell to the floor with a snap of the wrist.

        A thousand black bodies swept into a pile.
        ankle deep in raisin wings            flies         flies
        She shouted again,         flies
        She shouted,         flies
        shouted.         flies         flies

The flies are all over the sheets.            flies
He came and waved his arms.
He still had his arms. His breath. Stale air to breathe.     flies
luxuriant excess
slipping                 flies
slopping in a puddle of slick black blood
in the middle of the field
I am born and no one survives in one piece.

Father: a dust-encrusted memory.

The swarm dispersed for a moment and then swirled back around to feast on the upright. He beat the ceiling the walls the windows and made little progress, stunning but not destroying.

pale gray face, blank, staring out from inside the sheets

Mother: gone into the other night of mourning.

She located flies from her chair. There's one, in the corner, on the ceiling, right in front of you, now it's on your shoulder. Come on, you have to look for them. You have to sneak up.

flies from her chair

His field of vision one giant blind spot.

long leaps of blood finding a way back into the earth

Look with your spiritual eyes.

heat blackened field of fission; eye of the sun tearing at bleeding sheets

Can you see the enemy's hand at work here?

the sun cries only behind the cover of storm clouds

record heat and no rain in over two months

I sense in my spirit that this is the work of the enemy.

always

He's using flies to eat your father's blood.

hungry for light

the sun will not weep today

She began to cry and asked why the Lord allowed the devil to bring plague and pestilence upon them. *Now the blood shall be a sign for you on the houses where you are, and the plague shall not be on you to destroy you* . . . After everything we've been through.

He stopped waving and walked out.

Where are you going? Where are you going? Are you going to abandon me, too? I can't do this on my own.

He tossed the coiled paper on the counter and walked through the kitchen out the back door.

He returned with an orange cord and dropped the roll on the living room floor and walked out again.

She resumes her prayers.

Lord, hear our prayer:

. . . hide this house in the hollow of your hand . . .

He returned again, carrying the black mass of the bug zapper through the house. He plugged the cord in and hung the electric blue light in the corner.

pray to the blinding white heat

Heat stalks about like a roaring lion seeking that which it may devour.

Time comes to steal, kill, and destroy.

*a burnt offering to the Lord; a sweet aroma, an offering made by fire to the Lord*

She sits on erect and rigid in the deepening gloom. The snapping and buzzing, sizzling, goes on indefinitely and out of rhythm, flicking little flashes of light into the room, casting the shadows of her prayers against the walls.

Smoke hangs in the air:
> the smell of burnt flies:
> a fragrant incense bearing witness to her affliction.

[Night] The fields are screaming

[Night.] The fields are screaming. Crickets. Frogs. Lost and angry spirits. Crossing from the yard into the field, he thinks he hears Mother call him. He stops. Listens. A coal snaps in the fire pit. He watches the dull red murmuring embers. He watches the surrounding area and waits to see if the sperm of the sun found fertile ground in the dry grass; he waited for the birth of a flame. He watched for some time. He awoke again and remembered Mother. He had heard her. He hadn't heard her. The fields are screaming. The fields are moving, wandering. The fields are driving cars and getting drunk and fucking. The fields are sitting alone in the house, praying through the heat. Praying. The fields pray and scream. The fields will not witness the birth of the flame to cleanse and transform all things. Not tonight. Not until this night finally passes, however many days that will take. He looks toward the field, into the darkness hiding the combine, covering the soil containing his father's blood, the beginning and end and eternity of all things; the dawn and duration of this endless night. He squeezes the hungry mouth of the Mason jar in his hand; the jar containing air from a moment in time when none of this had yet happened and ceased to happen, sealing in time untouched, untainted by what was coming to kill it all together. It only took the right combination of elements meeting in the chaos to set things in motion. He starts into the field. He hears a murmur from somewhere as he crosses from the yard into the field. Mother calls him. He stops. He waits. He looks at the glowing dying embers left from burning another load. The coals might pop and light the straw grass on fire and maybe burn the whole yard, maybe burn the house and the barn, spread to the field, blow into town and choke the sky with a sooty eclipse. No, the glow retreats beneath a blanket of ash. He stands there and listens for Mother, watching the dying coals wink from under the ashes, a trace of what once was. His eyes drift out of focus. The fields are screaming. He hears nothing.

# Wash, Dry, Fold

## Myfanwy Collins

from *Mississippi Review*

Phyllis ran the counter at a dry cleaner three days a week. Other days she did odd jobs. Walked dogs. Brought meals to shut ins. That sort of thing. But the dry cleaner was her main employer. She processed orders, delivered laundered clothing back to its owners, answered the phone, made change for the washers and dryers. It was quick, tidy work. She enjoyed being on her feet and scanning the rack of clothing as it spun. She relished the crisp odor of starch. She was friendly with the customers, allowed them to feel heard when they bitched about stains and missing buttons.

Often, a man named Greg phoned the dry cleaners and when he did, Phyllis spoke with him briefly and after he hung up, five minutes later, Greg would call again and attempt to resume the conversation. They were in the same network on Facebook—Manchester, NH. "I liked your profile," Greg said when she questioned him about why he had started messaging her, the messages then leading to lengthy phone calls.

"What about my profile?" Phyllis asked, intrigued. She hoped he liked her favorite quote:

> *If you live to be a hundred, I want to live to be*
> *a hundred minus one day so I never have to live*
> *without you.*
> A. A. Milne

"You have high-brow taste in television," Greg said. "I thought you might be classy." She didn't really watch television. She checked out video tapes and DVDs from the library—most of them British shows from PBS: *The Black Adder. Are You Being Served?*

She lay on her bed with the phone up snug to her ear during this particular conversation and her room seemed smaller to her after he said this. She saw the light seeping around the edges of her light blocking shades. The way her double bed didn't seem big enough when she was in it alone. The sadness of her clothes folded neatly on her chair. She should have been untidy. She should have left her drawers ajar. If she smoked, she would have seemed more interesting, maybe. If her books were more intellectual.

Her apartment was three rooms. Kitchen/living space, bathroom, and this, her bedroom. Windows looked out onto the parking lot. Many young professionals lived in the building. It had seemed the perfect spot after her divorce, but now with this exciting young man in her life it felt dowdy.

From Greg's profile she learned that he enjoyed travel, Second Life, and foreign films. He listed his job as Professional Dreamer. His favorite quote:

> *The ladder of success is best climbed by stepping on*
> *the rungs of opportunity.*
> *Ayn Rand*

But there was more to why Greg contacted her. He wanted. He wanted her, he said, to help him, please. His mother was six feet tall. She had never cut her hair. Would Phyllis please come and wash and dry it? Run a comb through it? Brush it? His mother had such beautiful hair. Auburn or strawberry blonde. He wasn't sure the color exactly as it changed in the light. It changed with the years.

Phyllis said she would think about it, but Greg pushed to know when Phyllis would make her decision.

Soon, she said.

In her quiet moments, Phyllis composed an image of Greg's tall mother. Her loose hair. The ruddiness of her cheeks. The coarseness of her nipples from overuse. A wide, pale belly. A thicket of pubic hair.

But why had she assumed the woman would be naked? Less an assumption and more of a wish: The woman would be naked. Phyllis would enter the wide-plank, wood-floored kitchen and find the woman sitting on a hard-backed wooden chair, once painted red and now chipping. No cloth on the table, no dishes in the sink.

"My son brought you," the woman would say. She would stand then and turn, look back at Phyllis over her shoulder and then. And then. And then, Phyllis would see all of her beauty. "Come," the woman would say. And Phyllis would follow.

\*

Greg's dream was to produce a video called "Perfections/ Imperfections." The setting would be a strip club in Vegas. On one side of the club would be the naked imperfections: the legless, the flippered, the obese. The blind. The pregnant.

And on the other side, the buff, the blonde, the beautiful. No stretch marks. No dimpled asses.

Customers would start out on the imperfections and after they had had their fill, move over to the perfections side to cleanse the palate, if you will.

And what of Phyllis? He had only her profile photograph to go on. Which side was she? She wasn't a perfection, but then she wasn't exactly an imperfection either. He gazed at her Facebook profile photo. She appeared to have good hair. Thick, curly, long. Her eyes were washed out and verging on hopeless.

She might have had a few small acne scars on her cheeks concealed not so well with makeup. Her nose seemed knocked off-kilter. Oh, he didn't know. There was a lot, he supposed, that made her an imperfection.

Most importantly, she was dreamless, or at least this was what he gathered when he asked her what her hopes were.

"I'm not sure," Phyllis said. Too quickly. She didn't have any hopes, no dreams, but he knew that already. And this was a fatal flaw, making her the ultimate imperfection. All of the perfections had hopes and dreams; they were stripping their way through grad school in order to get their PhDs or they were in law school. They wanted a better life for their families. They would buy their mother a house. They would make sure their own kids never wanted for anything.

While the imperfections wanted little. They were dreamless. They were passing time.

*

Greg's mother left when he was nine. Gone. Packed up. Drove away. Left her dental practice. Left her piano. Left her sons and her husband. Gone, gone, gone.

Where did she go? West in her Honda Accord. She sent postcards from Glacier National Park where she summered and from Seattle where she wintered. "I sleep in my car," the summer postcards said, "and during the day, I hike."

She had seen Grizzly. In Yellowstone, she had seen wolves.

"I am happy," her postcards said. "Please do not miss me, because I do not miss you," the cards said.

Love,
Mom.

*

Phyllis said yes to Greg. "I will wash your mother's hair," she said and he hung up, then called back in three minutes. "I'm sorry I hung up on you," he said. "I got excited."

*

Of course, Greg went in search of his mother. When he was nineteen, he borrowed money from his father and bought a small truck. "I'm going to get mom," he told his dad. "I will bring her home."

Greg's father wasn't sure he wanted his wife back. Life was simpler without her. There was dust under the bed. He liked it there.

*

Phyllis agreed to meet Greg on a Thursday. The rendezvous was to take place outside the dry cleaner. Though he had never seen Phyllis but for her photograph, Greg said he would know her. "I feel you," Greg said.

What was his mother's name?

Madeline.

Maddy?

No. She prefers you use her full name, please.

The day was hazy. Phyllis huddled beneath the awning, staring out across the parking lot. A few cars dotted the landscape. It was 7:30 AM and none of the other shops were open yet. The supermarket opened at nine, but the dollar store didn't open until 10 and Mike's Subs at 10:30. The dry cleaner was open, though. Jeanie was working the counter. She chatted with Phyllis when she stepped out for a smoke but seemed uninterested in why Phyllis was there on her day off.

At five minutes past rendezvous time, she wondered if he would show up at all. She watched as a red SUV pulled into the lot. She hadn't expected him to drive a vehicle like that. The car circled the in front of the supermarket and then raced past her. The driver was a teenage boy. Not him. Greg was a man.

She shouldn't have said yes. She turned to check her face in the reflection of the window. She saw Jeannie leaning against a broom, staring up at the morning news on the television. There was a car accident on the screen. A medivac helicopter. Perhaps Greg was involved.

She returned her attention to her reflection. She saw him, then, walking across the parking lot. A baseball cap obscured his face in shadow. She turned to face him as he approached. He raised his hand in a wave.

*

Greg had an old photo of his mother taken just before she left home. She crouched awkwardly in their garden, planting impatiens. Her hands were bare and covered in dirt and she laughed as she turned to the camera. Her teeth were straight, barely any space between them to slide a piece of floss. The edges of the teeth were not flattened, rather slightly pointed. Predatory teeth. He would know her when he saw her. He would get her to smile and look for the sharpness.

Greg found his mother in West Glacier. It hadn't been difficult. It seemed everyone who worked in the park knew her, knew of her. She was something of a renegade. "She's had her run ins," one of the rangers told him, "but Maddy's good people." The ranger told him he'd find his mother's car in the parking lot of the general store near the campground. "She sleeps in her car," he said, "so either late night or early morning, she'll be there."

He found her car—a newer Accord than the one she'd

left home in—and waited beside it, hunched down, squatting on his heels. Where had she gotten the money for a new car? Probably his father had a hand in it. For a while Greg had suspected that his father was sending her money; this money kept her away from them, kept her living this transient lifestyle. Greg cupped a hand up to the glass and peered through the windows. The backseat was made up as a bed with a sleeping bag and pillow. The front passenger side held a plastic bin filled with papers—cards, bank statements, scribbles on loose leaf. Folks passing by eyeballed him like he was a criminal. "I'm waiting for my mother," he yelled after they passed, when no one was around to hear him.

By nightfall, she had not appeared, so he climbed into the cab of his truck to wait. He kept the window cracked open so he would hear her approach. He awoke in the night. His neck ached from how it had lain to the side on the seat back. He looked to his mother's car parked next to his. He saw the back of her head against the window. She was reading in the light of a lantern. She turned slightly and he saw her in profile. Yes. Yes, that was his mother.

He yearned to reach a hand out and touch her wiry hair. Mama, he thought. It wasn't what he had called her as a boy. She was Mom. But in his mind he heard Mama again and again, growing louder, more panicky.

Greg fumbled with his keys in the ignition. He started the truck and drove straight out of the parking lot without turning on his lights. It wasn't until he was miles away on a stretch of road dangerous for the free-range cattle that he turned on his lights again. There along the side of the road a dozen pairs of eyes were illuminated. Cows and their calves, sleeping, chewing. He slowed as he passed them, reverent. He drove on and on until the voice in his head quieted. Until he was away from the pull of her.

\*

Greg's body was slight. His hair red. How had he such a tall mother? But maybe the woman wasn't his mother. Maybe she wasn't six feet tall. Maybe it was all a lie. She should not have agreed to meet him.

"You came," she said, finally, after the silence of the two of them standing face-to-face became too much. Gone was the comfort of the computer screen, the ease of the phone.

"We should go," Greg said. She noted that his hands and forearms were tanned and freckled. That his sneakers were cleanly white. She was comforted then that he was okay. And she would simply wash his mother's hair and that would be the end of it. She could do that. She could offer such kindness.

"Yes," she said, "let's."

\*

The woman was bedridden. The mother. Maddy. Madeline. Her eyes were aware, showed gratitude, as Phyllis ran a comb through her drying hair. It had been a challenge to wash it. Phyllis had had to get in the tub with her and cradle the woman in between her legs as though she were giving birth to her. As if their embrace was anything other than out of utility. It was not the scene Phyllis had expected after all. There was nothing of the erotic she had anticipated, had craved.

The woman was aged. Her long hair was glorious but wiry. Her teeth, sharp. Greg had demurely left Phyllis to her work.

She felt for the woman. How to end up here living in a one-bedroom apartment with her son? He slept on the couch, he said. He made a point of saying.

Phyllis had answered Greg's call, this calling. She felt righteous and clean for serving this woman, but she could not do it again. She felt she had driven out her uglier thoughts. The ones involving her and the woman and their hands.

The air in the bedroom was overheated. Simply, Phyllis could not breathe. She looked out through the vast rectangle of the window. Beyond was the pale sky. Beyond that the stars and moon. Beyond and beyond and beyond this room there was air. This woman would die here. Phyllis knew that. She did not want to be there when it happened. She would satisfy herself that she had left this woman clean. It was enough.

*

Greg's mother wrote to him after he left Montana.

I waited for you. I stayed up all night. I was going to tell you about the huckleberries and where to find the best of them. You would have to share them with the bears, though, and so you might get eaten. But you drove away without even saying hello. Please do not miss me, because I do not miss you.

Love,
Mom.

## Notable Works

**Moby Dick**
Jason Bredle, *No Posit*

**Pocket Finger**
Ryan and Christy Call, *This PDF Chapbook*

**The Hobblers**
Dan Chaon, *SmokeLong Quarterly*

**They Are Feeling Good**
Chris Cheney, *Jellyfish Magazine*

**Eight Micros**
Kim Chinquee, *FRiGG*

**John Laroquette**
Thomas Cooper, *Memorious*

**Four Recent Apocalypses**
Lucy Corin, *Hobart*

**Opener**
Giancarlo DiTrapano, *Everyday Genius*

**Basics**
Gabe Durham, *Matchbook*

**As Gracefully as I Knew How**
Elizabeth Ellen, *Action Yes*

**The Beaten Path**
Elizabeth Ellen, *Lamination Colony*

**Going to Hell in Pieces**
Gary Fincke, *Green Hills Literary Lantern*

**Dog Catcher**
Brian Foley, *Front Porch*

**Seattle Gymnopédie**
Scott Garson, *SmokeLong Quarterly*

**Gratitude**
Molly Gaudry, *YB*

**Ginka's Perfume**
Anne Germanacos, *Swink*

**Three Little Stories**
Amelia Gray, *dispatch litareview*

**How He Felt**
Amelia Gray, *Wigleaf*

**The Gray**
Aaron Gwyn, *Esquire*

**Four Stories**
Evelyn Hampton, *Spork*

**Meat From a Meatman**
Lindsay Hunter, *Eyeshot*

**Sex: An Intercourse**
Bryan Hurt, *Barrelhouse*

**Hospitable Madness**
Jac Jemc, *featherproof Light Reading Series*

**The Crickets Try to Organize Themselves Into Some Raucous Pentameter**
Jac Jemc, *JMWW*

**Painted Faces**
Tim Jones-Yelvington, *Keyhole*

**Wedding Party**
Lily Ladewig, *Jellyfish Magazine*

**Creek Monster**
Jeff Landon, *Twelve Stories*

**Toast**
Darby Larson, *Keyhole*

**Maui Eyes**
Charles Lennox, *Corduroy Mountain*

**Shrub Prayer**
Cindy Loehr, *Everyday Genius*

**The Moon is a Star**
Peter Markus, *Necessary Fiction*

**Square in the Gut of Lovemaking Lessons**
Karyna McGlynn, *Siren*

**Six Micros**
Mary Miller, *FRiGG*

**This Isn't Like That**
Kyle Minor, *Waccamaw*

**Oklahoma**
Carrie Murphy, *Keyhole*

**I Use Commas Like Ninja Stars**
Sam Nam, *SmokeLong Quarterly*

**Trace**
Darlin' Neal, *SmokeLong Quarterly*

**Edward Wilson**
Linnea Ogden, *Harp & Altar*

**From "A Compendium of Domestic Incidents"**
Joanna Ruocco, *Conjunctions*

**Fervent Vows of Love**
Fortunato Salazar, *Wigleaf*

**We Will Take What We Can Get**
Matthew Salesses, *This PDF Chapbook*

**The Architects of the Dismantling**
Bradley Sands, *Mudluscious*

**Winter Register**
Jason Schwartz, *Failbetter*

**Film**
Claudia Smith, *Wigleaf*

**If Everything is Inevitable**
Angi Becker Stevens, *Monkeybicycle*

**The Sea Lions**
J.A. Tyler, *BluePrintReview*

**Jimmy, How He Wants a Piece of Sun Folded in His Hands**
J.A. Tyler, *You Must Be This Tall To Ride*

**Nines**
Anne Valente, *PANK*

**Carolina, Open Invitation**
Patrick Whitfill, *Abjective*

**A Pile of Shirts, Ripped from the Body**
Kevin Wilson, *Clapboard House*

**My Hand, Dead Tissue, Severed at the Wrist**
Kevin Wilson, *Hobart*

**Night Stand**
Daniel Woodrell, *Esquire*

# Contributors' Notes

**Chris Bachelder** is the author of *Bear v. Shark, U.S.!,* and the web novel *Lessons in Virtual Tour Photography.* His novel *Abbott Awaits* will be published in 2011. He teaches in the writing program at the University of Massachusetts.

**Brian Baldi**'s writing has appeared in *The Massachusetts Review, Denver Quarterly, Fairy Tale Review, SKEIN* and *Fourteen Hills.* His chapbook, *Lunar Asparagus,* was published by Invisible Ear in 2009.

Some say women aren't funny. They are wrong. **Elissa Bassist** is the editor of *Funny Women,* a popular and soon-to-be-critically-acclaimed column on TheRumpus.net, which offers an ever-widening space for women to submit and publish original humor pieces. She lives and works in her apartment, affectionally known as "The Bell Jar," in San Francisco. Please visit www. elissabassist.com to learn more.

**Jensen Beach** lives in Massachusetts with his family. He helps edit *Hobart web* and can be found online at jensenw.blogspot.com.

**Mary Biddinger** is the author of *Prairie Fever* (Steel Toe Books, 2007) and the chapbook *Saint Monica* (forthcoming, Black Lawrence Press). She edits the Akron Series in Poetry, co-edits *Barn Owl Review* and the Akron Series in Contemporary Poetics, and directs the NEOMFA.

**Kyle Booten** is currently a Helen Zell Fellow at the University of Michigan, Ann Arbor. He is co-editor of the online project *Just: Literature Under Severe Constraint,* and his poems have appeared in *Tin House, Guernica, Hotel Amerika,* and elsewhere.

**Robert Bradley** has been writing fiction on and off for ten years. He's been published in the *Apocalypse Reader* and on the net. This story was published at *Frigg Magazine*.

**Emily Bromfield** grew up and still lives in South East London. She's a graduate of the Creative Writing MA at Goldsmiths College and her short stories have been published in a number of anthologies. She currently works for an international writers' organization.

**Rachel Bunting** lives and writes in Southern New Jersey, between the Delaware River and the Pine Barrens. She is the author of two chapbooks, *Ripe Again* and *Imprimatur*, and her first full-length collection is in progress.

**Aaron Burch** is the author of the chapbook, *How to Take Yourself Apart, How to Make Yourself Anew* (PANK), and the full-length collection of short fictions, *How to Predict the Weather* (Keyhole Books). He is the editor of *Hobart*.

**Robert Olen Buter**'s latest novel is *Hell* and his third book of short shorts, *Weegee Stories*, is due later this year. He won the Pulitzer Prize for fiction in 1993. He teaches at Florida State University.

**Dan Chaon** is the author of several books of fiction, most recently the novel *Await Your Reply*. He lives in Cleveland, Ohio, and teaches at Oberlin College.

**Kim Chinquee** is the author of the collections *Oh Baby*, and *Pretty*. She has received a Pushcart Prize, and lives in Buffalo, New York.

**Myfanwy Collins** has been published in *The Kenyon Review, AGNI, Quick Fiction, Mississippi Review, Cream City Review, Potomac Review, Jabberwock Review, Monkeybicycle, SmokeLong Quarterly, FRiGG, Saranac Review* and other venues. She also has work included in *Rose Metal Press Field Guide to Writing Flash Fiction* (2009) and the 2008 Dzanc Books *Best of the Web* Anthology.

**Kristiana Colón** is an adjunct English professor at Malcolm X College in Chicago and an experienced poet, performer, and burgeoning playwright. She is an MFA graduate from the School of the Art Institute and has been seen on HBO's *Def Poetry Jam*. More information about Kristiana, as well as video, audio, and text samples of her work, can be found at www.kristianacolon.com.

**Thomas Cooper**'s fiction has appeared or is forthcoming in *Oxford American, Willow Springs, New Orleans Review, Sonora Review, Memorious*, and others. His chapbook of flash fiction, *Phantasmagoria*, was published by Keyhole Press in 2009. He is at work on a story collection and novel.

**Lydia Copeland**'s stories have appeared in the *Mississippi Review, Quick Fiction, Glimmer Train, the Northville Review* and others. Her chapbook, *Haircut Stories* is available from the Achilles Chapbook Series, as well as part of the chapbook collective *Fox Force 5* from Paper Hero Press.

**Elizabeth Crane** is the author of three collections of short stories, *When the Messenger is Hot, All this Heavenly Glory,* and *You Must Be This Happy to Enter.* Her work has appeared in numerous publications, been featured on NPR's Selected Shorts and adapted for the stage by Chicago's Steppenwolf Theater company.

**Michael Czyzniejewski**'s debut collection of short stories, *Elephants in Our Bedroom*, was released by Dzanc Books in 2009. He teaches at Bowling Green State University, serves as Editor-in-Chief of Mid-American Review, and is a 2010 NEA Fellow in Literature.

Despite this, or perhaps because of it, **Frank (Dahai)** is.

**Oliver de la Paz** is the author of three books of poetry: *Names Above Houses, Furious Lullaby,* and *Requiem for the Orchard.* He is the co-chair of the Kundiman.org advisory board and he teaches creative writing at Western Washington University.

**Alison Doernberg** grew up in Atlanta, Georgia, but has recently traded her native dogwoods for the palm trees of Oakland, where she works as a high school counselor and misses the sound of thunder. Her work has appeared or is forthcoming in *Eleven Eleven, Alehouse, Switchback, Inkwell, Fourteen Hills,* and *Redivider.*

**Kasandra Duthie**'s fiction has been published in *The Emerson Review, Hayden's Ferry Review, The Main Street Rag Fiction Anthology,* and *The Summerset Review.* She lives with her patient husband and two hysterical dogs in Minnesota where she teaches English at Saint Paul College.

**Elizabeth Ellen** is the author of *Before You She Was a Pit Bull* (Future Tense) *and Sixteen Miles Outside of Phoenix* (Rose Metal Press). She lives in Ann Arbor and is editor of Short Flight/Long Drive Books (a division of *Hobart*).

**Claudia Emerson** won the Pulitzer Prize in poetry for her book, *Late Wife,* and her most recent book publication is *Figure Studies*—both volumes are from Louisiana State University Press. She is Professor of English and Arrington Distinguished Chair in Poetry at the University of Mary Washington in Fredericksburg, Virginia.

**Brian Evenson** is the author of ten books of fiction, most recently the limited edition novella *Baby Leg,* published by New York Tyrant Press in 2009. In 2009 he also published the novel *Last Days* (which won the American Library Association's award for Best Horror Novel of 2009) and the story collection *Fugue State,* both of which were on *Time Out New York*'s top books of 2009. His novel *The Open Curtain* (Coffee House Press) was a finalist for an Edgar Award and an IHG Award.

**Lucas Farrell** is the author of two chapbooks: *The Blue-Collar Sun* (Alice Blue Books, 2009) and *Bird Any Damn Kind* (Caketrain Press, 2010). His first collection of poems, *The Many Woods of Grief,* won the 2010 Juniper Prize for Poetry and will be published by University of Massachusetts Press in 2011. He co-edits the poetry journal *Slope* and currently lives and works on a goat farm in Vermont.

**Sasha Fletcher**'s novella *When All Our Days Are Numbered Marching Bands Will Fill the Streets and We Will Not Hear Them Because We Will Be Upstairs in the Clouds* is due out from ml press in June. He is an MFA candidate in poetry at Columbia University in the city of New York.

**Scott Garson** is the author of *American Gymnopédies* (Willows Wept Press 2010). He edits *Wigleaf*.

**Molly Gaudry** is the author of the verse novel *We Take Me Apart* (Mud Luscious, 2009) and the editor of *Tell: An Anthology of Expository Narrative* (Flatmancrooked, 2010). Find her online at mollygaudry.blogspot.com.

**Matthew Glenwood**, 39, is a lifelong resident of Michigan's Upper Peninsula.

**Amelia Gray**'s writing has appeared in *American Short Fiction, Lamination Colony, DIAGRAM*, and *Caketrain*, among others. She is the author of *AM/PM*, published by Featherproof Books, and *Museum of the Weird*, which is due August 2010 through Fiction Collective 2.

**Mary Hamilton** is a writer, teacher, and optician living in Chicago. Her chapbook, *We Know What We Are* is forthcoming from Rose Metal Press.

**Leslie Harrison**'s first book, *Displacement*, won the Bakeless prize in poetry in 2008 and was published by Mariner Books. She lives and writes in rural western Massachusetts.

**Matt Hart** is the author of two previous books of poetry, *Who's Who Vivid* (Slope Editions) and *You are Mist* (Moor Books), with a third book, *Wolf Face*, on the way from H_NGM_N Books this Fall. He lives in Cincinnati, where he co-founded and edits *Forklift, Ohio: A Journal of Poetry, Cooking & Light Industrial Safety*.

**Christine Hartzler**'s essays and poetry have appeared in *Fiction Writers Review, Ninth Letter, Cream City Review, Michigan*

*Quarterly Review, Painted Bride Quarterly,* and *Mudlark.* She lives in Seattle with a physicist and two cats.

**Donora Hillard** is the author of the poetry collection *Theology of the Body* (Gold Wake Press, 2010). Her work is forthcoming *Hint Fiction: An Anthology of Stories in 25 Words or Fewer* (W.W. Norton & Company, 2010).

**Lily Hoang** is the author of the novels *The Evolutionary Revolution, Changing* (recipient of a 2009 PEN/Beyond Margins Award), and *Parabola* (winner of the 2006 Chiasmus Press Un-Doing the Novel Contest).

**Dave Housley**'s story collection, *Ryan Seacrest is Famous,* was published in 2007 by Impetus Press. His work has appeared or is coming soon in *Beloit Fiction Journal, the Collagist, Hobart, Nerve, Quarterly West,* and some other places. He's one of the editors at Barrelhouse magazine, and keeps his online stuff at davehousley.com.

**Jac Jemc** lives in Chicago. Her chapbook, *This Stranger She'd Invited In,* is due out from Greying Ghost this year and her first novel, *My Only Wife,* is forthcoming from Dzanc Books in 2012.

**Stephen Graham Jones** has six novels and one collection published, with another novel (*It Came from Del Rio*) and another collection (*The Ones That Got Away: Horror Stories*) on the way. "Modern Love" is maybe his hundred-and-tenth or so published story. He teaches in the MFA program at the University of Colorado at Boulder.

**Sean Kilpatrick**, raised in Detroit, is published in *Columbia Poetry Review, Fence, LIT, No Colony, Action Yes, New York Tyrant, Juked.*

**Matthew Kirkpatrick**'s writing has appeared in *Conjunctions, The Notre Dame Review, Harp & Altar, Center,* and elsewhere. He lives in Salt Lake City, UT.

**Stokely Klasovsky** is a veteran of the U.S. Navy and a graduate of the College of Charleston. He's also a huge fan of dogs and carrot juice, but not necessarily in that order.

**Kendra Kopelke** is founder and co-editor of *Passager*, a press and journal dedicated to promoting new older writers. The author of five books of poetry, she directs the MFA in Creative Writing & Publishing Arts at the University of Baltimore.

**Krystal Languell** is the author of *The Mean Particle*, a chapbook to be published this year by Tilt Press. Her poetry has appeared in *Denver Quarterly, H_NGM_N, No Tell Motel* and elsewhere. She also writes reviews for *NewPages*.

**Emma J. Lannie** lives in Derby, England, where she works as a librarian. You can read more of her stories at garglingwithvimto. blogspot.com.

**Charles Lennox** lives and loves in Orange, CA. His stories have appeared in *Quick Fiction, Smokelong, Mud Luscious, Wigleaf,* and *FRiGG*.

**Sara Levine**'s writing has appeared in *Nerve, The Iowa Review, Conjunctions, Fairy Tale Review*, and many other magazines. She won a 2008 Bridport Prize for Fiction, and her essays have been anthologized in *Best of Fence* and *The Touchstone Anthology of Creative Nonfiction: 1970 to the Present*. She is Chair of the Writing Program at The School of the Art Institute of Chicago.

**Jie Li** just completed her PhD in Chinese literary and cultural studies at Harvard. She has published several articles on Chinese cinema and made a documentary film in Cameroon.

**Sean Lovelace** has a flash fiction collection by Rose Metal Press titled *How Some People Like Their Eggs*. He likes to run, far.

**Josh Maday** lives in Michigan. His work has been published in *New York Tyrant, Phoebe, Action Yes, Keyhole, Apostrophe Cast, Word Riot, elimae*, and elsewhere.

**Ravi Mangla** lives in Fairport, NY. His short fiction has appeared in *Gargoyle, Annalemma, Gigantic,* and *McSweeney's Internet Tendency.* He is currently working on a story collection.

**Peter Markus** is the author of *Bob, or Man on Boat*, a novel brought out by Dzanc Books in 2008. His new book, *We Make Mud*, is forthcoming from Dzanc in March of 2011.

**Meredith Martinez** is a fiction student in the Warren Wilson College MFA Program for Writers. She lives with her husband in Mesa, AZ.

**James Scannell McCormick** holds a doctorate in creative writing-poetry from Western Michigan University. His works have appeared in *CutBank, The Lucid Stone, SLANT, Rattapallax,* and most recently in *Unsplendid.* His poem "Lot (Hermes in Tulips)" was nominated for a 2008 Pushcart Prize; his poem "Trouble" has been nominated for a 2009 Pushcart Prize. He currently lives and teaches in Rochester, Minnesota.

**Steven J. McDermott** is the author of the story collection *Winter of Different Directions* and the editor of *Storyglossia.* Find more of his work at stevenmcdermott.com.

**David McLendon** is an Edward F. Albee Foundation Fellow. He is the founder and editor of *Unsaid.* He divides his time between Ann Arbor and Brookyln.

**Mary Miller** is the author of a short story collection, *Big World*, and a chapbook, *Less Shiny.* Her stories can be found *in McSweeney's Quarterly, Black Clock, Indiana Review, Mississippi Review, Oxford American, Fiction, New Stories from the South 2008,* and many others.

**Kyle Minor** is the author of *In the Devil's Territory*, a collection of stories and novellas. Recent work appears in *The Southern Review, Surreal South, Fifty-Two Stories, Twentysomething Essays by Twentysomething Writers,* and *Best American Mystery Stories 2008.*

**Ander Monson** is the author of a host of paraphernalia including a decoder wheel, several chapbooks and limited edition letterpress collaborations, a website otherelectricities.com, and five books, most recently *The Available World* (poetry, Sarabande, 2010) and *Vanishing Point: Not a Memoir* (nonfiction, Graywolf, 2010). He lives and teaches in Tucson, Arizona, where he edits the magazine *DIAGRAM* and the New Michigan Press.

**Stefani Nellen** is currently at work on a collection of short stories about running and a science fiction novel about randomness and the mind. She had stories in *Web Conjunctions, Inkwell, Cosmos, Apex Digest*, and *Best of the Web 2008*, among other places. She lives in the Netherlands.

**Amber Norwood** received her M.A. in poetry from California State University, Northridge, where she is now a lecturer. Her work has appeared in *Barefoot Muse, Prick of the Spindle, Journal of Truth and Consequence* and others, and she has had work nominated for the Pushcart Prize.

**Cami Park** writes small things various. She keeps a blog at oddcitrus.wordpress.com.

**Jennifer Pieroni** is editor of the literary journal *Quick Fiction*.

**Julie Platt** was born and raised in Pittsburgh. She thinks a lot about writing, digital technologies, culture, poetry, materiality, and the imagination. You can visit her at julieplatt.com.

**Michelle Reale**'s fiction has appeared in *Smokelong Quarterly, elimae, Word Riot* and others. She has twice been nominated for a Pushcart Prize. Her fiction chapbook, *Natural Habitat* was published by Burning River in 2010.

**Nanette Rayman-Rivera**, three-time Pushcart nominee, winner of the Glass Woman Prize, is the author of the new memoir, *to live on the wind*, published by Scattered Light Publications. Her story is the first hand account of what really happens in the homeless shelters, food stamps, Medicaid and public housing projects, and how she got there.

**Dave Rowley** is originally from Sydney, Australia. He now lives in Seattle with his wife and two sons. Dave's poems have been previously published in *Mimesis, Juked,* and *Stirring.* He blogs at creativechai.com.

**Joanna Ruocco** co-edits *Birkensnake,* a fiction journal. She is the author of *The Mothering Coven* and *Man's Companions.*

**F. Daniel Rzicznek**'s books include *Divination Machine* (Free Verse Editions/Parlor Press, 2009), *Neck of the World* (Utah State University Press, 2007) and *Cloud Tablets* (Kent State University Press, 2006). He is also coeditor, with Gary L. McDowell, of *The Rose Metal Press Field Guide to Prose Poetry: Contemporary Poets in Discussion and Practice* (Rose Metal Press, 2010). He currently teaches at Bowling Green State University.

**Christine Schutt** is the author of two short story collections, *Nightwork* and *A Day, a Night, Another Day, Summer.* Her first novel, *Florida,* was a National Book Award finalist; her second novel, *All Souls,* a finalist for the 2009 Pulitzer Prize. Among other honors, Schutt has twice won the O.Henry Short Story Prize, as well as Pushcart and Mississippi Review fiction prizes. She is the recipient of NYFA and Guggenheim Fellowships. Schutt lives and teaches in New York.

**Amy Lee Scott** is a student in University of Iowa's Nonfiction Writing Program. Her work has appeared in *Brevity, Damselfly Press, The Daily Palette, Iron Horse Literary Review, Quarter After Eight,* and as a notable essay in *The Best American Essays 2009.* She has work forthcoming in *Fourth Genre.*

**Matthew Simmons** lives in Seattle with his cat, Emmett. He is the author of the novella *A Jello Horse (Publishing Genius Press),* and is The Man Who Couldn't Blog (themanwhocouldntblog. blogspot.com).

**Sarah J. Sloat** lives in Germany, where she works for a news agency. Her poems have appeared in *RHINO, Juked,* and *Bateau,* among other publications. Her chapbook, *In the Voice of a Minor Saint,* was published by Tilt Press in 2009.

**Sue Standing** is the author of four books of poetry, most recently *False Horizon*. She teaches Creative Writing and African Literature at Wheaton College (Norton, MA).

**Leigh Stein** is the author of the chapbook *How to Mend a Broken Heart with Vengeance* (Dancing Girl Press). She lives in Brooklyn, where she teaches drama to children.

**Angi Becker Stevens**' stories have appeared in recent or future issues of *Barrelhouse, The Collagist, Pank, SmokeLong Quarterly, Storyglossia, Necessary Fiction, Monkeybicycle, Wigleaf*, and more. She lives with her family in Michigan.

**Terese Svoboda**'s fifth book of fiction, *Pirate Talk or Mermalade*, will be published by Dzanc this fall. Bison Books will publish her sixth novel, *Bohemian Girl*, in 2011.

Four stories from **August Tarrier**'s collection (entitled *Are You Decent?*) have won national prizes—the Diagram Innovative Fiction Prize for "Field Notes" (published in *Diagram*, 2009); the Zoetrope Fiction Prize for "I Hold You Harmless" (2005), published in *Zoetrope: All-Story* (Spring 2006); the Tobias Wolff Award for "33 Swoonings" (2001), published in *The Bellingham Review*; and the Katherine Anne Porter Prize for "Dreaming in Color" (1989), published in *Nimrod*. "33 Swoonings" was also nominated for a Pushcart Prize. August lives in Philadelphia and is currently at work on a novel.

**J. A. Tyler** is the author six novel(la)s including *Inconceivable Wilson* (Scrambler Books, 2009),and the forthcoming *The Zoo, A Going* (Dzanc Books, 2013). His work has appeared recently with *Diagram, Sleepingfish, Caketrain, Fairy Tale Review, elimae,* & *Action, Yes*. He is also the founding editor of Mud Luscious Press. To read more, visit: www.mudlusciouspress.com.

Prize-winning writer **Pam Uschuk** is the author of five books of poetry, the latest, *Crazy Love* from Wings Press, 2009. Her work has been widely-published and translated into nearly a dozen languages. She teaches creative writing and environmental literature at Fort Lewis College in Durango, Colorado, and she makes her home with her husband, poet, William Pitt Root. Beginning in Spring 2011, she will be Visiting Poet at University of Tennessee, Knoxville.

**Anne Valente**'s stories appear or are forthcoming in *Unsaid, Annalemma, Keyhole, PANK* and *Monkeybicycle*, among others. She lives in Ohio.

**William Walsh** is the author of *Pathologies* (2010), *Questionstruck*(2009), *Ampersand, Mass.*(2011) and *Unknown Arts*(2011), all from Keyhole Press. His first novel, *Without Wax* (2008), is available from Cssperian Books.

**David Welch** has published poems in journals including *Kenyon Review Online, Gulf Coast,* and *Third Coast,* and the anthologies *Best New Poets 2007* and *Helen Burns Poetry Anthology: New Voices from the Academy of American Poets University and College Prizes, 1999-2008.* He currently lives in Chicago, Illinois.

**Brandi Wells** has fiction in or forthcoming *in Improbable Object, McSweeney's, Bust down the door and eat all the chickens, Smokelong Quarterly* and *Hobart.* She has a chapbook forthcoming as part of the chapbook collective *Fox Force 5,* which is being released by Paper Hero Press. She blogs at brandiwells.blogspot.com.

**Kevin Wilson** is the author of the story collection *Tunneling to the Center of the Earth* (Ecco/Harper Perennial, 2009). He lives in Sewanee, TN.

**Eleanor Wilner**'s seventh book of poems, *Tourist in Hell,* is due out this fall from The University of Chicago Press. Her most recent book, *The Girl with Bees in Her Hair,* is available from Copper Canyon.

**Angela Woodward** lives in Madison, Wisconsin. Her books include *The Human Mind* (Ravenna Press, 2007) and *The End of the Fire Cult* (Ravenna Press, 2010).

**Barbara Yien**'s poems have appeared in *42opus, Handsome, Meridian, ZYZZYVA, Hunger Mountain,* and *Indiana Review.* New work is forthcoming in *Cerise Press* and *Epoch.*

**Rachel Yoder** has written for the *New York Times, Sun Magazine, Missouri Review,* and *Kenyon Review.* She's Senior Editor for *Defunct Magazine* and an Arts Fellow in the Nonfiction Writing Program at the University of Iowa.

**Lisa Zaran** is an American poet, essayist and the author of six collections including *The Blondes Lay Content* and *the sometimes girl,* the latter of which was the focus of a year-long translation course in Germany. She is also the editor of *Contemporary American Voices,* an online journal of poetry. To see more of her work please visit her www.lisazaran.com.

# Index

**[out of nothing]**
www.outofnothing.org
Janice Lee, Eric Lindley, Joe Miazzo
shelling.peanuts@gmail.com

**>Kill Author**
www.killauthor.com
submissions@killauthor.com
sinister.cabal@killauthor.com

**10,000 Tons of Black Ink**
www.10ktobi.org
10KTOBI@literarywritersnetwork.org

**13th Warrior Review**
www.asteriusonline.com/13thWR/
theeditor@asteriusonline.com

**20X20 Magazine**
www.20x20magazine.com
Giovanna Paternò, Francesca Ricci
info@20x20magazine.com

**3:AM Magazine**
www.3ammagazine.com/3am/
Susan Tomaselli
andrew@3amMagazine.com

**322 Review**
www.322review.org
John Schoen
submissions@322review.org

**34th Parallel**
www.34thparallel.net
Trace Sheridan & Martin Chipperfield
submissions@34thparallel.net

**365 Tomorrows**
www.365tomorrows.com
Submissions through form on site

**42opus**
www.42opus.com
Brian Leary
brian@42opus.com

**5_Trope**
www.5trope.com
Gunnar Benediktsson
editor.5trope@gmail.com

**50 to 1**
50-to-1.blogspot.com
Glen Binger
50to1submit@gmail.com

**52 Stitches**
52stitches.blogspot.com
Aaron Paulson
52.stitches@gmail.com

**52nd City**
www.52ndcity.com
Thomas Crone
52ndcity@gmail.com

**5X5**
www.5x5litmag.org
Bradley Wonder, Mishon
Woolridge, Jory Mickelson
fiction@5x5litmag.org
nonfiction@5x5litmag.org

**63 Channels**
www.63channels.com
Glen Feulner
Submissions@63Channels.com

**7X20**
www.twitter.com/7x20
7x20mag@gmail.com

**The Abacot Journal**
abacotjournal.wordpress.com
Alexandra Ash
theabacotjournal@hotmail.com

**Abandoned Towers**
www.cyberwizardproductions.com/
AbandonedTowers/
Stephen Morgan
atsubs@gmail.com

**ABJECTIVE**
www.abjective.net
abjective.submission@gmail.com

**Able Muse**
ablemuse.com
Alex Pepple
www.ablemuse.com/submit-online

**Absent Magazine**
www.absentmag.org
Simon DeDeo
absentsubmissions@gmail.com

**Acentos Review**
www.acentosreview.com
Raina Leon, Eliel Lucero
acentosreview@gmail.com

**Action Yes**
www.actionyes.org
Johannes Göransson, Joyelle
McSweeney, John Dermot Woods
Not currently accepting submissions

**The Adirondack Review**
www.theadirondackreview.com
Colleen Ryor
editors@theadirondackreview.com

**AGNI**
www.bu.edu/agni
Sven Birkerts
agni@bu.edu

**AIM Magazine**
www.aimmagazine.org
Kathleen Leatham
editor@aimmagazine.org

**Alice Blue**
www.alicebluereview.org
Sarah Gallien
s.burgess@alicebluereview.org

**All Things Girl**
www.allthingsgirl.net
Deb Smouse
www.allthingsgirl.net/submit/

**Allegory**
www.allegoryezing.com
Ty Drago
submissions@allegoryezine.com

**Alternative Coordinates**
www.ac-mag.com
submissions@ac-mag.com
info@ac-mag.com

**The Altruist**
www.altruisticword.com/the_
ALTRUIST/Welcome.html
thealtruisticword@gmail.com

**Amarillo Bay**
www.amarillobay.org
Jerry Craven
comments@amarillobay.org

**American Short Fiction**
www.americanshortfiction.org
Dina Guidubaldi, Stacy Muszynski
Submit through form on website

**Ampersand**
www.ampersandreview.com
Jason Cook, Danny Lawless
ampersandsubmit@gmail.com
ampersandeditor@gmail.com

**Anastomoo**
www.anastomoo.com
Jesse Shipway
anastomoo@yahoo.com.au

**Anderbo**
www.anderbo.com
Rick Rofihe, June Eding
editors@anderbo.com

**Andromeda Spaceways Inflight**
www.andromedaspaceways.com
Nyssa
asimsubmissions@gmail.com

**Anemone Sidecar**
www.ravennapress.com/
anemonesidecar
Kathryn Rantala
editor@ravennapress.com

**The Angler**
angler.donavanhall.net
Donovan Hall
theangler@donavanhall.net

**Annalemma**
www.annalemma.net
Chris
chris@annalemma.net

**Another Realm**
www.anotherrealm.com
Gary Markette
editor@anotherrealm.com

**Anthurium**
scholar.library.miami.edu/
anthurium/home.htm
Coral Gables
anthurium.cls@miami.edu

**AntipodeanSF**
www.antisf.com.au
Ion Newcombe
editor@antisf.com.au

**Apex Magazine**
www.apexbookcompany.com
Jason Sizemore
apex.submission@gmail.com

**Aphelion**
www.aphelion-webzine.com
Daniel Ronga
shorts@aphelion-webzine.com
serials@aphelion-webzine.com
mare@aphelion-webzine.com

**Apollo's Lyre**
apollos-lyre.tripod.com
Kimberly Brown
kimberly@kimberlybrown.net

**Aposiopieces**
www.aposiopieces.com
aposiopieces@gmail.com

**Apparatus Magazine**
www.apparatusmagazine.com
Adam Hart
submissions@apparatusmagazine.
com

**Apple Valley Review**
www.applevalleyreview.com
Leah Browning
editor@leahbrowning.net

**Apt**
apt.aforementionedproductions.com
Randolf Pfaff
submit@aforementionedproductions.com

**Arabesques**
www.arabesques-editions.com/journal
Ali Alizadeh
submissions@arabesques-editions.com

**Arava Review**
aravareview.drupalcafe.com
Katie McClusky, Fiona Gardner,
Tova Gardner
katiemcclusky@gmail.com
fionagardner@gmail.com
tovagardner@gmail.com

**Arch Journal**
archjournal.wustl.edu
Haines Easton
archjournal.wustl.edu/submission

**Arkham Tales**
arkhamtales.com
arkhamtales@gmail.com

**Aroostook Review**
aroostookreview.umfk.maine.edu
Geraldine Cannon Becker
areview@maine.edu

**Ascent Aspirations**
ascentaspirations.ca
David Fraser

**At Large Magazine**
www.at-laargemagazine.com/Rohin
Guha, Niina Pollari
atlarge.editors@gmail.com

**Atom Jack Magazine**
www.atomjackmagazine.com
Adicus Ryan Garton
atomjackmagazine@gmail.com

**Audience Magazine**
www.worldaudience.org/pubs_aud_
mag_issues.html
M. Stefan Strozier
worldaudience@gmail.com

**Aurora Wolf**
www.aurorawolf.com
editor@aurorawolf.com

**Avatar Review**
www.avatarreview.net
art.editor@avatarreview.net
poetry.editor@avatarreview.net
prose.editor@avatarreview.net

**Babel Fruit**
web.mac.com/renkat/BABEL_
FRUIT/BabelFruit.htm
babelfruit@live.com

**Back Alley**
www.backalleywebzine.com
Richard Helmes
BarHallCom@aol.com

**Ballyhoo Stories**
www.ballyhoostories.com
Suzanne Pettypiece

**BAP**
www.bapq.net
Jennifer Bal
bapquarterly@yahoo.com

**Barcelona Review**
www.barcelonareview.com
Jill Adams
editor@barcelonareview.com

**Bare Back Magazine**
www.barebackmag.com
Natasha Brooks
editor@barebackmag.com

**Bare Roots Review**
www.smsu.edu/barerootsreview/
Mitchell Dahlhoff, T. J. Staneart
bareroot@smsu.edu

**The Barefoot Muse**
www.barefootmuse.com
Anna Evans
thebarefootmuse@gmail.com

**BarnStorm**
barnstorm.unh.edu
Bryan Parys
www.barnstormsubmissions.net

**Barrelhouse**
www.barrelhousemag.com
www.barrelhousemag.com/submissions/

**Bartleby Snopes**
www.bartlebysnopes.com
Nathaniel Tower
submissions@bartlebysnopes.com
contact@bartlebysnopes.com

**Bathhouse Hypermedia Journal**
www.bhjournal.com
EIC@BHJournal.com

**Battered Suitcase**
www.vagabondagepress.com
F.M. Neun
submissions@vagabondagepress.com

**Bear Creek Feed**
www.bearcreekfeed.com
editor@bearcreekfeed.com

**Bear Parade**
www.bearparade.com
bearparade@gmail.com

**The Beat**
www.the-beat.co.uk
Sean
sean@the-beat.co.uk
dissolutionword@yahoo.co.uk

**Beat the Dust**
www.melissamann.com/beat-the-dust.asp
Melissa Mann
www.melissamann.com/contact.asp

**Bending Spoons**
www.bending-spoons.com
Desiree Jensen
contact@spoonbenderpress.net

**Beneath Ceaseless Skies**
beneath-ceaseless-skies.com
Scott H. Andrews
submissions@beneath-ceaseless-skies.com

**Bent Magazine**
www.bent-magazine.com
submissions@bent-magazine.com
query@bent-magazine.com.

**Bent Pin Magazine**
puzzleddragon.blogspot.com/p/bent-pin-quarterly-author-index.html
Mar Walker
bentpin@me.com

**Bewildering Stories**
www.bewilderingstories.com
bwstories@gmail.com

**The BiblioFiles**
thebibliofiles.weebly.com
Andy Cerrone
submit.bibliofiles@gmail.com

**The Bicycle Review**
thebicyclereview.weebly.com
J. De Salvo
thebicyclereview@gmail.com

**Big City Lit**
www.nycbigcitylit.com
Nicholas Johnson
editors@nycBigCityLit.com

**The Big Jewel**
www.thebigjewel.com
Kurt Luchs
kurtluchs@aol.com

**Big Pulp**
www.bigpulp.com
submissions@bigpulp.com

**The Big Stupid Review**
www.thedrillpress.com/tex/tex.shtml
Tex
tex@thedrillpress.com

**The Big Table**
bigtablelit.blogspot.com
BigTableLit@gmail.com

**The Big Ugly**
www.biguglyreview.com
fiction@biguglyreview.com
nonfiction@biguglyreview.com
poetry@biguglyreview.com
fphoto@biguglyreview.com
music@biguglyreview.com
film@biguglyreview.com

**Birds By My Window**
birdsbywindow.blogspot.com
Michael Lee Johnson
promomanusa@gmail.com

**Birmingham Arts Journal**
birminghamartsjournal.com
Jim Reed
editor@birminghamartsjournal.com

**Black Heart Magazine**
www.blackheartmagazine.com
http://blackheartmagazine.com/
contact/

**Black Market Review**
www.blackmarketreview.com
Daniele Pantano
blackmarketreview@googlemail.com

**Black Petals**
www.blackpetals.net
T Stickl
tstickl@juno.com

**Blackbird**
www.blackbird.vcu.edu
T. Ransom
transom.vcu.edu

**Blink-Ink**
blink-ink.com/content
Lynn Alexander
submissions@blink-ink.com

**Blood Lotus**
www.bloodlotus.org
Stacia M. Fleegal, Teneice Delgado
bloodlotuspoetry@gmail.com
bloodlotusfiction@gmail.com

**Blood Moon Rising**
www.bloodmoonmagazine.com
A.L. Vermette
DemonicLord64@aol.com

**Blood Orange Review**
www.bloodorangereview.com
H.K. Hummel
submissions@bloodorangereview.com
hkhummel@bloodorangereview.com

**Blood, Blade and Thruster**
www.bbtmagazine.com
submissionsbbt@gmail.com

**Blossom Bones**
www.blossombones.com
Susan and Melissa
susan.blossombones@gmail.com
melissa.blossombones@gmail.com

**The Blotter**
www.blotterrag.com
Garry Somers
mermaid@blotterrag.com
chief@blotterrag.com

**Blue Print Review**
www.blueprintreview.de
Dorothee Lang
editor@blueprintreview.de

**Books For Monsters**
www.booksformonsters.com
editor@booksformonsters.com

**Booth**
booth.butler.edu
Robert Stapleton
booth@butler.edu

**Born Magazine**
www.bornmagazine.org
Ann Marie Trimble
http://www.bornmagazine.org/
submissions

**Boston Literary Magazine**
www.bostonliterarymagazine.com
Robin Stratton

**Bound Off**
www.boundoff.com
Mark Rushton
submissions@boundoff.com
inquiry@boundoff.com

**Brain Harvest Magazine**
www.brainharvestmag.com
Caren Gussoff, Shane Hoverston,
Eden Robins
submissions@brainharvestmag.com
brains@brainharvestmag.com

**Breath and Shadow**
www.abilitymaine.org/breath/
Chris Kuell
BreathandShadow@gmail.com

**Brevity**
www.abilitymaine.org/breath/
Chris Kuell
BreathandShadow@gmail.com

**Brink Magazine**
www.creativenonfiction.org/brevity
Dinty W. Moore
brevitymag@gmail.com

**Broadsided**
www.broadsidepress.org
Elizabeth Bradfield
broadsided@gmail.com

**Broken Pencil**
www.brokenpencil.com
fiction@brokenpencil.com

**Broken Plate**
www.bsu.edu/brokenplate/
Sean Lovelace, Mark Neely
brokenplate@bsu.edu

**BULL: Men's Fiction**
www.bullmensfiction.com
J. Haley, Tim Chilcote
BULLmensfiction@gmail.com

**Burst**
www.terra-media.us/burst/
Kevin
burst@terra-media.us

**Burst Fiction**
www.burstfiction.com
www.burstfiction.com/guidelines/

**Bust Down the Door and Eat All
the Chickens**
www.absurdistjournal.com
Bradley Sands
bust_submissions@hotmail.com
bradleysands@comcast.net

**Byzarium**
www.byzarium.com
L. Dragoon
byzarium@gmail.com

**Cabinet Des Fees**
www.cabinet-des-fees.com
Helen Pilinovsky, Erzebet YellowBoy,
Donna Quattrone, Nin Harris
cabinetdesfees@gmail.com

**Cadaverine**
web.mac.com/thecadaverine/
Wes Brown
thecadaverine@mac.com

**Cafe Irreal**
home.sprynet.com/~awhit
Alice Whittenburg
G.S. Evans
editor@cafeirreal.com

**Caffeine Destiny**
www.caffeinedestiny.com
Susan Denning

**Calabash**
www.nyu.edu/calabash/
Jacqueline Bishop
Calabash_journal@hotmail.com

**Callused Hands**
callusedhands.blogspot.com
editor.callusedhands@yahoo.com

**Camroc Press Review**
www.camrocpressreview.com
camrocpress@gmail.com

**Canopic Jar**
ww.canopicjar.com/c23/
editor@canopicjar.com

**Cantaraville**
www.cantaraville.com
Michael Matheny
cantaraville@gmail.com

**Carte Blanche**
www.carte-blanche.org
Maria Schamis Turner
submissions@carte-blanche.org
info@carte-blanche.org

**The Cartier Street Review**
thecartierstreetreview.blogspot.com
Bernard Alain, Joy Leftow
violetwrites@nyc.rr.com

**Carve Magazine**
www.carvezine.com
Matthew Limpede
www.carvezine.com/onlinesubmissions.html

**The Catalonian Review**
www.catalonianreview.com
catalonian.review@gmail.com

**The Cat's Meow**
www.rosannecatalano.net
Rosanne Catalano
www.rosannecatalano.net/submissions.htm

**Caveat Lector**
caveat-lector.org
Christopher Bernard, Ho Lin
editors@caveat-lector.org

**Cella's Round Trip**
www.cellasroundtrip.com
Rachel Hartley-Smith
reachcella@gmail.com

**Centaur Magazine**
www.centaurlit.com
Becky Erfph
Submit@CentaurLit.com

**Cerise Press**
www.cerisepress.com
Sally Molini, Karen Rigby, Fiona Sze-Lorrain
query@cezannescarrot.org

**Cerulean Rain**
www.ceruleanrain.com
Lindsey Webster
fiction@ceruleanrain.com
poetry@ceruleanrain.com

**Cezanne's Carrot**
www.cezannescarrot.org
Barbara Jacksha, Joan Kremer
query@cezannescarrot.org

**Cha: An Asian Magazine**
www.asiancha.com
Jeff Zroback
submissions@asiancha.com
eddie@asiancha.com

**Challenging Destinies**
www.challengingdestiny.com/
David M. Switzer
csp@golden.net

**Chaos Theory**
http://genspace.com/ctta/
A. A. Roberts, Dr. Jeffrey Shaw,
Dr. Arthur D. Roberts, Joyce Donohoo
ctta@genspace.com

**Cherry Bleeds**
www.cherrybleeds.com/
Du Shane
 dushane@gmail.com

**Chick Lit Review**
chicklitreview.org/default.aspx
Iris Green
 igreen@chicklitreview.org

**The Chimera**
www.the-chimaera.com/
SubmitOnline.html
editor@the-chimaera.com.

**Chimurenga**
www.chimurenga.co.za/
Ntone Edjabe
chimurenga@panafrican.co.za.

**Chiaroscuro**
www.chizine.com/
Brett Alexander Savory
savory@rogers.com

**Christian Perspectives**
1perspectives.webs.com/
christianperspectives.htm
Monique Berry
perspectivesmagazine@gmail.com

**Clapboard House**
clapboardhouse.wordpress.com/
Joe Frank Buckner
clapboardhouse@msn.com

**Clarkesworld**
clarkesworldmagazine.com/
Neil Clarke
neil@clarkesworldmagazine.com
sean@clarkesworldmagazine.com

**Clean Sheets**
www.cleansheets.com
Susannah Indigo
fiction@cleansheets.com
editors@cleansheets.com

**Clearfield Review**
www.clearfieldreview.com/
William Soule
cr.prose@yahoo.com
cr.fiction@yahoo.com
clearfieldreview@yahoo.com

**Clever Magazine**
www.clevermag.com/
Dianne K
editor@clevermag.com

**Clockwise Cat**
www.clockwisecat.blogspot.com/
Alison Ross
Fleurdumal666@gmail.com

**Clone Pod**
www.clonepod.org/
Zach, Abby, Forrest
fiction@thecoachellareview.com
poetry@thecoachellareview.com
nonfiction@thecoachellareview.com

**Coffee Cramp Magazine**
coffeecrampmagazine.tripod.com
Chick Lange
clangeditor@yahoo.com

**The Collagist**
www.thecollagist.com/
Matt Bell
fiction@thecollagist.com
poetry@thecollagist.com
nonfiction@thecollagist.com

**Collective Fallout**
collectivefallout.com/
submissions@collectivefallout.com
editor@collectivefallout.com

**Colored Chalk**
www.coloredchalk.com
Jason Helm
issue10@coloredchalk.com

**Columbia Review**
www.columbia.edu/cu/review/
about.html
Nellie Bowles, Stephanie Wu
columbiareview@columbia.edu.

**Concept Sci Fi**
www.conceptscifi.com/
submissions@conceptscifi.com

**Conifers**
www.pmc.edu/conifers
Lindsey Berndt
journal@pmc.edu

**Conjunctions**
www.conjunctions.com/webconj.html
Bradford Morrow
Postal mail: 21 E. 10th St. New York,
NY 10003

**Consequence Magazine**
www.consequencemagazine.org/
 George Kovach
consequence.magazine@gmail.com

**Conte Magazine**
www.conteonline.net/
Andrew Travel, Robert Lieberman
poetry@conteonline.net
prose@conteonline.net

**Contrary Magazine**
www.contrarymagazine.com/
Jeff McMahon
www.contrarymagazine.com/
Contrary/Submissions.html

**Convergence**
www.convergence-journal.com/
Cynthia Linville
clinville@csus.edu

**Copperfield Review**
www.copperfieldreview.com/
Meredith Allard
info@copperfieldreview.com

**Corduroy Mountain**
www.airforcejoyride.com/mtn.html
corduroymtn@gmail.com

**Cosmos Magazine**
www.cosmosmagazine.com/
Wilson Da Silva
www.cosmosmagazine.com/
contact/submissions/

**Coyote Wild**
www.coyotewildmag.com/
Laurie Basiewicz
editor@CoyoteWildMag.com

**Crash**
www.cra.sh/
David Elswick
crasheditors@gmail.com

**Creature Mag**
www.creaturemag.com/
creature@creaturemag.com

**Crime and Suspense**
www.crimeandsuspense.com/
Fred Snyder
submissions@crimeandsuspense.com

**Crossed Genres**
www.crossedgenres.com/
Bart R. Leib
www.crossedgenres.com/submissions/

**Crossing Rivers into Twilight**
www.critjournal.com/
Elizabeth Kate Switaj

**Cupboard**
www.thecupboardpamphlet.org
Dave Madden, Adam Peterson
submit@thecupboardpamphlet.org

**Cynic Magazine**
www.cynicmag.com
John Blackemore
submissions@cynicmag.com

**Daedalus Review**
www.daedalusreview.com
Andrew Wirzburger
submissions@daedalusreview.com
andrew@daedalusreview.com.

**Daikaijuzine**
www.daikaijuzine.com/dkz/
Richard S. Crawford
submit@daikaijuzine.com
editor@daikaijuzine.com

**Daily Tourniquet**
www.dailytourniquet.com/
Jeffrey Conolly
dailytourniquet@gmail.com

**Damazine**
www.damazine.com
Serene Taleb-Agha
Editor-in-Chief
poetry@damazine.com
fiction@damazine.com
nonfiction@damazine.com

**Danse Macabre**
dansemacabre.art.officelive.com
Adam Henry Carriere
dansemacabreonline@gmail.com

**Dante's Heart**
www.dantesheart.com/
Daniel Fusch
editors@dantesheart.com

**Dappled Things**
www.dappledthings.org
Mary Angelita Ruiz
dappledthings.editor@gmail.com

**Dark and Dreary Magazine**
darkanddrearymagazine.wordpress.com
darkanddreary.submission@gmail.com
darkanddreary.editor@gmail.com

**Dark Fire Fiction**
usersites.horrorfind.com/home/
horror/darkfire/home.html
Karonda and Dr. Jones
darkfireuk@gmail.com

**Dark Gothic Magazine**
bloodtouch.webs.com/
darkgothicmagazine.htm
gratistavampires@yahoo.com

**Dark Recesses**
http://www.darkrecesses.com/
M. Louis Dickson
submissions@darkrecesses.com

**Dark Sky Magazine**
www.darkskymagazine.com/
Brian Allen Carr
editor@darkskymagazine.com

**Dark Wine and Stars**
darkwineandstars.blogspot.com/
Mari Mitchell
aliceingoreland@yahoo.com

**Darwin's Evolutions**
darwinsevolutions.com/wordpress/
Darwin A. Garrison
editor@darwinsevolutions.com

**Dead Mule School of Southern Literature**
www.deadmule.com
Valerie MacEwan
submit.mule@deadmule.com

**Dead Paper**
deadpaper.org
Tim Gilmore
timgilmore@deadpaper.org

**Debris Magazine**
www.debrismagazine.com
Emily Bennett
editor@debrismagazine.com

**decomP**
www.decompmagazine.com
Jason Jordan
decomp.magazine@gmail.com

**Deep South**
www.otago.ac.nz/deepsouth/
Rhys Brookbanks
Deep South Department of English
University of Otago P.O. Box 56
Dunedin New Zealand

**Defenestration**
www.defenestrationmag.net/
Andrew Kaye
defenestrationmag@gmail.com

**Del Sol Review**
delsolreview.webdelsol.com
Lori Knight
knight.lori@gmail.com
poetry-dsr@webdelsol.com

**The Delinquent**
www.thedelinquent.co.uk/
submissions@thedelinquent.co.uk

**Della Donna**
delladonna.blogspot.com/
April
della.donna.zine@gmail.com.

**Demockeracy**
www.demockeracy.com/
www.demockeracy.com/contact

**Demonic Tome**
www.demonictome.com/
Jesse Dedman
Legato10@swbell.net

**Demon Minds**
www.demonminds.com/
J.P. Moore
submissions@demonminds.com

**Demonic Tome**
http://www.demonictome.com/
Jesse Dedman
Legato10@swbell.net

**Denver Syntax**
www.denversyntax.com
Jonathan Bitz
jonathan@denversyntax.com

**DesiLit**
www.desilit.org
Sumita Sheth
fiction@desilit.org
articles@desilit.org
humor@desilit.org
poetry@desilit.org

**Dew on the Kudzu**
www.dewonthekudzu.net/
dewonthekudzu@gmail.com

**DIAGRAM**
www.thediagram.com
Ander Monson
http://thediagram.com/
submissions/

**Diddle Dog**
www.diddledog.com/
Oz Lancombe
submissions@diddledog.com

**Digital Dragon**
www.digitaldragonmagazine.net/
T.W. Ambrose
digitaldragonmagazine@gmail.com

**Digitalis Obscura**
www.digitalisobscura.com/
D. Kai Wilson
fiction@digitalisobscura.com
poetry@digitalisobscura.com
nonfiction@digitalisobscura.com
editor@digitalisobscura.com

**The Dirty Napkin**
www.thedirtynapkin.com
J. Argyle Plath
http://thedirtynapkin.com/submit.php

## Dislocate

www.dislocate.org
dislocate.poetry.editor@gmail.com
dislocate.fiction.editor@gmail.com
dislocate.nonfiction.editor@gmail.com
dislocate.everythingelse@gmail.com
dislocate.everythingelse@gmail.com

## dispatch litareview

www.litareview.com/
dispatch@litareview.com

## Diverse Voices

www.diversevoicesquarterly.com/
Krisma
submit@diversevoicesquarterly.com

## Divine Dirt Quarterly

www.divinedirtquarterly.com/
A. Bowen, K. Dixon, S. Sheriff
abowen@divinedirtquarterly.com
kdixon@divinedirtquarterly.com
ssheriff@divinedirtquarterly.com

## Dog Oil Press

http://www.dogoilpress.com
submit@dogoilpress.com

## Dogmatika

www.dogmatika.com/dm/
Susan Tomaselli
dogmatika@googlemail.com

## Dogzplot

www.dogzplot.com
Barry Graham
www.dogzplot.com/submit.html

## Don't Look

www.dontlookzine.com/
Jack Lee, Linn Naess
jack.lee@dsidecreations.com
underthestairs@gmail.com

## Door Knobs and Body Paint

www.iceflow.com/doorknobs/DB.html
Leila Rae
leilarae@iceflow.com
doorknobsandbodypaint@gmail.com
riverbabble@gmail.com

## Double Room

www.webdelsol.com/Double_Room/
Peter Connors, Mark Tursi
double_room@hotmail.com

## Double Shiny

doubleshiny.com
doubleshinyreview@gmail.com

## Down in the Cellar

www.downinthecellar.com
admin@downinthecellar.com.

## Downgo Sun

www.northeastartskc.org/neartho2.htm
Missi Rasmussen, Curtis Urness
downgosun@aol.com

## The Drabblecast

www.drabblecast.org
Norm Sherman, Luke Coddington,
Kendall Marchman
drabblecast@yahoo.com
goatkeeper@hotmail.com
luketc@hotmail.com
kendallmarchman@yahoo.com

## The Drabbler

www.samsdotpublishing.com/
drabbler/main.htm
Terrie Relf
tlrelf@cox.net

**The Dream People**
www.dreampeople.org
Stanley Ashenbach
stanleyashenbach@yahoo.com

**Drops of Crimson**
www.gothhuntress.com/crimson/
homepage.html
editor@dropsofcrimson.com

**The Drunken Boat**
www.drunkenboat.com
Radha
http://www.drunkenboat.com/
submissions/index.php

**The Dublin Quarterly**
www.dublinquarterly.com/
Peter Anny-Nzekwue
fiction@dublinquarterly.com
poetry@dublinquarterly.com
features@dublinquarterly.com

**Ducts.org**
www.ducts.org
Jonathan Kravetz
www.ducts.org/content/submissions/

**The Dunesteef Audio Magazine**
www.dunesteef.com
Submissions@Dunesteef.com
Editor@Dunesteef.com

**East of the Web**
www.eastoftheweb.com/short-stories/
submissionsa@eastoftheweb.com

**Eat Your Words**
eatyourwordsjournal.blogspot.com/
eatyourwordsjournal@gmail.com

**Eclectica**
www.eclectica.org
Tom Dooley
submissions@eclectica.org
editors@eclectica.org

**Eclectomatic**
www.eclectomatic.net
Jim Zombie
jimmy@eclectomatic.net

**Edge of Propinquinty**
www.edgeofpropinquity.net/
Jennifer Brozek
gaaneden@gmail.com

**Einstein's Pocket Watch**
peafant.wordpress.com
Rob Crandall
Peafant@aol.com

**Electric Literature**
www.electricliterature.com/
Andy Hunter & Scott Lindenbaum
submissions@electricliterature.com
editors@electricliterature.com

**Electric Spec**
www.electricspec.com
Betsy Dornbusch
submissions@electricspec.com

**Eleven Eleven**
www.elevenelevenjournal.com
Hugh Behm-Steinberg
Eleven Eleven
California College of the Arts
1111 Eighth Street
San Francisco, CA 94107
eleveneleven@cca.edu

**Eleventh Transmission**
www.eleventhtransmission.org
Kirk Ramdath
submissions@eleventhtransmission.org

**Elimae**
http://elimae.com/
Cooper Renner
coop.renner@juno.com

**Eloquent Atheist**
www.eloquentatheist.com
Marilyn and Michael
http://www.eloquentatheist.
com/?page_id=4

**Elsewhere**
www.elsewherejournal.org
J.D. Schraffenburger
editor@elsewherejournal.org

**Elysian Fields**
www.efqreview.com
Tom Goldstein
P.O. Box 14385
Saint Paul, MN 55114-0385
info@efqreview.com

**EMG Zine**
http://emg-zine.com/
Ellen and Jennifer
editor@emg-zine.com

**Emprise Review**
www.emprisereview.com
Patrick McAllaster
 emppoetry@gmail.com
empreview@gmail.com
empriseeditors@gmail.com

**Emuse**
www.emuse-zine.com/
Submissions are closed

**Enscorcelled**
ensorcelled.berkeley.edu/
editors@ensorcelled.berkeley.edu

**Epicenters**
www.bc.edu/clubs/epicenters/
epicenters@gmail.com

**Epiphanyzine**
www.epiphanyzine.com
Willard Cook
www.epiphanyzine.com/submissions/
epiphany.magazine@gmail.com

**Errant Parent**
www.errantparent.com
submit@errantparent.com
editors@errantparent.com

**ESC! Magazine**
www.escmagazine.com
Michael Potter
submissions@escwebs.com

**Escape Pod**
www.escapepod.org
Jeremiah Tolbert
submit@escapepod.org
editor@escapepod.org **Escarp**
www.escarp.org
submit via Twitter

**Escarp**
www.escarp.org
www.escarp.org/submit.php

**Eskimo Pie**
www.eskimopie.net
eskimopi@jps.net

**Esquire**
www.esquire.com/fiction/
www.esquiresubmissions.com

**Evening Street Press**
webwiseboomersseniors.com/
eveningstreetpress/
Gordon Grigsby
editor@eveningstreetpress.com

**Evergreen Review**
www.evergreenreview.com
Barney Rosset
evergreensubmissions@gmail.com
evergreen@nyc.rr.com

**Everyday Fiction**
www.everydayfiction.com
Jordan Lapp
everydayfiction.com/authors/admin/
www.everydayfiction.com/contact-us/

**Everyday Genius**
www.everyday-genius.com
Adam Robinson
Subit via form on website

**Everyday Weirdness**
www.everydayweirdness.com
www.everydayweirdness.com/submit/
editor@everydayweirdness.com

**Ex Cathera**
theinfalliblechair.blogspot.com/
fromthechair@gmail.com

**Expanded Horizons**
www.expandedhorizons.net/magazine/
Dash
submissions@expandedhorizons.net

**Expat Lit**
www.expatlit.com
Joe Dugan
expatlit@gmail.com

**Expressions**
www.samsdotpublishing.com/
expressions/septemberexpressions.htm
Cathy
cathyartist@hotmail.com

**Exquisite Corpse**
www.corpse.org
Andrei Codrescu
submissions@corpse.org
acodrescu@gmail.com

**The Externalist**
www.theexternalist.com
Larina
www.theexternalist.com/ficguidelines

**Eyeshot**
www.eyeshot.net

**The Fabulist**
www.the-fabulist.org/yarns/
bibliopolis@the-fabulist.org

**Fact-Simile**
www.fact-simile.com/
Jen and Travis
travis@fact-simile.com
jenmarie@fact-simile.com

**Failbetter.com**
www.failbetter.com
Thom Didato, Andrew Day
submissions@failbetter.com

**Fairfield Review**
www.fairfieldreview.org
Edward Granger Happ
fairfieldreview@hpmd.com

**Faith, Hope and Fiction**
www.faithhopeandfiction.com
info@faithhopeandfiction.com

**Fantastic Horror**
www.fantastichorror.com
submissions@fantastichorror.com
info@fantastichorror.com

**Fantasy Gazetteer**
www.fantasygazetteer.com
editor@newfantasywriters.com

**Fantasy Magazine**
www.darkfantasy.org/fantasy/
rambo@fantasy-magazine.com

**Farmhouse Magazine**
www.farmhousemagazine.com/
submissions@farmhousemagazine.com

**Fawlt Magazine**
www.fawltmag.com/apathy/
editor@fawltmag.com

**Fear and Trembling Magazine**
www.fearandtremblingmag.com
Keenan Brant
editor@fearandtremblingmag.com

**Fear of Monkeys**
www.twinenterprises.com/the_
fear_of_monkeys/
widespread.fear.of.monkeys@gmail.com

**Featherproof**
www.featherproof.com
Jonathan Messinger
Submissions are on hiatus

**Feathertale**
www.feathertale.com/
Brent Popplewell
submissions@feathertale.com
bpopplewell@feathertale.com

**Fickle Muse**
www.ficklemuses.com
fiction2@ficklemuses.com
editor@ficklemuses.com.

**Fiction At Work**
www.fictionatwork.com
fictionatwork@gmail.com

**Fiction Circus**
www.fictioncircus.com
Miracle Jones, Stephen Future,
Goodman Carter, Xerzes Verdammt
submissions@fictioncircus.com.

**Fiction Weekly**
www.fictionweekly.com
Carver Waters
poetry.fieldstone@gmail.com
fiction.fieldstone@gmail.com
crenonfic.fieldstone@gmail.com

**Fiction Writers Review**
www.fictionwritersreview.com
Anne Stameshkin
fictionwritersreview@gmail.com

**The Fifth Dimension**
www.samsdotpublishing.com/fifth/
cover.htm
J. Erwine
jerwine@samsdotpublishing.com

**Fireside Lit**
www.firesidelit.com
submissions@firesidelit.com
query@firesidelit.com

**First and Last Sentence**
firstandlastsentence.blogspot.com/
Edward Simon
firstsentence@gmail.com

**Fishnet Mag**
www.fishnetmag.com
Greta Christina
fiction-editor@fishnetmag.com

**Five Chapters**
www.fivechapters.com
Fivechapters@gmail.com

**Flash Fiction Online**
www.flashfictiononline.com
Gary Cuba, Oliver House
submissions@flashfictiononline.
com

**Flash Me Magazine**
www.wingedhalo.com
Jennifer Dawson
submissions@wingedhalo.com.

**Flashfire 5000**
flashfire500.blogspot.com
editor.flashfire@gmail.com

**FlashScribe**
www.flashscribe.net
submissions@flashscribe.net

**Flashes in the Dark**
www.flashesinthedark.com
Lori Titus
submissions@flashesinthedark.com

**Flashing Swords**
www.flashingswords.com
A. C. Keller
submissions@flashingswords.com
flashingswordspress@gmail.com.

**flashquake**
www.flashquake.org
Sarah Black
submit@flashquake.org

**FlashShot**
www.gwthomas.org/flashshotindex.
htm
G.W. Thomas
ragemagsubs@yahoo.ca

**Flask and Pen**
www.flaskandpen.com
submissions@flaskandpen.com

**FlatManCrooked**
www.flatmancrooked.com
Deena Drewis
editors@flatmancrooked.com.

**Flurb**
www.flurb.net/
Rudy Rucker
rudy@rudyrucker.com

**Flutter Poetry Journal**
www.freewebs.com/rarepetal
Sandy
sandyb1070@msn.com
flashingswordspress@gmail.com

**A Fly in Amber**
www.aflyinamber.net/
www.aflyinamber.net/?page_id=37

**Fogged Clarity**
www.foggedclarity.com
Benjamin Decker
submissions@foggedclarity.com

**The Foghorn Magazine**
www.thefoghornmagazine.com
Summer Block
editor@thefoghornmagazine.com

**Foliate Oak**
www.foliateoak.uamont.edu
Travis Nicholson
foliateoak@uamont.edu

**For the Girls**
www.forthegirls.com
submissions@forthegirls.com
media@forthegirls.com

**Forge Journal**
www.forgejournal.com
Leif Milligan
forgejournal@gmail.com

**Forgot Magazine**
www.forgetmagazine.com
words@forgetmagazine.com

**Foundling Review**
www.foundlingreview.com
editor@foundlingreview.com

**Fractured Publisher**
www.fracturedpublisher.com
Tina Morgan
fpsubmissions@yahoogroups.com

**Fractured West**
www.fracturedwest.com
Kirsty or Helen
submissions@fracturedwest.com

**Framelines**
www.framelines.com.au
Sarah Nolan
submissions@framelines.org

**Freedom Friends**
www.freedomfriends.in

**Freight Stories**
www.freightstories.com
Andrew Scott and Victoria Barrett
submissions@freightstories.com
andrew@freightstories.com
victoria@freightstories.com

**Freight Train**
www.ftzine.com
Justin Hoffman
ftzine@gmail.com

**Fried Chicken and Coffee**
www.friedchickenandcoffee.com
Rusty Barnes
rusty.barnes@gmail.com

**Fried Fiction**
www.friedfiction.com
David Peters
submissions@friedfiction.com
feedback@friedfiction.com

**FRiGG Magazine**
www.friggmagazine.com
Ellen Parker
webmaster@friggmagazine.com

**Fringe Magazine**
www.fringemagazine.org
Lizzie Stark
FringeFiction@gmail.com
FringeNonFiction@gmail.com
FringePoetry@gmail.com
FringeTheMagazine@gmail.com

**Front Porch Journal**
www.frontporchjournal.com
Tom Grimes
www.frontporchsubmissions.com

**Frost Writing**
www.frostwriting.com
William Males
www.frostwriting.com/submissions/

**Full of Crow**
www.fullofcrow.com
Aleathia Drehmer, Lynn Alexander
fiction@fullofcrow.com
poetry@fullofcrow.com
aleathiadrehmer@fullofcrow.com
lynnalexander@fullofcrow.com

**The Furnace Review**
www.thefurnacereview.com
Ciara LaVelle
submissions@thefurnacereview.com

**Fusion Fragment**
www.apodispublishing.com/fusion/
Cavan Terrill
fusion@apodispublishing.com

**Future Earth Mag**
www.futureearthstudios.com/
future_earth_mag@yahoo.com

**Future Fires**
www.futurefire.net
fiction@futurefire.net
nonfiction@futurefire.net

**Futurismic**
www.futurismic.com
Paul Graham Raven
www.futurismic.com/guidelines/
fiction-submissions/
http://futurismic.com/contact/

**Galleys Online**
www.galleysonline.com
www.galleysonline.com/?page_id=9

**Gander Press Review**
www.ganderpress.com/review
Brant Goble
brant_goble@ganderpress.com

**Gangway**
www.gangway.net/magazine/
Gerald Ganglbauer
editors@gangan.com

**Gemini Magazine**
www.gemini-magazine.com
David Bright
submissions@gemini-magazine.com
editor@gemini-magazine.com

**Getting Something Read**
www.shortpoem.org
www.shortpoem.wufoo.com/forms/
submit-work/

**Ghoti Mag**
www.ghotimag.com
C. L. Bledsoe
editors@ghotimag.com

**Gigantic**
www.thegiganticmag.com/magazine
Ann DeWitt, Rozalia Jovanovic,
Lincoln Michel, James Yeh
Submissions through form on site

**Ginosko Literary Journal**
www.ginoskoliteraryjournal.com/
Robert Payl Cesaretti
Ginosko Literary Journal
Robert Paul Cesaretti, Editor
PO Box 246
Fairfax, CA 94978

**Girls With Insurance**
www.girlswithinsurance.com
T. Dean, D. Corrigan
tdean@girlswithinsurance.com
dcorrigan@girlswithinsurance.com

**Glasses Glasses**
www.glassesglasses.org
Rachel
rachel@glassesglasses.org

**Glassfire**
www.peglegpublishing.com/
glassfire.htm
Matt
submissions@peglegpublishing.com

**Gloomcupboard**
www.gloomcupboard.com
Dorla Moorehouse
aprilmaymarch777@yahoo.co.uk
dorlamoorehouse@gmail.com

**Glossolalia Flash**
glossolaliaflash.blogspot.com
Kristen Havet
glossolalia.productions@gmail.com

**Gnome**
www.asteriusonline.com/gnome/
theeditor@asteriusonline.com

**Gold Wake Press**
www.goldwakepress.org
J. Michael Wahlgren, Eric Beeny
submit@goldwakepress.org

**A Golden Place**
www.agoldenplace.com
Chrissy Jackson
editors@agoldenplace.com

**Golden Visions**
www.goldenvisionsmagazine.biz
www.goldenvisionsmagazine.biz/
Submission-form.html

**Gowanus Books**
www.gowanusbooks.com
Thomas Hubachman
tom@gowanusbooks.com

**Grain Short Grain Long**
www.sundress.net/
grainshortgrainlong/
www.sundress.net
grainshortgrainlong/tanoonan/
index.html

**Grantville Gazette**
www.grantvillegazette.com

**Green Hill Literary Lantern**
ghll.truman.edu
Adam Brooke Davis
Green Hills Literary Lantern
McClain Hall
Truman State University
Kirksville, MO 63501

**Green Silk**
www.thegsj.com/home2.html
hazekd@peoplepc.com

**Greenbeard**
www.greenbeardmag.com
Mariana Sabino
greenbeards@gmail.com

**The Griffin**
www.gmc.edu/students/
clubsorganizations/thegriffin.php
Dr. Donna M. Allegro
The Griffin
 c/o Dr. Donna M. Allego
Gwynedd-Mercy College
1325 Sumneytown Pike
P.O. Box 901
Gwynedd Valley, PA 19437-0901

**Grist Journal**
www.gristjournal.com
Charlotte Pence
Grist: The Journal for Writers
c/o Poetry, Fiction, or Nonfiction Editor
English Department
301 McClung Tower
University of Tennessee
Knoxville, TN 37996-0430

**Grumble Magazine**
www.grumblemagazine.com
submissions@grumblemagazine.com
mailbag@grumblemagazine.com

**Gud Magazine**
www.gudmagazine.com
Julia Bernd
editor@gudmagazine.com

**Guernica Magazine**
www.guernicamag.com
Robert Bly
editors@guernicamag.com
fiction@guernicamag.com

**Gulfstream**
w3.fiu.edu/gulfstream/index.asp
Peter Borrebach
gulfstreamfiu@yahoo.com

**H_NGM_N**
www.h-ngm-n.com
Nate Pritts
editor@h-ngm-n.com
matt@h-ngm-n.com
gina@h-ngm-n.com

**Hack Writers**
www.hackwriters.com
Sam North
hackwriters@gmail.com

**Halfway Down the Stairs**
www.halfwaydownthestairs.net
Stacy Brazalovich
submissions@halfwaydownthestairs.net
inquiries@halfwaydownthestairs.net.

**Hamilton Stone Quarterly**
www.hamiltonstone.org/hsr.html
Lynda Schor, Reamy Jansen
lyndaschor@gmail.com
reamyjj@gmail.com

**Harp & Altar**
www.harpandaltar.com
Keith Newton
editors@harpandaltar.com

**The Harrow**
www.theharrow.com
Jason Nolan
editor@theharrow.com

**Haruah: Breath of Heaven**
www.haruah.com
editor@haruah.com

**Heliotrope**
www.heliotropemag.com
Jay Tomio
Heliotropeditor@gmail.com

**Heroic Fantasy Quarterly**
www.heroicfantasyquarterly.com
Adrian Simmons
editors@heroicfantasyquarterly.com

**Hitotoki**
www.hitotoki.org
what@hitotoki

**Hobart**
www.hobartpulp.com
Aaron Burch, Jensen Beach
websubmissions@hobartpulp.com

**Horizons**
www.saltpublishing.com/horizon/
J. Holland
submissions-horizon@saltpublishing.com
j.holland442@btinternet.com

**Horror Bound**
www.horrorbound.com/news.php
Maria Grazia
editor@horrorbound.com

**Horror Garage**
www.horrorgarage.com
horrorgarage@horrorgarage.com

**The Horror Zine**
www.thehorrorzine.com
Jeanie Rector
thehorrorzine@gmail.com

**Hospital Drive**
hospitaldrive.med.virginia.edu/
Daniel Becker
hospitaldrive@virginia.edu

**Hot Metal Bridge**
www.hotmetalbridge.org
Amy Whipple
fiction@hotmetalbridge.org

**House of Horror**
www.houseofhorror.org.uk
Sam and Shane
horrorhouse.editor@yahoo.com
coeditor@yahoo.com
poetry_editor@yahoo.com

**Houston Literary Review**
www.thehoustonliteraryreview.com
Bill Brocado
assistant.editor@
thehoustonliteraryreview.com
poetry.editor@
thehoustonliteraryreview.com

**How to Write Stories About Writers**
www.dietsoap.org/category/
storiesaboutwriters/
Doug Lane
howtowrite@dietsoap.org

**Hub Fiction**
www.hubfiction.com
Lee Harris, Alasdair Stewart
fiction@therighthand.co.uk
nonfiction@therighthand.co.uk
als@therighthand.co.uk

**Hunger Mountain**
www.hungermtn.org
Caroline Mercurio
Hunger Mountain
Vermont College of Fine Arts
36 College Street
Montpelier, VT 05602
hungermtn@vermontcollege.edu

**Hypersonic Tales**
www.hypersonictales.com
http://hypersonictales.com/
tinc?key=aLd1KOYz

**Iddie**
www.iddie.net
Brian Cordell
iddie.submissions@gmail.com

**Identity Theory**
www.identitytheory.com
Matt Borondy
fiction@identitytheory.com
essays@identitytheory.com
editor@identitytheory.com

**The Idiom**
www.angelfire.com/poetry/
theidiommag/
theidiommag@yahoo.com

**Ignavia Press**
www.ignaviapress.com
ignaviapress@gmail.com

**Improbable Objects**
www.improbableobject.com
Jason Fraley
improbableobject@gmail.com

**In Posse Review**
www.inpossereview.com
Tatyana Mishel
http://www.inpossereview.com/
submissions.htm

**In the Grove**
www.inthegrove.net
Lee Herrick
In the Grove
(Genre Editor)
PO Box 16195
Fresno, CA 93755

**In the Mist**
www.inthemistmag.com
Ange Tysdal
inthemistmag@aol.com

**Indelible Kitchen**
www.popularink.com/ik/
submissions@popularink.com
info@popularink.com

**InDigest Magazine**
www.indigestmag.com
David Doody, Justin Nelson
submission@indigestmag.com
editors@indigestmag.com

**Indite Circle**
www.inditecircle.com
William Coleman
www.inditecircle.com/home/
index.php?option=com_
contact&Itemid=3

**Inertia Magazine**
www.inertiamagazine.com
J.M. Spalding
www.inertiamagazine.com/
submissions.php

**Infinite Windows**
www.infinitewindows.co.cc
info@infinitewindowspress.com

**Infinity's Kitchen**
infinityskitchen.com
Dylan Kinnett
www.infinityskitchen.com/
submissions/

**Ink, Sweat and Tears**
ink-sweat-and-tears.blogharbor.com
Charles
charles@legaltechnology.com

**Inkfilled Page**
www.inkfilledpage.com
inkfilledpage@indigoediting.com

**Innsmouth Free Press Zine**
www.innsmouthfreepress.com
H.P. Lovecraft
innsmouthfp@gmail.com

**Instant City**
www.instantcity.org
Eric Zassenhaus
http://instantcity.org/?page_id=9

**Interrobang**
www.interrobangzine.com
Christopher Curley
interrobangpvd@gmail.com

**Irish Playhouse**
www.irishstoryplayhouse.com
info@irishstoryplayhouse.com

**Istanbul Literary Review**
www.ilrmagazine.net
Etkin Getir
www.ilrmagazine.com/submissions/
www.ilrmagazine.com/contact/

**Jellyfish Magazine**
www.jellyfishmag.org
Eric Zassenhaus
jellyfishmag@gmail.com

**JMWW**
jmww.150m.com
Jen Michalski,
jmww.150m.com/Guidelines.html

**Journal of Truth and Consequence**
journaloftruthandconsequence.com
Miranda Merklein
journaloftruthandconsequence@
gmail.com

**Joyful!**
www.joyfulonline.net
Pamela Tyree Griffin
joyful_online@ymail.com

**Joyland**
www.joyland.ca/home/new_york
Emily Schultz
emilyschultz@rogers.com
joylandfiction@gmail.com
joyland.submissions@gmail.com

**JuiceBox**
www.squeezetheuniverse.com/juice
Jes. S. Curtis
submissions@squeezetheuniverse.com

**Juked**
www.juked.com
J. W. Wang
submissions@juked.com
info@juked.com

**Jupiter**
www.jupitersf.co.uk
www.jupitersf.co.uk/contact.htm

**Kakofonie**
www.brokendimanche.eu/kakofonie
editorkakofonie@googlemail.com

**Kalkion**
www.kalkion.com
Swapnil Bhartiya
submission@kalkion.com

**Kartika Review**
www.kartikareview.com
Christine Lee Zilka
fiction@kartikareview.com
poetry@kartikareview.com
nonfiction@kartikareview.com
editor@kartikareview.com

**Keep Going**
www.keepgoing.org
Tom Chilipala
thefarm@keepgoing.org

**Ken Again**
kenagain.freeservers.com
John Delin
olofblue@aol.com

**Kennesaw Review**
www.kennesawreview.org
Robert Barrier
kenrev@gmail.com

**Kenyon Review**
www.kenyonreview.com
David Lynn
kenyonreview.org/krsubmit/
submissions/

**Keyhole Magazine**
www.keyholemagazine.com
Peter Cole
submissions@keyholemagazine.com

**KGB Bar**
www.kgbbar.com/lit/
Suzanne Dottino
kgbbar@rcn.com

**Kimirial Ink**
bedazzledink.com/?page_id=137
editor@bedazzledink.com

**Kill Poet**
www.killpoet.com/ray/KillaP.swf
www.killpoet.com/new_pages/
submission.html

**Killer Works**
www.killer-works.com
Jude Mire
articles@killer-works.com
flashfic@killer-works.com
comments@killer-works.com

**Killing the Buddha**
www.killingthebuddha.com
submit@killingthebuddha.com

**Kissed by Venus**
www.kissedbyvenus.ca
Alexandra Wolfe
www.kissedbyvenus.ca/?page_id=9

**Kneejerk**
www.kneejerkmag.com
C. James Bye, Stephen Tartaglione,
Jonathan Fullmer
submissions@kneejerkmag.com

**Konundrum**
lit.konundrum.com
Pitchaya Sudbanthad
prose@konundrum.com
poetry@konundrum.com
lit@konundrum.com

**Kudzu**
www.hazard.kctcs.edu/jy5/
academicaffairs/Kudzu/
Kudzu2009/KudzuMagazine.htm
Donna Sparkman
HZ-HCTC-KUDZU@kctcs.edu

**Kweli**
www.kwelijournal.com/KWELI_
JOURNAL/Welcome.html
William E. Berry, Jr.
Kweli Journal
c/o William E. Berry, Jr.
Submissions Manager
P.O. Box 1813
Auburn, New York 13021
kwelijournal@me.com

**L Magazine**
www.thelmagazine.com
fiction@thelmagazine.com

**La Petite Zine**
www.lapetitezine.org
Melissa Broder, D.W. Lichtenberg
lapetitezine@gmail.com

**LabLit**
www.lablit.com
Jennifer Rohn
www.lablit.com/contact

**Labyrinth Inhabitant**
www.labyrinthinhabitant.com
Matt
labyrinthinhabitant@gmail.com

**Lacuna**
lacunajournal.blogspot.com
markenberg@yahoo.com

**Lamination Colony**
www.laminationcolony.com
Blake Butler
Submissions on hiatus

**Laughter Loaf**
www.molyworld.net/laughterloaf
Paul Molyneux
editor@molyworld.net

**Laura Hird**
www.laurahird.com
www.laurahird.com/submissions.html

**Leaf Garden**
leafgardenpress.blogspot.com
Melanie Browne, Robert Louis Henry
choicesreply@gmail.com

**The Legendary**
www.downdirtyword.com
submit@downdirtyword.com

**The Lesser Flamingo**
www.lesserflamingo.net
lesserflamingo@gawab.com

**Liar's League**
liarslague.typepad.com
liarsleague@yahoo.co.uk

**Limp Wrist**
www.limpwristmag.com
Dustin Brookshire, Heather Hughes
www.limpwristmag.com/Submissions.html

**Lines and Stars**
www.lineandstars.com
editor@linesandstars.com

**Linguaphobous**
lingua.phobo.us
editor@lingua.phobo.us

**The Linnet's Wing**
www.linnetswings.net
www.linnetswings.net/?stn=7221&mpageno=16&pageno=38

**The Lipstick Pages**
www.thelipstickpages.net
Danna Williams
editor@thelipstickpages.net

**Liquid Imagination**
www.liquid-imagination.com
Kevin Wallis, Chrissy Davis
lqeditor@gmail.com

**Listrophy**
www.listrophy.com
www.listrophy.com/submissionform.php

**Lit Up**
litupmagazine.wordpress.com
litupmagazine@yahoo.com

**The Litchfield Literary Review**
www.thelitchfieldliteraryreview.com
submissions@thelitchfieldliteraryreview.com

**Literal Latte**
www.literal-latte.com
Jenine Gordon Bockman, Jeffrey Michael Gordon Bockman
Postal Delivery Only

**The Literary Bohemian**
www.literarybohemian.com
Online Submissions Manager

**Literary Chaos**
www.litchaos.com
litk.os@gmail.com
submit.k.os@gmail.com

**Literary Fever**
www.literaryfever.com
www.literaryfever.com/?page_id=880

**Literary Mama**
www.literarymama.com
Caroline Grant
LMfiction@literarymama.com
LMpoetry@literarymama.com
LMnonfiction@literarymama.com

**LitNImage**
www.litnimage.com
Roland Goity
fiction@litnimage.com

**Litterbox Magazine**
www.litterboxmagazine.com
Allison Ritto, P.J. Martin, Penelope
Ingram, Becky Herd
fiction@litterboxmagazine.com
nonfiction@litterboxmagazine.com
poetry@litterboxmagazine.com

**Live Oak Review**
www.liveoakreview.com
Sabra Wineteer
editors@liveoakreview.com

**LoBrow Magazine**
www.lobrow.org
lobrowmagazine@gmail.com

**Loch Raven Review**
www.lochravenreview.net
Jim Doss, Christopher George,
Dan Cuddy
submissions@lochravenreview.net

**Locus Novus**
www.locusnovus.com
ulay@locusnovus.com

**Locust Magazine**
www.locustmagazine.com
lit@locustmagazine.com

**Logical Lust**
www.logical-lust.com
Jim Brown, Zetta Brown, Rachel
McIntyre
editor@logical-lust.com

**Lonesome Fowl**
www.lonesomefowl.com
lonesomepress@gmail.com

**The Long and Short of It**
www.longandshortreviews.com
www.longandshortreviews.com/
submissions.htm

**Long Story Short**
alongshortstory.homestead.com
Denise Cassino
alongshortstory.homestead.com/
SubmissionGuidelines.html

**The Lorelei Signal**
www.loreleisignal.com
Carol Hightshoe
submissions@loreleisignal.com

**LOST Magazine**
www.lostmag.com
Peter Joseph
nonfiction@lostmag.com
fiction@lostmag.com
artphoto@lostmag.com

**Lotus Reader**
www.lotusreader.com
www.lotusreader.com/index.
php?p=1_23_Submit

**Lowestoft Chronicle**
www.lowesoftchronicle.com
submit@lowestoftchronicle.com

**Lucrezia Magazine**
www.lucerziamagazine.com
Anastasia Mavromatis

**Lunarosity**
www.zianet.com/lunarosity/
Wayne Crawford
wayne1@zianet.com

**Lung Poetry**
www.lungpoetry.com
Alveraz Ricardez
info@lungpoetry.com

**LWOT**
www.lwot.net
Jared Young
lwoteditors@gmail.com

**M-BRANE SF**
mbranesf.blogspot.com
Christopher Fletcher
mbranesf@gmail.com

**M Review**
www.marylhurst.edu/mreview/
Vandoren Wheeler
mreview.editor@gmail.com

**Mad Hatters Review**
www.madhattersreview.com
Carol Novack
Online Submissions Manager

**Mad Swirl**
www.madswirl.com
Johnny Olson
submissions@madswirl.com

**Mangrove**
www.as.miami.edu/english/
mangrove/home.html
mangrove@miami.edu

**Mannequin Envy**
www.mannequinenvy.com
Jai Britton, Jennifer VanBuren, Alex
Nodopaka, Patrick Carrington
flash@mannequinenvy.com

**Many Midnights**
www.geocities.com/many_midnights/
many_midnights@yahoo.com

**Mare Nostrum**
www.writinwaterpress.com
Kevin Craft
submissions@writinwaterpress.com

**Marginalia**
www.marginaliajournal.com/iWeb/
Site%202/Home.html
Alicita Rodriguez, Joseph Starr
marginaliajournal@gmail.com

**Mary Magazine**
www.stmarys-ca.edu/external/
Mary/
Sara Mumolo
mary@stmarys-ca.edu

**Matchbook**
www.matchbooklitmag.com
submissions@matchbooklitmag.com

**Maternal Spark**
www.maternalspark.com/wp/
heddy.e@gmail.com

**The Maynard**
www.themaynard.org
Marc Serpa, Nicholas Hauck
fiction@themaynard.org
nonfiction@themaynard.org
poetry@themaynard.org

**The Mayo Review**
orgs.tamu-commerce.edu/
MayoReview/
Pamela Millar
mayoreview@gmail.com

**The McCroskey Memorial
Internet Playhouse**
www.theinternetplayhouse.com/
The_MMIP/The_McCroskey_
Memorial_Internet_Playhouse.html
Jim Snowden
submissions@theinternetplayhouse.com

**Media Cake Magazine**
www.mediacakemagazine.com
Lotta Tess
editor@mediacakemagazine.com

**Media Virus**
mediavirusmagazine.wordpress.com
Lawrence Gladeview, Stewart Grant
mediavirusmagazine@gmail.com

**The Medulla Review**
www.themedullareview.com
Jennifer Hollie Bowles, Gindy
Elizabeth Houston
medullafiction@gmail.com
medullapoetry@gmail.com

**Megan's Closet**
www.megans-closet.com
Becci Noblit Goodall
Forum Submission

**Melusine**
www.melusine21cent.com/mag
Janelle Elyse Kihlstrom
sub2melusine@gmail.com

**Membra Disjecta**
www.membradisjecta.com
submissions@membradisjecta.com

**Memorious**
www.memorious.org
Rebecca Morgan Frank
submit+poetry@memorious.org
submit+prose@memorious.org

**Menda City Review**
www.mendacitypress.com
Terry Rogers
editors@mendacitypress.com

**Metal Scratches**
www.metalscratches.com
metalscratches@metalscratches.com

**Metamorphoses**
www.cerrocoso.edu/
metamorphoses/index.htm
Gary Enns
met@cerrocoso.net

**Metazen**
www.metazen.ca
Frank Hinton
editor@metazen@gmail.com

**Mezzo Cammin**
www.mezzocammin.com
Kim Bridgford
kbridgford@yahoo.com

**MFA/MFYOU**
www.mfamfyou.com
Ashley Cowger
submissions@mfamfu.com

**The MFA Whidbey Student Community at Northwest Institute for Literary Arts**
www.whidbeystudents.com/poetry/

**Mi Poesias**
www.mipoesias.com
Didi Menendez

**Mickle Street Review**
micklestreet.rutgers.edu
Geoffrey Sill
mstreetr@camden.rutgers.edu

**Micro 100**
micro100.blogspot.com
Dustin LaValley
dustin_lavalley@yahoo.com

**Microhorror**
www.microhorror.com/
microhorror/
Nathan Rosen
microhorror@gmail.com

**Midnight Echo**
www.australianhorror.com/index.
php?view=115
Marty Young
midnightecho@australianhorror.com

**Midnight In Hell**
www.midnightinhell.com/index2/
index.html
subs@midnightinhell.com

**Midnight Times**
www.towerweb.net/mt/midnight_
times.shtml
Jay Manning
editor@midnighttimes.com

**Midway Journal**
www.midwayjournal.com
Justin Maxwell, Rebecca Weaver,
Ralph Pennel, Nathan Thompson
Postal Submissions Only

**Milk Magazine**
www.milkmag.org
Larry Sawyer
milkmag@rcn.com

**Milk Money**
www.milkmoneymag.com
Marija Zummo
submissions@milkmoneymag.com

**Mindflights**
www.mindflights.com
Scott Appleton
Online Forum Submission

**Minima Magazine**
www.magazineminima.
com/4kontent.html
Jonathan Carr
minima@negativespacemedia.com

**Miranda**
www.mirandamagazine.com
submissions@mirandamagazine.com

**Mirror Dance**
mirrordancefantasy.blogspot.com/
Megan Arkenburg
markenburg@yahoo.com

**Mirrors**
www.mirrorsmag.com
Julie Yi, Sandy Chao
info.mirrors@gmail.com

**Mississippi Crow**
www.mississippicrow.com
Nadia Giordana
mississippicrow@msn.com

**Mississippi Review**
www.mississippireview.com
Frederick Barthelme
editors@mississippireview.com

**Mixtape Journal**
mixtapejournal.blogspot.com
themixtapejournal@gmail.com

**Mobius**
www.mobiusmagazine.com
Fred Schepartz
fmschep@charter.net (fiction)
demiurge@fibitz.com (poetry)

**Modern Haibun and Tanka Prose**
www.themetpress.com/
modernhaibunandtankaprose/
Jeffrey Woodward
mhtp.editor@gmail.com

**Moloch**
www.moloch.ie
Ailbhe Darcy, Clodagh Moynan
editor@moloch.ie

**The Mom Egg**
www.themomegg.com/themomegg/
Home.html
Marjorie Tesser
themomegg@gmail.com

**Monkeybicycle**
www.monkeybicycle.net
Jessa Marsh, Steven Seighman
websubmissions@monkeybicycle.net

**Monongahela Review**
www.monreview.com
Luke Bartolomeo
mononghelareview@gmail.com

**The Monsters Next Door**
www.themonstersnextdoor.com
LB Goddard
monstereditor@yahoo.com
tmndshorts@yahoo.com

**Moon Drenched Fables**
www.capriciousquills.com/
moondrenchedfables/index.html
Sarah, Carol
fablefictionsubmissions@yahoo.com

**Moondance**
www.moondance.org
Loretta Kemskey
submissions@moondance.org

**Moonshot**
www.moonshotzine.com
JD Scott
submissions@moonshotzine.com

**The Moose & Pussy**
www.themooseandpussy.com
submissions@themooseandpussy.com

**Morbid Outlook**
www.morbidoutlook.com/home/
section/home.html
Laura McCutchan
submissions@morbidoutlook.com

**Moria**
www.moriapoetry.com
William Allegrezza
submissions#moriapoetry.com

**Morpo Review**
www.morpo.com
Robert A. Fulkerson
Online Submissions Manager

**Mosaic**
www.mosaicmagazine.org
Ron Kavanaugh
info@mosaicmagazine.org

**Mud Luscious**
www.aboutjatyler.com
J.A. Tyler
author@aboutjatyler.com

**Mudlark**
www.unf.edu/mudlark/
William Slaughter
mudlark@unf.edu

**Mung Being**
www.mungbeing.com
Mark Givens
Online Submissions Manager

**Muscadine Lines**
www.asouthernjournal.com
Kathy Rhodes
kathy@asouthernjournal.com

**Mustachioed**
www.mustachioed.com
submissions@mustachioed.com

**Mysterical-E**
www.mystericale.com
submissions@mystericale.com

**Mystery Authors**
mysite.verizon.net/mysteryauthors/
Lisa Logan

**Nanoism**
www.nanoism.net
Ben White
nanofic@gmail.com

**Narrative Magazine**
www.narrativemagazine.com
Carol Edgarian, Tom Jenks
Online Submissions Manager

**The Nautilus Engine**
rnwrrn.googlepages.com
rondwarren@hotmail.com

**Necessary Fiction**
www.necessaryfiction.com
Steve Himmer
editor@necessaryfiction.com

**Necrotic Tissue**
www.necrotictissue.com
R. Scott McCoy
editor@necrotictissue.com
Submissions currently closed

**Ne'er Do Well**
www.theneerdowell.com
Laura Bogart

**Neon**
www.neonmagazine.co.uk
neonmagazine@ymail.com

**New Bedlam**
www.newbedlam.com
Jodi Lee
Online Submissions Manager

**New Ceres**
www.newconceptspublishing.com
Alisa Krasnostein
ceressubs@gmail.com

**New Fairy Tales**
www.newfairytales.co.uk
editor@newfairytales.co.uk

**The New Flesh**
newfleshmagazine.blogspot.com
eyesliketwenty@hotmail.com

**New Myths**
www.newmyths.com
Scott T. Barnes
editor@newmyths.com

**New Vilna Review**
www.newvilnareview.com
Daniel E. Levensen
editor@newvilnareview.com

**New Works Review**
www.new-works.org
Jonathan Sanders
brettalansanders@gmail.com

**The New Yinzer**
www.newyinzer.com
Kristofer Collins
submit@newyinzer.com

**Newport Review**
www.newportreview.org
Kathryn Kulpa
submissions@newportreview.org

**Nexus**
www.wsunexus.com
Aaron Larson
wsunexus.submissions@gmail.com

**Night Train**
www.nighttrainmagazine.com
Rusty Barnes

**Nimble**
www.thenimblefew.com
Travis E. J. Taylor
submissions@thenimblefew.com

**Niteblade**
www.niteblade.com
fiction@niteblade.com, poetry@niteblade.com

**No Posit**
kenbaumann.com/noposit.html
noposit@gmail.com

**No Record**
www.no-record.com
submit@no-record.com

**No Tell Motel**
www.notellmotel.org
Reb Livingston
submit@notellmotel.org

**Noctober**
noctober.wordpress.com
Rebecca Weybright

**Noneuclidean Café**
www.noneuclideancafe.com
James Swingle
submissions@noneuclideancafe.com

**NOÖ Journal**
www.noojournal.com
Mike Young
submissions@noojournal.com

**Normal Words**
www.normalwords.com
submissions@normalwords.com

**The Northville Review**
www.northvillereview.com
Erin Fitzgerald
northvillereview@gmail.com

**Northwords Now**
www.northwordsnow.co.uk
Rhoda Michael
Online Submissions Manager

**Nossa Morte**
www.nossamorte.com
Melissa De Kler
submissions@nossamorte.com

**Not a Paper Plane**
www.notapaperplane.com
notapaperplane@gmail.com

**Not just Air**
www.notjustair.org
Christina Donnelly, Parris Garnier
transom@notjustair.org

**Notes from the Underground**
www.notesfromtheunderground.co.uk
Chris Vernon, Tristan Summerscale
info@notesfromtheunderground.co.uk
poetry@notesfromtheunderground.
co.uk

**Novelletum**
www.novelletum.com
Dr. Katricia G. Pierson
chief@novelletum.com

**The November 3rd Club**
www.november3rdclub.com
Carlye Archibeque
nov3rdsubmissions@yahoo.com

**Nth Position**
www.nthposition.com
Val Stevenson
rquintav@gmail.com

**Nth Word**
www.nthword.com
Ryan O'Connor
submissions@nthword.com

**Oak Bend Review**
www.oakbendreview.com
Sandee Lyles
sandeelyles@yahoo.com

**The Oddville Press**
www.theoddvillepress.com
Patricia Hurst
submissions@theoddvillepress.com

**Off Beat Pulp**
www.offbeatpulp.com
Nigel, Jacob, Otto
submissions@offbeatpulp.com

**Offcourse Literary Journal**
www.albany.edu/offcourse/
I. Nirenburg
offcourse@albany.edu

**OG's Speculative Fiction**
www.cameron.edu/okreview/
Seth Crossman
poetry@theopinionguy.com
submissions@theopinionguy.com

**The Oklahoma Review**
www.cameron.edu/okreview/
Dawn Bona
okreview@cameron.edu

**On the Page Magazine**
www.onthepage.org
Nada Von Tress

**On The Premises**
www.onthepremises.com
Tarl Roger Kudrick
entries@onthepremises.com

**One Page Stories**
www.onepagestories.com
Christy Schick
Online Submissions Manager

**Open Letters Monthly**
www.openlettersmonthly.com
John Cotter
submissions@openlettersmonthly.com

**Open Thread**
www.openthread.org
Cecilia Westbrook
Online Submissions Manager

**Ophelia Street**
www.opheliastreet.com
submissions@opheliastreet.com

**Oregon Literary Review**
orelitrev.startlogic.com
Charles Deemer

**Orion's Child**
galadarn.com/OrionsChild.html
Gabriel Cole
editororionschild@galadarn.com

**Orson Scott Card's Intergalactic**
Medicine Show
www.intergalacticmedicineshow.com
Online Submissions Manager

**Otoliths**
the-otolith.blogspot.com
Mark Young
otolitheditor@gmail.com

**Our Stories**
www.ourstories.us
Alexis E. Santi
Online Submissions Manager

**Outsider Writers Collective**
www.outsiderwriters.org
Pat King, David Blaine, Caleb
J. Ross, Tim Hall, Victor
Schwartzman, Lena Vanelslander
prose@outsidewriters.org

**Outwardlink**
www.outwardlink.net
reginedelune@outwardlink.net

**Oxford Magazine**
community.muohio.edu/oxmag/
Rachel Ewing
oxmagessayseditor@muohio.edu
oxmagfictioneditor@muohio.edu
oxmagmediaeditor@muohio.edu
oxmagpoetryeditor@muohio.edu

**Ozone Park**
www.ozoneparkjournal.org
Deonne Kahler
fiction@ozoneparkjournal.org
nonfiction@ozoneparkjournal.org
poetry@ozoneparkjournal.org
translation@ozoneparkjournal.org

**Pagan Imagination**
www.paganimagination.com
Kerry Morgan
submissions@paganimagination.com

**Painted Bride Quarterly**
http://pbq.drexel.edu/index.php
Panamowa

**Pangur Ban Party**
www.pangurbanparty.com
deejburndt@gmail.com

**PANK**
www.pankmagazine.com
M. Bartley Siegel
Online Submissions Manager

**Pantechnicon**
www. pantechnicon.net
Trudi Topham, Alasdair Stuart

**Paper Street**
www.paperstreetonline.org
Arlan Hess
editor@paperstreetonline.com

**Paper Wall**
www.paperwall.org
Sam Cole, Katie Cole
submit@paperwall.org

**Parables and Pearls**
www.parablesandpearls.com
admin@parablesandpearls.com

**Paradigm**
www.paradigmjournal.com
Matthew Norris
submissions@paradigmjournal.com

**Paradigm Shift**
sites.google.com/site/
theknightsdomain/paradigm-shift-
online
Topher Scott
thx_cvs@yahoo.com

**Past Simple**
www.pastsimple.org
Marcus Slease, Jim Goar
submitto7@pastsimple.org

**Pax Americana**
www.paxjournal.com
Ben Mirov
submitonline@paxjournal.com

**Pebble Lake Review**
www.pebblelakereview.com
Amanda Auchter
submissions@pebblelakereview.com

**The Pedestal Magazine**
www.thepedestalmagazine.com
John Amen
pedmagazine@carolina.rr.edu

**Pemmican**
www.pemmicanpress.com
Robert Edwards
pemmicanpress@hotmail.com

**The Pennsylvania Review**
www.pennreview.com
Reginald Maria Huntley
pennsylvaniareview@gmail.com

**Pens on Fire**
www.pensonfire.com
Samantha Viles
fictionsub@pensonfire.com
poetrysub@pensonfire.com

**Pequin**
www.pequin.org
pequin1000@gmail.com

**Per Contra**
www.percontra.net
Miriam N. Kotzin, Bill Turner
percontrafiction@yahoo.com

**Perigree**
www.perigee-art.com
Robert Judge Woerheide
info@perigree-art.com

**Persimmon Tree**
www.persimmontree.org
Nan Fink Gefen
submissions@persimmontree.org

**Perspectives Magazine**
1perspectives.webs.com
Joy Harpo
perspectivesmagaine@gmail.com

**Philadelphia Stories**
www.philadelphiastories.org
Carla Spataro, Christine Weiser
Online Submissions Manager

**The Piker Press**
www.pikerpress.com
Alexandra Queen
poetry@pikerpress.com

**Pindeldyboz**
www.pindeldyboz.com
Whitney Steen, Grace Bello, Nora
Fussner, Rohan Bassett, Andrew
Borgstrom, Nicole Derr, J. A. Tyler
submissions@pindeldyboz.com

**Pine Tree Mysteries**
www.pinetreemysteries.com
Morgan Drake
drakeditor@gmail.com

**Pink Mouse Pub**
www.pinkmouseonline.com
ghb@pinkmouseonline.com

**Place Magazine**
www.placemag.org
Jennifer Hamilton, Amy Vickberg
submissions@placemag.org

**Planet Magazine**
planetmagazine.wordpress.com
editor@planetmag.com

**Please Don't**
www.please-dont.com
Pete Coco, Scott Stealey
submissions@please-dont.com

**Plots With Guns**
www.plotswithguns.com
Anthony Neil Smith
a.neil.smith@gmail.com

**The Pocket Review**
www.pocketreview.org

**Pocono Armchair Review**
poconoarmchairreview.com
editor@poconoarmchairreview.com

**Pod Castle**
www.podcastle.org
submit@podcastle.org

**Poemeleon**
www.poemeleon.org
Cati Porter
Online Submissions Manager

**Poetic Legacy**
www.poetriclegacy.mysite.com
Michael Lee Johnson
poetrymanusa@gmail.com

**PoeticDiversity**
www.poeticdiversity.org
Marie Lecrivain
Online Submissions Manager, or
marie@poeticdiversity.com

**Poetry Midwest**
poetrymidwest.blogspot.com
Matthew W. Schmeer
submit@poetrymidwest.com

**The Poetry Warrior**
www.thepoetrywarrior.com
thepoetrywarrior@gmail.com

**The Poet's Haven**
www.poetshaven.com

**Pollifax**
www.vajrtennis.com/pollifax/
Christine Train, Kevin Oltan, Monica
Lowstuter
pollifax.submit@gmail.com

**Polluto**
www.polluto.com
Adam Lowe
editor@polluto.com

**Polu Texni**
www.polutexni.com

**Pond Ripples**
www.pondripplesmag.com
Rebecca Burgenor
rebeccaburgenor@pondripplesmag.com

**Poor Mojo's Almanac**
www.poormojo.org
Dave Nelson, Morgan Johnson, Fritz
Swanson, Erik Garner Warren
Online Submissions Manager

**Postcard Shorts**
www.postcardshorts.com
Online Submissions Manager

**The Potomac**
www.thepotomacjournal.com
Charles Rammelkamp
Charles/Rammelkamp@ssa.gov

**Powder Burn Flash**
www.powderburnflash.com
powderburnflash@sbcglobal.net

**A Prairie Journal**
www.aprairiejournal.com
LeAnn Spencer
editor@aprairiejournal.com

**Press 1**
www.leafscape.org/press1/
Arlene Ang
press1editorial@hotmail.com

**Prick of the Spindle**
www.prickofthespindle.com
Cynthia Reeser
pseditor@prickofthespindle.com
emcknight@prickofthespindle.com
eweinstein

**Prima Storia**
www.primastoria.com
writers@primastoria.com

**Prism Review**
www.laverne.edu/academics/arts-sciences/prism-review/
prismreview@laverne.edu

**Pseudopod**
www.pseudopod.org
Ben Phillips
editor@pseudopod.com

**Publishing Genius**
www.publishinggenius.com
Adam Robinson
editor@publishinggenius.com

**Pulp Net**
www.pulp.net
Lane Ashfeldt
Online Submissions Manager

**Pulp Pusher**
www.pulppusher.com
pulppusher@yahoo.co.uk

**Purdee**
purdeemag.yolasite.com
purdee.mag@gmail.com

**Pure Francis**
www.purefrancis.org
Elizabeth Wylder
purefrancis.mag@gmail.com

**Qarrtsiluni**
www.qarrtsiluni.com
Beth Adams, Dave Bonta
qarrtsiluni@gmail.com

**Quantum Kiss**
www.quantumkiss.com
Mary Jo, William Ledbetter
submissions@quantumkiss.com

**Quantum Muse**
www.quantummuse.com
Michael Gallant
editors@quantummuse.com

**Quarterly Conversation**
www.quarterlyconversation.com
Scott Esposito
scott_esposito@yahoo.com

**Quarterly Literary Review Singapore**
www.qlrs.com
Toh Hsien Ming
Online Submissions Manager, or
editors@qlrs.com

**The Quay**
www.quayjournal.org
Jennifer Pattison Rumford, Shawn
Kerivan, Betsy Self Elijah, Karen Terrey
editor@quayjournal.org
fiction@quayjournal.org
nonfiction@quayjournal.org
poetry@quayjournal.org

**Quicksilver**
academics.utep.edu/Default.
aspx?alias=academics.utep.edu/
quicksilver
Nick Ripatrazone, Brian Anderson
quicksilver@utep.edu

**Quill and Parchment**
www.quillandparchment.com
Sharmagne Leland-St. John
qpsubmissions@
quillandparchment.com

**The Quills Quarterly**
www.thequillsquarterly.com
K.C. Crawford
submissions@quillsquarterly.com

**The Quirk**
www.thequirk.org
editors@thequirk.com

**R.K.V.R.Y.**
www.rkvry.com
Victoria Pynchon
jdeutsch@dslextreme.com
victoria.pynchon@gmail.com

**Radioactive Moat**
www.radioactivemoat.com
P. Edward Cunningham
radioactivemoat@gmail.com

**Raging Face**
www.ragingface.com
master@ragingface.com

**Rain Fade**
www.rain-fade.com
Bryan Coffelt
submissions@rain-fade.com

**Ramble Underground**
www.rambleunderground.org
fictioneditor@rambleunderground.com

**The Random Eye**
pinkbagels@gmail.com

**The Ranfurly Review**
www.ranfurly-review.co.uk
Colin Galbraith
submissions@ranfurly-review.co.uk

**Raphael's Village**
www.raphaelsvillage.com
fictioneditor@raphaelsvillage.com

**Raving Dove**
www.ravingdove.org
Jo-Ann Moss
ravingdove@gmail.com

**Raygun Revival**
www.raygunrevival.com
Johne Cook
overlords@raygunrevival.com

**Read This Magazine**
www.readthismagazine.co.uk
Claire Askew
submissions@readthismagazine.
co.uk

**Real: Regarding Arts & Letters**
real.sfasu.edu
Christine Butterworth-McDermott

**Reconfigurations**
reconfigurations.blogspot.com
W. Scott Howard
showard@du.edu

**The Recusant**
www.therecusant.org.uk
Alan Morrison
therecusant@yahoo.co.uk

**Red Fez Publications**
www.redfez.net
Michele McDannold
Online Submissions Manager

**Redivider**
www.redividerjournal.org
Matthew Salesses
Online Submissions Manager

**Reflection's Edge**
www.reflectionsedge.com
Sharon Dodge
fictionsubmissions@reflectionsedge.com
editor@reflectionsedge.com

**Residential Aliens**
www.resaliens.com
Lyn Perry
lyn@resaliens.com

**Retort Magazine**
www.retort.brentley.com/retort.htm
Brentley Frazer
submissions@retortmagazine.com

**Revenant**
www.revenantmagazine.com
Geoff Bough
rd@revenantmagazine.com

**Reverie**
www.aquariuspressbookseller.net
Randall Horton
reverie.journal@gmail.com

**Review Americana**
www.americanpopularculture.com/
review_americana.htm
Leslie Wilson
editor@americanpopularculture.com

**Revolution SF**
www.revolutionsf.com
revolutionsfsubs@gmail.com

**Rhythm**
rhythmpoetrymagazine.english.dal.ca/
Mary Kathryn Arnold
rhythm@dal.ca

**The Right Eyed Deer**
therighteyeddeer.webs.com
Doug Pugh
therighteyeddear@gmail.com

**Right Hand Pointing**
www.righthandpointing.com
Dale Wisely
righthandpointing@gmail.com

**Rise Converge**
riseconverge.blogspot.com/
Jeff Crook

**River & Sound Review**
www.riverandsoundreview.org
Jay Bates
rsrfictioneditor@hotmail.com
rsrhumoreditor@hotmail.com
rsrnonfictioneditor@hotmail.com
rsrpoetryeditor@hotmail.com

**River Babble**
iceflow.com/riverbabble/Welcome.html
Leila Rae
riverbabble@gmail.com

**River Poets Journal**
www.riverpoetsjournal.com
Judith A. Lawrence
judithlawrence@comcast.net

**Rivets**
www.rivetslitmag.com
Christy Frantz, Dale Debakcsy
editors@rivetslitmag.com

**Roadrunner Journal**
www.roadrunnerjournal.net
Scott Metz
scott@roadrunnerjournal.net

**Robot Melon**
www.robotmelon.com
Steven Lew
robotmelon@gmail.com

**Rogue Blades Entertainment**
www.roguebladesentertainment.com
Jason M. Waltz
Online Submissions Manager

**Rope and Wire**
www.ropeandwire.com
Scott
Online Submissions Manager

**The Rose & Thorn**
www.theroseandthornezine.com
Barbara Quinn
rose-andthorn@live.com
poetryeditor@hotmail.com

**The Rose City Sisters**
rosecitysisters.blogspot.com
Paula Johnson
rosecitysisters@mac.com

**Rotten Leaves Magazine**
www.rottenleaves.com
Axel Hassen Taiari, Christopher J. Dwyer
submissions@rottenleaves.com

**Rougarou**
www.louisiana.edu/Academic/
LiberalArts/ENGL/Creative/
Rougarou/Rougarou.html
Jerry McGuire
rougaroufiction@gmail.com
rougarounonfiction@gmail.com
rougaroupoetry@gmail.com

**Rough Copy**
www.roughcopy.net
Janet Freeman
fiction@roughcopy,net
nonfiction@roughcopy.net
poetry@roughcopy.net

**Round**
www.roundonline.com
Beth Bayley
isubmit@roundonline.com

**Rumble Magazine**
rumble.sy2.com
Craig Snyder
rumble.microfiction@gmail.com

**The Rumpus**
www.therumpus.net
Stephen Elliott
tips@therumpus.net

**Rustblind**
www.rustblind.com
Ben Pealer, Jacinta Meyers
ben.pealer@rustblind.com
j.meyers@rustblind.com

**Ruthless Peoples Magazine**
www.ruthlesspeoples.com
Submissions on hiatus

**The Saint Ann's Review**
www.saintannsreview.com
fiction@saintannsny.org
poetry@saintannsny.org

**Salome Magazine**
www.salomemagazine.com
Colette Brown
gatekeeper@salomemagazine.com

**Salt River Review**
www.poetserv.org
James Cervantes, Greg Simon,
Lynda Schor
cervantes.james@gmail.com
greg.simon@comcast.net
lynda.schor@gmail.com

**Saltgrass Journal**
saltgrassjournal.blogspot.com
Julia Cohen (poetry), Abigail
Holstein (fiction)
saltgrass.journal@gmail.com

**Sangam Literary Review**
www.sangammagazine.com
Munir Muztaba Ali
editor@sandammagazine.com

**Saw Palm**
www.sawpalm.usf.edu
Alicia Thompson
sawpalm@cas.usf.edu

**Scalped**
www.scalpedmagazine.com
Erin Rodino
Online Submissions Manager

**Scapegoat Review**
www.scapegoatreview.com
Erika Lutzner
Online Submissions Manager

**Scawy Monstur**
www.scawymonstur.com
Pat Moran
MrMonstur@scawymonstur.com

**Schuylkill Valley Journal**
www.manayunkartcenter.org/svja.html
Peter Krok
svjpoetry@yahoo.com

**The Scrambler**
www.thescrambler.com
Jeremy Spencer
editor@thescrambler.com

**Scribal Tales**
www.scribaltales.com/
Daniel Olarnick
Dolarnick@aol.com

**Scribblers On The Roof**
www.jscribes.com
Kelly Hartog
submissions@jscribes.com

**Scruffy Dog Review**
sdr.colingalbraith.co.uk
Brenda Birch
submissions@thescruffydogreview.com

**Second Run**
www.secondrun.org
Jim Coppoc
submissions@secondrun.org

**Segue**
www.mid.muohio.edu/segue/
Eric Melbye
segue@muohio.edu

**Sein Und Werden**
www.kissthewitch.co.uk/
seinundwerden/sein.html
seinundwerden@gmail.com

**Semaphore**
www.semaphoremagazine.com
Marie Hodgkinson
semaphoremagazine@gmail.com

**Sensorotika**
www.sensorotika.com
submissions@sensorotika.com

**Seven Letter Words**
www.sevenletterwords.com.au
Rohan Bassett
editor@sevenletterwprds.com

**Sex and Murder**
www.sexandmurder.com
Douglas Allen Rhodes
editor@sexandmurder.com

**SF Zine**
www.shadeworks.org
C. E. Ramirez
submissions@sfzine.org

**SFWP**
www.sfwp.org
Andrew Gifford
sfwritersproject@gmail.com

**Shade Works**
www.shadeworks.org
Gordon Clemmons
editors@shadeworks.org

**The Shadowcast Audio Anthology**
shadowpress.wordpress.com
shadowcast@mcsi.com

**Shady Side Review**
www.shadysidereview.com
Sarah Grubb, Amy Holwerda, Teresa
Petro-Michelli
fictioneditor@shadysidereview.com
nonfictioneditor@shadysidereview.com
poetryeditor@shadysidereview.com

**Shaking Like A Mountain**
www.shakinglikeamountain.com
Wayne Cresser, Vito Grippi
editors@shakinglikeamountain.com

**Shalla Magazine**
www.shallamagazine.com
Carolyn DeGrasey, R. W. Weber,
Keith Burke, Paul Gough, Cynthia Alvarez
shalla_editor@yahoo.com

**Shatter Colors Literary Review**
www.shattercolors.com
Robert Scott Leyse
editor@shattercolors.com

**Shelf Life Magazine**
www.shelflifemagazine.com
Messina, Ryan Dilbert
contact@shelflifemagazine.com

**Sheroes Rag**
www.freewebs.com/sheroesrag/
sheroes_rag@hotmail.com

**The Shine Journal**
www.theshinejournal.com
Pamela Tyree Griffin
shinesubmit@fastmail.us

**Shipwrights**
webzone.imer.mah.se/projects/
shipwrights/frontpage.aspx
Darius Degher
shipwrights@mah.se

**Shit Creek Review**
shitcreek.auszine.com
Angela France, Nige Holt, Rose
Kelleher
Online Submissions Manager

**Shock Totem**
www.shocktotem.com
K. Allen Wood
submissions@shocktotem.com

**Shofar Literary Review**
www.shofarlitreview.com
shofarlitreview@shofarlitreview.com

**Shoots and Vines**
www.shootsandvines.com
Crystal Folz
submissions@shootsandvines.com

**The Shore Magazine**
www.theshoremag.com
Shane Sinnott
submissions@theshoremag.com

**The Short Humour Site**
www.short-humour.org.uk
Brian Huggett
submissions@short-humour.org.uk

**Short Story Library**
shortstory.us.com
Casey Quinn
submit@shortstory.us.com

**Shots Magazine**
www.shotsmag.co.uk
Mike Stotter
stories4shots@yahoo.co.uk

**Shred of Evidence**
www.shredofevidence.com
Megan Powell
editor@shredofevidence.com

**Side of Grits**
www.ruralmessengerspress.com
Michele McDannold
editor@ruralmessengerspress.org

**Sidebrow**
www.sidebrow.net
submit@sidebrow.net

**Sideshow Fables**
www.sideshowfables.com
Paul Eckert
sideshowfables@gmail.com

**Silenced Press**
www.silencedpress.com
submissions@silencedpress.com

**Silver Blade**
www.silverblade.net
Karl Rademacher
submissions@silverblade.net

**Siren: A Journal of Literature and Art**
www.sirenlit.com
Sara Kearns
sirenlit@gmail.com

**Sirens**
www.sirensmag.com
Heather Wood Rudolph, Jennifer
Armstrong
heather@sirensmag.com
jennifer@sirensmag.com

**Six Little Things**
www.sixbrickspress.com
Bard Cole
editor@sixbrickspress.com

**Six Sentences**
sixsentences.blogspot.com
sixsentences@yahoo.com

**Sixers Review**
www.sixersreview.com
Natalie Yasmin Soto, Tomas C.
Batista, Olivia Isabel M., Shola
Webion, Kemsa Kems, Safiyah Umar
sizersreview@yahoo.com

**Sleet Magazine**
www.sleetmagazine.com
Susan Solomon
editor@sleetmagazine.com

**Sliptongue**
www.sliptongue.com
Robert Scott Leyse
sliptonguemag@gmail.com

**Slope**
www.slope.org
Brandon Shimoda, Greg Hill Jr.

**Slow Trains**
www.slowtrains.com
Susannah Indigo
editor@slowtrains.com

**Slurve**
www.slurvemag.com
tryouts@slurvemag.com

**Slush Pile**
slushpilemag.com
M.R. Branwen
slushpilemag@gmail.com
slushpilepoetry@gmail.com

**Smashed Ink**
www.smashedink.com
Maxwell Rutherford
gwolas@smashedink.com

**Smokebox**
www.smokebox.net
fuel@smokebox.com

**SmokeLong Quarterly**
www.smokelong.com
Randall Brown
Online Submissions Manager

**The Smoking Poet**
www.thesmokingpoet.net
Zinta Aistars
thesmokingpoet@gmail.com

**SN Review**
www.snreview.org
Joseph Conlin
editor@snreview.org

**Sniplits**
www.sniplits.com
acquisitions@sniplits.com

**SNM Horror Magazine**
www.snmhorrormag.com
Steven N. Marshall
snmeditor@yahoo.com

**Snow Monkey**
snowmonkeyjournal.blogspot.com
John Burgess
snowmonkey.editor@comcast.net

**Snow*Vigate**
www.snowvigate.com
Doug Martin
snowv@snowvigate.com

**So You Think You Can Write**
sarahjoyya.wordpress.com
Sarah Joy Freese
sarahjoyyas@gmail.com

**Softblow**
www.softblow.org
Christopher Ujine Ong, Eric Low,
Gwee Li Sui, Jason Wee
editor@softblow.org

**SoMa Literary Review**
www.somalit.com
Kemble Scott
submit@somalit.com

**Something Wicked**
www.somethingwicked.co.za
Joe Vaz

**Sonar 4 Ezine**
www.sonar4publications.com
Shells Walter
sonar4publications@gmail.com

**Sorcerous Signals**
www.sorceroussignals.com
Carol Hightshoe
submissions@sorceroussignals.com

**Sotto Voce**
www.sottovocemagazine.com
Emily Thorp
Online Submissions Manager

**Soundzine**
www.soundzine.org
Charles Musser
submissions@soundzine.org

**South Jersey Underground**
www.southjerseyunderground.com/
Home_Page.php
Jim Blackburn
southjerseyunderground@comcast.net

**Southern Women's Review**
www.southernwomensreview.com
Alicia K. Clavell
southernwomensreview@gmail.com

**Southpaw**
www.southpawjournal.co.uk
southpawjournal@hotmail.co.uk

**Southword Journal**
www.munsterlit.ie
James Harpur
poetryeditor@munsterlit.ie
fictioneditor@munsterlit.ie

**Space Squid**
www.spacesquid.com
squishy@spacesquid.com

**Space Westerns**
www.spacewesterns.com/
N.E. Lilly
submissions2018@spacewesterns.com

**Spaceports & Spidersilk**
www.samsdotpublishing.com/
spacesilk/cover.htm
Marcie Lynn Tentchoff
spacesilk@yahoo.com

**Spark Bright**
www.freewebs.com/sparkbright/
Emily Smith
spark_bright7@yahoo.co.uk

**Spec The Halls**
www.aswiebe.com/specthehalls.html
Abra Staffin Wiebe
specthehalls@gmail.com

**SpecFic World**
www.specficworld.com
Doyle Eldon Wilmoth, Jr.
subs2009@specficworld.com

**Specs**
www.specsjournal.org
Vidhu Aggarwal
editors@specsjournal.org

**Speechless Magazine**
www.speechlessthemagazine.org
Suzanne Lummis
suzanne@speechlessthemagazine.com

**SPHERE**
www.spheretlr.org
Brandon C. Battersby, Ryan Elwood
Online Submissions Manager

**Spindle**
www.spindlejournal.org
Serena Epstein, Dresden Glover, Grace
Harris, Michelle Labbe, Katie Walsh
submit@spindlejournal.org

**Spindle Magazine**
www.spindlezine.com
Guy LeCharles Gonzalez
submissions@spindlezine.com

**Spindrift**
www.shoreline.edu/spindrift/
Lucy Weiland
spindrift@shoreline.edu

**Spinetingler Magazine**
www.spinetinglermag.com
Sandra Ruttan
spinetinglermag@mysterybookspot.com

**The Splinter Generation**
www.splintergeneration.com
splintergeneration@gmail.com

**Spooky Boyfriend**
spookyboyfriend.weebly.com
Nathan Logan
spookyboyfriend@gmail.com

**Spork Press**
www.sporkpress.com
Richard, Drew
submit_fiction@sporkpress.com

**Springgun Press**
springgunpress.com/issueone.html
Erin Costello, Mark Rockswald
editor@springgunpress.com

**The Square Table**
www.thesquaretable.com
Dina DiMaio
editor@thesquaretable.com

**Squid Quarterly**
www.squidquarterly.com
Beth Couture, Jeffrey Tucker
submissions@squidquarterly.com

**The Squirrel Cage**
www.thesquirrelcage.co.uk
Matt Brolly
submissions@thesquirrelcage.co.uk

**Staccato Fiction**
www.staccatofiction.com
submissions@staccatofiction.com

**Staffs & Starships**
www.staffsandstarships.com
James Boone Dryden
submissions@sheerspeculation.com

**Static Movement**
www.staticmovement.com
Chuck Turner
printstaticmovement@gmail.com

**Steel City Review**
www.steelcityreview.com
Julia LaSalle
editor@steelcityreview.com

**Stepping Stones Magazine**
www.fspressonline.org
fiction@fpressonline.com
nonfiction@fpressonline.com
poetry@fpressonline.com

**Stickman Review**
www.stickmanreview.com
Anthony Brown, Darrin English
fiction@stickmanreview.com
nonfiction@stickmanreview.com
poetry@stickmanreview.com

**Still Crazy**
www.crazylitmag.com/index.php
Barbara Kussow
submissions@crazylitmag.com

**Stirring**
www.sundress.net/stirring/
Josh Webster, Erin Elizabeth Smith
stirring.fiction@gmail.com

**Stone's Throw Magazine**
www.stonesthrowmagazine.com
Russell Rowland, Tami Haaland
stonesthrowmagazine@gmail.com

**Stop Buying Stuff Magazine**
www.stopbuyingstuffmagazine.com
stopbuyingstuffmagazine@gmail.com

**Stories For Children Magazine**
www.storiesforchildrenmagazine.org
Claudette Hegel, Gisele LeBlanc
sandielee@storiesforchildren.com
GiseleLeblanc@storiesforchildren.com

**Stories That Lift**
www.storiesthatlift.com
www.storiesthatlift.com/index.php/site-
specific/submission-guidelines.html

**Story*GLOSSIA***
www.storyglossia.com
Steven J. McDermott
Submissions are currently closed

**Story Quarterly**
www.camden.rutgers.edu/
storyquarterly/
J.T. Barbarese
story.quarterly@camden.rutgers.edu

**Storyscape**
www.storyscapejournal.com
Anne Hays
storymaster@storyscapejournal.com

**storySouth**
www.storysouth.com
Terry Kennedy
terry@storysouth.com

**StoryTime: African New Fiction**
publishyourstory.blogspot.com/
postonstorytime@gmail.com

**Strange Horizons**
www.strangehorizons.com
Susan Marie Groppi, Jed Hartman,
Harold Bowes, M.R. James, Niall Harison
articles@strangehorizons.com
fiction@strangehorizons.com
poetry@strangehorizons.com
reviews@strangehorizons.com

**Strange Road**
www.strangeroad.com
editor@strangeroad.com

**Strange World**
strangeworldmagazine.blogspot.com
strangeworldmag@gmail.com

**Strangeweirdandwonderful.com**
www.strangeweirdandwonderful.com
D. L. Russell
submissions@
strangeweirdandwonderful.com

**Streets of Chiba**
streetsofchiba.wordpress.com
Joseph T. Christopher
socssubmissions@gmail.com

**Stride Magazine**
www.stridemagazine.co.uk
Rupert Loydell
submissions@stridemagazine.co.uk

**Stymie**
www.stymiemag.com
Erik Smetana
stymiemag@gmail.com

**Sub-Lit**
www.sub-lit.com
Amber Brooks, Laurah Norton
Raines, Michael Ogletree
amberbrooks@gmail.com
fiction@sub-lit.com
nonfiction@sub-lit.com
poetry@sub-lit.com

**Subtle Tea**
www.subtletea.com
David Herrle
doomsinger@subtletea.com

**The Summerset Review**
www.summersetreview.org
Joseph Levens
editor@summersetreview.com

**Sunday Salon**
www.sundaysalon.com/zine
Nita Noveno
currently not accepting

**Sunken Lines**
www.sunkenlines.com
Austin Cambridge, Minty Snuff,
Dogger Banks
editor@sunkenlines.com
minty@sunkenlines.com
dogger@sunkenlines.com

**Sunsets and Silencers**
www.sunsetsandsilencers.com/home
Chuckie Campbell
sunsets.silencers@gmail.com

**Super Arrow**
superarrow.blogspot.com
Amanda Goldblatt
superarrowfliestrue@gmail.com

**SUPERficial Flesh**
www.superficialflesh.com
Lauren Dixon
submission@superficialflesh.com

**Superstition Review**
www.asu.edu/superstitionreview/
n3/index.html
Patricia Colleen Murphy
superstitionreview@asu.edu

**Survival By Storytelling
Magazine**
sbsmag.wordpress.com
Shaun Duke, Imelda
sbsmag@yahoo.com

**Survivor's Review**
www.survivorsreview.org
Sheree Gaudet Kirby
sheree@survivorsreview.org

**Suss**
www.sussitout.org
Dan Manchester
dan@lintelsashandsill.org

**Susurrus: The Literature of Madness**
www.susurrusmagazine.com
Brian Worley
editor@susurrusmagazine.com

**Swell**
www.swellzine.com
swelleditor@yahoo.com

**Swink**
www.swinkmag.com
Darcy Cosper
swinkonline@gmail.com

**Switchback**
www.swback.com
Kelly Krumrie
submissions@swback.com

**Sybil's Garage**
www.sensesfive.com/publications/
sybils-garage-no-6/
Matthew Kressel
info@sensesfive.com

**Sycamore Review**
www.sycamorereview.com
Anthony Cook
www.sycamorereview.com/
submissions

**The Sylvan Echo**
www.sylvanecho.net
editor@sylvanecho.com

**Taddle Creek**
www.taddlecreekmag.com
Conan Tobias
editor@taddlecreekmag.com

**Tales From A Small Planet**
www.talesmag.com
Patricia Linderman
editor@talesmag.com

**Tales From the Moonlit Path**
www.moonlit-path.com
submissions@moonlit-path.com

**Tales of Moreauvia**
www.moreauvia.com
Pete S. Allen
submissions@moreauvia.com

**Tales of the Zombie War**
www.talesofworldwarz.com
west@talesofworldwarz.com

**Tarpaulin Sky**
www.tarpaulinsky.com
Christian Peet
*snail mail only

**Tattoo Highway**
www.tattoohighway.org
Sara McAulay
submissions@tattoohighway.org

**TeenAge Magazine**
teenage.doubleedgedpublishing.com
Michele Archer
teenage_editor@
doubleedgepublishing.com

**Temenos**
www.chsbs.cmich.edu/creative_
writing/temenos.htm
Mike Shafer
temenoscmu@gmail.com

**Terracotta Typewriter**
www.tctype.com
tctype@gmail.com

**Terrain.org**
www.terrain.org
Simmons B. Buntin
contact2@terrain.org

**Tertulia Magazine**
www.tertuliamagazine.com
Rosa Martha Villarreal
submissions@tertuliamagazine.com

**Thaumatrope**
thaumatrope.greententacles.com/
Nathan E. Lilly
thaumatrope@greententacles.com

**The**
welcometoyethe.blogspot.com
Craig Sarnotti
craigtheeditor@gmail.com

**Theaker's Quarterly Fiction**
http://www.silveragebooks.pwp.
blueyonder.co.uk/mag/tqf/tqf.htm
Stephen Theaker
silveragebooks@blueyonder.co.uk

**Thick With Conviction**
www.angelfire.com/poetry/
thickwithconviction/
Kayla Middlebrook
twczine@yahoo.com

**Thieves Jargon**
www.thievesjargon.com
Dan Scannell
submissions@thievesjargon.com

**Third Order Magazine**
www.thirdorder.org
Karen Osborne
thirdordereditor@gmail.com

**Thirst For Fire**
www.thirstforfire.com
Devan Sagliani
fire@thirstforfire.com

**Thirteen Myna Birds**
13myna.blogspot.com
julietx@bust.com

**Thirty First Bird Review**
www.thirtyfirstbird.com/
contactinformation.htm
Edward Simon
thirtyfirstbird@yahoo.com

**This PDF Chapbook**
www.publishinggenius.com/2009/
01/chapbook-genius.html
Adam Robinson

**This Zine Will Change Your Life**
thiszinewillchangeyourlife.blogspot.com
Ben Tanzer
thiszinewillchangeyourlife@yahoo.com

**A Thousand Faces**
www.thousand-faces.com
Frank Byrns
submissions@thousand-faces.com

**Three Crow Press**
www.morriganezine.com
Reece Notley
submissions@morriganezine.com

**Three-Lobed Burning Eye**
www.3lobedmag.com
Andrew S. Fuller
www.3lobedmag.com/submissions.
html

**Thrillers, Killers & Chillers**
thrillskillsnchills.blogspot.com
Matt Hilton
matthiltonbooks@live.co.uk

**Thrilling Detective**
www.thrillingdetective.com
Kevin Burton Smith
kvnsmith@thrillingdetective.com

**Thug Lit**
www.thuglit.com/home.html
Todd Robinson
submissions@thuglit.com

**The Tide Pool**
www.tidepoolfiction.com
Shari Green
tidepoolfiction@gmail.com

**Tiferet**
www.tiferetjournal.com
Donna Baier Stein
editors@tiferetjournal.com

**Titular**
www.titular-journal.com
titularjournal@yahoo.com

**Toasted Cheese**
tclj.toasted-cheese.com
Stephanie Lenz
submit@toasted-cheese.com

**Tom's Voice**
www.tomsvoicemagazine.com
Vanessa Gebbie
editor@tomsvoicemagazine.com

**Tonopah Review**
www.tonopahreview.org
tonopahreview@gmail.com

**Torch**
www.torchpoetry.org
Amanda Johnston
prose@torchpoetry.org
shorts@torchpoetry.org
poetry@torchpoetry.org

**The Toronto Quarterly**
thetorontoquarterly.blogspot.com
Darryl Salach
thetorontoquarterly@hotmail.com

**Touch: The Journal of Healing**
www.thelivesyoutouch.com/
touchjournal/2009/Home.html
O.P.W. Fredericks
prose@thelivesyoutouch.com
poetry@thelivesyoutouch.com

**The Town Drunk**
www.towndrunkmag.com
Brit Marschalk

**Tower of Light**
www.tolfantasy.com
Michael Southard

**Trickhouse**
www.trickhouse.org
Kristen Nelson
info@trickhouse.org

**Trillium Literary Magazine**
www.trilliumliteraryjournal.org
James L. Myron
submissions@trilliumliteraryjournal.org

**Triple Canopy**
www.canopycanopycanopy.com
Sam Frank, Alexander Provab
submissions@canopycanopycanopy.com

**Troubadour 21**
www.troubadour21.com
Carlton Lloyd Smith
submission@troubadour21.com

**Tulip**
tulipweekly.wordpress.com
tulipsubmissions@gmail.com

**Turbine**
www.victoria.ac.nz/turbine/
turbine@vuw.ac.nz

**Turn of the Screw Serial Fiction**
www.aturnofthescrew.com
M. Rhode
submissions@torquerepress.com

**Tweet the Meat**
tweetthemeat.blogspot.com
tweetthemeat@gmail.com

**Twelve Stories**
www.readtwelvestories.com
Molly Gaudry, Blythe Winslow
twelvestories@gmail.com

**Twilight Tales**
www.twilighttales.com
Ed DeGeorge
features@twilighttales.com

**Twilight Times**
www.twilighttimes.com
Lida Quidden
publisher@twilighttimes.com

**Twisted Dreams**
www.myspace.com/
twisteddreamsmagazine
Andrea Dean VanScoyoc
murgaine@yahoo.com

**Twisted Tongue**
www.twistedtongue.co.uk/
creativestaff.htm
Claire Nixon
twistedtongue@blueyonder.co.uk

**Two Hawks Quarterly**
twohawksquarterly.com
fiction@twohawksquarterly.com
creativenonfiction@
twohawksquarterly.com
poetry@twohawksquarterly.com
genrex@twohawksquarterly.com

**Two Sentence Stories**
www.twosentencestories.com
Mathew Ferguson
mathew@twosentencestories.com

**Two With Water**
www.twowithwater.com
Denise Dooley
submissions@twowithwater.com

**U.M.P.H.**
www.umphprose.com
Mignon Ariel King
umphsubmits@yahoo.com

**Ugly Cousin**
www.uglycousin.com
Scott Topping, Angie Curneal
Palsak
scott@uglycousin.com
angie@uglycousin.com

**Umbrella Journal**
www.umbrellajournal.com
Kate Bernadette Benedict
umbrellajournal@gmail.com

**Uncharted Sky**
www.unchartedsky.com
submissions@unchartedsky.com

**Under This Red Rock**
http://www.underthisredrock.com/
submissions@underthisredrock.com

**Underground Voices**
www.undergroundvoices.com
uveditor@undergroundvoices.com

**Unlikely 2.0**
http://www.unlikelystories.org/
Jonathan Penton
jonathan@unlikelystories.com

**Untitled Books**
http://www.untitledbooks.com/
Viola Fort
fiction@untitledbooks.com

**Up The Staircase**
http://www.upthestaircase.org/
mainpage.htm
April Michelle Bratton
upthestaircase@gmail.com

**UpRightDown**
http://www.uprightdown.com/
Lee Berman
plot@uprightdown.com

**Vain Magazine**
www.callmevain.com
Tia Orian
submissions@callmevain.com

**Valparaiso Poetry Review**
www.valpo.edu/vpr/
Edward Byrne
VPR@valpo.edu

**Velvet Mafia**
www.velvetmafia.com
Sean Meriweather
editor@velvetmafia.com

**Verb-Ate-Him**
verbatehim.wordpress.com
submissions.verbatehim@gmail.com

**Verbsap**
www.verbsap.com
Laurie Seidler
editor@VerbSap.com

**Vestal Review**
www.vestalreview.net
Mark Budman
submissions@vestalreview.net

**Vibrant Grey**
www.vibrantgray.com
Cannon Roberts
cannon@vibrantgray.com

**The View From Here**
www.viewfromheremagazine.com
Mike French
viewfromhere@primemail.com

**The Vocabula Review**
www.vocabula.com
Robert Hartwell Fiske
editor@vocabula.com

**Vulgata Magazine**
www.vulgatamagazine.org
Melinda Selmys
slushpile@vulgatamagazine.org

**Waccamaw**
www.waccamawjournal.com
Dan Albergotti
waccamawjournal@gmail.com

**Wag's Revue**
www.wagsrevue.com
Sandra Allen
editors@wagsrevue.com

**Wamack**
wamack.blogspot.com
Grant Wamack
grantwamack@gmail.com

**Wanderings**
www.wanderingsmag.com
Mike Wever
editor@wanderingsmag.com

**War, Literature and the Arts**
www.wlajournal.com
Donald Anderson, Jesse Goolsby,
Glenn Dayley, Will Hochman
editor@WLAjournal.com
jesse.goolsby@usafa.edu
glenn.dayley@usafa.edu
hochmanw1@southernct.edu

**Ward 6 Review**
www.ward6review.com/
contentsV2I2.htm
Les Kay
submissions@ward6review.com

**Waterlogged August**
www.waterloggedaugust.com
Dan Cavallari
waterloggedaugust@gmail.com

**Wazee**
www.wazeejournal.org
Noelle Nicholson, Mimi Schaefer,
Roger Wehling
fiction@wazeejournal.org
nonfiction@wazeejournal.org
poetry@wazeejournal.org

**Weber Journal**
www.weber.edu/weberjournal
Michael Wutz
mwutz@weber.edu

**Weird Tales**
www.weirdtales.net
Ann Vandermeer
weirdtales@gmail.com

**Well Told Tales**
welltoldtales.com/originals
welltoldtales.com/submissions-policy

**West Goes South**
www.westgoessouth.com
Gwen M. Cassidy
wgsfiction@gmail.com
wgspoetry@gmail.com

**The Western Online**
www.thewesternonline.com
Matthew Pizzolato
submissions@thewesternonline.com

**Whatever Is Pure E-Zine**
psalm121.ca/edify.html

**Wheelhouse Magazine**
www.wheelhousemagazine.com
David Michael Wolach
wheelhouse@wheelhousemagazine.com

**Whispering Spirits**
www.whisperingghosts.com
Diana Cacy Hawkins
whisperingspirits@gmail.com

**Whispers From the Unseen**
www.unseenwhispers.com
submit@unseenwhispers.com

**Whistling Shade**
www.whistlingshade.com
Joel Van Valin
fiction@whistlingshade.com

**White Whale Review**
www.whitewhalereview.com/home
Jim Cronin
fiction@whitewhalereview.com

**Why Vandalism?**
www.whyvandalism.com
submissions@whyvandalism.com

**Wicked Alice**
www.sundress.net/wickedalice/
Kristy Bowen
wickedalicepoetry@yahoo.com

**Wigleaf**
www.wigleaf.com
Scott Garson
wigleaf.fiction@gmail.com

**Wild River Review**
www.wildriverreview.com
Joy E. Stocke
submissions@wildriverreview.com

**Wilde Oats**
www.wildeoats.com/MainPage
editors@wildeoats.com

**Wilderness House Review**
www.whlreview.com
Steve Glines
editor@whlreview.com

**William's Fortnightly Word**
www.williamswebsite.se
William Males
william@williamswebsite.se

**Willows Wept Review**
willowsweptreview.blogspot.com
willowsweptreview@gmail.com

**Winamop**
www.winamop.com
editor@winamop.com

**Wings ePress**
www.wings-press.com
Lorraine Stephens
subs@wings-press.com

**Withersin**
withersin.com/withersin.htm
Misty Gersley
withersin@hotmail.com

**Witness**
witness.blackmountaininstitute.org
Amber Withycombe
witness@unlv.edu

**Wizards of the Wind**
wizardsofthewind.blogspot.com
Michael Lee Johnson
promomanusa@gmail.com

**Woman Writers**
www.womenwriters.net/
Ann Margaret Bogle, Kim Wells,
Michelle Detorie
Fiction_Editors@womenwriters.net
poetry_Editor@womenwriters.net
wombpoetry@gmail.com

**Word Catalyst**
www.wordcatalystmagazine.com/
Shirley Allard
editor@wordcatalystmagazine.com

**Word For/ Word**
www.wordforword.info
Jonathan Minton

**Word Riot**
www.wordriot.org
Martha Clarkson, Kevin O'Cuinn,
Timmy Waldron
wr.poetry@gmail.com
wr.submissions@gmail.com

**Word Slaw**
wordslaw.blogspot.com
Ryan P. Standley
wordslaw@gmail.com

**Words Beats & Life**
wblinc.org/Journal.htm
Mazi Mutafa
submissions@wblinc.org

**Words Without Borders**
www.wordswithoutborders.org
Alane Salierno Mason
submissions@wordswithoutborders.org

**Work Magazine**
workmagazine.wordpress.com
Julie Mae Madsen, Claire Rudy
Foster
workzine@gmail.com

**The Workshop**
www.theworkshopmagazine.com
Lisa Gordon
submit@theworkshopmagazine.com

**Writer's Bloc**
www.writers-bloc.net
editor@writers-bloc.net

**The Writer's Bloc (Rutgers)**
www.writersblocmag.org
Kevin Dickinson
editor@writersblocmag.org

**The Writers Block**
www.thewritersblockmagazine.ca
Ben Gehrels
the.writers.block@hotmail.com

**Writer's Dojo**
www.writersdojo.org
James Bernard Frost, Kerry Cohen,
Kirsten Rian
fic@writersdojo.org
essay@writersdojo.org
poetry@writersdojo.org

**Writer's Eye**
www.thewriterseye.com
Amber Lea Starfire
amber@amberstarfire.com

**Writer's Ink**
thewritersink.wordpress.com
Ahuva Goldstand, Itai Rosenbaum
Submissions.WritersInk@gmail.com

**Writers' Stories**
www.writersstories.com
writersstories.com/page/submission-
guidelines.aspx

**Writing Raw**
www.writingraw.com
Weeb Poker, Rib Poker, Ditch Poker
submissions@writingraw.com

**Writing Shift**
www.writingshift.com
Justin Schwan
submissions@writingshift.com

**The Wrong Tree Review**
www.wrongtreereview.com
Sheldon Compton, Jarrid Deaton
editors@wrongtreereview.com

**wtf pwm**
www.wtfpwm.com
submit@wtfpwm.com

**Xelas Magazine**
www.xelasmagazine.com
Margaret Clark, Jennifer Armentrout
prose@xelasmagazine.com
poetry@xelasmagazine.com

**Xenith**
www.xenith.net
Kelly Joi Phelan
patrick.nathan@gmail.com

**Yankee Pot Roast**
www.yankeepotroast.org
Josh Abraham, Nick Jezarian,
Geoff Wolinetz
hasselhoff@yankeepotroast.org

**YB**
ybjournal.blogspot.com
Rose Hunter
rosehunter400@yahoo.com

**Yellow Mama**
blackpetalsks.tripod.com/
yellowmama/index.html
Cindy Rosmus
crosmus@hotmail.com

**Yellow Medicine Review**
www.yellowmedicinereview.com
editor@yellowmedicinereview.com

**The Yellow Room**
www.theyellowroom-magazine.
co.uk/www.theyellowroom-
magazine.co.uk/Welcome.html
Jo Derrick
*snail mail only

**Yemassee Journal**
www.yemasseejournal.org
Darien Cavenaugh, Bhavin Taylor
*snail mail only

**You Are Here**
www.u.arizona.edu/~urhere/
Rafael Routson
urhere@u.arizona.edu

**You Must Be This Tall To Ride**
www.youmustbethistalltoride.net
B.J. Hollars
editor@youmustbethistalltoride.net

**Young Adult Literature Review**
www.yaliteraturereview.com
Ragu
litmag@yaliteraturereview.com

**Young Writer**
www.young-writer.co.uk
youngwriter@writersnews.co.uk

**Young Writers' Literary Journal**
www.youngwriterssociety.com/
forum184.html
Brad Stanley

**Yuan Yang**
www.hku.hk/english/yuanyang/
yuanyang.htm
Paige Richards, Marina Ma,
Nathaniel Lee Caldwell
yuanyang@hkusua.hku.hk

**Zafusy**
www.zafusy.org
Jody Porter

**Zahir**
www.zahirtales.com
Sheryl Tempchin
*snail mail only

**Zaum**
www.zaumpress.net
Reilly Nolan
zaumpress@gmail.com

**Zeek**
www.jewcy.com/zeek
Jo Ellen Green Kaiser
submissions@jewcy.com

**The Zip-Book**
www.thezipbook.com
submit@thezipbook.com

**Zoetrope All-Story**
www.all-story.com
Michael Ray
*snail mail only

**Zone 3**
www.apsu.edu/zone3/
Susan Wallace
*snail mail only

**Zumaya Publications**
www.zumayapublications.com
acquisitions@zumayapublications.
com

**Zygote In My Coffee**
www.zygoteinmycoffee.com
Brian Fugett, Karl Koweski, Aleathia
Drehmer, C. Allen Rearick
submissions@zygoteinmycoffee.com